"Intrigue, romance, a clandestine kiss . . . all cast in a Regency setting so magnificently detailed I could see the fabrics and feel the glow of another era. Secrets and past disappointments keep Céline and Rees apart, not to mention the largest chasm of all—class. A wonderfully romantic and memorable read!"

—**Maureen Lang**, author of *Bees in the Butterfly Garden*

"The first paragraph drew me into the story, and the next twist held me there to the end."

—**Laurie Alice Eakes**, author of *A Flight of Fancy*

"*Moonlight Masquerade* is a wonderful romance, graced with expert detail of the Regency period, as well as with Ruth Axtell's usual flair for intensely romantic situations between characters so real I couldn't stop thinking about them. *Moonlight Masquerade* is an exciting romantic adventure of spies, forbidden love, and happily-ever-after that I thoroughly enjoyed."

—**Melanie Dickerson**, two-time Christy Award finalist and author of *The Healer's Apprentice* and *The Merchant's Daughter*

Moonlight Masquerade

A REGENCY ROMANCE

RUTH AXTELL

Revell

a division of Baker Publishing Group
Grand Rapids, Michigan

Published by Revell
a division of Baker Publishing Group
P.O. Box 6287, Grand Rapids, MI 49516-6287
www.revellbooks.com

Printed in the United States of America

Library of Congress Cataloging-in-Publication Data
Axtell, Ruth.
    Moonlight masquerade : a Regency romance / Ruth Axtell.
      pages cm
    ISBN 978-0-8007-2089-6 (pbk.)
      1. Aristocracy (Social class)—Fiction. 2. London (England)—Social life and customs—19th century—Fiction. 3. Great Britain—History—George III, 1760–1820—Fiction. I. Title.
    PS3601.X84M66 2013
    813'.6—dc23   2012042129

This book is a work of fiction. Names, characters, places, and incidents are the product of the author's imagination or are used fictitiously.

13 14 15 16 17 18 19   7 6 5 4 3 2 1

I'd like to thank my agent Chip MacGregor.
He took me on during a transition time in my writing career
and believed in my stories.

Thanks to my daughter, Adaja, and to my email friend,
Patricia. They're my first readers and gave me
the thumbs-up on my opening scenes.

1

Rees had never seen so many female baubles in his life. Ropes of pearl, gold chains, jeweled tiaras, and bracelets of every description lay nested in their satin surroundings.

The Countess of Wexham's jewelry box contained enough precious stones to feed half of London.

But he wasn't interested in what her jewels would fetch on the market. He was searching for something else among the lady's belongings. Something infinitely more precious—and damaging—if it were found.

Information.

Rees glanced quickly over his shoulder—having imagined the sound of footsteps behind him all evening—before lifting each article of jewelry to make sure nothing lay beneath. He replaced them one by one, endeavoring to leave everything as he had found it. Conscious that the seconds were ticking by, he was still not certain what he was looking for, only that he would recognize it when he saw it.

He lowered the lid and relocked it. Next, he slipped his skeleton key into the narrow drawer in the lower part of the jewelry box and opened it. Rows of amethyst, topaz, ruby, and emerald earrings and rings glinted back at him from the light of his candle.

He went through every item, probing the satin beneath. Nothing out of the ordinary . . . for a lady of the fashionable world of the London *ton*.

He slid the drawer closed and locked it, expelling a breath. He glanced at the brass clock beside the jewelry box. Ten precious minutes had passed since he'd entered the lady's dressing room. He'd already searched her bedroom and found nothing. He calculated he had at least another hour before she or her maid returned for the evening.

He eyed the piece of furniture the jewelry box sat upon. A mahogany bowfront chest of drawers with brass lion's head pull handles. Forcing himself to continue the disagreeable task of going through someone's personal belongings, he grasped the top two handles and opened the first drawer. Stacks of handkerchiefs sat in neatly folded squares, of every texture and description from snowy white to pale cream and sheerest lawn edged in a wide swath of lace to heavy cambric, monogrammed in the corner, as plain as a man's.

The latter were at odds with their owner, a lady of utmost femininity.

Rees went through each pile, feeling for any object, anything suspicious—a folded piece of paper, a scroll, something cylindrical into which a document could be slipped.

The scent of mahogany and lavender drifted to his nostrils. His fingers encountered a few sachets tied with satin ribbons. He examined each one but felt only the tiny lavender pellets beneath his fingertips.

He reached the bottom of the drawer and touched the paper lining, probing each corner, going so far as sliding his hand under the paper while holding the piles of handkerchiefs in place with the other.

He repeated this motion on each side of the drawer, left, front, rear, and right, then gave it a careful look to ascertain that its contents looked undisturbed before softly pushing the drawer closed.

Where would he hide something if he were a fashionable lady? His narrowed gaze roamed the dainty dressing room, taking in its furnishings—two large wardrobes along one wall, the chest of drawers he stood in front of, a dresser with a mirror, two comfortable armchairs flanking it, a large, plush carpet in shades of rose and green covering most of the floor. A faint scent of perfume permeated the air, nothing cloying, but light, reminding him of a Sussex village in high summer when the roses festooned the hedgerows, casting out their fragrance when one brushed by them.

He turned back to face the chest of drawers. No help for it but to go methodically through every drawer, every item, just as he'd done in the bedroom.

He hated this aspect of the job—snooping through a lady's private things. A bloody naval battle, crossing swords on the deck of a frigate, was preferable.

The ticking clock reminded him again that he'd better get to it or he'd end up discovered before his first week was up.

Steeling himself for the task, he slid open the next drawer. Thank goodness everything in the lady's terrace house was new and well maintained. He needn't fear any sticking drawers or squeaking hinges. He knew from her dossier that Lady Wexham had only moved here after her widowhood three years ago.

He eyed the drawer's contents in dismay. Silk and lawn undergarments.

Without meaning to, he envisioned the lady they belonged to.

A beautiful woman, dark of hair and eye, more elegant and well-bred than any woman of Rees's acquaintance. And, for the foreseeable future, his employer.

And very possibly a spy against Great Britain.

It was his task to find out.

He stared at the lacy chemises and silk stockings, curling his fingers into his palms.

He reached out, knowing each minute was precious. He must finish his search, no matter how distasteful, and leave the room before anyone chanced by.

Focusing on the task at hand, Rees plunged his hands into the drawer, going through every item as he had in the drawer above, feeling to the bottom for anything tucked beneath the paper lining.

Halfway down the length of the drawer, reaching a pile of stays and corsets, he heard the door click open in the next room.

He froze, this time his ears not deceiving him. It couldn't be Valentine, the lady's maid. He had heard her tell the cook that she was going out. As for Lady Wexham, she never returned before midnight, and it was scarcely ten o'clock.

But the soft sound of footsteps like a lady's evening slippers on the floorboards was unmistakable. Rees snuffed out his candle even as his glance darted about the four corners of the dressing room, memorizing the placement of the furniture before being plunged into darkness.

His only hope was one of the armoires. He crossed the room in a few long strides and reached for the second one, the farthest one from the door to the bedroom, calculating it would be the least likely to be opened if the person entered the dressing room. He opened one of its doors, thankful for its well-oiled hinges. In another second, he had the other side opened and was crouching down, feeling for the bottom shelf. It was wide and deep, at least two feet in height. Shoving aside the clothes, he hunched into it, barely able to squeeze his six-foot frame into its confines.

Hearing further movement in the next room, he hugged the candle to his chest, stifling an exclamation as hot wax spilled onto his hand. Quickly, he shoved some of the garments over himself and drew the two doors closed from within. Would the person smell the scent of burning wax from a recently doused candle?

He wasn't able to latch the doors from where he lay on the bottom. The best he could do was grip the second door with his fingertips, praying no one would come into the dressing room or notice that one door was slightly ajar.

His spine pressed against the rear of the armoire, his knees were drawn almost to his chest, the toes of his shoes touched one end of the armoire, the crown of his head the other. Closing his eyes, he strained to hear, praying he wouldn't be discovered.

Who could have come into the lady's bedroom? It couldn't be Lady Wexham herself. As for her maid, he had seen her leave the house as soon as her mistress departed in her carriage. A Frenchwoman, she was scornful of the other servants except for the French cook, treating the British ones as beneath her notice.

For a long time there was only silence in the stuffy space. Perspiration broke out on his forehead and neck. The scent of walnut mingled with rose and starch of whatever article of clothing he held against himself. He loosened his hold on the candle and rubbed the edge of the garment between thumb and forefinger to distract himself from his uncomfortable position. Silk.

In the scant week he'd been employed in the Countess of Wexham's household, he'd seen her wear a dozen different outfits, changing at least three times in a day. Morning gowns, riding habits, calling outfits, evening gowns. He compared her to his younger sister, Megan, who always looked pretty but who didn't own a fraction of the gowns of his employer. Megan's were simple cotton gowns, copied from a fashion magazine and made at home. But Megan lived in the country and never aspired to the heights of Lady Wexham.

Despite Rees's efforts to distract himself from his cramped confines, the minutes stretched out. He heard nothing more beyond the thick walnut panels of the armoire.

His feet grew numb, then his fingertips from the strain of holding the door in place. Drops of perspiration began to course down his temple and trickle into one eye. He dared not move to wipe it away. The air grew thick and stuffy. He wondered idly if a person could be asphyxiated inside a wardrobe.

He imaged the headlines: "Lady's Butler Found Dead in Her Walnut Armoire Among Her Petticoats."

Don't be so chickenhearted. It's no worse than sleeping in the hold of a ship. You survived enough years of that. Of course, he'd been more than a decade younger and a few pounds lighter when he'd been in His Majesty's navy.

Perhaps another maid had come in to turn down the bed and she'd be gone in a few minutes.

At the sound of the door to the dressing room opening, his body tensed anew, every sense on alert. A few footsteps followed by silence. The intruder must have stepped on the carpet. *Intruder?* Rees caught himself. *He* was the intruder.

A soft humming came through the crack in the door.

He knew that hum. He'd heard it before. Lady Wexham stood on the other side of the armoire's doors, just inches from where he lay crammed like a sausage in a bun.

What was she doing home at this hour? Perhaps she'd forgotten something and returned to fetch it?

It didn't make sense. Valentine was there to ensure that her mistress had everything she needed when she went out.

Or could it be that she was home for a reason that had nothing to do with her social life . . . but with something clandestine?

His heart began to pound as anticipation grew at the thought that perhaps this evening he'd uncover something tangible about Lady Wexham's loyalties. If he could prove she was a French spy, he'd be done with this cursed assignment.

The next instant he pictured the sly look of triumph on the senior clerk's face and realized he would get little credit for his discovery. His excitement faded, replaced by disgust at the depths his job had forced him to.

Playing a servant in a countess's household just so his superior at the Foreign Office, young Alistair Oglethorpe, could boast of the accomplishment to the foreign secretary.

"Tsk!"

His senses back on high alert, he strained to hear more. Lady Wexham sounded vexed.

Wishing he could peer through the crack, he remained as still as stone, not moving so much as an eyelid.

"Drat!"

What was she doing?

Then footfalls again and silence.

Had she left? He waited, still not daring to move. His neck developed a crick from the angle it was bent. His feet ached from lack of circulation, and he was forced to shift them a fraction.

What seemed an eternity but was probably only several minutes later, the sound of two female voices neared the wardrobe.

"I do beg your pardon for getting you out of bed, but I find I can't manage these stays myself."

"Of course not, my lady, with all the lacing down the back."

It was one of the young housemaids with the countess. He still didn't have all of their names straight. Was it Virginia or Sally?

"I'll undo it for you in a thrice."

"Valentine's not here and I really didn't want to disturb anyone else."

"It's no bother at all, my lady. I went to bed because I didn't expect you home. But I'd a' waited up if I'd known you'd be home this early."

"Indeed you shouldn't have, since there was no way for you to have known I couldn't abide the crush at Princess Esterhazy's." There was wry amusement in Lady Wexham's tone.

A few seconds later, the maid spoke again. "There you go, my lady."

"Thank you," the countess breathed out in obvious relief.

"Is there anything else you need, ma'am?"

"I hate to be a bother, but perhaps some tea. I have a bit of a headache. I daresay it's this wretched fog. That's really why I came back so early."

The maid clucked her tongue. "I'm sorry you're feeling poorly. You do look a mite pale. I'll fetch you that tea straightaway."

The maid's voice came from different distances as if she were moving around. He imagined she was putting things away. As long as she didn't decide to put her mistress's gown in the wardrobe . . .

"I think one of those tisanes would be better for me. Perhaps a chamomile?"

"Very well, my lady. There you go, you'll probably feel a lot more comfortable in your nightgown."

"Oh yes, much, thank you, Virginia. You're a dear."

So it was Virginia who had responded to the lady's summons.

"Let me get your wrap."

"There is no need. I am going right to bed as soon as I wash my face and clean my teeth."

"When I come back, I'll brush out your hair, my lady."

"Thank you, but I can manage that myself tonight."

"Very well, I'll return in a moment."

Rees waited, expecting the door to the wardrobe to be thrust from his fingertips at any moment. But all he heard was water poured from the pitcher and then some splashing.

Again, he waited what seemed an age before he heard the maid's voice. "I've put a mug beside your bed." Her voice moved away from him. "Here, let me plait your hair."

Lady Wexham said through a yawn, "No, I shan't bother tonight."

"Oh, my lady, are you certain? It'll take me only a moment."

"That's quite all right. It's only for tonight."

"If you're certain, my lady." The maid sounded doubtful.

Rees pictured Lady Wexham's chestnut locks, which she usually wore coiled or braided above her head with shorter curls left loose around her face as was the fashion. How long would it fall? At least to her waist, he calculated. He forced such unseemly thoughts from his mind.

"I'm certain, Virginia." Lady Wexham's voice was firm. "I shall drink the tisane you were such a dear to prepare for me at this hour."

"Very well, my lady."

Suddenly Rees heard Virginia's voice right outside the wardrobe door. "Let me know if you should need anything else."

"Oh, don't bother with those. Valentine will tidy everything in the morning."

"I'll just put this gown away, my lady."

Rees's heart thudded in his chest loudly enough to vibrate the door panels. Would she notice that the door was not latched?

"Just drape it across the chair for now. Valentine will have a fit if things are not done precisely to her liking. Now, you run along to your own bed. It will be light soon enough."

"Very well, my lady. Good night then, if you are sure you don't require anything more."

"Nothing more tonight. Thank you."

The voices faded from the room.

Rees counted a full minute in his head before allowing his body to relax the least bit.

Now, to find a way out of this room. There was only the door through Lady Wexham's bedroom. How long would it take for her to drink her tea and fall asleep?

Clearly, he was in for a long wait yet. He daren't tiptoe through her room until she was in a deep slumber.

Praying that chamomile tea had sedative properties, Rees eased his cramped feet and loosened his hold on the door. He flexed his fingers to restore feeling to them.

How long he lay curled up in the armoire, he had no idea. He must have dozed eventually. He awoke with a start, dreaming of something. He strove to remember, and it came back to him. He'd been in a coffin, everything completely black before his eyes.

He blinked, realizing just as in the dream, he couldn't see a thing. Then he remembered where he was and why.

Hearing nothing, he pushed open one of the wardrobe doors a few inches. More darkness and stillness greeted him, so he pushed it a little farther.

Seeing no light from the other room, he dared to open the other door all the way and stretch his legs out of the wardrobe. Immediately pins and needles shot through his feet.

He had to wait a moment for the sensation to ease. Then he set his candle on the floor and eased his body out of the confining shelf space the rest of the way.

He paused, cocking his ear. Still nothing. The countess must have fallen asleep.

He crouched on his hands and knees, rolling his head around to ease the kinks from his neck and shoulders. Then he attempted to put some semblance of order to the shelf he had lain in for some hours. What would Valentine think when she saw the rumpled clothing? Would she ask her mistress about it? He tried to fold the garments in the dark and pile them atop one another.

Then he stood, picking up his candle and its holder and placing them in his pocket. Pausing again to listen, he carefully closed the doors, quietly securing them.

His eyes, adjusted to the dark, made out the shadowy space of the open door to the bedroom. Feeling in front of him with his outstretched arms, he made his way there step by hesitant step. His feet made no sound on the carpet, but when he reached an area of floorboard right before the door, he slowed his pace even more.

Finally, he was through the door. Now, the faint sounds of even breathing came to him. The curtains around the wide, four-poster bed had been drawn, hiding its occupant.

Rees reached another carpet and was able to walk more easily until reaching floorboards again as he neared the door to the hallway. Two steps later, a loud creak sounded under his sole. It reverberated in the still night. He held his breath, not moving a muscle.

Lady Wexham didn't stir.

Rees shifted his weight to his other foot and slowly eased his first foot—heel, ball, toe—off the noisy floorboard, expecting another creak.

"You mistake me, sir."

Rees froze, turning halfway and peering at the shadowy bed.

Lady Wexham mumbled something in French, and he realized she was talking in her sleep. Her bedclothes rustled, and she sighed.

Rees waited, counting the seconds until deeming her fully asleep.

He reached the door with no further creaks and paused, his hand wrapped around the brass knob. He turned it a fraction. It gave easily. Completing the revolution, he pushed the door open a crack. A second later, he widened it just enough to ease his body through.

He was in the corridor. A faint light from a street lamp at the front of the house shone through the window at that end of the hallway. He shut the door behind him, taking extra care in turning the knob back to its original position. Just the faintest "click" signaled it was fully closed.

He allowed himself to rest a moment against the hallway wall and wipe his brow with his hand, not daring yet to grope for his handkerchief. Time enough when he reached his room below stairs.

The night had proved fruitless. He hadn't been able to complete his search of Lady Wexham's rooms, and who knew when he'd be given another opportunity. Valentine guarded her mistress's rooms like a jail keeper. Tonight had been unusual for them both to be out. If Lady Wexham had anything to hide, the likeliest place would be in her private quarters.

If the maid had opened the wardrobe this evening, how would he have explained his tall form huddled on the bottom shelf? His body shuddered.

He'd have to be more careful. He couldn't afford to be suspected by anyone of the household, least of all by its mistress. Everything depended on her believing him to be nothing but a butler.

2

*C*éline's headache was completely gone by morning. She blinked at the clock on her night table. Seven o'clock. She must indeed have fallen asleep right away to be up so early.

Yawning and stretching her arms above her head, she thought about the day ahead. Her best ideas came upon just awakening, so she burrowed back among the pillows and bolsters, reveling in that feeling of relaxation and well-being after a sound night's sleep.

Her lips twisted at the thought of the previous evening. First a long dinner, then a rout. For engagements which promised brilliant company and conversation over the table and in the drawing room, each had proved sadly flat. When was it that each London season had begun to blur into the preceding one?

Perhaps that's why she'd agreed to Roland de Fleury's request.

She punched at one of her pillows, not wanting to think about that, preferring instead to berate the English.

They tried so hard to surpass their rivals across the Channel in thought and manners, but all they succeeded in doing was transforming the dining table into a feeding trough, and as for conversation—she wrinkled her nose. *On-dits* and innuendos instead of stimulating discussion. What did they know of salons where not only the best and brightest convened to debate ideas, but public policy was even shaped? Céline had grown up on her mother's tales of the brilliant company gathered in those Parisian parlors.

Holland House was the closest the British came to the French salons of Madame Necker, Madame de Roland, and Sophie de Condorcet. But it was all the way out in Kensington. Paris boasted its best literary and political salons in its heart. Even the Terror had not succeeded in closing down this avenue for the exchange of ideas.

She sat up in bed and tugged on the bell pull. It was likely time for another dinner party. It had been over a fortnight since her last, what with poor Mr. Rumford injuring himself and sending his nephew as replacement butler. She hadn't dared a dinner party with an untried butler.

In the intervening time, she'd scarcely heard any news worth passing along to Roland. Perhaps it was time to stir the pot and see if anything rose to the top. By gathering a select company of politicians, journalists, and artists around a dinner table, one never knew what one might hear.

Céline studied her nails, wondering whether to have Valentine buff them again. The soft peach color and shine of the oil rubbed into them was already fading, and the pretty almond shape could certainly use a bit of reshaping.

She brought a forefinger up to her lips and bit on the nail, her thoughts returning to that which she'd rather avoid.

Even after six months, she did not like—or feel at ease with—the task of collecting information. But the cause was a worthy one, as Roland had pointed out. Not only worthy but of the utmost urgency. France needed her help. Whatever happened to Napoleon, the royalists must not regain power.

Céline shuddered, picturing the fat, aging Comte de Provence living in exile at Hartwell House, just beyond London, waiting to return to France as Louis XVIII if ever Napoleon should fail.

With the abysmal news from the Russian front, that likelihood was growing stronger each month. She sighed, not liking to think what would happen to her beloved France in the aftermath of this wretched war. She longed for the day of peace, but at what price would it come?

She forced her finger from her mouth, looking in dismay at the damage she'd done. Valentine would scold and file her nails with enough vigor to draw blood.

Napoleon would *not* fail. He had always managed to overcome his adversaries, and he would do so again.

Céline threw aside the bedcovers just as her maid entered the chamber with a can of hot water in one hand and a pile of towels in the other.

"*Bonjour.* How are you feeling this morning?"

"Perfectly fine." She yawned. "I haven't slept so well in an age. Virginia fixed me a tisane."

Valentine stopped before her, eyeing her critically. "You look as pale as bleached muslin."

"*Merci, chérie*, for your fortifying words." Even though Céline strove to speak English with her two French servants whenever anyone else was around, in private they usually lapsed into French.

Valentine ignored her sarcasm. "And the headache?"

Céline waved a hand. "Completely gone. But it was enough to make me ill disposed to stand the crush at Princess Esterhazy's last night."

Valentine harrumphed. "And your hair! *Quelle horreur!* Couldn't that good-for-nothing maid manage a simple plait?"

Céline touched her loose locks. When she tried to run her hand through them, she understood Valentine's horror. "I sent her to bed. The poor girl had been asleep when I rang for her—and I only did so because I couldn't manage my stays. My head was certainly not up to having someone pull a hairbrush through it," she ended with a significant look at her maid.

Valentine appraised her a few seconds more, *tsk-tsking* before she was satisfied that Céline was not suffering from a worse ailment than a head of tangled hair. "*Bien.* I will pour this water. Sally is bringing your *chocolat* and croissant. I hope that will do something for your looks."

"Am I that washed out?" Céline walked to the dressing table in the next room and peered into the mirror. "Oh, my." Her hair did indeed look a fright.

Valentine poured steaming water into her pitcher and mixed it with cold. "*Pardonnez-moi* that I was not here when you came in. If I'd known you'd return so early, I, too, would have come back."

"How were you expected to know?" Céline leaned over the porcelain basin, lathering her hands and face with the lavender-scented soap and then rinsing them off. She grabbed up a towel and patted them dry. "Pray, how was your evening?"

Valentine paused from shaking out Céline's gown and gave a Gallic shrug. "Bah! The usual. Those English, they are so *bêtes*!"

Céline laughed. "Stupid only in that they don't appreciate your French charm?"

Her maid picked up her garments from the chair where Virginia had laid them. "What can one expect from a land so drenched in fog? Where people eat roast mutton and boiled potatoes without a hint of herbs or wine?" She examined the overskirt of the lemon-yellow gown for any stains or rips.

"Well, you cannot complain in this household. Gaspard is an excellent Provençal cook."

Valentine checked the chiffon slip. "If one can overlook his tantrums, then, yes, his cooking is worth it." She frowned at a stain. "You spilled something on this."

Céline glanced over the towel. "Likely champagne. That bumbling fool Orrington bumped into me before dinner. I think he was already foxed long before he arrived."

Valentine sniffed her displeasure and set the gown aside. She picked up the silk petticoat and muslin shift from the chair and slung them over her arm.

Céline turned back to her washstand and attempted to run a hand through her hair again. What a tangled thicket. Hopefully, she wouldn't end with another headache brought on by Valentine's comb and brush.

Her hair fell to her waist, and sometimes she was tempted to hack it all off like Lady Caroline Lamb. Valentine would have a fit.

"C'est quoi cette saloperie?"

She turned at her maid's exclamation of outrage. "What's the matter now? Have you discovered my shoes to be soiled or my tippet to have lost some feathers?"

Valentine was kneeling before the lower shelf of one of the armoires. Céline frowned. "What is it?"

An unintelligible sound issued from the abigail's throat as she gestured at the rumpled mound of garments spilling out onto the floor.

"Don't glare at me. I haven't been rummaging about in there! I know better than to do any such thing."

"Then it must have been that lazy, good-for-nothing Virginie. I knew I couldn't trust her to take my place for one evening."

"I assure you, my dear, poor Virginia had nothing to do with it. I dismissed her as soon as she'd helped me undress and brought me a tisane. I know how particular you are about my clothes, so I told her you would see to everything on the morrow."

The news did not allay Valentine's ire. She began pulling out the garments one by one, muttering Gallic imprecations. "Then who made such a mess of your gowns?" Angry sounds issued from between her teeth as she began refolding the gowns. "Do you think I would leave things in such a state? I shall have to iron these anew. Ohh!"

Céline turned at the sudden exclamation. "What is it now?"

Valentine's mouth a thin, hard line, she said nothing but marched to where Céline sat and thrust a pale blue satin gown under her nose.

Céline stared at the blotch of hardened wax the size of a button on the bodice. "Oh, dear." She took the gown from her maid. "What a pity. Do you think it will come out?"

"It is ruined." Valentine's chin trembled with ire. *"C'est abominable."* Once again, a string of French imprecations followed, among them how one couldn't trust this household of English pigs.

She narrowed her eyes at Céline. "I will find who was responsible, and they will pay!"

"I wish you luck, since the maids know enough to leave my things alone. They go in too much fear of you, *ma chérie*, to risk your displeasure."

Valentine said no more, her back rigid as she put things back to order. Céline returned to her bed and picked up a writing tablet and pencil to begin composing a guest list.

A few moments later, Sally, the other housemaid, entered with Céline's breakfast tray.

"Thank you. It looks delicious." Céline pulled the tray toward her and unfolded the napkin, realizing how hungry she was since she had scarcely enjoyed her dinner last evening.

She pulled apart a croissant and inhaled its buttery fragrance. "Nothing like the French to produce a pastry that melts in the mouth." Spooning a small dollop of marmalade onto the piece of croissant, she anticipated the first bite. "At least the British know how to make jam." She smiled at the young maid.

The girl smiled back at her. "That they do."

"I'm glad you brought me my tray and not Virginia."

Sally stopped in the act of plumping a pillow. "Why is that, my lady?"

"Valentine is quite cross with her—without cause, please assure her."

The young maid's eyes widened with worry. "Oh no. What did she do?"

"Nothing at all. Valentine is likely just jealous that I had to ring for Virginia last night when I returned early. Anyway, it's nothing for her to worry herself about. Just tell her to stay out of Valentine's way for a few hours."

"Yes, ma'am, I'll be sure to warn her." Sally returned to her task, her tone still betraying concern.

Céline poured out a cup of steaming hot chocolate from the silver pot and unfolded the edition of the *Morning Post*. No earth-shattering news on the front page. "Speaker Addresses Committee in Opposition of Catholic Relief Bill"; "Ackermann's Repository Illuminated by Gas Light." Hmm. At least the prints would be more visible. She would judge for herself at Wednesday's literary reception. She wondered whether the poor émigrés employed in the back room painting screens and flower stands would benefit from this new lighting.

Céline continued perusing the headlines and skimming through the articles that interested her. "Sense and Sensibility: Princess Charlotte Ignores Father's Advice and Visits Her Mother after Grandmother's Funeral."

Céline's lips curved into a smile at the revised account of the crown princess's visit to her mother despite the Regent's estrangement from his wife. Only a few days ago, the *Morning Chronicle* had published an account of Princess Charlotte throwing herself upon her father's chest in gratitude for allowing her to attend her maternal grandmother's funeral.

Who knew what to believe in the newspapers? One paper was Tory, the other Whig, the one defending the Prince Regent, the other decrying all his excesses.

Her smile grew at the next story. "Russian Cossack Gives Riding Exhibition in Hyde Park." She read the article of the visiting military hero performing stunts in his baggy trousers, red tunic, and fleece hat, his shashka at his side, his musket slung on his back.

Despite the amusing account of the man's skill and bravado, a wave of sadness passed over Céline at the thought of how many brave young Frenchmen had so recently perished in the forests and fields between Moscow and Minsk. How many at the hands of this one Cossack?

All the more reason she must help her countrymen.

Céline laid aside the newspaper and returned to thoughts of a dinner party. Parliament was in session. By now, everyone who was anyone in politics and foreign affairs was in town.

She sipped her chocolate, ticking names off in her head. Yes, Castlereagh and Lady C., Lord Wellesley—perhaps she'd learn something of his brother on the Peninsula. Would he bring Lady Hyacinthe? She was scorned by all, but at least Céline could speak French with her. Poor woman, if she had lived in France, she would have been accepted everywhere. Even though Wellesley had finally married her, the *ton* still snubbed her because she was a former actress at the Palais Royale. Of course, it didn't help that she didn't make the effort to learn English.

Planning successful dinner parties took the skill of an officer laying out a battle strategy.

Sighing, Céline moved aside the tray and rose. "Valentine, set out my habit." She would go for a ride in the park then go over the dinner preparations with her housekeeper and butler at their morning meeting. Would her new butler be up to a dinner party? He'd scarcely been here a week.

"Are you sure you are well enough?"

Céline laughed aside her maid's concern.

"All that bouncing around in a saddle could bring on the headache again."

"Nonsense. The fresh air will dissipate any lingering effects of that stuffy drawing room last night."

Valentine sniffed and flounced back to the dressing room.

 **3**

*I*t was a quarter after ten when Rees opened the front door to his mistress. He'd sent both the footmen from this post, setting them to polish the silver, even though it looked perfectly shiny to his untrained eye.

He wanted to assure himself that the countess had seen or heard nothing suspicious in her bedroom the night before.

He inclined his head to Lady Wexham as she entered. "Good morning, my lady. Did you have a pleasant ride?"

She handed him her crop with a smile. "Good morning, Mr. Mac-Kinnon. Yes, it was lovely, thank you. How are you this fine morning?"

Her smile never failed to disarm him. It had nothing haughty or sly about it. He hadn't known what to expect of a possible lady spy, but it wasn't the open, friendly look she bestowed on him—and on every one of the servants, as far as he'd observed in his short stay in her household.

She was also the loveliest woman he'd ever met. Her skin was like a porcelain figurine's, though unlike the pale and pink coloring of one of those, her cheeks were duskier, betraying her southern French heritage. Her hair was a rich chestnut brown. His gaze slipped a notch to her lips, which were generous. Her even white teeth made a lovely contrast to the light olive tone of her skin.

"I am perfectly well, thank you. And yourself, my lady? Virginia said you suffered from a headache last night?" Would her old butler have asked her such a question, or would she think him too forward? But Rees wanted to gauge her reaction to mention of last evening. He watched her face closely.

She laughed—a sweet, tinkling sound—as she untied the filmy pink scarf that wound loosely around her neck and removed the top hat perched at a jaunty angle on her dark locks. "I am pleased to hear that you are well. As for me, it was nothing—a very slight headache. Completely gone, thank you." She glanced around. "Where is William?"

It never failed to surprise him how much notice she took of each servant no matter how lowly the position. "He and Thomas are polishing the silver."

"Wonderful." She handed Rees her soft kidskin gloves and turned to pat her hair in the glass. "I always enjoy the park at this hour. Hardly a soul except the squirrels scampering up the trees and the livestock grazing in the distance."

"Indeed, my lady." What more could he say, never having had the leisure nor opportunity to own a horse in London to ride in Hyde Park?

Her gaze met his in the glass. "I have decided to hold a dinner party, perhaps Thursday next? That gives us almost a week." She gave a final pat to her curls and turned back to him, tilting her head to one side, her strong, black eyebrows arched upward. "Think you are up to it, or would you prefer I wait until you are more familiar with the running of this house?"

He blinked, wondering how to respond. Her glance and tone held a mixture of inquiry and amusement—and just a hint of challenge. Or was he reading too much into them?

He realized she was awaiting his opinion. "Thursday? As you wish, my lady," he replied with a slight dip of head, as he deemed a proper butler would.

She gave a slight laugh. "At least I can be assured the silver will be at its best."

"The silver? The silver, yes, of course. Indeed." What a dunderhead she must take him for. How did one behave as a butler? Staid and dignified, like Rumford, he imagined. His own conduct fell far short. Poor old Rumford had only had a few days to take Rees through his paces.

Lady Wexham placed a slim forefinger to her slightly pursed lips, emphasizing their pretty bow and crimson shade. "I shall discuss the dinner party with you and Mrs. Finlay when we get together this morning. Will you let her know?"

He stepped back from her, sensing dismissal. "Yes, my lady. At the usual time?" One of the duties of butler and housekeeper, he'd quickly come to learn, was a meeting each morning with the mistress of the house to go over her day.

She smiled in reply—a devastating smile that always left Rees weak in the knees. Was that how she wangled state secrets from highly placed officials? "Yes. I shall be in the morning room as soon as I change out of this outfit."

"Very well. We shall await your convenience."

"Thank you, Mr. MacKinnon." Unlike most employers, she always addressed him by "mister," which he found oddly respectful. He'd fully expected to be ordered hither and thither as "MacKinnon." It had made it more difficult to dislike this suspected traitor.

She walked around him, and he quickly backed out of her way as she headed for the staircase.

Under the guise of placing her hat and riding crop on the side table for the odious lady's maid to pick up later, Rees watched Lady Wexham ascend the stairs from his vantage near the mirror. Her every movement was graceful. Was it because she was French by birth? Or was it simply because she was the daughter of a marquis and the widow of an earl?

When she disappeared from sight, Rees caught his own reflection in the glass so lately occupied by Lady Wexham's image. Did he really look so forbidding? He made a conscious effort to ease the frown from his forehead.

But it did nothing to alter the knot of disgust in his chest at the appearance he presented. How he hated this uniform of butler! He must be grateful that a butler was not obliged to wear knee breeches and powder his hair the way footmen must—although Lady Wexham did not require the latter of those in her employ. According to Tom, Lady Wexham said it reminded her too forcibly of why the French had revolted.

No, Rees brought his thoughts back to his own appearance. A gentleman would never wear black trousers with his black coat unless it was for evening wear. Neither would he wrap a black neck cloth around his shirt collar. Although the black, long-tailed coat and pants and the starched white shirt were finely cut, they were the distinguishing features of a manservant. They set him apart from any gentleman walking past the bow windows that fronted this large terrace house in Mayfair.

A gentleman's neckwear was bleached white, with an occasional spotted or printed one, especially if the gentleman considered himself a sporting man. His waistcoats ranged from the snowiest white to every hue of the rainbow, of the finest cloth and silk thread. And his pantaloons or breeches were buff or fawn colored.

But black was the color of service.

Rees would rather go back to the baggy trousers and striped jersey of a simple sailor in His Majesty's navy than sport this frieze coat provided for him by Rumford.

If his mother or sister should ever chance to see him—heaven forbid!

Thankfully, they were safely tucked away in a village far enough from London that they rarely came to town. He was not at liberty to tell anyone of the double life he was leading. It would only cause disbelief and anguish to his poor widowed mother if she thought Rees's father had toiled so long and hard to provide his son with a gentleman's upbringing to see him now working as a butler, no matter how fashionable the establishment. No, his mother's patriotism would not extend so far.

Rees turned away from the mirror. It would do no good to chafe at his circumstances. He was here for a reason, and see it to its conclusion he must.

Céline faced her butler and housekeeper across the small round table in the breakfast room, a notepad in front of her. "I have compiled a list of twenty, including myself. I shall send the invitations out today."

"Very good, my lady." Mrs. Finlay was keeping her own list of what must be done in preparation for the dinner party. Céline knew she could trust her. She had proven an excellent housekeeper since the day Céline as a young bride had first met her.

Céline laid down her gold pencil. "I shall discuss the menu with Gaspard as soon as we finish here. By the by, I shall not be dining in this evening. I'm expected at Marlborough House for dinner and then shall be attending the opera."

Mrs. Finlay made a note. "I shall inform Gaspard." She glanced at MacKinnon. "You will let Jacob know to have the carriage ready."

"The rest of the servants may have the evening off as soon as I leave," Céline told her butler. "You, too, for that matter."

"But the door—"

Céline waved aside his concern. "The groom will take care of that." She tapped her pencil against her notepaper. "For the dinner party, I think the blue Sèvres service?"

"Yes, my lady." Mrs. Finlay made another notation.

Céline turned her attention back to her new butler. If only old Mr. Rumford hadn't taken that fall. He'd be out six weeks, at least, the physician had told him. But he'd insisted that his nephew, Harrison MacKinnon, was up to the task.

He's been footman at Telford House in Derbyshire these last eight years, and now he's been made under-butler. It's a large estate, my lady, with upward of a hundred servants, so he can be spared, her old butler had written her. *The butler and I are old friends. He wouldn't begrudge lending me Harry for a few weeks.*

She hadn't the heart to refuse old Rumford, and a few days later, his nephew had arrived. Thus far, she conceded, Mr. MacKinnon had proven satisfactory—unobtrusive and efficient, keeping away unwanted callers. She'd had no complaints from the staff, either—excluding Valentine, who was rarely pleased with anyone.

This dinner party would test his mettle. "I will look over the wines with you directly we finish here," she told him now. Would he be like the typical Englishman, knowing only port and brandy?

"I am at your service."

There was something vaguely unsettling about the man's gray eyes. Too steady in the way he regarded her even after they'd both finished speaking. It wasn't insolent by any means, just observant. It made her think he saw more than she cared to let the world see.

He was certainly good-looking—and much too young to be a butler. He could be anywhere from twenty-eight to thirty-two, she estimated, tilting her head and studying him. He had a full head of dark brown hair and well-proportioned features from a wide forehead to a determined-looking chin.

Most butlers were in their fifties or sixties, attaining their situation after decades in service.

But perhaps this man's relative youth and looks would be an asset, if they impressed her guests and caused them to overlook any shortcomings. Then again, he wasn't a footman, hired as much for his figure as for his abilities. A butler must be discreet, dignified, and most of all, trustworthy. She trusted him only because she trusted Rumford.

She sighed inwardly. As long as her temporary butler didn't commit some unforgivable blunder as mangling the names of her guests or botching the precedence of those entering the dining room.

She spoke to Mrs. Finlay. "We shall expect the guests here between half past seven and eight. We will gather in the drawing room." She addressed MacKinnon. "You may announce dinner at eight. If Lord Castlereagh accepts, he will accompany me to the dining room. We may put Lady Castlereagh with the Tory, Huskisson." She glanced down

31

at her list then back at MacKinnon. "And the Countess Wentworth can be escorted by her husband the earl . . . then Colonel Percy with his wife, and perhaps Wilberforce with his wife across from his fellow Whig, Lord Althorp. That should provide for some lively debate on both politics and morals.

"And my sister-in-law, Lady Agatha, we'll need someone to escort her. We'll round out the list with the Duc de Berry. I believe he's in town," she added to herself, then more briskly to the butler, "but I shall review the final list with you when I receive their replies."

"Yes, my lady."

She discussed a few more things with him concerning the table arrangements and silver to be used then pushed away from the table. "Very well. I shall go over the menu with Gaspard. We shall order some pheasant from Wexham Hall." At least the new earl didn't begrudge her the bounty from the estate.

Mrs. Finlay collected her notes and stood. "Very good, my lady. The steward shall be glad to send a brace or two, I'm sure."

"They will do well for the second course with a roast of lamb or beef. Perhaps some lobster or prawns and a soup for the first." She turned to MacKinnon. "Would you care to accompany me to the wine cellar and we can make some preliminary selections?"

He rose and gave a slight nod. "As you wish, my lady."

Despite his words, she couldn't help sensing something behind those smoky gray eyes that belied the tone of utmost respect.

She just couldn't quite put her finger on what it was.

Rees waited until Lady Wexham stood, then went to hold the door open for her. His thoughts were still wrapped around the fact that her guest list held a significant number of highly placed government officials and members of Parliament, including the foreign minister. If they indeed accepted her invitation to dinner, the Home Office had not exaggerated her influence.

He followed her down the hallway then preceded her down the

flight of stairs to the basement, collecting a branch of candles and tinderbox on his way down.

Before he could place the candelabra on the floor, Lady Wexham took it from him, while he dug in his pocket for his key ring.

"Thank you, my lady."

"Do you know anything about wines?"

Her question took him off guard. He unlocked the door to the wine cellar, a room situated beside his sleeping quarters, taking a few seconds to compose his answer. "I have . . . a little knowledge of spirits." Not quite the truth, not quite an untruth.

She stepped past him into the shadowy interior as he held the door open for her.

Stone walls and floor made the chamber noticeably cooler. Wooden shelves lined the walls from floor to ceiling. Dark green and brown bottles filled them, their thick bottoms facing outward.

On his first day of employment, when he'd been shown around, he'd been astounded at the vast collection stored in the cellar. When he was handed its key, he wondered idly what was to be done in the event of someone breaking into its stores. Was he expected to defend the wine, whose value was incalculable since the blockade with France? But thus far, there had been no incidents and he'd become accustomed to selecting a bottle for the chef, who didn't seem to be able to cook without wine.

Rees stepped in after Lady Wexham and left the door wide open behind him. He set the branch of candles on a table and proceeded to strike the tinder. When the room glowed with a soft radiance, he joined his employer where she stood in front of a rack.

"How are you finding it after a week?"

He was still nervous every time she addressed him, afraid he would betray by his words the fact that he was no butler. "I am getting my bearings, thank you, my lady."

He made a pretense of examining a shelf of bottles, turning one slightly to the right, another to the left. He'd learned about wines from working in his merchant father's warehouses in Bristol when he was a youth.

"Has the staff been helpful to you?"

He watched her, without seeming to, out of the corner of his eye. She stood not more than a foot away from him in the confined area. "Yes, very helpful."

"This is your first time as a full-fledged butler, is it not?"

What was she getting at? "Yes, my lady."

"You needn't 'my lady' me after every reply, you know."

His fingers stopped in the act of rubbing off a bit of dust from a bottle. Was his ignorance of how to address the peerage so obvious? "I beg your pardon, my l—" He couldn't help the warmth stealing into his cheeks.

She chuckled. "You probably feel the way I did when I was first married. I was very intimidated by so many servants. I had never lived in such a great household. And yet, at eighteen, as the new mistress, I was expected to assume responsibility for them all."

Her confession surprised him. "Is that why you address me as 'mister' and not merely 'MacKinnon'?"

Her eyes widened a fraction as if the question had caught her off guard. In the candlelight, her irises looked translucent, like an aged Calvados brandy. Then her lips quirked upward, perfectly delineated curves the color of pomegranate, a fruit he'd seen for the first time in Gibraltar, when his ship had been in port.

"Perhaps it is. A new endeavor can be terrifying."

He cleared his throat, wondering if this was a typical conversation between a lady of the house and her butler. "You seem to have succeeded admirably."

She gave a slight inclination of her head. "Thank you, sir. It has taken many years."

They continued regarding each other for a few seconds longer until she said, "You have only been in the position for a week."

"Yes. The other servants have been very kind."

"Even Monsieur Gaspard?"

His own lips crooked upward on one side. "He has not yet thrown any saucepans at me, at any rate. Only mutterings in French."

"Oh, do you understand French?"

"No," he said quickly. "No more than a word or two." He must not lose the advantage of understanding the language while they had no knowledge of his ability.

"You are fortunate indeed, then, if that is all you have endured. Wait but a fortnight."

"I shall hope to be agile enough to duck in time."

Her clear laughter echoed in the stone enclosure.

Why was he finding it so easy to talk this way with her? He had never been one to engage in lighthearted repartee, least of all with so highborn a lady.

Her expression sobered. "But perhaps the size of your previous household makes this one small by comparison. Your uncle said you have worked your way up the ranks to under-butler. You must be used to many dinner parties and catering to a variety of guests."

He hedged, choosing his words carefully. Whatever story he wove, he must remember its details in the future. Thankfully, he was a person mindful of details—one of the principal reasons he had been chosen for this task. "It was a large estate, but we saw few visitors. My employer was . . . a gentleman of advancing years who seldom entertained. Moreover, he and the . . . uh, mistress spent long periods of time absent from the household. It was not their—er—principal seat. That was in . . . Buckinghamshire."

She lifted a brow. "Indeed? Whereabouts? I go frequently to the Aylesbury Vale area."

Why had he chosen that county? He thought quickly of an area far removed from the area she mentioned. "It is near Beaconsfield."

She nodded. "Hartwell House is near Aylesbury. Are you familiar with it? It is where the Comte de Provence resides."

The Count of Provence, the self-appointed future king of France should Bonaparte ever fall. "Very little. I myself have never been to Buckinghamshire."

"My mother spends most of her time at Hartwell House. She forms part of the small French court which surrounds the count. It reminds her of how her life used to be in France."

He was not sure how to read her tone. Ironic or sympathetic? "Yes, I understand, my lady." Would Lady Wexham go to Hartwell while he was in this household? And if she did, how could he arrange to be taken along? As butler, he would be expected to remain behind, taking care of the house in its mistress's absence.

She pursed her fine lips. "Still, you seem much too young to be a butler. I hope my dinner party will not rattle you."

He thought of the guest list. Would anyone recognize him? Important members of government frequently came through the Foreign Office, where he had worked a number of years until being loaned to the Home Office for this spying assignment. Rees shook aside his worries, doubting anyone would recognize a lowly clerk as a butler in a West End residence.

Lady Wexham turned her attention back to the rack of bottles. "Well, I suppose we should put our minds to the upcoming dinner party. Your footmen will wonder what is keeping you."

He brought his thoughts back to the present. "You said you wished for shellfish and soup for the first courses?"

"Yes. I shall see what Gaspard finds at Billingsgate when he goes, then a joint of lamb, one of beef or veal, and the pheasant for the second course, accompanied by vegetables and aspics." She tapped a finger against her lips. "Asparagus would be nice this time of year, and then fruit and jellies or perhaps a trifle to finish."

He was perusing the bottles as she spoke and now removed one at his eye level. "May I suggest a 1771 Château Margaux claret with the lamb?" He took out his handkerchief and rubbed the dust from the bottle's label before placing it before her. "And perhaps a Calon-Ségur with the beef and veal, 1784. Both excellent years and ready to uncork if your guests merit such wines." His eyes met hers.

She arched her dark eyebrows as she took the first bottle from him. "Lord Castlereagh I should think does. The man has traveled widely and appreciates a good French wine."

Rees removed another bottle from its cradle on a higher shelf, thanking himself that he had inspected the cellars when he'd first come on the job. "There are some good Pavillon Blancs for the pheasant and fish."

"You seem to know more of French wines than you let on, unlike most of your countrymen," she added with a low chuckle that skittered over his nerve endings like a silken cloth.

His gaze continued perusing the racks, pretending nonchalance as he berated himself for showing off. "The butler at my . . . other place of employment taught me."

"I shan't deny I was doubtful when your uncle recommended you, but I see I was wrong . . . at least when it comes to selecting wines," she said in an amused tone.

He thought it prudent to make no reply. Instead he handed down another bottle, taking the first from her. "Madeira to begin with and let's see . . . some Armagnac and port for the gentlemen after dinner. Unless, of course, you prefer exclusively French cognac." He met her gaze once more.

"The Portuguese make a fine brandy." She took the bottle from him. "Just because I was born across the Channel does not mean I think only French products are superior."

"You were fortunate to stock your cellars so well before the blockade." Or did she patronize the smugglers' trade?

"My late husband the earl had the foresight to arrange imports from Bordeaux and Bourgogne during the short peace." Her lips twitched. "I think he must have brought over a boatload before the blockade was resumed."

"A wise gentleman." His mind couldn't help calculating. The countess had not been married to the old earl then but had been a young lady in Paris during those nine months of the Peace of Amiens.

What had she been doing there? The question had intrigued him when he'd first read her file, and did so now as he gazed into her beguiling eyes.

"He was wise in certain things." Her words seemed to contain more than the mere surface meaning. She handed the bottle back and rubbed her fingertips.

He quickly proffered his handkerchief. "Excuse the dust."

She wiped her hands off with the white cloth. "That is quite all right. Thank you," she said, returning it. "I see that I can leave the selection of wines safely in your capable hands. You may confer with Gaspard on the final choices."

He inclined his head.

"Good. Make sure you request the proper service from Mrs. Finlay the day before the dinner party. She will have the kitchen maids wash everything before your footmen lay the table. You can give her any silver that needs washing."

"Yes, my lady." Whatever brief moment of informality had trans-pired between them was clearly over and she had returned to her brisk tone of mistress of the house.

"You may rest assured, my lady, that everything will be ready for your guests. I will be on hand to receive them and have them shown up to the drawing room. We will announce dinner as soon as everyone has arrived and make certain all covers are removed with as little encumbrance to your guests as possible."

"Excellent. I will make an inspection of the dining room before they arrive."

"Very well." He sounded like the perfect butler. Perhaps he would even end up fooling himself.

Her gaze rested on him once more. "If this dinner party goes off well, I shall be forever in your debt."

Once again her words arrested his attention as if they were speaking on two different levels. Was there more behind them than a simple exchange between butler and mistress?

Before he could analyze it further, Lady Wexham backed away from him and exited the cellar, leaving a variety of impressions in her wake.

Rees stood, a bottle in his hand, breathing in the faint scent of roses on the air, a welcome antidote to the damp smell of mortar permeating the small cellar.

A lady being gracious to her new butler, or a French spy suspecting any new person in her household of being a counterspy?

He looked down at the bottle he was still holding in his hands, realizing how easy it was going to be to let something slip and give himself away.

Part of it was pride—a good part, he admitted to himself, disliking intensely this lowly role he must play for the duration of his sojourn in this house. He should have shown himself ignorant of wines. Thankfully, she seemed to accept his explanation.

As a Christian man, he didn't like untruths, but this assignment would involve nothing but untruths, so he'd better steel himself to weaving them. He'd always heard that the closer one stuck to the truth, the more believable one's lies. Well, he would put that theory to the test in the coming days or weeks.

He thought about Lady Wexham's dinner party—with a guest list of distinguished individuals from the highest levels of government. This was exactly the kind of social event Rees was here to witness, to keep his eyes and ears open for any whisper of just what Lady Wexham's game was. Where did her true sympathies lie, with the Comte de Provence, who lived in exile just outside London, and who soon might be the new king of France—or with Napoleon Bonaparte, who still held the vast majority of Europe in his grasp and was Britain's greatest foe?

If Lady Wexham was guilty of any treason to the British government, Rees would find out, cost him whatever dignity it might.

4

*L*ater that day Céline scowled at her maid through the dressing table mirror. "Careful, my hair is attached to my scalp."

Valentine's reply was to grasp a hank of her locks and pull the brush even harder.

"Ouch!"

Valentine ignored her exclamation. With firm, dexterous motions she took up Céline's hair and twisted it into a knot atop her head and proceeded immediately to stick pins into it. "If you want to look presentable this evening, you must pay the price."

Céline yawned. "Another tedious dinner. Though I have heard favorable things about the opera *Artaxerxes*." The mention of the dinner she was attending reminded her of the one she was planning.

She glanced at Valentine's reflection in the mirror. "What do you think of Mr. MacKinnon?"

Valentine snorted. "He is no butler."

The statement brought her up short, forcing her to remember the strange way he'd made her feel in the narrow confines of the wine cellar. She'd pushed aside the sensations as soon as she'd left the cellar, preferring not to dwell on them.

Céline raised her eyebrows now at her maid. "No butler? Why, what has he done?"

"What hasn't he done?" she scoffed. "He is too young to know anything of heading a house of consequence."

Céline relaxed at Valentine's words, seeing the woman had no unusual qualms about the new servant. "Well, we had no choice in the matter really. I couldn't refuse Rumford's offer. He felt so badly already, I didn't want to add to his burden."

"Bah! He should not have forced you to take a family member in his place. I'm sure we could have done well without a stranger coming in."

"We didn't know how long Rumford would be laid up. It is no light matter, to fall like that at his age. If he weren't so far away, I would pay him a visit, but his sister assured me he is receiving the best of care."

"To go to Yorkshire on holiday! He had no business going so far."

"He cannot help it if his family lives there. If you had your way, none of the servants would ever have a holiday or visit their relatives, eh?"

"They don't know how good they have it with you as their mistress—and they take full advantage!" She ran the comb through the hairbrush to clean it out and placed the two back on the dresser. "If you didn't have me to look after your interests, they would have long since robbed you of all the earl left you."

Céline laughed aloud at that. "That would take some doing."

Valentine curled a ringlet of Céline's hair around her finger. "Still, it is not right to travel so far. What if I were to demand to go to France?"

"Well, it would hardly be practical with the blockade. If we weren't at war, I should by no means forbid you to return to France for a visit."

Valentine merely sniffed and continued fiddling with Céline's coiffure. "There, that should do. Is Lady Agatha accompanying you tonight?"

Céline made a face at the mention of the late earl's spinster sister who lived with her. "Yes, she'll probably complain of the food and then chatter without pause through the opera."

"Why do you continue to suffer that woman under your roof?"

Céline sighed, often wondering at the same thing herself. "Because she has nowhere else to go."

Valentine snorted. "No one else would take her in!"

Céline rose and smoothed the ivory-colored gown. A square emerald glinted in a pearl choker at her throat. Valentine handed her a pair of ivory kid gloves. Céline pulled them on and walked to the pier glass, preferring not to discuss her sister-in-law. Agatha was her cross to bear, as she called it privately. At least she no longer had to suffer the earl.

She gave herself a final inspection in the long glass, pinching her cheeks. "I am not so pale now, am I?"

"No, you have achieved a bit of color since this morning."

She touched the thin strand of pearls interwoven in her hair. "Will I do?"

Valentine fussed some more with the skirt of her gown. Finally, she stepped back and nodded abruptly. "You'll do. The color becomes you."

"Yes, Madame Delantre has the right touch."

"I still think you should have found a replacement for Rumford through an agency."

Céline blinked at the sudden return to the topic of butler. Her hand went to the choker at her neck, touching the stone. "An agency? Dear me, no. Not when Mr. MacKinnon comes so highly recommended by his uncle. If he shouldn't live up to the task, he knows he'll have to answer to him. So, I am sorry, Valentine, but you will have to put aside your prejudices for a few weeks."

"A man so good-looking has no right to be a butler!"

Céline felt a warmth rise to her cheeks. She, too, had noticed MacKinnon's looks, especially when he'd stood so close and made that strange remark about her addressing him as "Mr. MacKinnon." She looked at her reflection, pretending to adjust the lace trim edging her neckline. "Why, Valentine, it's not like you to be so dead set against anyone for his looks." She smiled inwardly. Mr. MacKinnon had probably rebuffed one of Valentine's overtures, for her to hold him in such contempt.

She met her abigail's gaze in the mirror. "In any case, I shall judge Mr. MacKinnon's abilities for myself at my dinner party next week."

"Let us hope he does not embarrass you with some clumsy faux pas among your guests."

Céline laughed and left her maid straightening up her clutter, though inwardly she couldn't help a worry that her temporary butler might not prove up to the task of a dinner party full of important guests.

Rees awoke the next morning with a start, his heart racing with fear. Lady Wexham was calling to him and he was trying to reach her.

He closed his eyes again, trying to recapture the scene. She'd been in trouble of some sort. Rarely did he dream so vividly. His hand reached out as if to recall the dream. It had been dark. They'd been riding—or had it only been he and she in a carriage? He'd seen her pale face as if through a glass.

He rubbed his hand across his face to awaken himself fully, but it only caused the images to further fade.

It had only been a dream. It held no significance, no doubt brought on by his worry over the coming dinner party he would be responsible for as butler. His heart gradually subsided to its natural rhythm, but the sense of foreboding didn't leave him.

Lord, show me what, if anything, this means. He listened but sensed only stillness. He continued praying a few moments longer.

Finally, knowing he wouldn't fall asleep again that morning, he pulled off the bedcovers and grabbed his dressing gown from the straight-back chair beside his narrow bed. He glanced at his pocket watch lying atop his neatly folded clothes on the chair. It was only half past five, still too early to rise. As butler, he was also privileged with later hours than those under him, who would be stirring soon. He was not required to make an appearance until breakfast time—for the servants between eight o'clock and nine—depending on when each one had finished his morning chores. He'd also been greatly relieved to discover that as a butler, he was privileged with a room to himself apart from all the other servants, who lived on the top floor. Only Mrs. Finlay and the French cook shared the basement

43

floor, but their quarters were at the opposite end of the basement at the rear, near the kitchen.

Although it was referred to as the basement, it really was only a half basement, two-thirds submerged underground, but with enough room aboveground to afford a narrow horizontal window at street level by the service entrance.

He stood at the window now, pushing aside the filmy curtain—another sign of his employer's thoughtfulness, in providing a servant's room with privacy from passersby. The view from his window was of the concrete bay containing the service stairs to the sidewalk. The clomp of the milkmaid's clogs sounded on the street above, fading as she moved on to the next house after filling up their can of milk. The lamplighter climbed up to the lamp, dousing its flame. Everything else on the street was quiet.

His thoughts drifted to the strange twists and turns of life that had brought him to this fashionable address from the small cell he'd called his office in the bowels of the Foreign Office.

There he'd sat translating and cataloging documents and deciphering messages intercepted by their agents across the Channel. Painstakingly preparing reports for Lord Castlereagh, and for Mr. Fox before him, hoping someday to catch someone's eye and be promoted into the realm of real diplomacy, perhaps as a chargé d'affaires in some foreign embassy or post.

But after ten years, Rees had lost hope of advancement. Then scarcely a month ago, the promotion he'd been striving for had been dangled before him like the French fleet before Nelson.

But it came at a price. A steep one.

Rees rubbed the bridge of his nose, still not sure if he'd done the right thing in accepting the assignment thrust upon him. Not that he'd been given much choice.

He remembered his initial excitement at the senior clerk's words: "I have a new assignment for you. One that can yield high dividends if you play your cards right."

Rees said nothing at first, distrustful of the young man's words. Alistair Oglethorpe, third son of a baronet—as he'd let Rees know his first day at the Foreign Office and at every opportunity since then—had come in only a few months ago and been put in charge of the junior clerks, who had a much longer tenure.

Oglethorpe raised a pale brown eyebrow. "Well, aren't you interested? Or do you prefer to continue toiling away at your desk in obscurity?"

Rees ignored the question, having grown inured to the man's barbs. "Very well, what is it you wish me to do?"

Oglethorpe twirled a quill between his fingers. "Too much information is going across the Channel and getting to Bonaparte. We need to tighten our scrutiny of the émigré community."

Rees frowned. While the Foreign Office supervised all British spies on the Continent, the Home Office was responsible for monitoring any spying activities in the British Isles.

Oglethorpe's next words captured Rees's full attention. "We're sending you over to the Home Office."

"I beg your pardon?"

Oglethorpe smiled, an expression that always came across as a smirk to Rees. "It's quite simple, old boy. They have oversight over all the French émigrés living in England and you know French."

Rees's childhood French had been honed by the months he'd spent in a French prison when his frigate had been sunk off the coast of Brest.

"They need someone who knows how to ferret out anything peculiar." Oglethorpe shrugged. "You have been able to break codes. I told Lord Sidmouth I had a man who could fill the requirements of what they're looking for."

Rees's excitement began to grow. Perhaps a real opportunity for promotion was presenting itself.

Oglethorpe leaned forward, placing his elbows on his desk and tapping its surface with the tip of the quill. "We'd like you to play at butler in a prominent French household in Mayfair."

Rees grappled to understand what Oglethorpe was telling him. "You want me to what?"

Oglethorpe's smirk deepened. "To spy. You'll assume the role of a butler. It shouldn't be too difficult for you. Just look stiff—the way you're accustomed to around here—and stand at attention."

When Rees had dared to question the orthodoxy of such an assignment for a clerk, Oglethorpe leaned back in his chair and eyed him through his glass. It irked Rees that his superior was but three-and-twenty—eight years his junior.

"It's this way, Phillips. Anyone we have with the skills for such an assignment is either over in France already or would be recognized in a fashionable house in the West End." He chuckled. "Who would recognize a junior clerk with your—ahem—background?"

Oglethorpe loved to lord his aristocratic standing over Rees's middle-class one—ignoring the fact of how recent his father's minor title was. He rubbed his hands together as if he had thought of the scheme himself. "It's a perfect ruse. You know French and excel at trifling details. You have a talent at seeing patterns where others don't. It must have to do with staring at those scribbles all day. If there's anything out of the ordinary in that household, you'll be the one to spot it."

He yawned behind a pale, manicured hand. "Really, you should be honored. You can enter that tonnish realm and partake of its splendors, as a butler, of course." He laughed then shuffled the papers on his desk—reports Rees had been up late to compile—and adopted a dismissive tone. "It shouldn't take you long, if indeed Lady Wexham is sending information back to Boney's people. You're to report to the Home Office tomorrow morning. They'll fill you in on everything."

As Rees stood to leave, Oglethorpe threw out the last inducement. "You'll be well rewarded. Sidmouth told me himself, if you help draw out a French spy, the Crown will show its appreciation."

So, it came to lowering himself to masquerading as a butler for a few weeks in a countess's London establishment, or spending the rest of his days in a basement cubicle in Whitehall answering to a pompous ignoramus.

From one basement to another.

Céline rang for a fresh pot of tea before returning her attention to her guests. "Tell me, Kimberley, how have you been amusing yourself since you've arrived in London?" She was fond of her niece, even though she was only related to her by marriage. She and her mother had come to pay a morning call.

They talked for several minutes about the different balls and routs Kimberley had attended since her coming out.

"I am so relieved she had her presentation before Princess Augusta's death," her mother, the new Countess of Wexham, said. Céline retained the title only as a courtesy. "Can you imagine if we had waited until now when they are all in mourning?" She shuddered. "As it was, the Queen's Drawing Room was well attended when Kimberley made her debut."

"There is nothing like a young lady's presentation," Agatha simpered, looking up from her tambour screen.

Since Kimberley and the countess were her direct relations and the new heirs, Agatha fawned over them. Céline suspected she was hoping to be invited to live with them in their Grosvenor Square mansion—the house that had been Céline's home until the old earl's death.

Bernice, the countess, folded her hands in her lap. "Since then, Kimberley has received so many callers." She smiled indulgently at her daughter. "Such nice young gentlemen like the Duke of Devonshire and Lord Delamere have been quite assiduous in their attentions."

The color rose in the girl's cheeks.

Céline smiled. "Have any of them found favor with you or are you keeping them all at bay for the moment?" she teased.

Kimberley looked down at her gloved hands, which clutched her reticule. "I don't know . . . they've all been so civil."

"There is no rush to settle on any one gentleman yet," Céline hastened to assure her. "You're but seventeen and in your first season."

Kimberley's blue eyes widened. "But Lady Wexham, didn't you wed during your first season?"

Céline smoothed the worked muslin of her gown. "Yes, that is so. But I hold that a young lady has plenty of time and should enjoy her first season."

Agatha pulled her embroidery needle up from the frame. "A young lady can't afford to let a good offer pass. More than two seasons and she is in danger of being considered on the shelf."

Céline reined in her irritation at her sister-in-law. It seemed whatever she said, Agatha would take the contrary position.

Bernice sniffed. "Plenty of young women marry at Kimberley's age. Why, I myself made what my parents considered a very good match at eighteen. As did you," she added with a pointed look at Céline.

Céline's sympathy for young Kimberley grew. Between her mother and great-aunt Agatha, they would have her married to the highest bidder, regardless of how suited the couple was to each other. She hated the thought of young ladies being forced into marriage against their will with no thought to their future happiness. To be shackled to someone merely for sake of name or fortune could become a nightmare once the vows were exchanged and the couple settled down to married life.

She laughed to lighten the atmosphere. "You must enjoy your seasons, Kimberley, and trust that you'll meet the right young man in good time whether it's one season or several."

"Several? I should think not!" Agatha declared, knotting her thread. "I'm sure Kimberley will meet nothing less than a duke or marquess this very season."

Céline eyed her sister-in-law, wondering what possessed her seamstress to suggest that particular shade of evening primrose against her complexion. "I'm certain she shall meet many young gentlemen. She has no need to fear being left on the shelf." She gave Agatha a pointed look. The earl's sister had never married. No man would offer for so disagreeable a personality regardless of her portion.

Agatha pinched her lips together and concentrated on her stitch, an ugly flush staining her sallow cheeks.

Céline considered taking a hand in young Kimberley's season. At least she could help the poor chit broaden her opportunities before she was forced into some loveless marriage. She considered what to do as she poured the tea William had just brought in.

When they had all been served, she eyed the ladies over the rim of her cup. "I should like to give you a ball, Kimberley."

The girl gasped. "A ball? Truly, Aunt Céline?" She turned to her mother, a smile breaking open on her mouth. "Did you hear that, a ball for me!"

"How very thoughtful of you, Céline." Despite her words, the new countess's words held a complacency that showed she considered it a matter of course that Céline should host a ball for her daughter. Céline tried not to let it annoy her. By now she should be used to the fact that if she had borne the late earl a son, Bernice with her bobbing ostrich feathers would not be flaunting her status in Céline's drawing room.

"When is it to be?"

Kimberley's tone held such enthusiasm that Céline's irritation disappeared. "Let's see . . ." She tapped a finger against her chin. "We need time to get out the invitations. It needs to be a large ball. We'll clear the drawing room and the rear sitting room as well, and open the connecting doors. I shall hire musicians, we need flowers, and of course, a theme."

"Oh yes, a theme!" Kimberley leaned forward. "Lady Thorncroft's ball was fairies and sprites."

Céline nodded, casting about for something original. Although she was used to entertaining, she hadn't held a ball since long before the earl had passed away.

As the ladies took up the discussion, deciding whom to invite and when to hold the ball, Céline continued pondering. She wanted to attract the best crowd and make sure enough eligible bachelors showed up for Kimberley's sake. If her mother was going to pressure her into a betrothal her first season, the least Céline could do was ensure the poor girl would have a wide array to choose from.

She turned her thoughts to the ball's theme. Hmm. What would be a good draw this season? A fête of flowers, a rite of spring, Arabian nights? She discarded them as already having been done or too ostentatious in a time of mourning for Princess Augusta.

She continued thinking. What was on everyone's mind?

The war.

That was a depressing thought. But wait, why not turn it around? A patriotic ball. Decorate the drawing room with the colors of various regiments. Celebrate some of the Peninsular victories. Invite the Horse Guards and whichever other officers were on leave.

It would certainly draw everyone. A sort of morale boost.

And with so many military figures in her ballroom, who was to say what bits of information she might glean?

She smiled at Kimberley. "I have an idea for the theme . . ."

The next afternoon, Céline had a hard time sitting for her portrait. Her mind flitted from one thing to another—from details for the upcoming dinner party to the many tasks to be done for Kimberley's ball.

She half-regretted her impulsive gesture to host the ball. But she quickly shook away any qualms, reminding herself sternly of the reasons. She would not have the poor girl subjected to the same fate she had been forced to endure.

"My lady, if you could erase the scowl from your pretty features and look this way, please."

She smiled at the artist, one of the most renowned in the country. "Forgive me, Mr. Lawrence."

"You are too beautiful a lady to appear to all posterity as if you were forever having the blue devils."

"Indeed not." She straightened her shoulders, attempted to lighten her features, and glanced in the direction the portraitist indicated, wondering why she had agreed to this portrait. Perhaps because in a couple of years she would be thirty.

A soft knock interrupted the depressing thought.

Trying not to move from her pose, she called, "Enter."

"Excuse me, my lady, you rang for me."

At the sound of MacKinnon's voice, she turned just enough to face him. "Yes. Please, don't stand there in the doorway, come in."

His glance shifted to the painter. "I can return at a better time. I don't wish to disturb you."

She waved aside his concerns. "Nonsense. Mr. Lawrence can continue working as we talk." She motioned to the silver salver her butler carried in one hand. "Good, you brought my visitors' cards. I wish to go over them with you. Could you be so kind as to read the names for me?" She had only just returned half an hour ago from her own morning visits and needed to continue familiarizing her new butler with those visitors for whom she was in and those to whom she was unavailable.

"Certainly." He picked up the first card. "Lord Dunston."

She wrinkled her nose. "When did he call?"

"Shortly after noon. It was his second visit today."

She sighed. "Very well. If he calls again, show him up." Prosy old bore.

He picked up the next card. "Countess Wexham and her daughter."

"Oh, I am sorry I missed them. I'm sure they are here to discuss the ball." At the lift of his dark eyebrow, she added, "I have decided to hold a ball here in Lady Kimberley's honor." Her butler really did have fine eyebrows, she noted as she spoke—straight and heavy and very dark. They set off his light-colored eyes to distinction, making them appear all the more deep set.

She tilted her head, unmindful of the portraitist's impatient throat-clearing. "Do you think you are up to a ball, Mr. MacKinnon?"

Her butler inclined his head a fraction. "I shall endeavor to do my best."

He certainly had all the imperturbability of a butler in the making. And yet . . . there was something behind that steady regard. "That is all I can ask. In any case, I shall be discussing it further with you and Mrs. Finlay."

"Very good, my lady." He read another card. "Mrs. Morrison. She called about an hour ago."

"I'm in for her."

"Mr. Smythe-Wiley and his sisters."

"No," she said promptly.

"Miss Jamieson."

"Yes."

"Lord Marley."

"Hmm . . ." She pursed her lips, considering. "Yes."

He set the last card back down. "Those are the individuals who called when you were out."

"Good, that takes care of the first lot for today. You shall have to bring the other cards to my sitting room as visitors arrive." Her lips curled upward. "Don't worry, soon enough you'll know who are the dead bores, who *must* be received, and those I take pleasure in receiving." She couldn't help a laugh. "The latter list is quite short, so you shall have no problems with that one."

His own lips quirked upward at one corner, but then he quickly cleared his throat, erasing all amusement from his features. "Yes, my lady."

Valentine's words drifted into her thoughts. She could well understand how her abigail had found this man's looks and understated charms irresistible. "I shall be going out again, so please tell the coachman to have the phaeton ready at five."

"Yes, my lady." Although the words were spoken in a calm way that revealed nothing, the butler's gaze held an intensity that not only intrigued her—but drew her.

She tore her gaze away with effort, looking instead to her portraitist. He was tapping his paintbrush against his palette. "I must resume my pose for the long-suffering Mr. Lawrence. He is much sought after, and I mustn't waste his time."

MacKinnon took a step back and bowed. "I beg your pardon, my lady."

Before she could make any reply, he turned away, leaving her feeling as if something unfinished lay between them.

5

The next morning, Rees left his room and headed down the basement corridor to the rear of the house for breakfast. He entered the servants' dining room adjacent to the kitchen to hear Valentine speaking to one of the chambermaids. "You zink you can get in her ladyship's good graces with zis?"

The lady's maid jabbed her finger in the chambermaid's face. Rees paused on the threshold, observing the two, who had not heard him come in.

"You had better watch yourself, you stupid girl, or you'll be scrubbing ze scullery floor—"

Rees coughed, hastening forward. "What has Miss—Virginia," he remembered in time, "done to cause you displeasure?" He tried to look his frostiest as he eyed the Frenchwoman.

Valentine glared at him. "This slattern who calls herself a parlor maid has made a mess of her ladyship's belongings. I am absent for an evening, and she cannot serve her ladyship without leaving everything in disarray."

He held up his hand to silence her and turned to the girl, who looked hardly more than seventeen, her eyes large with fright. "What is it that you have—ahem—supposedly done?"

"Supposedly done!" Valentine's dark eyes flashed at him. "There is no supposed about it. She is a clumsy, ignorant—" Valentine lapsed into a string of French, ending with the clear *"cochon!"* Pig.

Rees could not let on that he understood her insults. "That is enough, Valentine." He gave the other maid his attention once again. "Virginia, please continue." He waited, his hand still held up to keep the other woman silent. Valentine only fumed at him, her arms crossed.

"If you please, Mr. MacKinnon . . . I've done nothing wrong." The young woman was near tears. Casting fearful glances at Valentine, she continued at Rees's nod. "Mlle. Valentine accused m-me of l-leaving a mess in her ladyship's room the night h-her ladyship came home early, but, sir, Lady Wexham insisted I leave her things as they were. I-I tried to tidy up, sir, honestly I did, but she wished only for me to leave. She said that Valentine would take care of things in the morning—"

Valentine harrumphed. "I'm sure ze countess did not mean for you to rummage about in her armoire and wrinkle her gowns when she told you to leave her things."

Rees swallowed, realizing exactly who had left the disorder. "Ahem. Did you leave her armoire in the state Valentine describes?"

Virginia shook her head vigorously. "Oh no, sir, indeed I did not. Her ladyship didn't even permit me to open it."

"Very well."

"Is zat all you can say!" Valentine spat at him. "You will let her get away with zis because she is a silly young thing—"

Before she began to hurl insults at him, he pulled himself up, towering over her. "That is enough! If Virginia says she did not do what you accuse her of, that is final. You will have to see to the tidying up yourself."

"How—how dare you!"

"Because I am butler in this household. If you do not like that fact, we will go to Lady Wexham and ask for her account. If she did indeed tell Virginia not to open the armoires, then she did not." He knew full well Valentine was not going to want to go to the countess. But he didn't like having to make more an enemy of her than he already had.

He had not been in the household more than a day when she had sought him out in a dim passageway of the house and begun to flirt with him. The last thing he needed was an entanglement with a French lady's maid.

Valentine continued eyeing him with malevolence in her dark eyes. She was not an unattractive woman, slim, of medium height, with dark hair and eyes. He judged her to be around his own age, thirty or so. But he found nothing attractive in her disdainful attitude.

It had crossed his mind that to enter into a flirtation with her would possibly help him ferret out information about the countess. Didn't they say that servants were privy to most things in a household—and a trusted lady's maid to her mistress's most guarded secrets?

But Rees had drawn the line at going to those lengths. If there were secrets to be discovered, he wasn't going to dally with a maid to uncover them. The fact that she, too, was French meant that she could very well be working with the countess.

He nodded in a clipped fashion to the women. "Very well, be about your business, the two of you." One benefit of being butler was that his word was law.

Valentine sniffed and flounced away. Virginia smiled gratefully and bobbed a curtsy before backing away. "Thank you, sir. Honestly, I didn't do anything but what I was supposed to—"

He smiled in reassurance. "It's all right. I'm sure there is a logical explanation for it all." *Which none of you will ever discover.*

Mrs. Finlay entered from the kitchen, ushering them to the table. "Breakfast is served."

With a gesture to Virginia to precede him, Rees made his way to the head of the long table. It was set with a white cloth and a place for each of the servants. The two scullery maids were scurrying from kitchen to table with steaming dishes.

The footmen, other maids, housekeeper, and outdoor staff found their places and stood behind their chairs, waiting for his appearance before taking their seats. It had been both humbling and daunting to realize his position as butler. He was only a servant above stairs. An ineffaceable line of demarcation existed between him and the world of his employer.

But below stairs he was king, all of the other servants deferring to him, even Mrs. Finlay, though as housekeeper she was almost his equal, the chatelaine key ring at her waist marking her position. Everyone respected Rees's word . . . except the two French servants, Valentine and the cook, Gaspard, who insisted on being called a chef.

"Good morning," Rees greeted the servants around the table, then with a nod to them all, he signaled his permission for them to be seated. In the few days he'd had to receive his training from Mr. Rumford, the old butler had informed Rees on the precise hierarchy that governed this large household.

Rees let his gaze wander over the faces gazing back at him, waiting for him to bless the food so they could begin to eat. The chef sat to his immediate right, Valentine to his left, Mrs. Finlay at the foot of the table. Ranged down the length of the table were the other servants in order of importance and seniority. A dozen besides himself, footmen, parlor maids, kitchen maids, coachman, groom.

When the scullery maids had brought in the last dishes, they, too, took their places at the very end of the table.

Rees bowed his head. "Bless, O Father, thy gifts to our use and us to thy service, for Christ's sake. Amen."

The servants joined him in the amen then immediately unfolded their napkins and began passing plates. He was in charge of dishing out the main servings, a mixture of French and English-style fare, so he took up the plates as they were handed to him and spooned out the fluffy eggs, slices of fried ham, sautéed mushrooms, and cold pâtés. Baskets of bread were passed amongst the servants.

Gaspard snapped open his own napkin and took the first plate Rees filled. With a look of disdain from under his heavy black eyebrows and nary a "*merci*," he bent over his plate and began to eat.

One of the scullery maids soon got up and began pouring tea or coffee for everyone else.

Rees compared this household of servants to those at his mother's house. These days his mother and sister relied on only a cook and a woman of all work. When his father had been alive and they'd lived in the prosperous port city of Bristol, there had been a couple of additional servants. But he'd never lived in a household with so many to do for so few.

Taking his first forkful, Rees glanced at the chef. Gaspard was a gifted cook, he had to concede. He was perhaps in his midforties with lank black hair and a pale, almost sickly complexion. Perhaps he spent too much time at his stove and very little out of doors.

Rees only half paid attention to the servants' talk around him as he pondered his next move in this game of stealth he was embarked upon. He let his gaze roam slowly over the members of the staff. He'd only searched Lady Wexham's rooms—and not even finished those. Perhaps he should go through the two footmen's. Not that he suspected them of anything. Tom and William, strapping young men of equal height and build, were thoroughly British, and if by some stretch of the imagination he could conceive of their behaving traitorously, they weren't smart enough. They were the ones he worked closest with and he'd had their measure in the short time he'd been in the household.

Tom was chatting in a lively manner with Virginia and Sally across from him, while William, the other footman, looked on, injecting a comment now and then. Tom was almost holding court, Rees observed with amusement, the young maids looking as spellbound as if he were recounting a fairy tale.

Tom poked a fork toward Sally. "I had it from the head footman at Melbourne House that Lady Caroline is once again making a cake of herself over Lord Byron now that she is back from her exile."

William chortled over a mouthful of scrambled eggs. "I heard when she asked for a lock of his hair, he sent her one of Lady Oxford's."

The young footmen guffawed. "He said it was lucky coincidence that its color and texture were the same!"

One of the scullery maids looked round-eyed. "Poor Lady Caroline. Isn't Lady Oxford old?"

Tom gave her a pitying look. "Not so old . . ." he added in a suggestive way.

Rees glanced down to the end of the table to Mrs. Finlay, who was eating in the methodical way she did everything, addressing only an occasional comment to the scullery maids and the chambermaids nearest her. She was a woman of around fifty, with a trim figure and serious demeanor, her honey-brown hair half mixed with gray.

She looked up from her plate and said in a voice to be heard above the footmen, "Mr. Gaspard, did Lady Wexham discuss the menu for the dinner party with you?"

He wiped his mouth with his napkin. "*Certainement.*"

Mrs. Finlay gave no sign that she noticed his scornful tone. "I should like to talk with you about it after breakfast. I must decide on which service to use for each course."

"*Bien sûr.*" His eyes snapped to the scullery maids. "Ellie, Sarah, you will accompany me to the market this morning. We must look for ze *truffes*, ze lobster, ze morels"—he waved a hand—"and everyzing else for ze dinner."

"Yes, sir," the two girls murmured.

Rees fixed his attention on cutting a piece of ham on his plate. If Gaspard was at the market later in the morning, and the two footmen were busy blacking boots, perhaps he could do a quick search of the chef's room. It would only be a small window of time, but he could at least do a cursory inspection.

He brought the piece of ham to his mouth and chewed it thoughtfully, studying the man out of the corner of his eye.

If anyone in this household was a spy, he'd lay odds it was Monsieur Gaspard.

Or perhaps he was merely an arrogant French chef, for whom only food was worthy of respect. Rees suspected that even Lady Wexham was careful in her treatment of him. If he were the least ruffled, he could threaten to quit. A good French chef, no matter how temperamental, would be snapped up by another hostess in Mayfair before teatime.

As if sensing his observation, Gaspard turned his black eyes to him, a scowl creating a deep furrow between the heavy black brows. Rees held up his fork. "Delicious ham."

"Humph!" he snorted.

Spy or chef, Rees intended to discover which.

Rees hid his impatience as he waited for Gaspard to leave for the market. At intervals, he found excuses to wander down to the kitchen, but each time, to his growing uneasiness, the man was still bustling about, showing no signs of departing.

Soon the footmen would be finished with their morning tasks, and a search would be too risky.

It wasn't until the servants had partaken of their midmorning tea that Gaspard finally left with the two scullery maids in tow.

Rees wiped at an imaginary smudge on a brass doorknob before addressing the two footmen. "The wine cellar is in abysmal condition. I want each bottle wiped clean with a rag."

Tom and William gaped at him. "The wine cellar, sir?" Tom, the boldest, dared ask.

Rees gave him a quelling look. "That is correct. When I was in there last with Lady Wexham, I was appalled at how dirty everything was."

"B-but, sir, old Rumford never permitted us in there. He preferred the bottles to show their age. We cleaned them, o' course, whenever he brought one up."

"Be that as it may, I would prefer you wipe every bottle off." He plowed on, sounding as uncompromising and obdurate as he imagined a good butler would. "I was obliged to lend Lady Wexham my handkerchief to clean her fingers after taking down a bottle."

Tom shut his mouth on whatever he was going to say. "Very well, sir, if you think we ought. I just hope Rumford doesn't chew us up for meddling in his cellar."

"I shall speak to Mr. Rumford myself upon his return and explain whatever additional duties I have required of you." He turned away from them. "Very well, be about the task."

"Sir—"

He swiveled around, allowing just a trace of impatience in his tone. "Yes?"

William cleared his throat. "The key. We can't get in otherwise."

He felt the flush along his jawline. "Yes, of course. Come along."

He marched down the stairs, as if they had been at fault. The two followed at his heels.

He left them with plenty of clean rags, staring slack jawed at the rows of bottles, and felt only a slight qualm. Hopefully, he wouldn't return in an hour to find bottles missing or telltale signs that they had been imbibing. He tried to think of a way to warn them that he'd be aware of how many bottles there were. Mr. Rumford kept a detailed account book cataloging every bottle, but Rees was not such a mutton head to think he'd be able to tell upon a quick inspection.

"Very well, carry on. I shall be down by and by to check on your progress."

"Yes, sir," they both chimed in.

Rees made his way back down the dim corridor then up the service stairs to make them believe he was going to the upper part of the house.

The chambermaids were busy cleaning the upstairs receiving rooms. He could hear them chattering in the parlor.

He had little time to lose. He retraced his way down the stairs to the basement and headed toward Mrs. Finlay's sitting room.

He knocked smartly and poked his head in the door at her immediate reply to come in. "Lady Wexham wishes to see you in her sitting room." That much was true as the countess desired to go over dinner party details.

The housekeeper was sitting at her account books. "Very good, sir. I shall go straightaway." She closed the ledger and rose, her keys jingling at her waist, and straightened her starched white cap.

He held the door for her and closed it after her.

As she walked away from him toward the service stairs, he jangled his own set of keys and pretended to head toward the wine cellar, but as soon as the housekeeper was out of sight up the stairs, he did an about-face and continued past her room. He glanced quickly into the kitchen, but it was empty, everything tidy. He paused in front of the servants' dining hall then walked through it to the room in the rear used by Gaspard.

He knocked, although he didn't expect any reply.

After a few seconds of silence, he glanced behind him then quickly turned the knob, but it resisted his pressure.

He paused, not expecting to find it locked. Why would a servant lock his room?

Quickly, Rees dug into his own pocket and took out his skeleton key. His palms starting to sweat, he slid it into the keyhole. He breathed a sigh of relief when it turned easily.

He pushed the door open and peered into the crack. Finding the room empty, he entered and shut the door softly behind him, pocketing his keys. He'd have to make sure to lock the door behind him again.

Taking a deep breath, he let his eyes roam more slowly around the perimeters of the narrow room, picking out the details. The first thing that struck him was how untidy it was.

Like his own, this chamber had only enough room for an iron bedstead, narrow chest of drawers, and a corded trunk at the foot of the bed. Some wooden knobs on the wall opposite the bed held some aprons and clothes.

The resemblance to his room ended there. The bed was unmade, dirty linen and aprons formed a pile in the middle of the floor, a stack of newspapers filled one corner of the room, the window facing the back of the house was grimy. Dirty plates and cups lay about.

Wrinkling his nose against the stale smell of an unventilated room, he trod silently forward to the bed. He lifted the crumpled bedsheets and glanced down to the foot. Then he dropped them and felt the mattress through the sheets. Kneeling down, he lifted the straw-filled mattress and glanced under it. Trails of dust covered the floorboards visible through the ropes holding up the mattress. He let it fall and bent down to the ground and eyed the entire expanse of floor beneath the bed. Something caught his eye. Flattening his length, he reached out to the far end and grasped what looked like a corner of paper caught between the floorboards.

It proved to be only a torn scrap. He retrieved it and smoothed it out.

His eyes quickly read the scrawled jottings in French, which appeared to be in verse. *Le roi toujours. Toujours le roi.* The king always. Always the king.

A royalist sentiment. Hardly seditionary.

Hard-pressed to know whether the note was important or not, he stuck it in his pocket. He'd show it to his contact from the Home Office.

He stood back up, dusting off his trousers, and continued his search. The newspapers were also in French though printed in London. After perusing a few of the front pages, he concluded that they, too, were royalist in tone. Nothing surprising. Most of those forced from France during the revolution yearned for a return of the monarchy.

Rees turned to the chest of drawers. The top held a couple of cookbooks. He picked up one, its cover dirty, its pages stained and torn, its binding coming apart. It was all in French. Thin, folded pieces of paper were lodged here and there, but he saw that they, too, were mere recipes.

Pâte Brisée. His eyes scanned the list of ingredients. Flour, lard, salt. A recipe for pastry dough. He stuck it back in the book and set it down and proceeded with the other. Another well-used French cookbook. He bent down to the chest of drawers.

He should be used to this task by now, but his hands still shook as they searched through Gaspard's personal belongings, expecting at any moment for someone to enter behind him. He found stacks of starched white aprons, handkerchiefs, and shirts. Knitted stockings and undergarments.

An extra blanket lay in the bottom drawer. Under it he found a stack of postmarked envelopes tied with a string. He took it to the bed, cocking an ear toward the door, thinking he heard a sound. But only silence greeted him. He sat down on the only chair and quickly untied the bundle. The envelopes were postmarked and originated in France. He opened the first and tried to decipher the handwriting.

After skimming through the top ones, he saw that they were from a wife and a mother, but they were dated twenty years ago. So, he had corresponded with family members during the Directorate. But what had happened to those family members in the meantime?

He retied the bundle and placed it back in the drawer and shut it. Then he examined the few items of clothing hanging on the pegs, felt the ledge of the narrow window above, and glanced into every corner of the small room. Nothing suspicious. The room was curiously bare of personal effects for someone who had been in the same household for so many years. Perhaps he spent most of his time creating dishes in the kitchen, so he didn't need a roomful of things.

He certainly appeared to be an ardent royalist. For that matter, Lady Wexham was probably one as well. It was hard to imagine her a spy. She seemed much too open, much too nice.

He reined in the direction of his thoughts. Too many of his waking hours were spent dwelling on his employer's attributes.

Rees exited the room as quietly as he had come. As he locked the door and turned around, his breath caught. Valentine stood in the doorway to the servants' dining hall, her arms folded, her feet planted apart. He knew she hadn't been there when he'd first opened Gaspard's door.

He assumed his most haughty stare to match her sharp, narrowed gaze. "Yes, what is it?"

Ignoring his question, she lifted her chin. "What are you doing in Gaspard's room?"

His mind scrambling for possible replies, he said with quiet dignity, "That is between Gaspard and me." Feigning indifference to her presence, he walked toward her, hoping she would move out of his way before he reached the doorway.

She remained motionless, her eyes boring into him.

He looked down his nose at her. "Haven't you anything to do?"

She said nothing, her nostrils flaring. They stood eye to eye, barely a foot from each other.

"Excuse me, mademoiselle, but if you do not have any other occupation, I do. Please move aside."

Her lips flattened, her eyes mere slits. She finally took a step back.

As he passed, she hissed, "If you wish me to be quiet, it will cost you something." The "something" came out sounding like "somesing."

Rees stopped halfway through the doorway. "I beg your pardon?"

She tossed her head. "You understand me!"

Perspiration began to roll down the center of his back. He lifted his chin. "I have no idea what you are implying. Good day." He left her and strode out of the dining room and through the kitchen, not stopping until he reached the wine cellar, his heart thundering in his chest.

He'd have to think of a plausible excuse if the maid told Gaspard or Lady Wexham of his snooping. He had no doubt that she would tell one or both of them, since he hadn't stooped to bribery. Not that he hadn't considered it for a split second. But her offer probably consisted of more than just money. And it would probably buy him little security. She would be the kind to play both sides.

How soon would she tell her mistress? He could brush Gaspard off with some haughty tale of inspection and tell him his room was a disgrace.

But as for Lady Wexham—Rees imagined the polite look of inquiry in her brandy-hued eyes. He'd have to elaborate on the inspection excuse, make something up about touring all the servant's quarters— that it was part of the under-butler's regular duties at Telford House.

He ran a hand along his collar, his neck cloth constricting him. Would she believe such a flimsy explanation?

6

*C*éline returned exhausted from a short trip to Hookman's Library and some of the shops on Bond Street. She still had to change for dinner and Almack's later in the evening for her niece's debut there. Perhaps she'd have enough time for a cup of tea and a quick nap.

MacKinnon opened the door for her, relieving her of her packages as soon as he had closed the door behind her.

He placed them on the side table and took her gloves. "Thank you," she murmured.

She unbuttoned her pelisse. "Send a footman up with my parcels. Tell Valentine I'm home. And please request a cup of tea from the kitchen."

He helped her off with the pelisse. "Yes, my lady."

"Thank you." For some unaccountable reason, her cheeks felt warm. Perhaps because she found herself standing so close to her butler. He had such penetrating gray eyes. They were almost silver. Her gaze moved downward over his features, his straight nose and firm lips to his strong chin. A small pale scar like the slimmest of new moons drew her gaze. The crescent was on one side of his chin, partly under it . . . yet instead of marring his features, it added to his attractiveness.

"My lady?"

Her gaze flew to his before she pivoted away from him, flustered that she'd been caught staring. She directed her attention to untying her bonnet though her fingers fumbled with the knot.

"You had several calls while you were out. And Lady Agatha wishes to see you."

"What?" His words served to snap her out of the strange spell he seemed to wrap her in. Silly woman. She was no longer an impressionable young girl making her debut.

With a glance at the full tray of calling cards, she headed toward the staircase. "Very well, bring them up to me with the tea. I shall look through them in my room." She sighed. "Tell Lady Agatha I shall be in my room."

Once in her room, she sat in a comfortable armchair and removed her half boots. In a few minutes Valentine knocked softly and entered.

She knelt by Céline and took over the task. "The tea will be up shortly."

"Good, I'm parched. My, but shopping is exhausting, especially when one must stop every few feet and greet someone or other of one's acquaintances."

Once she was comfortably attired in a silk peignoir, another knock signaled Sally, who brought in the tea tray. Obviously, Virginia was still staying out of Valentine's sight.

Valentine met William at the door and took the purchases from him.

Céline motioned for Valentine to bring them to her. "Good, my books. I want to begin one right away." She snipped the string of her parcel as Sally set down the tea tray. The maid took the paper wrapping and string away as soon as she had removed the books.

Céline opened each one with a loving hand, reading the titles once again and enjoying the feel of new leather covers, before setting them aside on the table beside her chair and taking the one she wanted to read onto her lap.

"Will you be needing anything else, my lady?"

She glanced up at Sally with a smile. "No, thank you."

Finally, only Valentine remained, and she continued puttering around as Céline cut the pages of the new novel by Maria Edgeworth and sipped her tea.

She was engrossed in the first chapter of *The Absentee* when she heard her abigail clearing her throat for the second time. "Yes, what is it?" she asked without looking up from her book.

When her question was met with silence, Céline looked up.

Her maid and longtime companion stood with her hands folded before her, a grim expression on her face. "I told you that man was no good."

Céline laid her book down on her lap, knowing she would have no peace until Valentine unburdened herself. "What man?"

"That one who calls himself a butler."

The steady tick-tock of the clock penetrated her hearing as her eyes narrowed on her maid. "MacKinnon? What has he done?"

"He was in Gaspard's room." Valentine rocked back on her heels, her nostrils flared in outrage.

Céline closed her book, no longer able to ignore her maid's misgivings concerning her butler. "How do you know this?"

"I saw him coming out of it with my own eyes. With a key in his hand," she added ominously.

"Did he see you?"

"Of course. I made sure he did."

Céline frowned. "When exactly was this?"

"This morning after Gaspard had left for the market."

"What did MacKinnon say?"

"He was as brazen as brass. He told me to go about my business!"

Pursing her lips, Céline tried to think of a logical explanation. "He must have had some reason for being in there."

"I'm sure he did. Snooping around, that's what it was."

"But he didn't behave as if he had anything to hide?"

"Of course not. He's too astute to behave scared. He's a sly one, he is!"

Céline considered. "I don't know . . . he hasn't struck me as 'sly.'
Observant, yes, and quite respectful and respectable-looking. After
all, he *is* the butler. He has a right to inspect any room he wishes.
I'm sure there is some acceptable reason." Why was she loathe to
believe MacKinnon capable of some underhanded behavior in her
household?

Valentine tossed her head. "Oh, he'll likely have some excuse to
offer. He'll have had time to come up with something."

"Have you told Gaspard?"

"Of course. He says luckily he keeps nothing written in his room.
He will be more cautious from now on *naturellement*."

Céline nodded, thankful her chef was so resourceful.

"What I say to you is watch that one. He's a slippery one."

Céline chewed on her lip, puzzling it out. "Yes, indeed, I shall," she
murmured, turning back to her book. She'd have to take a closer look
at her new butler. Not that he didn't already intrigue her.

As Valentine was leaving the room, Agatha appeared at the door.
She pushed past Valentine and strode to Céline's chair, a sheet of
paper in her hand.

Céline looked up from her book. "You wished to see me?"

"I want to discuss the ball for Kimberley."

Céline closed her book with a sigh. "Of course."

"I have made up a guest list. The countess and I have singled out
which eligible gentlemen should be invited."

Her sister-in-law loved to lord over the fact that Céline was no
longer the true Countess of Wexham. How little she realized the title
meant to Céline. For her it held nothing but bitter recollections. "Very
well." She held out her hand for the list.

Agatha blinked as if not expecting such immediate capitulation.
"Well, I—I shall have to recopy it."

Céline raised an eyebrow. "Do you think I will not follow it to the
letter?"

"It took us time and effort to compose it. I shall not risk its being mislaid somewhere among your papers." She gave a pointed look toward Céline's desk piled high with invitations.

"Then I suggest you send out the invitations yourself. Let me know how many to expect." Céline was too weary at the moment to wage an argument over something as trivial as a guest list. She would send out her own invitations to those she thought her young niece would enjoy.

"Very well. Now, I wish to discuss the supper menu with you. The countess and I thought—"

Céline touched her fingertips to her temples. "I have a bit of a headache. If you wish to sit with Mrs. Finlay and me in the morning, I shall gladly do so."

Satisfied, her sister-in-law left at last. Céline rested her head against the chair. She had not lied about her head. Somewhere between Valentine's disturbing report on MacKinnon and Agatha's insistence on her guest list, Céline's temples had begun to pound. Her life was suddenly becoming overly complicated.

The clink of silver against china mingled with the babble of voices across the dinner table. The night of the dinner party had arrived.

The three chandeliers above the twenty-foot table glowed with dozens of beeswax candles. Elaborately carved bronze wall sconces added to the light.

The crystal goblets gleamed. Silver vases were filled with hothouse flowers. The center epergne was heaped with an artistic arrangement of sugared fruits.

The guests were engaged in animated conversation as they partook of Gaspard's rich food and the late earl's fine wines. After the flurry of last-minute arrangements before the guests arrived, Rees had undergone the nerve-racking task of receiving the distinguished personages, praying he would not fumble over their names.

Bringing in the first course had gone without a hitch. Finally, now, Rees had a few moments to catch his breath. He was positioned against the wainscoted wall of the dining room, his responsibility for the present to observe the footmen, making sure they replenished servings of food and drink, while awaiting Lady Wexham's signal to remove the covers and bring in the next course.

Rees couldn't help glancing at her. She presided over the long table like a queen, her dark hair dressed in an elaborate coiffure high on her head, diamonds glinting among the glossy locks.

At least Valentine must have said nothing to her about his presence in Gaspard's room. Or had she? He was not naïve enough to think Valentine was through with him. Likely she would strike when he least expected it. But Lady Wexham had not intimated by word or look that she knew anything of the incident.

A hint of a smile graced her fine lips. She bestowed the barest of nods, as if to reassure Rees that she found everything to her satisfaction.

And then her attention was taken once again by Lord Castlereagh, who sat at her right. Her smile broadened and a sparkle came into her eyes. "So, you only come to my table to partake of my French chef's delicacies?"

The distinguished-looking foreign secretary smiled. "Have pity on a man who sometimes goes days without arriving home in time for dinner." He glanced across the table at his wife. "The affairs of state have no respect for a wife's dinner hour."

The handsome woman whose diamond choker and bracelets flashed in the light of the chandeliers smiled indulgently. "If Robert can make it home one evening in five, it is the most I can hope for—and then we usually have an engagement elsewhere."

"Then I am doubly grateful that you deigned to sit at my table this evening."

Castlereagh chuckled and patted Lady Wexham's hand. "But, as you say, it is solely due to your French chef! This lobster veritably melts upon the tongue." He took a generous mouthful of the seafood in velouté sauce.

At the middle of the table, the conversation turned to the war.

"Now that Prussia has declared war on France and joined the Coalition, their army will soon have Napoleon in flight."

Rees's glance shifted to the two members of the House of Lords who sat directly in front of him.

"With Tsar Alexander hot on his heels after routing him from Russia, there's reason to hope for the liberation of Europe."

The Duc de Berry across the table raised his glass. "Could it be that this year we'll see the Corsican upstart finally overthrown?"

Colonel Percy, a well-fed, gray-haired gentleman whose gold buttons and epaulettes shone brightly against his red coat, spoke up. "It depends on his army. As long as he has their undying loyalty, it will be hard to depose him."

"But that army was decimated in Russia," the Tory, Huskisson, put in, thrusting his fork at the other two.

Rees glanced toward Lady Wexham to gauge her reaction, but she seemed serene enough, and after listening to these remarks, turned to address something to Lady Castlereagh.

The conversation continued, from the war in America and the swearing in of Mr. Madison for a second term to the war in Mexico and how this might affect the Peninsular War in Spain.

"Wellington has had the winter to reorganize the troops. The French are in for a surprise if they think they will see him withdraw again to Portugal."

The Whig, Althorp, held up his glass of wine for Tom to refill. "Let us hope so. Last autumn proved disastrous what with having to abandon Madrid and retreat all the way back to Ciudad Rodrigo. The Iron Duke lost all he had gained at such a price."

Tom and William removed the covers. The guests sat back, their conversation ebbing and flowing as freely as the wine, the edge of their hunger satisfied.

Once the guests were served and Rees had helped replenish everyone's glass, he stood once more to observe and, more importantly, listen.

But as the dinner dragged on, it was easy for his thoughts to drift. Nothing of dire national security seemed to be exchanged. The conversation turned inconsequential, from the latest *on-dits* to the leading dancer at the ballet.

His glance strayed the length of the table, alighting briefly on each guest in their brilliant jewels and fashionable garments, every face animated in convivial conversation. Finally, his gaze came to rest once more on Lady Wexham as it had been all evening.

After a fortnight of observing her, he was more intrigued than ever. Who was she? A simple society lady or a French spy? She'd been widowed three years. Why hadn't she remarried? As much as the notion was abhorrent to him and as far as he could ascertain, she had no lover. It was well known a lady of her rank and fortune would not be restrained by moral conventions. But she was never absent an entire night, nor was there any particular gentleman caller on closer terms to her than any other.

Neither did she seem to have any close female friends or relations. A host of acquaintances, yes, a round of social engagements, but no confidante or intimate like females were so fond of having.

He thought of his own sister and her closest friend, Jessamine. Scarcely a day went by when they didn't visit with each other, not only talking of commonplaces but confiding their deepest secrets.

Perhaps that was a girlish thing to do, outgrown once a woman married, as the countess had. But he thought of his own mother. Though she was widowed now over a decade, she had a circle of friends who helped her through the trials of life.

He glanced at Lady Agatha, Lady Wexham's sister-in-law, a thin woman with a haughty expression and glittering jewels against her wrinkled neck. All he'd observed between the two ladies was a chilly formality.

His thoughts returned to Lady Wexham. For a woman who appeared friendly to all and courteous and considerate to even the lowest servant, Lady Wexham seemed to have no intimates. From Rees's observation she spent her days and evenings in a busy round of engagements only to return alone to a mansion, her only companions a sister-in-law who preferred her own quarters and a surly French maid.

A tug of compassion nipped his heart as he watched Lady Wexham smile at a guest. Was she deep down a lonely person?

But no, Lady Wexham's aloofness was only further proof that she was a spy, he maintained.

Rees shifted his weight, his feet aching. He'd been up early after a restless night. After years of employment that required sitting for hours, he'd had to accustom himself to stand at attention, keeping his face expressionless. The latter should be easy, he told himself, having to practice the same tight control every day at the Foreign Office.

But those things were endurable. No, what he found most exhausting this evening was his dual role of butler overseeing the other servants' comings and goings and undercover agent for the British government.

Not that it was the least tiresome to keep watch over Lady Wexham. He'd never met a lady like her before. He'd *read* about them, certainly, in the few novels his sister had pushed on him and the occasional social column of the newspaper, but he had never actually been around one.

Enchantress. The word came to him. Observing her interact with her guests, he saw her captivate the gentlemen around her. Their age mattered little, from the pimply faced young Baron von Klemperer, who hailed from the Duchy of Saxony, to the septuagenarian colonel. They all sat enthralled by her words.

Yet she listened more than she spoke.

The longer he observed her, the harder it was to put it down to merely looks or charm. There was a keen intelligence behind those expressive eyes.

Rees ticked through the list of facts he'd memorized from the dossier kept on Lady Wexham and all French émigrés of any consequence living in the British Isles.

Widow of the late Earl of Wexham. Age twenty-eight, born in the southwestern French province of Périgord but living in England from the age of seven, when she and her mother had escaped the Terror. Her father, the late Marquis de Beaumont, had perished under Madame Guillotine in September of 1792, only a few months before his king.

But the dry facts told Rees little about the lady behind those brandy-hued eyes and that generous smile.

It was one thing to read the bare bones of a person's life history, but quite another to behold the person in the flesh. Nothing had prepared him for that, and he began to doubt that his particular skills would avail him for this job.

On the surface, it would seem that, having lost her father to the fanatical tyrants of the Revolution, Lady Wexham would be a die-hard royalist. And having spent her formative years in Britain and married a wealthy peer of the realm, that she would have become a loyal British subject.

Rees looked over the long table of guests, hard-pressed to know why he wasn't satisfied with the logical conclusions to be drawn.

There were, for instance, those nine months Lady Wexham had spent in Paris with her mother during the short Peace of Amiens in '02. Of course, she'd been only seventeen and not even presented yet. She'd returned to London at the renewal of hostilities between the two countries, and made her coming out at eighteen.

The announcement of a brilliant match at the end of her first season had been testimony to her beauty and charm, since, as to portion, she was but an impoverished émigré, despite being of noble birth.

Oglethorpe had merely laughed when Rees had pointed out this short interlude. "A mere chit then. What could she know about any-thing? No, dear man, you are grasping at straws. If she is a spy, it is of recent origin, as an independent widow of means."

Rees's attention went back to Castlereagh, who was speaking gravely to Lady Wexham and showing her marked deference. Lord Castlereagh was known to be devoted to his wife. His head would not be easily turned by a mere pretty face. He clearly respected Lady

Wexham's opinions. Rees heard snatches of conversation about the European continent and its future division in a post-Napoleonic world.

This was the discussion he longed to participate in. Instead, he must stand mute as a post, pretending he hadn't an idea in his head beyond counting the silver and pouring the port.

At least Castlereagh had not recognized him from the Foreign Office—or if he had, had made no sign of it. Earlier, Rees had allowed the two footmen to do the honors at the door and had tried to stay in the background, overseeing everything between foyer, drawing room, and now dining room, hoping to efface himself as much as was possible for someone of his height.

His ears caught the words of William Wilberforce, member of the House of Commons and leading evangelical of the day. Rees had been surprised by his inclusion in Lady Wexham's guest list. After years fighting in parliament for the abolition of the slave trade, he was now in failing health, his eyesight poor. But he was a man greatly admired by Rees, and it had been an honor to help him up the stairs.

The elder statesman was addressing Lady Wexham with a smile. "My dear, I know your skepticism, but it is only in the Gospels that we find the eternal truths that enable us to carry on through life's struggles." He gently thumped the silver handle of his knife against the white linen cloth. "I am certain that it is their faith that gets our young soldiers through the horrors of war."

Lady Wexham took a sip of wine before replying. "That may be, but I am sure the young recruits facing them on the other side of the battlefield are praying to the same God. How do you reconcile that dilemma?"

"Ah, but only One who died and suffered for all our sakes can understand the suffering of each one, regardless of which colors they are flying."

"But why permit this carnage in the first place?"

"It is not God's doing, but man's greed and avarice."

Someone else spoke, but Rees couldn't forget the brief exchange so easily. Lady Wexham had raised a valid point. No matter that Napoleon had been the aggressor, dragging a generation of young men to their death on the battlefield. Had she lost someone dear to her? Was that what caused the trace of cynicism in her tone when asking about God's role in all this?

For a brief moment Rees wished he could reveal himself and offer Lady Wexham the kind of solace that Wilberforce was able to. Rees could tell her about sorrow and loss and finding the answers in eternal things.

Reality reasserted itself and he exhaled silently, resigned to playing the role of butler, there to see that the dishes on her table were served hot and in the proper order.

7

In the wee hours, long after the last guest had departed, Céline sat at her escritoire writing, her script small and neat from her days at the fancy young ladies' boarding school her mother had sold her jewelry to pay for. All to groom Céline for an advantageous marriage after they'd left France, her father killed, their wealth lost.

Shaking aside the past, she focused on the message she was composing. It had taken her a while to memorize the code, but she no longer had to keep checking for letters and numbers.

She sat back and set down her quill pen. That should do it. She hadn't gleaned much at the dinner, but perhaps the different views of the war from the various members of parliament and the foreign secretary would give the French an indication of which way the wind was blowing from Prime Minister Liverpool's administration.

She picked up the pounce box and sprinkled some of the fine powder over the paper to blot the ink. Then she shook off the excess and rolled it up, securing it with a piece of string. She rose from the desk, placing the small scroll in the pocket of her peignoir, and picked up the large India shawl from a chair.

Wrapping it around herself, she went to the door and opened it softly. Good, everyone was abed. She quickly stepped into the hallway and closed the door behind her. Listening another second but hearing nothing, she made her way to the staircase. Enough lamplight from the street illuminated her way.

She paused at the entry hall. Everything was put back to rights. The dinner party had gone well, she thought. A good mixture of guests. She began to look forward to her young niece's ball.

Céline headed to the back of the house, to the service stairs to deliver the ciphered message to Gaspard. Now, the going would be trickier, if a step were to creak, or a servant to still be about. She paused at the top of the narrower, uncarpeted stairs. All was quiet.

She stepped onto the first step then the next. Midway, she stopped, hearing the sound of footsteps.

They were heading away from her, toward the front of the house. Who could still be up? It had been almost three in the morning when she'd left her room.

She heard the sound of another door and realized the front service entrance was being opened. Quickly, she retraced her steps and made her way to the front door.

There she paused and inched forward. Keeping close to the wall, she peered out the lacy curtain covering the front window by the door.

A tall, shadowy figure appeared up the steps leading to the street. She drew back. Mr. MacKinnon. No one else was as tall as the silhouette she made out, not even Tom or William. Despite the cloak, she was sure it was her butler.

She inched back toward the sliver of window. He had reached the pavement and, with a quick look around him, made his way down the street, his stride long.

She stood, her heart pounding, hardly daring to breathe, until he disappeared around the corner.

Céline returned back to the service stairs, Valentine's warnings about the butler coming back to her. What had seemed nothing more than spiteful tales from a spurned maidservant took on a more ominous cast. Who was this man who had so recently entered her household?

Where had he gone? Merely to a nearby tavern to have a drink with his fellow servants after the rigors of his first dinner party in her household? But how many of his cronies would be up at such a late hour? She could not have asked for a better substitute for Rumford. MacKinnon had performed his duties flawlessly this evening, keeping calm, remembering everything that needed to be done.

He was everything that was dignified and unobtrusive, ever watchful, anticipating when a guest needed a glass refilled or a second helping from a dish beyond his reach.

Céline had been watching him, whether he realized it or not, during the dinner party, her maid's words never far from her mind. She'd seen that barely visible nod of his square chin to William or Tom, and the footman would scurry forward to offer the guest what was needed.

He was a man who knew how to command without seeming to. What a waste for him to aspire to a mere butler.

And such a fine, distinguished-looking man. He looked more like a statesman than a butler. If he'd been in France . . . With the right clothes, this man would pass for a gentleman.

Where could he have gone at this hour? Céline's thoughts strayed to another possibility. An assignation? Her frown deepened, not liking the thought.

But worse than those possibilities was the one she didn't want to contemplate.

Could someone suspect her activities? Had they sent someone into her household to spy on her? Was MacKinnon related to old Rumford at all? But Rumford had written her himself . . .

She had known Rumford since she'd come to the earl's house on her marriage. Even though the butler had intimidated her with his frosty manner, it hadn't been long before she'd earned his respect . . . even his sympathy.

She trusted him. He'd never given her reason otherwise.

She shook her head. She could not believe that he would betray her. No, it couldn't be. Her fingers clenched around her shawl. Could the old, stalwart butler have been bought off? Was MacKinnon even his nephew? Both men were tall and broad-shouldered, but there was no other resemblance that she could discern. But how much would a man of nigh on seventy resemble one of thirty?

Having come to no conclusions, she arrived in front of Gaspard's door and knocked softly. There was no response. Hoping he was not yet asleep, she knocked a little louder.

Finally, the door opened a crack. Her chef's eyes sharpened at the sight of her, and he opened the door wider. "You have something for me?" he asked her in French.

In reply, she handed him the paper.

He took it without a word. A second later, he closed the door. Céline turned away and headed back up to her room.

It wasn't until she was there that she realized she had not mentioned MacKinnon's strange departure to Gaspard. She must do so at the earliest opportunity. He could keep a closer eye on her butler.

She and her compatriots would have to watch their steps even more closely within their own house.

"Well? What have you found?" the soft-spoken man, his gray hair half hidden by his low-crowned hat, asked Rees.

Rees sat facing his contact across the table in the tavern not far from the Thames. The man he knew only as Bunting sat hunched over his pewter tankard, the collar of his coat turned up around his ears.

Rees had only met with him once, right before taking on his assignment. "Nothing much," he said quietly. "Lady Wexham is not the only French person in the household."

The man merely raised a shaggy gray eyebrow, waiting.

Rees cleared his throat. "There is her abigail, one Valentine Simonette, and her cook, Gaspard Guignoret. They have both been in her service several years as far as I can ascertain. I was able to search both rooms."

"Well?"

He extracted the bit of paper he'd found in Gaspard's room. "The chef appears to be a royalist. His room is full of royalist newspapers. I found this." He handed the scrap to the man, who took it in his hand and studied it a moment.

He didn't return it to Rees but pocketed it. "It could be a front."

"Lady Wexham had a dinner party this evening, the first since I've been in residence. She is well connected."

Bunting listened as Rees recounted who had attended and what was discussed. "Very good," Bunting said, sitting back. "I'll be here next week. Keep your eyes and ears open. If anything should prevent you from meeting me here, come to my lodgings." He gave him the address.

Rees left the tavern, taking in gulps of the cool night air, feeling as if he'd been through the Inquisition even though Bunting had been mild-mannered and silent for the most part. Was it only Rees's own ambivalence regarding Lady Wexham that was making him overly sensitive, as if he were holding something back from his contact? But he'd told him everything he knew.

Everything but the way Lady Wexham made him feel when he stood behind her taking off her cloak or when he looked into her inquiring gaze as she handed him her gloves.

The next afternoon Rees took advantage of some free time to visit his own lodgings, a brick building on a narrow street not far from the government buildings of Whitehall. He couldn't be gone from the house long, having told Tom he was going out to buy a newspaper.

Thankfully, he didn't run into anyone he knew. He went quickly up the stairs, unlocked his door, and slipped into his room. Although it was risky to be seen about, he needed to check for any correspondence from his family, who had no idea about the double life he was leading.

Rees had explained to his landlord that he'd be gone a few weeks to help an ailing relative but that he would be by from time to time to check for any post. He had kept his rent up so that his lodgings would be held for him and any letters he received slid under his door.

Stooping to pick up the mail, he saw at once he had received two letters, one from his mother and one from his sister. He crossed the small parlor adjoining the even smaller bedroom, breaking open the seal on his mother's first. He scanned the contents quickly.

It was a chatty letter bringing him up to date on the household goings-on and the village gossip. Nothing much changed there from season to season, for which he was thankful. His mother had had enough sadness and upheaval in her life with the death of Rees's father and the loss of his business.

It wasn't until the last line of her note that Rees felt any undue curiosity.

> *I shall let your sister tell you her news. Both hers and Jessamine's. They can speak of nothing else.*
> *Jessamine has grown into a lovely young woman. She is a dear girl, such a comfort to us.*

His frown deepened at his mother's less-than-subtle hint. He smoothed the frown away, wondering why the news should be disagreeable to him. He'd grown to admire their neighbor and his sister's closest friend Jessamine each time he was home on a visit. Hadn't he begun to consider in the last year or so that perhaps she would make him a fine wife?

Wondering what his sister and her closest friend had gone and done, Rees laid down his mother's letter and broke open his sister's.

> *Dearest of dear brothers,*
> *We are coming to see you!*

Alarm shot through him at the first words. Quickly, he read on.

> *Jessamine and I are coming to <u>London</u>, I should say.*

His sister's exuberance was transferred to her letters with lots of underlining and exclamation points.

Mother has surely filled you in on all the news in our sleepy village, so I will skip right to what occupies <u>all my attention</u> at the moment.

Jessamine's mother is <u>taking her to London</u> for a se'night and she <u>has invited me along</u>! I can hardly sleep for the anticipation! They are visiting a brother of Mrs. Barry's who is on leave. She has long been planning a visit to town . . .

The letter went on to describe how the trip came about. His heart sank with each passing exclamation of enthusiasm.

You may begin to plan all kinds of outings for us. I will tell you right now, I wish to see <u>at least two plays</u>. Isn't there a Scott drama performing? I also wish to see the animals at Astley's Amphitheatre, and the Bullock Museum. I read they just opened. And <u>Farraday's</u>. I have heard you can try the laughing gas and make yourself silly. I can't imagine you, dear brother, losing your dignity to such a degree.

Mrs. Barry has bespoken rooms for us at Grillon's, so I shall be living in fine style. I hope that is convenient for you. We are to leave on <u>Friday the twenty-fifth</u>. I do hope you may call on us the next day.

Perhaps you can rent us a chaise to ride in Hyde Park at the fashionable hour. I am sure you are privy to such things and can help acquaint us with all the <u>subtleties</u> of the West End.

I so look forward to seeing you, and I know Jessamine does as well. She doesn't say it, but I know she misses your company. Not as much as I!

Please say you have some time from your work at the Foreign Office to ferry us about a bit. We shall undoubtedly spend the mornings visiting the shops. At least Mrs. Barry assures me the hotel is in close proximity to Bond Street.

Rees refolded the letter. Since he couldn't take it back with him, he placed it along with his mother's on the desk. He glanced at his pocket watch. He'd have to reply now before his sister appeared in town.

He hated not being able to see her, but there was no help for it. He could not let her discover what he was about.

He picked up his pen and dipped it into the inkwell.

Dear Mother and Megan,

I was both pleased and chagrined to receive your news, Megan, that you were coming up to town at the end of next week. How I would love to see you. I would certainly make time to escort you and Mrs. Barry and Jessamine about.

He paused, having to think of some valid excuse why he wouldn't be able to see her. Taking a deep breath, he re-dipped the pen and began again.

However, I am sorry to have to tell you that I will be away from London for—

Again he hesitated, his pen hovering above the page. Better play it safe, since he didn't know how long this assignment would last.

—a few weeks. The Foreign Office is sending me to an M.P.'s country house to act as his secretary. He is involved in some work on a pending bill and needs help in the research and drafting of it.

Strange how easy lying was becoming to him, he who had always striven to be honest and aboveboard in all his dealings. He read over what he had just written.

Would his sister believe his explanation? He didn't even know if such a reason was plausible. But he couldn't think of anything better on such short notice. If he pleaded indisposition, both his mother and sister would be upon him, wanting to nurse him.

He scribbled a few more lines, adding some newsy bits about life in town and the latest excesses of the Prince Regent. He promised to write more at a later date, making it sound as if his job was keeping him particularly busy at the moment. He expressed his disappointment at not seeing them—being able to be genuine in this—and finally sat back, feeling as if he'd completed a grueling obstacle course.

Would either of them read something between the lines? His mother was very discerning. Would she sense he wasn't being candid? If so, hopefully, she would attribute it to the sensitive nature of his work at the Foreign Office.

Sensitive. That's exactly what it was, he thought, picturing Lady Wexham.

He heard a clock tower chime the hour in the distance and realized with a start he needed to get back.

He reread the note, folded it up, and proceeded to melt some wax to seal it. He'd have just enough time to post it.

And he'd have to pray that when his sister was in town, he wouldn't run into her. His lips turned downward at the little likelihood of her running into a butler. Though they would both reside in Mayfair, their two worlds would be at the opposite ends of the spectrum.

As he made his way to the post office, his thoughts turned to Jessamine. He felt only a mild regret, that of not seeing an acquaintance who was coming up to town.

Why wasn't he more anxious to see her?

He'd had little time and opportunity to form any romantic attachments in his life. Only now, at thirty-one, after a decade of toil, did he feel prepared to support a wife. He'd managed to put aside a little money—what he didn't send to his mother and sister—by scrimping on his own life.

He didn't go out into society, so the only woman who held any interest for him was his sister's closest friend, Jessamine, a young girl who'd lived in the same village all her life. She'd made his sister's acquaintance when his widowed mother had resettled in her girlhood home.

Rees had never seen Jessamine as anything but a girl until just recently, as both she and Megan had blossomed into young women. Whenever he managed to get home for a visit, she was there. Somehow, without any effort, they had formed a friendship. His sister and mother certainly seemed to encourage it.

She was a well-behaved young lady, quiet, unassuming, all that a man would want in a wife.

Any thoughts he might have had earlier in his life of settling down had been put aside, first because of the war, and then until his sister was provided with a respectable dowry and his mother for her old age. Without conscious intention, the idea had taken shape, so gradually he could hardly pinpoint when he'd first entertained it, that Jess would make him a suitable wife.

He hadn't gone so far as to court her formally, much less propose. But he had thought she seemed willing enough, if he were only to hint at a deeper friendship. There was nothing to displease, so he'd allowed himself to be led along with the notion, only making it clear to his sister and mother that he would not ask for anyone's hand until he had paid off his father's debts and saved enough to be able to provide for a wife and eventual offspring.

Yet, now, he felt only a mild regret that he would miss Jessamine's visit to London. Shouldn't a man feel a woman's absence more keenly?

His thoughts turned to Lady Wexham, and he felt an ache so acute he came to an abrupt stop on the street. What was he thinking?

He shook his head, determined to cast such thoughts of his employer—his *temporary* employer—far from his mind.

Too many things were at stake right now—on a national and international scale—for him to be pining for a woman he had no right to be thinking of.

Céline stood back to survey the effect of the red, white, and blue swags and banners draped across the top of the drawing room walls. The union jack hung at one end of the room.

Sighing with satisfaction at how patriotic it all looked, she turned to William. "I want the lilies here, in front of the potted greenery." She indicated a corner of the drawing room, then addressed Virginia, who stood with a feather duster in her hand. "Mind you clear all the trinkets from the tabletops before the footmen move them."

The room was in disarray as they removed most of the furniture from the drawing room in preparation for the ball. Céline craned her neck at Tom, who was on a stepladder cleaning the chandelier. "Tom, I want you to help William carry up the flowers that have been delivered."

She glanced at MacKinnon, who was perched on another ladder under another chandelier. "I am sure Mr. MacKinnon will excuse you for a few minutes."

The butler nodded. "Of course, my lady." For a second their eyes met, and she wondered what was going on behind those watchful gray ones. She had come to no conclusions yet about his late-night errand, the preparations for the ball having taken up all her thoughts in the intervening time.

The next moments were spent in consultation with Mrs. Finlay, directing the footmen in placing all the potted plants that had been ordered from Tubbs' Nursery Gardens in Chelsea.

"What do you think?" She stood back, observing the effect of all the greenery and colorful lilies and orchids gracing the various corners of the spacious room. "The orchestra will sit there between those rows of ferns and palms," she said, pointing. "We'll set the chairs over that way for the dowagers and these doors to the sitting room will be opened for refreshments." She turned to the footmen.

"Very good, ma'am." Mrs. Finlay followed her indications. "It has been some years since you have given a ball."

She smiled ruefully. "Yes, I'm not sure whether I would have suggested it if I'd remembered the work involved."

Mrs. Finlay gave one of her rare smiles of approval. "Oh, my lady, I'm sure it is good to see the room being put to such advantage. No doubt, the late earl would have been pleased with all the effort you are putting forth for his young relative."

Céline smiled briefly but made no reply. The servants had been devoted to the old earl, and she had never by word or deed given any indication that her feelings were otherwise. She glanced at MacKinnon, who now stood at the base of one of the stepladders, wiping his hands on a rag.

"Mr. MacKinnon?"

He turned to her attentively. "Yes, my lady?"

Although she was of medium height, standing beside him made her feel small. His shoulder was at about the height of her temple. "I wish to go over the guest list with you. I realize you have not presided over a ball in London and want to make sure you feel comfortable in your mind about it. Do you have a moment?"

"As you wish." He followed her to her sitting room.

When he remained standing as she took her seat at the escritoire, she motioned to a nearby chair. "I really don't want you towering over me," she said with a smile.

He brought over the straight-back chair and sat beside the desk.

She pulled her guest list forward to where he could see it as well. "I have listed them in order of rank. I will have William receive the guests at the door. Tom can escort the ladies to Virginia or Sally in the retiring room where they can leave their wraps. When they arrive at the drawing room, you will announce them right at the entrance. Have you done this at all in your other position?"

"I confess that I have not."

She moistened her lips. "Let us take the first names, the Duke and Duchess of Marlborough. You must speak loudly enough to be heard above any din or music. The most distinguished guests tend to arrive quite late, you know."

"I understand, my lady."

His eyes met hers, and once again she felt caught by their steady gaze. For an instant, she felt the overwhelming urge to ask him straight out what game he was about. But no, she mustn't be so foolish. Hers was not the only life at stake. She must protect Gaspard and Valentine at all costs.

But she couldn't resist testing him a bit. She set down her list of names and sat back in her chair. "How is your uncle?"

There was the merest flicker in his gray eyes, as if her words had thrown him. "On the mend, thank you."

He was quick to recover, she'd give him that. She smiled. "Perhaps I should visit him. He has been in the family so many years—long before I ever came to this household."

His eyes widened for a fraction of a second—in alarm?—then just as quickly were shuttered as he looked down at her guest list. "I am sure my uncle would be touched, but I assure you it is not necessary. You have your ball. I am certain he would be distressed to know you had taken so much time and effort to travel to Yorkshire on his behalf."

He looked once more at her, his gaze as calm and steady as before.

"I didn't realize in all these years he had a niece, isn't that funny? She must be a comfort."

"She is his sister, actually."

Point scored for MacKinnon. "Yes, of course." She picked up a quill pen and ran it along her cheek. "I'm sorry he was so far he wasn't able to return here after his fall. We would have looked after him . . . and you would have him close by."

His gaze didn't waver. "That is most kind of you, my lady, but really he is quite comfortable in . . . Leticia's home."

She arched her brows. "Your Aunt Leticia?"

"Yes."

"Your family is numerous?" she asked innocently, intrigued by the tension she sensed in him. Perhaps he was only nervous because he still considered himself new in her household and under her protection. A part of her wished it were so . . . that he was only a simple butler.

"Ye—no. That is to say," he said with a slight clearing of his throat, "there are few offspring of—of—my generation, but we are scattered." A faint color tinged the upper portions of his cleanly shaven cheeks.

"Does Leticia have any children?"

The flush had spread to his jawline—a fine, strong jaw. She rested her chin in her hand, more intrigued than ever by this mysterious stranger in her household. "No," he said after a few seconds had passed.

His slight hesitation and embarrassment, instead of diminishing his appeal, added to it. Her own cheeks grew warm at the thought. She realized she was enjoying the game—enjoying it too much.

She folded her hands and sat straight, focusing back on her list. "Very well, I shall endeavor to get through this ball first. Perhaps afterwards . . ." Let him believe she still intended a visit to his "uncle."

"Now, when the duke and duchess arrive, you will announce them as His grace and . . ."

8

$\mathcal{R}$ees stifled a yawn. He was tired of standing there like a statue, surveying the dancers on the floor.

One thing he had learned over the past few weeks in her ladyship's household. The butler and footmen did a lot of standing at attention.

Lady Wexham's ball was a grand success if measured by how crowded the room was—and how warm. Rees longed to tug at his tight cravat, but he must continue dignified and unmoving.

The place overflowed with distinguished guests from dukes and marquesses, officers of the Horse Guards, members of parliament, and all the bedecked and bejeweled ladies they escorted.

Would Lady Wexham use such a venue to glean state secrets? He doubted it. He'd seen her do nothing but greet the guests he'd announced and make certain no one stood alone. He watched her skill in making her guests feel comfortable, bringing people together, then moving off after ensuring they were engaged in conversation. She seemed to float through the throng of people.

Floating was an appropriate word, he conceded, watching the airy gown swirl around her as she danced. He knew little of women's fashions, but she never failed to impress him with her appearance. This evening, she wore some sort of filmy white overskirt over a pale pink gown.

Ostrich feathers of the same shade of pink graced her dark hair. Pearl drop earrings dangled from her earlobes, and ropes of pearls graced her neck.

Even though she directed everyone's attention to the guest of honor, a shy young blonde who smiled at everyone presented to her but spoke little in return, it was Lady Wexham who outshone her, whether she meant to or not.

He deliberately looked away from the countess, disturbed with how much notice he was taking of her. He could no longer fool himself that he was merely keeping his eyes on her to catch her in any suspicious behavior.

She drew him with her beauty and femininity, with her charm and intellect, as no woman ever had. Sometimes, he had the sense that the attraction was mutual. He would catch her looking at him as if assessing him. The other day, sitting beside her desk, he felt as if she had been toying with him in some way. Or was it because her maid had caught him snooping?

He had prayed for wisdom and discernment. He mustn't let himself be swayed by her beauty. He must watch his step very carefully. Why hadn't Lady Wexham confronted him about it? Was she playing a game with him?

Was that why she looked at him in that thoughtful way?

Abruptly, he left the ballroom, deciding to check on Tom, who was still at the front door for any late arrivals. Rees glanced into the dining room on his way, where the table was set for a midnight supper.

In the entryway, he caught Tom yawning and smiled in sympathy. "Think you'll make it to the end?"

Expecting a scold, Tom had snapped his mouth shut and straightened. Now his lips relaxed into a grin. "Yes, sir. Gaspard has a full table laid for us below for later." He gestured up the stairs. "How are things on the dance floor?"

"Fine." To relieve his own fatigue, Rees opened the door onto the mild night. The street lamps were lit. A carpet had been set over the steps and down the walkway to the street and torches placed there to help light the way to the entrance.

Carriages lined the street with coachmen waiting for their employers. "Have they been offered refreshment?"

"Oh yes. The kitchens have seen a steady stream of coachmen and grooms for the last few hours."

Rees glanced up and down the street. Things seemed relatively quiet. He paused at the outline of someone standing in the shadows near the corner. The person took a step, disappearing farther into the shadows.

Rees quirked an eyebrow at Tom. "How long has he been hanging around?"

Tom turned from looking at one of the carriages. "Who?"

Rees indicated with his chin. "Down there, see that person?"

Tom squinted. "No."

"Just wait. He moved into the shadows."

Rees engaged Tom in commonplace conversation, instructing him to keep his eyes in that direction, while Rees deliberately looked away.

After a few moments, Tom said in a low tone, "Yes, I see someone."

"Notice him before? Perhaps one of the coachmen?"

"No, I don't think so. But it's hard to tell, with so many people coming and going."

"Of course." He pondered what, if anything, he ought to do.

"Maybe he'll move away when the watch comes along."

"Maybe." Rees checked the case clock in the hall. "It will be another quarter of an hour. I'll come back then. Let me know what happens."

"Yes, sir."

Rees made a tour of the downstairs rooms, and then walked to the basement to check on the activities in the kitchen. Although the maids and housekeeper were bustling about, and Gaspard was directing them like a captain from the quarterdeck, things seemed to be running smoothly. Rees stepped past them into the scullery and out into the backyard. Unlike most houses, where the backyard was used for storing coal and other things, this one contained a large area devoted to both a kitchen garden and some ornamental ones.

The air was pleasant after the stuffy indoors. Rees made his way down a gravel path until he reached the alley separating the yard from the mews. A few lights still burned in the living quarters above the stables.

Finding nothing out of the ordinary, he peered down the alley in the direction where he had seen the shadowy figure. No one was about.

He made his way cautiously down the dark alley until he reached the end of the block, turned, and made his way toward the street, keeping his footsteps as silent as he could the closer he got to the corner.

He paused, seeing a figure lounging against the building.

Giving the man no time to react, he quickly stepped in front of him. The man flinched and took a step away.

"Good evening, sir," Rees said, looking him up and down. He appeared a gentleman, though wearing riding clothes—a dark cutaway, buckskin breeches, and tall boots.

The man nodded curtly. He wore a hat so it was hard to make out his features in the shadows.

"I am butler at the house yonder." He indicated the lighted entry. "I couldn't help but notice your presence in the vicinity. Are you a guest?" he asked, although it was obvious from the man's lack of evening clothes that he was not.

The man hesitated a few seconds then said, "No—that is, I am acquainted with . . . Lady Wexham, but I see she is entertaining." He spoke with a French accent. He motioned to his garments. "As you can see, I did not come prepared."

Rees debated. "If you care to wait, I can give Lady Wexham your card."

Again, the man considered. All the while, Rees was growing more and more suspicious of his behavior. Finally, he nodded. "Very well, I shall accompany you to Lady Wexham's residence and await her word. But, I do not wish to disturb her if she is engaged."

They walked along the pavement until they reached the front entrance. Tom gave a start of surprise to see Rees coming from the street. "Good evening again, Tom. If you would show this gentleman to the front sitting room, I shall inform her ladyship of his presence."

He took the card the man handed him, and with a bow left him in the footman's care. It was not until he was up the stairs, out of sight of the man, that Rees glanced at the card.

Roland de Fleury.

He entered the drawing room and scanned it. He finally located Lady Wexham standing with a gentleman in uniform. A Major Clarendon, if Rees remembered correctly.

He made his slow way across the room until he reached her. She met his eye while still in conversation. He bowed his head and waited.

They weren't talking of anything pertaining to the war but of the merits of the spa town of Bath versus that of Cheltenham.

When there was a lull in the conversation, she touched the major's arm. "Excuse me a moment, sir."

"Certainly, certainly, dear lady."

When she turned to Rees, he leaned closer to her, breathing in a whiff of her perfume. "There is someone to see you." He gave her the card. "He says he does not wish to disturb you."

She barely glanced at the card before slipping it away somewhere in the folds of her gown. "Where is he?"

"In the sitting room below."

"Very well. You may tell him I shall be down presently."

Just as Rees was about to turn away, she spoke his name.

"Yes, my lady?"

She smiled, and he felt his gut tighten with longing. "Thank you, Mr. MacKinnon, for all your help with the preparations." She looked around the room. "It is going well, don't you think?"

Struggling against his inclination to stare at her, he followed her gaze. "Yes, quite."

His glance returned to her, and for the next few seconds, neither looked away.

With a great effort of will, he managed to bow and walk away, shaken at the encounter.

Céline watched her butler depart. Only part of her mind wondered what he made of her mysterious French caller. The greater part was still caught up in the look they had exchanged.

It seemed that every time she had caught a glimpse of him this evening, he was observing her.

A part of her had felt almost . . . protected. But that was absurd.

Now, she had read admiration in his eyes . . . and longing. She was old enough to recognize that in a man's eyes. She rarely paid attention, having grown inured to men's flattery since her coming out. But life had taught her to view such displays with cynicism. Men were rarely what they appeared.

What shocked her now was her own response to Harrison Mac-Kinnon. It was immediate and visceral and shook her to her very core, making her wonder if she knew herself at all.

She was no Valentine, ready to assuage her loneliness with any attractive man.

Céline had led a perfectly chaste life since the earl's death. She had grown to conclude since her marriage that she was merely a cold woman. The earl had certainly accused her of it after she failed to produce an heir for him.

But this—what was this sudden longing she felt whenever her eyes met MacKinnon's, to be caught up in his embrace? A butler, or a spy? She must be mad.

Feeling the calling card he had handed her, tucked now in the folds of her gown, she glanced around her to see if anyone had noticed her exchange with MacKinnon. It was Roland, her contact. She could scarcely believe he had risked coming openly to her house. The fact that he had, told her it must be important.

She pretended to take notice of someone across the room and made her way in that direction. At the last moment, she veered toward the doorway and slipped out of the drawing room before anyone could waylay her.

By the time she arrived at the closed door of the small sitting room at the front of the house, where guests were usually asked to wait, she had had a chance to think.

Mr. MacKinnon stood only a few feet away near the front door with Tom. It would be too dangerous to talk with Roland here.

Seeing her, MacKinnon sprang forward to open the door to the sitting room for her. She nodded briefly and entered the small room.

Roland turned away from the mantel at the sound of the door. He was a man about her age. He had been a comrade-in-arms of Stéphane's when she'd met him that year in Paris.

At the sight of her, Roland broke into a wide smile and stepped toward her.

They both waited a moment to ensure they were alone. Then reaching up, Céline embraced him, whispering, "What brings you here?"

He gave her a quick peck on both cheeks. Before pulling away, he whispered back, "Your butler caught me loitering down the street. I had little choice."

Her eyes widened in alarm. "How on earth . . . ?"

"Come." He took her hand and led her to the settee by the fireplace well away from the door. "I told him I didn't wish to intrude since I could see you were occupied. I mustn't stay. I meant to come in later and see Gaspard. I didn't realize you were entertaining on such a scale."

She sat beside him, hardly hearing his words, too rattled by the fact that MacKinnon had been the one to discover him. She would have to do something about her butler . . .

"Who is that fellow, anyway?"

She blinked, forcing her attention back to Roland. "Who?"

"That butler."

"He's here only temporarily." She pursed her lips, wondering how she was to neutralize MacKinnon's presence. She could no longer ignore the fact that he must have been sent into her household to spy on her. Perhaps even Rumford wasn't aware of his real identity. Could his nephew have been recruited by the government as a spy and not told his uncle? But that made no sense.

Moistening her lips, she told Roland about her butler's injury.

The Frenchman rubbed his chin. "His nephew, eh?"

"How did he come upon you?"

"He came up behind me from the alley. Resourceful fellow."

Céline puckered her brow. "Yes." Searching her chef's room, going out in the wee hours . . .

Roland waved a hand. "No matter. You may tell him I am a distant cousin bringing you word that a dear aunt in France is gravely ill, and I risked a crossing to bring you a message from her and to take one back."

"Very well. Is she ill enough to warrant my return?" They had discussed the possibility that Céline might need to escape to France if her role were discovered.

He smiled. "Not at present. It is still much too dangerous to attempt a crossing. Too many British cutters ready to stop any French vessel they detect. But 'Tante Bette' will appreciate any word of comfort you send her." He gave an exaggerated sigh. "I only pray she will last until my return. She is failing."

Céline searched his face, wondering if he was referring now to the state of things in France. "Oh, dear. Is there anything to be done?"

"Not tonight, my dear. You may return to your party and perhaps write to her tomorrow." He stood and bowed over her hand. "I shall bid you good night." As he leaned over her hand, he whispered, "Meet me tonight after your guests have left, at the Boar and Rabbit. Is two o'clock sufficient time?"

It was their usual meeting place, although usually it was Gaspard who ventured out. "Better make it three before everything quiets down here." Her mind considered the options. "Wait," she whispered, touching his forearm. "I might be followed by my 'resourceful' butler." She brought her face up to his ear and whispered some instructions.

He squeezed her hand and let it go, taking a step back. "I can see myself out. Do not trouble yourself."

Before she could move, he had already crossed the room and opened the door. "Ah, my good man, I shall be on my way."

MacKinnon was standing close to the door, which wasn't unusual in itself, Céline told herself.

As he escorted Roland toward the front door, Céline rose and made her way to the foyer, waiting until MacKinnon had shut the door.

He cocked an eyebrow. "Is anything amiss?"

She clasped her hands, looking up in mute appeal. "I have just received some . . . disturbing news."

"What is it—my lady?"

She drew out a breath. "Mr. de Fleury came to bring me word of a family member's illness—an aunt of mine." She sniffed, digging for her handkerchief. "He risked much to make the crossing."

"I am sorry, my lady. Is it very serious?"

"Yes. I was quite close to her when I spent some time in Paris." She moved away from him. "I must return to my guests. Thank you, Mr. MacKinnon, for alerting me to Mr. de Fleury's visit. I will be in the drawing room if anyone else should call."

"Very well, my lady."

She climbed the stairs, feeling her butler's gaze on her until she was out of sight. Had he believed her tale? She'd hardly been able to keep her thoughts straight with his eagle eyes homed in on her.

Now she must ensure that all went according to plan at the rendezvous with Roland. Céline entered the drawing room, her mind already planning the details for the meeting in the tavern after the ball.

If her butler was indeed someone planted in her house to spy on her, tonight would confirm it beyond a doubt.

Rees stood in the basement corridor just outside his door, his ears cocked for the slightest sound of movement. He would have to meet Bunting again tonight.

He hadn't been able to hear what had transpired between Lady Wexham and the mysterious Frenchman this evening. He dismissed at once her tale of a sick aunt. It was too obvious a story. The whole visit had been odd to begin with.

The house had finally settled down for the evening. He knew it was almost three. The guests had not begun leaving until after one. Then the servants had been busy putting everything to rights. The drawing room still stood bare of most of its furniture, but they had swept the floors and tidied everything.

Rees and the footmen had finally locked up all the doors and checked the windows. He had heard the servants trudge up the back stairs to their rooms.

He had sat for some minutes in his own bedroom, fully dressed, though he longed to stretch out on his bed.

Had the Frenchman come to give Lady Wexham a message? How could he discover it? Lady Wexham had gone back to her ball and behaved like any hostess, continuing to circulate among her guests, rarely dancing and never stopping too long with any one person.

Rees froze, hearing a step on the stair above him.

Yes, someone, a female by the lightness of the tread, was coming down the main staircase.

After a few seconds, the footsteps continued. If he hadn't been so alert, he would probably not have heard them.

A minute later he heard the front bolt being drawn and then the door opening.

Could Lady Wexham be leaving? At this hour? His heart thundering so he could barely make out anything more, he walked up the service stairs.

He reached the top in time to hear the front door close with a soft thud.

Giving the person only time to leave the immediate area, Rees hurried forward and opened the door a crack. Seeing and hearing nothing, he widened it and made his way up the steps to peer down the street.

He managed to make out a cloaked figure striding down one end. A second later, she turned the corner.

Was it Lady Wexham? Was she going to meet Monsieur de Fleury? Or, someone else? Without waiting to think things through, he slipped out, shutting the door behind him as silently as she had. He didn't bother to hide himself as he rushed down the street, since she was already out of sight.

But as he turned the corner, he paused. She was walking rapidly eastward along a side street. He assessed the street, determining how to follow her without being detected. Thankfully, a mist had risen, and the sections of street between the street lamps were dark.

Once she was about a block ahead of him, he made his way after her, thankful for the soft pumps he wore as part of his butler's uniform. Boots would have kept his feet drier but would have made too much sound against the pavement stones.

Instead of following a clear course, she kept turning, left then right as if in a zigzag pattern. She avoided the watchmen's boxes. Rees finally realized she was heading toward Piccadilly. She frequently looked over her shoulder, so Rees had to stay a good block behind her and out of the orbs of the street lamps.

But once she reached Piccadilly, she stayed on it, continuing to head eastward. If she went much farther, she'd leave the West End and enter less savory neighborhoods.

His concern deepened. The normally heavily trafficked street was almost deserted. Only those with shady business were about now. Didn't she realize how exposed and vulnerable she was, out by herself at this hour? How could the Frenchman send her out on so dangerous an assignation?

He fumed, his alarm and anger growing as she left the relative safety of Mayfair and skirted around Leicester Square. She scanned the area, as if aware of the dangers lurking in corners, and kept her pace up.

Once someone called out from the shadows, and she hurried on.

Rees wondered what he'd do if someone tried to molest her. Try his best to save her although he carried no weapon.

What he could do now was pray for her—and for himself.

His breath was coming fast and furious and still no signs of her slowing. They entered the darker and more dangerous area surrounding Covent Garden. The theater was long over, and the only activities remaining at this hour were women plying their nightly trade in alleyways and patrons staggering from disreputable gaming houses and seedy taverns.

A stray dog crossed his path, and the smell of rotting fruit and vegetables filled his nostrils as they neared Covent Garden market. The stalls were dark square silhouettes rising from the piazza, waiting for dawn to come to life again.

Rees's quarry turned so abruptly down a narrow side street that he almost missed her. She stopped in front of a tavern and entered it. Rees waited outside for some minutes before approaching the heavy studded door, hardly believing Lady Wexham would come to such a place. He wished he'd thought to bring a cloak to draw up around his face. The night air was cool, but he was sweating from the long, brisk walk.

Uttering a quick prayer for guidance, he entered the taproom. The noise and smoke hit him like a heavy curtain. Thankfully, the room was poorly lit and still full of people. Knowing his height would draw attention, he quickly looked for an empty seat where he could conceal himself.

Only after wedging himself between two others on a rough-hewn bench did he allow himself to look more carefully around him. It was difficult to make out people in the murky light. He craned his neck to look into the farthest recesses of the room. Where had she gone? He didn't dare stand up again. Had she gone into the back, he wondered, seeing a waitress slip through a doorway there.

"What'll ye have?" A large-boned waitress stood beside him, wearing an apron smeared with soot and grease.

"A half pint of porter."

She left him, and he continued his scrutiny of each customer's face. The search only deepened his fear for Lady Wexham's safety.

He jumped as a pewter tankard was plunked down in front of him. Quickly, he dug into his pocket for a coin.

At least now he would blend in better with the crowd, he thought as he brought the dark brew to his lips.

His gaze stopped then doubled back to a cloaked figure in a shadowy corner of the tavern. The person moved, and he caught the outline of a smooth cheek. Was it a lad or lady?

He continued staring over the rim of his tankard at the figure hunched over the dark table, growing more and more certain it was the same person he had followed across town.

He couldn't help the unpleasant jolt at finding the beautifully attired and coifed Lady Wexham of the ballroom transformed into this . . . this woman sitting in a disreputable tavern, speaking with who knew what suspicious character. If it was the Frenchman—and who else could it be?—then Rees would have a hard time refuting the evidence before him.

It was only then he realized how much he had not wanted Lady Wexham to be a spy.

He tried to get a glimpse of her companion, but his view was blocked. He didn't dare make himself too visible. He'd just have to be patient and wait until they got up to go. Meanwhile, he continued sipping his tankard slowly, keeping the brim of his hat low over his forehead.

He only had to wait a few minutes before the cloaked figure raised her hands and drew off the hood.

Rees sucked in his breath.

It was Valentine.

Céline planted her forearms on the tabletop, facing Roland. "Well? Did he come?"

Roland merely smiled and slid a tankard toward her. "Here, it will help take the chill off you."

She fanned her face with her hand. "Refresh me, you mean. It was a long ride from Berkeley Square in a stuffy hackney." Taking a sip, she focused on what was uppermost in her mind. "What happened earlier? Did Valentine spy anyone following her?"

Roland smiled. "Yes, she is quite certain your tall butler was on her heels. I did as you suggested and had someone come in my place as well." His smile deepened. "I think they both found it a lark. She said she did as you instructed and kept her head covered until certain your man could see her."

Céline sucked in her breath. Could MacKinnon really have followed her? Even now, she found it difficult to believe.

"You shall have to ask Valentine for details. I spoke to her but a moment. But she seemed vastly entertained."

Céline could well imagine. Valentine had been waiting for her revenge from whatever perceived slight she had suffered at MacKinnon's hand. Céline herself had not liked resorting to these tactics but had seen no alternative.

She took a long draft of the bitter ale then set it down carefully. "Now, please tell me why you risked coming to the house earlier. It will soon be dawn and I must return."

Roland sat back, a smile still playing around his lips. "Calm down, I will see you home. Valentine said she will be on the lookout for you to let you in. You are safe."

"Thank you, but there is no need. I asked the driver to wait."

"*Bon.*"

He leaned forward, lowering his voice. "We know Bonaparte's days are numbered. There is a growing royalist faction in Paris." His expression turned grim. "Unfortunately, they are backed by the British. If Louis returns and is crowned king, it is the end of democracy for France. We must prevent that at all costs."

She nodded, knowing already what he was telling her.

Glancing around him, he lowered his voice to a bare whisper. "We need you to go to Hartwell House."

Her lips turned downward, the very thought of that place lowering her spirits. "Must I?"

He nodded. "We must know what the Comte plans. You are in his favor. Lord Liverpool and Castlereagh are working ever more closely with him as the successor in France once Napoleon is defeated."

She could see no way out of it. "Very well. When do you wish me to go?"

"Immediately."

9

As Rees made his way home more slowly this time, the night air felt cool against his cheeks. He stuck his hands in the pockets of his pantaloons and quickened his stride, no longer worried about following his quarry. The fog hung thick, and he knew dawn was just over the horizon. He'd get no rest this night.

Alone now, he continued puzzling the event. Had Valentine gone in Lady Wexham's place? But it didn't seem to have been more than an assignation. When she'd risen from the table, the man accompanying her had not been Monsieur de Fleury, but a stranger. Rees had only followed them to the corner, where the two had embraced before heading off in a different direction from Mayfair. Their deep kiss had left little doubt to the nature of their relationship.

The fog around him was lightening by the time Rees reached Lady Wexham's house. Shivering against the damp, he glanced up at all the windows, making sure no one was yet up before walking to the front door.

With a start, he realized it was locked. He tried it again, but to no avail. How could that be, when Valentine had not arrived ahead of him?

With little hope, he walked back down to the service entrance, but that, too, was locked and bolted, the way he had left it earlier in the night.

With a resigned sigh, he tried all the ground floor windows, but they too were shut tight. The back door as well as the stable doors in the mews were also bolted.

He finally ended up at the back kitchen garden and lay down on a cold, damp bench facing a flower bed, curling his body against the chill. It would not be long before one of the housemaids or footmen was up and unlocked the doors.

He woke to the sound of the scullery door opening. Quickly, he unfurled his body and crouched low behind the bench, but it was behind a screen of shrubbery.

He yawned and rubbed his hands together to warm them. He dug his watch from his pocket and rewound it. Five minutes later, he made his way to the front service entry, endeavoring to stay out of sight.

To his relief, it was unlocked. Quickly, he opened it and glanced down the basement entryway. He heard some servants' voices in the distance, but the coast to his room was clear. Once again, he was thankful that he was at the front end of the house.

Once in his room, he shed his clothes. A maid had left a can of water for him outside his door, as was her habit. Thankfully, she would not have noticed that he had been absent from his room.

He washed and dressed. He hung up his black suit, eyeing it critically. A night at large and an hour sleeping in it had left it damp and wrinkled. He'd wait till it was dry and give it a good brushing.

Then he took up his Bible and prepared for his morning devotions. It would be a long day, and he needed all the strength he could get.

When Céline returned to the house, Valentine opened the door to her and bustled her in.

Céline leaned against the door a moment. "Am I ever exhausted!"

Valentine took her cloak from her and bolted the door behind her. "Come, I have your bed turned down and your nightgown laid out."

Once they were in Céline's room, Valentine quickly began to help her off with her gown.

Céline brushed her hands aside. "Tell me first about your evening. Roland said MacKinnon followed you."

Valentine shrugged. "If it was not he, it was his twin."

"Tell me exactly what happened. Roland could give me few details."

Valentine stifled a laugh. "I led him all about Mayfair. What an *imbécile* to be so easily fooled. If that is what the Home Office employs, no wonder the British have not beaten us."

"Never mind that, what happened when you arrived at the tavern?"

Valentine folded her arms across her chest, a satisfied smirk on her lips. "He took the bait. I spied him the moment he entered the tavern. There he sat across the taproom, trying to look as if he belonged there." Her maid's dark eyes gleamed. "I waited until sure he must have seen me, then"—making the motions with her hands, she pretended to draw back the hood of a cloak—"*voilà*, I revealed myself."

Realizing she had been holding her breath, Céline released it. "Do you think he saw you?"

She gave an emphatic nod. "*Mais oui!*"

Céline suspected there was more by the sly look in her eyes.

Valentine kept her waiting. "When we left again, I made certain he saw us." Her lip curled upward. "I kissed Antoine full on the lips." She cackled then, clapping her hands. "Arm in arm, we went off. I am certain MacKinnon saw us. He could suspect no spying activities after my display."

Céline folded her arms, her lips pursed in thought. Would it suffice?

"*Eh, bien*, you and I are both exhausted." Once again, Valentine began to undo the buttons on her gown.

Céline acquiesced without a word, too preoccupied to say anything more.

When she was under her covers and beginning to feel drowsy, Valentine gave one last chuckle. "I think you have had your revenge, madame, on your snooping butler."

Céline's eyes widened. "What do you mean?"

"I made sure to lock the door when I came in."

"What do you mean?" Before Valentine had a chance to reply, the significance dawned on her. "You mean . . . ?" She drew in her breath. "Mr. MacKinnon had no way to get back in the house?"

Valentine nodded, looking self-satisfied. "I made sure to arrive before he did. He might have thought I was going off with my *amour*. Instead, I took a hackney back here. Hah, hah!"

Céline remembered how hard he had worked since daybreak for the ball. "Poor Mr. MacKinnon."

"Bah! He is out to do you harm, *ma chérie*. You must have no pity on that man."

Why did she? Her butler was clearly out to expose her and yet she felt a twinge of compassion for him.

Why was her heart softening after all these years?

As Rees feared, it was a long morning, in which he was kept running up and downstairs, delivering bouquets and cards to Lady Wexham's private sitting room from the many guests who had been at her ball.

She, on the other hand, had still not stirred by noon. How nice to have the luxury of sleep after all those hours on the dance floor, he thought sourly. At least she hadn't had to traipse across town and then be locked out of her house.

Rees stifled another yawn and brought in another posy of flowers. He glanced at the card, indifferent by now to all the gentlemen who had sent their compliments.

Lord Delamare thanked her for a delightful ball and hoped to call on her at another date, the note read.

Rees set the bouquet down beside the dozens of others adorning the tabletops. The maids were busy setting them in vases of all shapes and sizes. The sitting room looked like a hothouse.

What a debauched, idle life.

But better than a traitorous one, he kept telling himself.

He should be relieved that it hadn't been Lady Wexham last night at the tavern.

Yet, he couldn't quite shake the feeling that she was involved in something clandestine. His mind kept returning to the mysterious caller. What astonished him more—which he had been unable to deny any longer to himself—was how much Rees wanted an honorable explanation.

The fact that she hadn't been the one in the tavern didn't clear her. It just seemed too coincidental that the same night she'd had a mysterious French caller, her maid would go out for a rendezvous.

It was just too convenient. He didn't doubt Valentine had a lover. But why would she choose a night after a long ball? All the servants were exhausted after the preparations. Of course, a lady's maid did nothing more than get her mistress ready for the occasion. Still, it just didn't feel right . . .

Another knot he was trying to unravel was what he was to tell Bunting when he next reported to him. After last night's debacle, Rees had come straight home. Bunting would wonder why he hadn't been at the tavern. He'd have to go out again tonight, hoping his contact would be there again. If not, he'd have to try his lodgings.

What would he tell Bunting about Monsieur de Fleury?

How could he not mention him? The man was a Frenchman. If Lady Wexham's story were to be believed, he'd just crossed the Channel to bring news of a sick aunt.

He harrumphed, stooping to pick up a fallen card from one of the bouquets.

He turned at the sound of a footstep, expecting for some reason to see Lady Wexham, as if thinking about her so much should make her appear. But it was only her sister-in-law. He pushed aside the disappointment he felt. Lady Agatha looked at him but gave no acknowledgment that she actually saw him. She wandered through the room, picking up a card here and there to read it, uttering an occasional "hmph!" Rees pretended to rearrange a bowl of white roses, all the while observing her.

But after circling the room once, she left without a word. How different her conduct from Lady Wexham's, he couldn't help thinking, who always spoke a friendly word of greeting to her servants. Rees could have been an armchair or divan for all the notice Lady Agatha had taken of him.

A few moments later, Valentine entered the room. The abigail, too, ignored him and began to inspect the bouquets, openly reading the cards. Finally, selecting two she turned to leave the room again.

"Her ladyship is up?" The words were out before he could consider them.

She stopped, looking at Rees with disdain and a certain something else—amusement?—in her eyes. "Zat is not your affair. When my lady needs you, she will call for you."

Before he could reprimand her, she flounced out of the room.

Anger flared in him. He had a short fuse today, his head pounding, his feet sore.

Dismissing the insolent maid as not worth the bother, he made his way back downstairs.

The front door rang again, and he yanked it open only to find a gentleman he recognized from Lady Wexham's coterie—those for whom she was "in."

Rees stepped back, his expression stiff. "Good day, my lord."

Baron Winifred Shelbourne lifted his monocle. "Good day . . . MacKinnon, isn't it?" he asked, stepping in.

He handed Rees his top hat and malacca walking stick. With a flourish, he swung off his greatcoat and held it out to Rees. "Be so good as to let Lady Wexham know I am here."

Grinding his teeth against the man's conceit, Rees took the things without a word. The man was a fop with his pomona-green cutaway and patterned waistcoat. His starched white neck cloth looked so stiff he could not bend his head, but stood looking downward at Rees even though Rees was taller by an inch or so.

"Her ladyship is not receiving."

The young baron let his monocle fall, continuing to dangle it by its velvet ribbon as he eyed Rees. "She'll receive me."

Rees eyed him in what he believed was his frostiest butler stare. "I believe she is not yet up, my lord."

The dandy smothered a yawn behind a gloved hand. "Oh, do be a dear man and announce me. She'll see me in her boudoir if she is up, and in her bedroom if she is not."

Rees reined in his anger with effort. "Very well, my lord. If you would care to wait in the sitting room." He led him to the same room he had escorted the Frenchman to the evening before and opened the door.

At least it gave him an excuse to go to Lady Wexham's room and inquire after her.

He knocked on her bedroom door, hearing a murmur of voices behind it. About time she was up.

Valentine opened the door a crack. "You? What do you want?"

"Baron Shelbourne is below and insists on knowing if her ladyship is receiving."

Before she could reply, Lady Wexham spoke from within the room, "Who is it?"

Valentine shut the door in his face.

A second later, she reopened it. "Very well, show him up."

She shut the door once again before he had a chance to ask where to show him. Surely not to her bedroom? He hadn't believed Shelbourne when he'd suggested it. Perhaps to the hothouse of her private sitting room.

When he returned with Baron Shelbourne in tow, the dandy took the decision out of his hands, walking ahead of him as they reached Lady Wexham's door and standing before it. "You may announce me."

Rees knocked once more. Valentine opened at once, if not with a smile, then at least without the scowl or smirk she reserved for Rees. She dropped a curtsy, opening the door wider. "My lord, please come in."

Rees managed to see Lady Wexham sitting up in bed against a pile of pillows. "Good morning, Winnie," she called out cheerfully, "you may chat with me while I finish my chocolate."

The door shut in Rees's face once again.

How was it possible for a woman to receive a gentleman in her bedroom? Rees was unable to imagine his mother or sister—or any respectable lady—heaven forbid, Jessamine—behaving so indecorously.

His sensibilities were in for further shocks as the afternoon wore on. A few more callers were allowed upstairs. This time, he escorted the gentlemen into Lady Wexham's boudoir, the room he had searched, where she sat at her dressing table, Valentine arranging her hair.

She was wearing a lacy, frilly garment that looked more like nightwear than a morning gown. But everyone seemed to take it in stride, the gentlemen beckoned to comfortable armchairs where they lounged and gossiped about the previous evening.

Rees left disgusted, determined to expunge this woman from his thoughts. He knew the French had different ideas, but this was going too far.

If not a traitor, then she was certainly a woman of loose morals, someone he had no business thinking about—much less obsessing over—the way he had begun to in recent days.

He must make every effort to report to Bunting as quickly as possible. He would tell him everything he knew. The sooner he was finished with this assignment, the sooner he could quit this unholy household and receive his promotion, and, God willing, do some work that had real value to the nation's security.

Céline sat at her writing desk, flipping a quill pen back and forth against her cheek as she thought about what to write her mother.

Since she was obliged to go out to Hartwell House, she must inform her mother, who disliked unannounced visits.

How Céline hated visiting the large estate leased to the Comte de Provence for the last several years of his exile from France. Surrounding him there were several members of the émigré community, all titled families who had fled France during the Terror.

In the years since her marriage, Céline had distanced herself from the French community in England. To her, they represented all that was old and regressive of her country. *L'ancien régime.* Impoverished aristocrats who thought themselves better than everyone, living off past glories. They spent their days on the fringes of the Comte de Provence's expectations, pinning their hopes and ambitions upon his ascension to the throne.

What France needed was true democracy, to go back to the ideals of the Revolution without reverting to all the excesses that had resulted from leaders who had taken control and brought on the awful Reign of Terror.

She still believed there were men and women who could be trusted to lead the nation.

Men like Stéphane, the one and only man she'd loved, but whose life had been cut short in battle, and now Roland and others who were fighting to keep democracy alive in France. Men whose ideals would not be corrupted by power.

Stéphane had been such a man—idealistic, yet with the strength and pragmatism to build a nation where all could have fair and equal treatment under the law.

She sighed, bringing her thoughts back to the present. It would do no good to think about things that had happened so long ago. *Chère Maman,* she began her letter.

> *I shall be arriving to visit you in a few days. Please do not put yourself out. You know I bring my own retinue of servants. Please tell the Comte of my arrival.*

She paused again, thinking of all the preparations to be made. When she went out to Hartwell House, it was as if she were temporarily moving house. They needed to take their bed linens, a small contingent of servants, a carriage and horses, even food.

Those servants left behind would enjoy a bit of a holiday, since there was little to do when she was not in residence except wait on her sister-in-law. Céline made a moue of distaste. Perhaps she could foist Agatha as a houseguest on one of her friends . . .

Her thoughts returned to her impending trip to Hartwell House.

Which of the servants would she take this time? It had been several months since the last trip. The servants didn't like to go, since all the servants at Hartwell were French and the British felt out of place there, as if they were on foreign soil.

Well, Valentine would go along, of course, and Jacob, her coachman, with a groom, as well as either Tom or William. One of the chambermaids and one kitchen maid. Mrs. Finlay would stay and look after Agatha and the house.

And her butler? If Mr. Rumford were here, she would give either him or Mrs. Finlay a holiday. There would need to be very little done at the house. If Agatha did stay, she would do no entertaining, so she required very little staff.

But what of Mr. MacKinnon? Should she make him stay on here or take him with her?

She rubbed the quill pen against her cheek, considering. She could keep an eye on him at Hartwell—or leave him behind, and ensure that he couldn't keep an eye on her.

Even while her reason told her to keep him in London, another part of her wished to have him along.

She told herself he could do little harm at Hartwell. He understood no French, the language spoken almost exclusively there. She hadn't had a chance to talk to MacKinnon since the ball last evening. She felt guilty about the wild-goose chase he had been sent on, even though she knew it had been a necessary step.

Ignoring the voice in her head, she came to her decision. MacKinnon would go along.

She would tell him to prepare for the trip. He would be in charge of the other servants. That should keep him too busy to observe her every move.

Céline finished her letter and then began a list of preparations before the trip.

Rees was in his butler's pantry with William, inspecting the silver that had been used at the ball's supper, when they were both surprised by the appearance of Lady Wexham.

"Good afternoon."

"Good afternoon, my lady," they both answered, standing at attention.

As usual she looked lovely, her peach-colored gown brightening the surroundings immediately.

She turned with a smile to the footman. "Would you excuse us a moment, William?"

"Yes, my lady."

"Thank you."

When the young man had left, she faced Rees with another smile, her hands clasped loosely in front of her. She wore a matching peach ribbon in her rich chestnut hair, bringing out the warm tints in it.

He had a hard time reconciling the lovely, innocent-looking woman who looked more like a girl than a woman of eight-and-twenty with one who would receive gentlemen callers while still abed.

He cleared his throat, trying to dispel the image that had plagued him all day from his mind. "Yes, my lady?"

"I am going out to Hartwell House."

"Indeed?" It was a country estate not far outside of London, where Louis XVI's brother had finally found lodging after years of living in exile across the Continent at the largesse of various heads of state.

She moistened her lips, enhancing their rosy hue. "I usually go out there several times a year to visit my mother. There is a large French community there," she added in a wry tone.

He remained silent, wondering where she was leading. Was she going to leave instructions for him while she was absent? He curled his fingers into his palms, trying to think how he could get himself included.

"I usually take a small number of servants with me. It is quite a vast estate, and the émigrés there are for the most part impoverished. Thus, any household help is usually a necessity for visitors."

"Which servants do you intend to take with you, my lady?"

She ticked them off on her slim fingers. "Valentine, Sally, one of the kitchen maids, a scullery maid, Tom—since William accompanied me the last time—and Jacob, and a groom. I shall take my traveling carriage and hire another with postilions for the servants."

"Yes, my lady." He asked, trying to conceal any disappointment he felt at being excluded, "And Gaspard?"

She shook her head. "No. The Comte has his own cook, and the two clash terribly whenever I've made the mistake of taking Gaspard along. You may tell the servants to begin preparations for the trip. They know what to do. We need to bring linens and provisions. Enough for a fortnight at least."

"Yes, my lady."

"I wish you to accompany me as well."

He couldn't help registering his surprise. "Me?"

"Yes. You can help Tom with any of his duties." Her eyebrows drew together, her amber eyes holding a question. "Do you ride?"

The question caught him unaware since his thoughts were still adjusting to the news that he was to go to Hartwell. "Yes."

Her eyes widened slightly. "Indeed? That is good. You and Tom may ride alongside the equipage. I wish to take along my mare, of course. Since we are taking such a small staff, you may help Tom with the duties of footman, and give Jacob any assistance with the horses, if you don't object."

"No, my lady, why should I?"

Her full lips curved slightly upward. "Because you are the butler, are you not?" Her tone was teasing, the same tone she had used in conversation with the gentlemen in her boudoir.

He didn't respond to the smile, instead saying stiffly, "I am here to serve you in any capacity you require while my uncle is laid up."

The humor evaporated from her expression. "I didn't offend you, did I?"

He blinked at her gentle tone. Except she had no idea why he was offended—nor must she ever. Until he discovered the truth of Lady Wexham's loyalties, he must act out his role of simple butler. "Of course not. I shall be perfectly happy to assist Tom and Jacob."

"Good. You may confer with Jacob concerning the travel arrangements. Mrs. Finlay will show you what needs to be packed."

"Very well, my lady."

"In recompense for these added duties, you shall find that you have much more free time at Hartwell than you do here. I require very little, so the servants who accompany me find it to be more of a holiday than a hardship."

"I see."

"Be sure to pack some suitable attire for the country. There are miles of parkland and we are not far from the market town of Aylesbury. There is also a small village nearby."

"Very well, my lady. When should we be ready to depart?"

"As soon as possible. Perhaps the day after tomorrow?"

When she had left the small room, Rees found it hard to collect his thoughts. Why was it every time he spoke to her, no matter how brief the exchange, he felt himself once again ensnared by her charm? He needed to keep his focus on his assignment.

Despite this, all he felt was an overwhelming sense of relief. For whatever the reason, Lady Wexham had decided to take him along to Hartwell.

The next day Rees spent crisscrossing London with a list of commissions. Her ladyship needed a special blend of tea from Fortnum and Mason's, a pair of shoes she had had made at Wood's, a parasol from Cohen's, the latest novels from Lackington Allen & Co.

With the house in upheaval, he was doing what he would normally have the footmen do. But they were busy packing up the crates of food and wines under Gaspard's watchful eye.

Rees exited the Pantheon Bazaar where Lady Wexham had sent him to pick up a pair of lady's gloves and stepped onto Oxford Street.

"Rees!"

His head snapped up at the feminine voice.

Midway down the next block, his sister hailed him. "Rees!" she repeated, waving her arm. Right behind her stood Jessamine and her mother, Mrs. Barry.

All three stared at him, surprise and disbelief in their eyes.

He'd forgotten his sister's impending visit. In the same instant he remembered his butler's garb. He'd been so caught up in carrying out Lady Wexham's errands that he'd overlooked the fact that he was in the precise neighborhood where his sister and Jessamine were most likely to be.

Panic held him rooted to the pavement.

And Jessamine! What would he say to her?

Without thinking, he swiveled around and pushed past the exiting shoppers and reentered the Pantheon. He could use it as a shortcut to the other side of the block, his only thought that they mustn't see him.

A few minutes later, he reached Marlboro Street. Then he broke into a run, turning corners until he was almost to Seven Dials, a neighborhood they were sure not to enter.

He halted to catch his breath, keeping a sharp eye for pickpockets.

Had they seen him clearly, or had he been far enough away to pass for someone who only resembled him? How was he to explain when Megan next wrote him? Thank goodness he'd be leaving town the next day for Hartwell. He'd write his sister as soon as he arrived to tell her he'd been sent there by the Foreign Office.

His mother and sister would be pleased, thinking he was receiving a promotion with all this traveling he seemed to be doing. If only they knew the truth. A butler!

His thoughts returned to the encounter. He'd just set his hat on his head, so his features would have been hard to distinguish. But they'd seen his eyes. If Megan wrote him about the encounter, he'd be forced to deny having been in the city. His postmark from Hartwell would prove it. At least he'd already warned her he would be out of town. That should certainly convince her she had been mistaken.

But what if all three of the ladies agreed that it had been he?

How he hated this masquerade!

With a sigh, he turned back toward Mayfair. The sooner he returned to the house, the safer he'd be.

He would have to report this evening to let Bunting know of his departure for Hartwell House.

That should keep the man satisfied for the time being.

$\mathcal{T}$he trip to Hartwell House did not take more than a few hours even though they had not had an early start, with so many things to be seen to.

The carriages assumed a leisurely pace, stopping at two posting houses on the way, to change horses. By early afternoon, they were passing through Aylesbury, then on through the picturesque countryside beyond it. By midafternoon they turned into the gate to the vast parklands surrounding the French comte's residence.

Céline pushed aside the curtain of the carriage window, watching the scenery. She had not been out here to see her mother since February when everything had been covered with snow.

With each passing mile, her spirits sank a notch. It was so each time she came. It reminded her too much of the past.

At least now the countryside was green, the leafy forests of beech creating a dappled effect of light and shadow upon the carriage. After miles of parkland, they at last entered the Grand Avenue leading toward the palace.

A mile or so farther, the carriage drew up before the large golden ashlar stone structure. Canted bay windows at either end balanced out the Jacobean and Georgian mansion.

A pity that since its owner had leased the palace to the Comte de

Provence, the handsome mansion had fallen into decay. The shrubbery needed trimming, flocks of chickens and small livestock squawked and squealed from the parapet surrounding the lead roof, and the overall appearance looked shabby.

The carriage came to a stop at the main doorway. A footman in faded livery and powdered wig opened her door and let down the step.

Two more footmen stood at attention at the door. The butler, whom she knew well, came to greet her.

"*Bonjour*, madame." He bowed. "Welcome back. Your mother informed us of your arrival. We have put you in your usual suite in the east wing, if that is to your liking."

"Yes, of course, Monsieur Denfort. My servants will see to the bags. Is my mother about?"

"Yes, in her rooms. Tea will be served at five."

"Is the Comte well?"

"Yes, my lady, I am happy to report. His gout is not troubling him overmuch. I believe he will make an appearance at tea."

"I shall greet him then. You will see to my servants, will you not?"

"Of course, madame."

She was led up the wide staircase and down a long passage to her mother's rooms. Hartwell House had dozens and dozens of rooms.

The footman knocked at her mother's door and announced her. She must grow accustomed to the formal pace of things here. It was, after all, a royal court—or pretended to be.

When her mother saw her, she smiled and held out her hands. "Ah, Céline, you are here at last."

The two barely touched cheeks and drew apart. "Hello, *Maman*. You are well?" She eyed her mother, who was dressed in the older fashion, her brown silk open robe gown displaying a deeper yellow petticoat beneath. She wore a high, frilly lace fichu around her neckline, and her graying brown hair was powdered and covered in a lacy mobcap.

Her mother sighed. "As well as can be expected for one of my years."

Her mother indicated Céline take the seat beside her on the settee. "How was your journey?"

"Uneventful." The two exchanged pleasantries after her mother gave instructions for refreshment to be brought up to her.

Céline didn't worry about her own servants, who knew what to do. Valentine would oversee Sally in the unpacking and making up of beds, the kitchen and scullery maids would make themselves useful in the kitchen. As for MacKinnon, she hoped he would not be at loose ends, especially among so many French people, but doubtless Tom would show him the ropes.

She would go down and check on him—on all her servants—later. But first there was this interview to be gotten over and then tea. She turned to her mother. "Is there anything new?"

"My dear, there is always something new. Our hopes are growing that soon that monster Bonaparte will be defeated. I pray every day that our own Louis will be sitting on the throne that upstart dared to crown himself emperor upon. What conceit!"

Before her mother grew agitated, Céline turned the conversation to more mundane matters. "How is *Tante* Louise?" she asked, naming the close friend of her mother's who was not related by blood, but whom Céline had grown accustomed to calling aunt.

"Oh—as always, complaining . . . if it's not gout, it's rheumatism."

They talked some more of the various long-term residents of Hartwell House before Céline brought up a less pleasant subject. "*Maman*, I received your request for an advance upon your next quarterly allowance."

Her mother motioned with her fine hands. "And what of it? Why should I not appeal to my only child if I run short? You have been well provided for. Why should you deny your poor mother anything? I who sacrificed everything for you." She put a hand to her forehead. "All those years after your dear papa was taken and I was alone in the world, friendless with not a penny after those scoundrels took everything from us—"

Céline sat back, resigned to the familiar tirade against the Jacobins who had appropriated their family's lands and wealth. When her mother paused for breath, she quickly filled in the silence. "I begrudge you nothing, *Maman,* you know that. What I do object to is having you spend your *generous* allowance on gambling debts. Why can't you be content with those pensioners who only play for pennies?"

Her mother waved a hand scornfully. "You wish me to appear like those beggars!" Her voice rose. "Why you begrudge me the few pleasures that are left in my life! I cannot appear a miserly widow at the table when everyone knows my daughter is the wealthiest Frenchwoman in London!"

"I would wish no such thing. I merely ask you to exercise self-restraint and get up from the card table when your luck runs against you."

The interview ended badly, with her mother in tears, as Céline had known it would. She finally excused herself with "Do not upset yourself, *Maman.* I shall write you a bank draft."

After her visit with her mother, Céline was at last free to go to her own suite of rooms, on another floor, removed from those of her mother, who was a permanent resident of the palace.

"There you are at last," Valentine said as soon as she entered. "You will be late for tea. How was Madame de Beaumont?"

"Fine." Céline would dearly have loved to sit in an armchair and not do anything for a while, but she knew Valentine would not allow that, so she submitted meekly to being undressed.

"I have laid out the blue Indian muslin with the cream sash. There is hot water for you to wash, if it hasn't grown cold by now."

"Very well." Céline walked behind the cloth screen to wash the travel dust off herself.

An hour later, washed, trussed, and coiffed, Céline left her chambers to make her way back down the myriad passages and staircases to the main salon, where she knew the old Comte received his visitors in the late afternoon.

When she arrived, there were already several guests and habitués whom she recognized gathered in the marble-floored corridor.

After greetings, they passed into the salon, where they stood or sat about the spacious room with its floor to ceiling bay windows overlooking the parkland while waiting for the Comte to appear.

A quarter of an hour later, he entered, accompanied by his closest retinue of advisors and servants. After he was settled on a velvet settee, Céline approached him. One foot, plagued by gout, rested on an embroidered footstool in front of him. White silk stockings covered thick ankles and calves.

He was almost sixty. His girth filled the settee made for two. Gray powdered curls framed his face. He wore his hair long, in a queue in the back. His face was round with jowls, his nose hooked, his eyes and eyebrows dark, contrasting to his powdered hair.

His eyes lit up in recognition. "*Ma chère* Céline, my child!" He held out a plump, beringed hand.

Céline took his hand and curtsied deeply. "My lord."

"Come, tell me the news from town."

A footman brought a chair and she sat beside him for a while, telling him all the news she knew would amuse him.

"And the Regent is still misbehaving?"

"As usual. He hardly dares show his face in the streets for fear of the mobs. But he spends most of his time in Brighton these days."

"Ah, the seaside. If I could travel, I am sure it would do me good." He motioned to his foot. "But you see how I am held captive here."

She murmured sympathetically. "And Madame Royale, I trust she is well?" she asked, referring to the Comte's niece, the only remaining offspring of the beheaded Louis XVI.

"She is very well. You shall see her for yourself." He made a motion toward the room. "And the Duc d'Angoulême is here from London. We are all, as you can imagine, looking forward to our return to France."

"You think it will be so soon?"

"No one can say, but our hopes are quite high now that the Corsican has suffered such reverses on the Russian front."

After chatting with him a few more minutes, Céline paid her respects to the other members of the royal household. Her mother appeared and took her to greet a few more of her old acquaintances.

A weak tea was served. Céline looked forward to several days of tedium. She doubted she would discover much news of value in this environment where everything was steeped in the past.

After greeting the only people who interested her, she made her way out to the terrace, feeling stifled inside. The gardens, despite signs of neglect, still displayed an air of elegance.

Perhaps she could enjoy some good rides and walks if the weather held. Though it was hard to ride unaccompanied at Hartwell. The ladies usually rode or drove in groups. Since her widowhood, Céline was no longer used to such a formal way of life, where every activity was regulated and overseen.

The memories she rarely indulged in London always thrust themselves into her thoughts when she came to Hartwell. She could never forget her mother's role in breaking up the one and only love she had experienced in her twenty-eight years. Stéphane Delacroix.

Céline had met the young French cadet during the brief peace, when she and her mother had returned to Paris, her mother hoping to regain some of the family's wealth lost during the Revolution.

Céline believed her mother's hatred of Bonaparte had as much to do with his government's unwillingness to return her husband's ancestral home as for political reasons.

Céline had been introduced to the handsome cadet at the home of one of her mother's friends. Possessing neither the title nor wealth to satisfy her mother's ambitions, Stéphane had been rejected out of hand as a suitor. With Valentine's help, however, Céline continued to meet Stéphane in secret. When her mother discovered it, she cut short their stay and brought Céline back to London posthaste, unmindful of Céline's threats, hysteria, or sullen silence.

Hostilities between the two countries had soon resumed. Once back in London, her mother had used every penny she had for Céline's coming out, impressing upon her the need to make a brilliant match.

"You have looks and charm, *chérie*. Use them to advantage, if you don't want us both to spend the rest of our days eking out an existence in some milliner's back shop."

As the season advanced and no suitable young gentleman proposed, her mother had paced the floor, wringing her hands. "You must do more to encourage them. You cannot stand looking such a tragic figure, as if you are already in decline. You must put yourself out."

But Céline found it impossible to behave lively like the other debutantes that season, when her heart was broken.

The memory of her emotional state at seventeen only drew a shudder of distaste from her vantage of eight-and-twenty. Older and wiser, she could only feel pity for that green girl who had shed so many useless tears.

Valentine had been her lifesaver, the one who arranged a secret correspondence for her and Stéphane.

But her mother had not given up. With no young men coming up to scratch, she had fixed her sights on an older man, someone for whom her daughter's youth and beauty would outweigh her lack of dowry sufficiently to extract a proposal of marriage.

After carefully taking stock of the wealthy bachelors past their prime, her mother had selected the Earl of Wexham, a widower with a vast fortune. It mattered little that he was three times Céline's age.

When Céline balked at having to entertain the old earl, her mother's anger had given way to palpitations and swoons. She had taken to her bed, crying out that Céline would be responsible for her death and blaming her for their precipitous return to England before she could regain their family's wealth and ancestral home. Céline had countered that she'd rather do anything than sell herself to a man she found repugnant.

Things had been at a stalemate, her mother refusing all food, when Céline had received news of Stéphane's death. It was Roland who had written to Céline. Stéphane had fallen at the Battle of Ulm in Bavaria, a national triumph for Napoleon, a personal tragedy for her.

Valentine had held her in her arms as Céline sobbed, her dreams and hopes shattered by one simple sentence. *Fallen in battle, a hero's death, but he is no more . . .*

Valentine had been her only confidante. She was the one who'd made her get up in the morning; dressed her in the finery her mother insisted she wear, when all she wanted was to wear black; lectured her that she must smile and go on no matter what she was feeling inside.

"You must think not only of your own survival but of your mother's. What will become of her if you should succumb to self-pity? You will find yourselves on the street," she spat, her eyes filled with a venomous light as if she had firsthand experience. "You think you are the first girl to fall in love and lose her young man? Bah! You will survive a broken heart—but you may not survive the streets, *ma chérie*. In a few years your body will be broken—and then you will wish for a wealthy man to offer you his hand—but you will find only those who will take from you without a wedding ceremony!"

In the end, Céline accepted the earl's marriage proposal. There seemed little choice. Only later did she discover the hard bargain her mother had driven, extracting a generous marriage settlement for her only child.

Old enough to be her father—even older than her own father would have been—the earl had been, nevertheless, unfailingly attentive and kind to her during his courtship.

Innocent that she was at the time, she was lulled into believing that a paternal figure like the earl would make no demands on her as wife.

How naïve she'd been.

At first she had tried to love him, doing her best to hide any distaste or failure to reciprocate his feelings.

But in the end, it had mattered not. When after a year, then two, she had failed to produce an heir, his own devotion had cooled until all that was left was a cold disdain in private and a brittle politeness when the two were in public. He had occupied his time in the House of Lords and on his country estate, hunting with his cronies.

It was only by chance that she heard of his mistress, the first of a string of actresses or dancers. Céline could be sure that some well-intentioned friend would make sure she knew the latest gossip. She'd felt relief, believing he would leave her alone, but to her chagrin, the earl continued making demands on her at regular intervals though with no success. She continued barren, and he railed against having been fooled by her and her mother.

For seven long years, she had endured her existence, going about society as if everything was well, though she knew from the looks in people's eyes that they were assessing her. Where was the heir? It was no secret that the earl had married because he needed a son. His first marriage had produced no children.

No one would fault him. It was the bride's duty to increase.

Then she'd had to ignore the rumors about her own life, whenever she seemed to give her attention to some gentleman over another. Being French, naturally she was assumed to have a string of paramours. After a while she became indifferent to the gossip and learned to ignore the murmurs behind her back, laughing and shining in society as a leader of fashion as her dreams died and her soul dried up within her.

But her mother had been well provided for, moving out to live at Hartwell House with the cream of the émigré society, while Céline spent her days in town, preferring to cultivate the British *ton*.

When the earl had dropped dead of a heart attack during a hunt, at first Céline had felt nothing but shock, followed by numbness. The relief had not come until later as she realized what widowhood with wealth could bring—not happiness but independence.

Gradually, she began to enjoy that independence. The only thing marring it was the earl's sister coming to live with her.

Agatha had been a thorn in the flesh since then—albeit a minor one.

In compensation, Céline was left a sizeable fortune. The bulk of the estate had been entailed, passing on to his nearest male relation, a nephew, the new Earl of Wexham. But Céline had been given life use of a townhouse, as well as a generous jointure.

Suffering the vapors and prone to hysterics, Madame de Beaumont had proven herself a tough negotiator when agreeing to Céline's betrothal.

But all that was in the past. Céline shook off the recollections, a conscious effort she had to undergo each time she came out to Hartwell.

"You have come from town?" a pleasant, masculine voice spoke over her shoulder.

She turned from her contemplation of the gardens to face another habitué of Hartwell House, Monsieur de la Roche. He was one of the close circle surrounding the would-be king. "Yes, to visit my mother."

"Of course," he murmured. "Such a devoted daughter."

"And you are still at Hartwell?" she asked, eyeing him. She'd never felt comfortable around de la Roche. He was perhaps in his sixties, slim and of medium height. He had thin, gray hair, and his skin seemed to stretch too tightly over what had once been a handsome face.

His eyes of indeterminate color, a washed-out blue or green or gray with flecks of yellow, gazed back at her. "Yes. Serving our future king."

Her gaze went to the old Comte. "Do you think his return is imminent?"

"Perhaps by the end of the year or early the next."

She raised an eyebrow. "So soon?"

"Soon? I would say he has waited too long."

"Yes, when measured by the years of his exile. But when one reads news from the Continent, it seems Napoleon is still unchallenged."

"But that is changing."

"Since his invasion of Russia, yes . . . it does appear so." She smiled. "If you will excuse me, monsieur, there is someone I must greet."

He bowed over her hand. "Of course, my lady."

She probably should have stayed to ferret out more information from de la Roche, but something about him made her nervous. It was as if everything he said had a double meaning. With so many residents at Hartwell, it should be easy to avoid him during her stay.

By the time the long dinner was over, Céline was exhausted from making small talk and not being truly honest in anything she said —especially when it pertained to events in France, around which the bulk of the émigrés' conversation revolved.

Valentine was waiting for her and rose as soon as Céline entered her room.

"You look tired, madame."

"If I do, it is because I am," she said, dropping into a chair with a weary sigh.

"*Non, non,*" Valentine scolded. "Come, let me help you off with your dress first. You will feel better in a dressing gown."

"Very well."

As Valentine helped her undress, Céline asked her, "Are the servants all settled in?"

"Yes. They have their usual rooms."

"Is Mr. MacKinnon finding his way?" She realized she hadn't had a moment to look for him nor had she seen him at dinner.

Valentine sniffed as she began to let down Céline's coiffure. "That one seems to blend in wherever he's placed."

"I did not notice him waiting at table during dinner, so I wondered where he might have got to."

"They put him to work in the kitchens overseeing the serving dishes." She yanked at Céline's hair. "Why have you allowed that man to come with us here?"

She was too tired to argue with her abigail. "I thought it best."

"Hah!"

"Ouch!" Céline brought a hand up to her hair where Valentine pulled at it again with the hairbrush.

It was probably too late to send for MacKinnon now. First thing in the morning. She met Valentine's gaze in the mirror. "Please have him come to me in the morning."

Valentine's lips tightened into a line of displeasure, but she said nothing more.

Afterward, as Céline lay in bed, her thoughts returned to MacKinnon. The man had certainly acquitted himself on horseback on the trip out to Hartwell. She couldn't help but notice the fine figure he cut on her roan mare as he and Tom accompanied the carriages. She could see he was an accomplished horseman. At the posting houses, he had been attentive, coming up to her coach before the inn servants to ask her if she cared for refreshment. Was Valentine right and it had been a mistake to bring him out to Hartwell? Was she only giving him more opportunity to catch her in her spying activities and turn her in?

Céline turned in her bed, seeking a comfortable position on the strange mattress. She would have to alert Roland to put an escape plan in place should the worst happen.

She sighed, too weary to think of that now. Once again her mother had lost a sizeable amount at cards after dinner. If only she could keep an eye on her mother in the card room. From the woman who'd been so strong and domineering in her life, her mother had become increasingly childish and dependent. It was as if she'd deliberately misbehaved this evening after Céline's remonstrances against wagering such large sums.

She gazed into the darkness, wondering what to do. Sometimes the weight of responsibility became too much . . .

Late the next morning, when Lady Wexham descended for breakfast, Rees was waiting for her outside the morning room.

"You wished to see me, my lady?"

As usual she looked as if she had just stepped off a fashion plate from the kinds of lady's magazines his sister was fond of. This morning, she wore a pretty gown of pink and green sprigged muslin with a light green sash tied high above her waist.

She smiled at him. "Yes." Motioning a little ways down the corridor, she led him out of the way of the servants carrying in replenishments of food, to a small alcove overlooking the side lawn. "I didn't have a chance to see you yesterday and wished to ask how you were getting on."

Once again she had surprised him. Since arriving at this French enclave, he had been astounded at both its size and the number of servants and retainers. Yet, she had remembered him. "Fine, my lady, I thank you."

"Is the staff treating you well? I apologize that they are all French. I do hope it's not too inconvenient." Her honey-hued eyes showed genuine concern.

"No, my lady. We . . . make each other understood."

"That's good." She stood regarding him a moment longer until he had the sense there was more she wished to say to him.

"I wanted to tell you that you may make use of the grounds as if you were a guest. They are quite extensive with many walking trails through the forests. Tom can show you about."

He felt a surge of disappointment that that was all it had been. He inclined his head. "Thank you for your kindness, my lady."

"And of course, you may ride. I see that you are an accomplished horseman. Did you ever work in the stables at Telford?"

He thought quickly. "Yes, when I was quite young."

"Well, as you will soon see, apart from helping to serve at mealtimes, your time is pretty much your own."

"Thank you." Had she really taken the time to think of his free time? He thought of Oglethorpe and wondered if the young dandy ever thought about how Rees spent his Sundays.

They each paused. She looked ready to dismiss him when he spoke. "If I may ask you something."

She blinked her pretty eyes. "Of course."

"I noticed some creeks on our way here. Would I be permitted to fish?"

She pursed her fine lips. "I do not see why not. I shall inquire, but in the meantime, you have my leave."

He inclined his head once again. "Thank you, my lady."

"You are welcome."

Before he could move away, she held up a finger. He waited for her to speak, but she didn't do so right away.

She moistened her lips, and he noticed a slight flush of color on her cheeks. "I have another request."

Sensing it was something she was having trouble articulating, he waited.

"It is my mother."

He blinked, not having expected that. "What is it you wish me to do?" he asked softly, wondering why she hesitated.

"She enjoys playing cards."

He lifted his brows. "That is usual, is it not, for someone of her station?"

"Oh yes." Her lips twisted. "Unfortunately, unlike the English, the passion for betting among the French is shared equally between men and women."

He wondered why she would be telling him this.

"She plays very deep."

Understanding filled him. Was she worried about how much her mother was losing? "How may I help?"

She smiled ruefully. "I'm not sure. She spends her evenings in the game room."

He pondered. "You wish her to refrain from the table?"

"That would be impossible. What I wish is . . ." Again she moistened her lips, and he felt a burst of compassion for the trouble she was having in making her request. She drew in a breath. "What I wish is for someone to distract her . . . or . . . or warn me when she is losing more than she can afford. Perhaps you could station yourself beside her table in the evenings and come to me if you see her going beyond a certain amount?" She hastened on, "It is not that I wish to curtail her pleasure, but she—"

He bowed his head, not obliging her to finish. "I shall do as you request."

"Thank you." The words were uttered on a breath of relief. He wished he could offer more. "If there is nothing else?"

She started, as if realizing she had been staring into his eyes. "No, nothing else." With a nod, she dismissed him.

Rees felt her gaze as he walked off, even as he wondered how the deuce he was going to keep an avowed gambler from squandering her money . . . at the same time wishing for more dragons to slay for his lady.

11

*R*ees had been at Hartwell House a few days. He couldn't complain. The grounds were beautiful, and he had ample time to explore them. The weather had been warm and sunny, the mists usually clearing by midmorning.

In addition, Tom had been helpful the first day or so in showing him around.

"We all look forward to comin' out to Hartwell. Except for all the Frenchies we have to endure," he said, "it's more a holiday than anything else."

Rees saw Lady Wexham at the evening meal, where he assisted the footmen in serving. She always made a point of stopping briefly before him and Tom to ask how they were. He couldn't help but be touched by her solicitude toward her servants.

For the rest of the time, he caught only glimpses of her in the distance—out riding with a group of ladies, or walking the gardens with a pair of gentlemen, or playing croquet with a mixed group.

He was hard-pressed not to let on to the servants of the vast estate that he understood their language, especially with Tom, who found it tedious to be "among so many frogs." He and the other servants from Lady Wexham's household spent their free time together like aliens in a foreign land. Even if they might quarrel or not get along in London, here they stuck together like bosom friends.

The French staff, for their part, were disdainful of these "ignorant *Anglais*."

Valentine was in her element, nattering away in French and flirting with the male household servants. She would cast Rees baleful looks, as if to say, *Look what you deprived yourself of.*

Rees felt no inclination to hobnob with his fellow servants. He had to maintain his distance, in order not to slip and give away the fact that he could perfectly understand French.

Thus, he found himself on his own a good deal of the time. He'd walked to the village and gone fishing a couple of times by the banks of a stream that ran through the property. More importantly, he'd explored the mansion and grounds thoroughly, always keeping an ear and eye out for anything suspicious.

But, in all, he was frustrated not to have better access to Lady Wexham or those close to the Comte. For all he knew, she was gathering information and passing it on and he would have no clue.

If Lady Wexham had meant to tie his hands, she had done an effective job by asking him to look after her mother. After dinner, he had to position himself near her card table. It was a wonderful vantage for overhearing their talk—useful if it weren't a foursome of older persons who spent the hours bickering over their play or reminiscing about their life in France.

So far he had not had to report Madame de Beaumont to her daughter. Céline's mother had had a streak of luck, walking off with a tidy sum each evening. She'd taken a fancy to him, which helped him convince her to leave the tables while her luck held.

He had made a habit of patrolling the grounds at night, once the dinner was over. This was usually not until very late, since first he usually accompanied Madame de Beaumont for a turn or two the length of the terrace. He had seen little of Lady Wexham herself, unless it was on the terrace with a guest or guests, but for all he could make out, it was in lighthearted conversation.

What was left for him, if he did not complete this assignment with satisfactory results?

He could always advertise as a butler.

The bitter jest did nothing to alleviate his pessimistic thoughts.

Without a promotion, he could never hope to have a career on the diplomatic field.

His thoughts turned to Jessamine. Without a job with prospects, he would never be able to marry. Another dead end faced him, and he had no inkling of which way to turn or what was the answer.

He had spent hours sitting on the banks of the creek, walking or riding the fields and forest, his thoughts going around and around, praying for direction, and all he felt was he must wait.

Wait and see things through, even when he saw nothing good ahead.

Céline guided her mare through the sparse trees of a wooded area along the stream. She had finally escaped the rest of the company and gone on a ride by herself.

The trees were in full leaf, though they retained the tender green color of spring, and the ground was soft and moist from the rains.

She wondered when and how she would be approached by Roland.

She had plenty to tell him, although she didn't know how much was accurate or even useful. The Comte and those closest to him spent their days planning their triumphant return to Paris. Louis trusted her because both her parents came from long and noble lines and he had known them in France.

She felt no qualms about informing on what went on at Hartwell. She didn't consider it part of the British government but of the old French regime. Only England and the other Allies would wield power on the Continent once Napoleon fell. Louis depended completely on their sovereigns, particularly England's, to obtain the throne in Paris.

Although fond of him, Céline thought the Comte would be disastrous for France. He really had no right to the throne. He'd declared himself the regent before ever his brother or the crown prince had been executed, and had been jockeying ever since to claim the title of king.

But more importantly, it would be a step back for France. Being at Hartwell House convinced her that to return to the old ways, after so much sacrifice and bloodshed to do away with the injustices of the *ancien régime*, would be France's death knell.

Bonaparte had turned into nothing but a despot, but at least he had kept much of what the Directory had voted into law.

Céline sighed, wondering what was to become of France, and what, if any, role she might have. Would she end her days in London, on the endless round of social calls, living in town during the season, traveling about from country house to country house in the warm months and hunting season, no longer able to claim the earl's country seat as her own, since the new heir had taken occupancy? Or worse, would she end hanging from a noose?

Pushing aside the morbid thought, she made an effort to take in the lovely scenery.

She brought a hand up to shade her eyes, detecting someone fishing along the bank of the stream. Perhaps it was MacKinnon. She had given him permission. But the low-crowned, wide-brimmed hat shaded his features.

Feeling an unaccountable lightening in her spirit, she nudged her mare in his direction.

She smiled when he looked up, enjoying the sight of someone completely at ease in his surroundings. "Good afternoon." How different he appeared from the dignified butler—and yet how well—in his country buckskins, high boots, and dark blue jacket.

He made as if to get up, and she motioned him back. "Stay put, you might disturb the fish." Without giving him a chance to react, she slid off her horse and tossed the reins over the saddle. "Catch anything?"

"No, nothing today, but I have caught some carp on other occasions, which has made me popular with the chef."

She found a nearby rock and decided to join him awhile, telling herself this was a good time to discover a little more about him. She ignored her quickened pulse at his proximity in this more relaxed setting away from everyone.

Seeing her intent, he again began to stand. "Here, let me put my jacket on the rock if you are to sit."

"No, please don't bother. It's perfectly clean." She demonstrated by removing a glove and dusting its surface with her bare hand. Settling upon it, she pretended to enjoy the scenery as she decided how best to proceed.

They sat in silence as he resumed fishing.

"How is your uncle?"

The question brought no reaction. MacKinnon continued looking out at the water, the long fishing pole in his hands. "He is well."

"Does he say when he will be back?"

His gaze flickered to hers. "He is anxious to come back. Perhaps in a fortnight."

Instead of relief, Céline felt an instant of alarm at the thought that MacKinnon would leave her household so soon. "Please tell him not to fret . . . a man his age . . . it takes more time for bones to knit. There is no need to rush things." She smiled, slowing her words. "You must reassure him that his nephew is filling his shoes splendidly."

"I thank you, my lady. I must confess I was . . . nervous of taking over his position, albeit temporarily." He focused on the cane pole as he spoke.

She removed her other glove and set the two on her lap. "Well, you have done an excellent job." After a pause, she continued. "Are you happy here at Hartwell?"

"Yes." Was it her imagination or was there a wariness in his tone?

"I'm glad of that," she repeated, thumping her gloves against her knee. She knew her emerald-green riding habit suited her. What did he think of her appearance? Oh, dear, what a silly thought. To hide her confusion, she concentrated on her gloves, folding them together as she cast about for another line of questioning. "Did you always wish to go into service?"

He regarded her sidelong. "Why do you ask?"

She eyed the length of him, her lips pursed. "You don't strike me as a butler."

He said nothing, continuing to watch her in that steady way he had.

"I mean, you perform the duties flawlessly, don't misunderstand me. It's just that you seem . . . how shall I put it—" She brought a finger to her lips. "More than a butler? Your speech is refined, for one thing." Her lips curled up in a smile. "You could pass for a gentleman."

Something flickered in his gray eyes. "I had good teachers."

She cocked an eyebrow, wondering if he would be forthcoming with more personal information. "Did you?"

"I mean those above me always corrected my speech," he hastened to add. "I think my mother did wish me to do more. She always admonished me to . . . to emulate my betters."

She tried to picture what kind of mother he had had. "She must be a remarkable woman. She was also in service?"

"Yes." Before she could ask him something more about his relations, he said, "I was not always in service." His voice was low, as if the words were dragged out of him against his will.

"I knew it!" She leaned forward, her elbows on her knees, her excitement rekindled. "What else have you done?"

"I was in His Majesty's navy as a youth."

"How romantic." A sailor. "Were you very young?"

He shrugged. "Fifteen—not so very."

"Did you fight under Nelson?"

He gave a brief nod of his chin.

She was more intrigued than ever. "How utterly fascinating. Tell me what he was like."

His gaze strayed beyond the water, as if he were picturing the admiral. "He was a brave commander, utterly fearless. His men would trust him in any battle, no matter how outnumbered we seemed at the outset."

She nodded. "I met him in London once during my first season. He was being fêted by all the *ton* after his victory on the Nile. But he had eyes only for Emma Hamilton. Such a dashing figure he cut, even with the loss of an arm and eye."

When MacKinnon said nothing more, she prodded gently, "But you didn't continue in the navy?"

She waited several seconds.

"I was wounded."

She drew in a breath. "Dear me, was it serious?"

"Serious enough." After a moment he added, "I was some months recovering."

"Were you discharged?"

He nodded.

"Was that when you became a footman? Was there nothing else to do?"

He focused once more on the fishing pole. "My mother needed me home by then."

"Were you her only son?"

"Yes."

Her curiosity was growing. "Do you have any sisters?"

His answer seemed long in coming. "One."

"How nice that must be," she said wistfully.

"Are you an only child?" He looked at her now and she felt the tables turned on her, as if in that moment she would tell him anything he wished to know. "Yes." The word came out a whisper.

He looked away, and she could breathe again. "Forgive my impertinence." His butler tone was back.

"There is nothing to forgive."

He shrugged again. "I was only a seaman. During the peace, there was no hope for advancement. My father, who was in service as a groom, found me a position as footman at Telford House, where I have been ever since."

Disappointment surged in her breast. When had his words become a fabrication? How much was truth? Was any of it? "It must not have been easy after a life at sea . . . to be bound to one place, one household."

"Not so very different. A ship is a confined space, and the discipline, by consequence, very rigid, even harsh at times." He shrugged again. "Life on a large estate in the country offers certain benefits as well." His tone was expressionless.

"Yes, that is so." She bit her lip, wondering how to get him to tell her more. "If you had been born in France, you would have achieved something greater, perhaps even a position in government."

"If I hadn't been conscripted into Bonaparte's war machine."

Well, she could see he was British to the core, judging Napoleon as only a monster. She sobered, remembering Stéphane's untimely death. "Yes, that is so. Likely you would have been killed on the battlefield."

Again, there was silence. A cricket chirped around them.

"Do you miss France?"

Was he going to ferret out whether she was a Bonapartist? She took her time responding, rubbing at the stone she sat upon. "It has been so long since I left. I was only a child." She shook her head with a smile. "So, no, I do not miss France day by day. I consider myself British in many ways."

"Would you go back now, if not for the war?"

When had her interrogation been taken over by him? She was more amused than alarmed. There was an underlying force to the man, and she wished to pursue whatever game they were playing. "For a visit, I would undoubtedly go." She sighed, letting her gaze drift over the dark water. "Though I dread what I would find."

At the question in his eyes, she explained. "The war has undoubtedly devastated the country, but it has survived much in its long history. I know it will recover." She smiled. "Yes, I should like to visit it again. And, of course, Paris is a beautiful city. Very different from London. Have you never been?"

He shook his head. "We blockaded many French ports."

"The British navy certainly wreaked havoc on the French."

"If Bonaparte hadn't been so unreasonable in banning all trade . . ."

"It is a pity he came when he did. Who knows where France might be today had she been allowed to develop as a . . . republic." She had to tread carefully or he would suspect her loyalties. "There might have been a chance for footmen to become statesmen . . . and thousands of young men's lives would have been spared."

Their eyes met. "Yes, it is a pity . . . But then France might have continued in her extreme Jacobinism."

"My father was a victim of the Terror," she said softly.

"I'm sorry."

In that moment she thought she read sympathy in his eyes but was no longer sure what was real and what was part of his masquerade. If he was indeed a spy, he undoubtedly knew everything about her past. It would be easy enough to feign the appropriate emotion.

Why was there this yearning in her heart for something genuine and honest from him?

Rees walked back from the stream, carrying his fishing pole, unmindful of the vegetation around him, his thoughts filled with his encounter with Lady Wexham.

The woman fascinated him more than ever. What other highborn lady would spend an hour talking with a servant? Was it because she was indeed a French Republican, seeing no class difference between the two—or was it that she knew he was no butler? More likely the latter.

His hand clenched around the fishing pole. He had been foolish to share those bits and pieces of his past, interweaving the truth with fabrication. It was easy to tell himself she'd ensnared him with the sympathetic look in those darkly fringed eyes. She'd shown herself such an attentive listener that he'd wanted to tell her more about himself—the real him, not a man pretending to have been raised as a servant. Vain, foolish man! Was she playing with him as a cat with a mouse?

At least he'd stopped himself before revealing his time in the French prison.

He neared the various outbuildings surrounding Hartwell House. Many of the impoverished émigrés living on the count's generosity had been permitted by him to convert the outbuildings into shops of all kinds, from artisanal specialties like lace making and painted porcelain vases to more practical businesses like a bakery and pastry shop to serve the main house.

Rees had never been to Versailles but imagined this as a scaled-down version from what he had read of it.

His thoughts returned to what he'd gleaned from Lady Wexham. Most of all, they focused on one remark of hers. She seemed no lover of Bonaparte. Most remarkable of all, she'd posed the question, what if the emperor had never been?

The more he mulled over her words, the more they sounded like that most appalling of French political factions, the Jacobins. His jaw tightened at the thought of those revolutionaries who had torn down all the traditions of France, killing their own king and sending all who disagreed with them to the guillotine.

But he could hardly believe it of Lady Wexham, whose own father had been sentenced by those radicals.

She and her mother had had to flee France, leaving their home and lands behind to live as impoverished immigrants in a strange land.

He sighed, reaching the main house. It was past time to put aside personal thoughts of Lady Wexham and focus on relaying this information to Bunting.

Rees entered one of the side wings of Hartwell House and headed to the storage room from where he had borrowed the fishing pole. It was filled with all sorts of sporting and hunting equipment, boots, umbrellas, and croquet sets, everything jumbled and covered with dust.

He set the pole on a rack with all the others, the Scripture "be not unequally yoked with unbelievers" flitting through his mind. He had no idea what Lady Wexham's spiritual beliefs were, but he had seen no evidence of her attending church while in London.

He knelt down to put away his fishhook in a box of tackle. Looking at an array of fishing lures, he stiffened when he heard a masculine voice just outside the door.

"I am watching her."

The words were in French. Without thinking, Rees ducked lower, crouching behind a stack of crates.

The men's footsteps sounded entering the room. "Céline Wexham? Do you think that is necessary?"

Rees's heart began to pound.

"I don't trust her."

He tried to place the soft-spoken tone.

The other masculine voice protested. "But she is one of Louis's favorites. She is Sophie's daughter! There is no more loyal subject. No, this time you've let your suspicious nature run away with you."

"We shall see." The man's tone remained cool.

Since their voices indicated they stood on the other side of the small room, Rees dared inch forward around the crates. The two gentlemen were facing a window.

Monsieur de la Roche. The other one, a short, stout man in a dark blue frock coat, he didn't immediately recognize. He must be a visitor. Rees eased back behind the crates.

The shorter man spoke. "Has she done anything to warrant your distrust?"

"Perhaps. What I am certain of is we are reaching a critical time and must not allow any information to leak out. We cannot let anyone stand in our way. Many do not want to see the House of Bourbon reascend the throne."

The other man sighed. "A pity the lovely Céline should prove a traitor to our cause."

"Whether or not a pity, she must not be allowed to hinder it. I will continue watching her, and if she should prove detrimental, she will be stopped."

The words sent a chill down Rees's spine.

The men turned and left the room.

As the echoes of their footsteps faded, Rees eased back on his haunches, his heartbeat gradually easing.

What was Lady Wexham involved in? Didn't she realize the danger?

An image of her flashed into his mind—her smiling face, those golden eyes alight with amusement as the sunlight shone on her chestnut locks.

His chest constricted at the thought of anything evil befalling her.

It couldn't be possible.

He clenched his hands.

He couldn't allow it.

Not only would he have to shadow her now to watch her movements.

He must shadow her to protect her.

12

*C*éline wandered through the salons, feeling restless after dinner. She entered the card room, her eyes scanning the various tables for her mother.

She felt an immediate sense of ease at the sight of Mr. MacKinnon standing a few feet behind her. Ever since she had asked him to look after her mother, her mother had left the tables at a decent hour.

"*Ma chérie*, what a lovely man your new butler is. *Que beau! Que large! Que gracieux!*" her mother had told her the day after meeting MacKinnon.

Céline forced a careless laugh at her mother's raptures. "Yes, he cuts quite a handsome figure."

"You must find a way to keep him when your old butler returns." She wagged a finger at Céline. "Perhaps I can keep him on here." She winked at her daughter. "If you would give me an allowance for a manservant."

"I will gladly do so, but I fear MacKinnon is merely on loan to me. He has his own situation, which I believe he is quite satisfied with." A position she feared had something to do with the Home Office.

Now, she observed the two. Her mother turned to say something to MacKinnon, and he bent toward her, nodding his head slightly, his demeanor looking as if he took everything she said with utmost absorption.

She must remember to do something for him for being so thoughtful to her mother. She mentally shook her head, reminding herself that he was no servant and likely would not be with her household long. The question was—who would have the upper hand when he left?

She approached her mother's table, nodding to the company who greeted her cheerfully. Lastly, she glanced at MacKinnon, with a brief smile and nod.

Old Monsieur Villiers looked up from his hand. "*Ma chère* Céline, what do you think?"

She glanced at his cards. "Hm. *Maman*, you shall have to have a care."

Her mother tossed her powdered curls. "Bah, he is bluffing. I know all his tricks."

Céline moved to stand beside MacKinnon, knowing she mustn't single him out any more than any of her servants, yet feeling drawn to him as an animal to a lure. "I hope this is not too tedious for you."

"Not at all. Lady de Beaumont will play only a hand or two more and then ask me to promenade her on the terrace."

"Thank goodness she is no longer playing faro."

"Yes. She was persuaded to stick to quadrille with these fine gentlemen," he murmured with an indication toward the pensioners seated at the table with her.

She dared glance at him under her lashes. "I am sure you are responsible for that. I can only offer you my deepest gratitude."

He kept his eyes on the card players. "She was convinced of the healthful benefits of a promenade on the terrace before retiring."

She swallowed a laugh at his acumen. "Let us hope the weather remains clear."

"Yes." His tone echoed the amusement in her own. "I have not yet thought what to do if it should rain."

"Oh, there are miles of galleries you can stroll."

He chuckled.

She quickly scanned the room to make sure no one had noticed the enjoyment they were exhibiting in their conversation. She caught sight of Monsieur de la Roche, who had looked up from his hand of cards across the room.

Quickly, she erased her smile and fixed her gaze on her mother. "I do thank you for watching out for my mother. You have eased my mind immensely."

"It is my pleasure." They kept their tones low as if by mutual consent.

Knowing she must soon excuse herself and move on, she nevertheless added, "My mother is figuring out a way to have you stay on at Hartwell when we leave."

"I am perfectly happy where I am."

At the Home Office or in her household? Despite her realization that it must be the former, she couldn't help the gratification that spread through her at his simple words. Once again, she felt they were talking on two different levels. "That is what I told her," she answered lightly, although her heart was thumping.

"Do you have any idea when you are returning to London?"

She glanced at him, but he continued looking forward. "Not as yet." She moistened her lips. "Are you anxious to return to town?"

"I was merely enquiring"—he cleared his throat—"to be able to inform the servants—"

Was he feeling as nervous as she, as if they were both walking a tightrope yet neither would welcome the safety of the net below? With reluctance she took a step away from him. "Well, I shall not distract you any longer. I just wanted to thank you—for your patience with my mother." She lifted her gaze to his. "Good evening."

His gray eyes locked with hers and he nodded once. "There is no need . . . my lady."

She inclined her head in response.

Assuming a lighthearted tone, she bid her mother and her cronies good night and moved to another table as if she hadn't a care in the world. As she greeted another old lady, she allowed herself to search for Monsieur de la Roche.

He was playing to the trick. As if sensing her gaze, he looked up just as he laid down his card and lifted a brow. She nodded, forcing a stiff smile before turning away.

She left the card room, keeping her pace slow, though she felt more than one person's attention directed toward her.

MacKinnon and de la Roche? And other potential enemies?

Later in the evening, she made her way to the terrace, telling herself it was not to catch a glimpse of MacKinnon accompanying her mother.

But there was no sight of him or her mother. They must have gone up. She shook aside her disappointment.

She walked the terrace's wide perimeter. She stopped and chatted with the few individuals who still lingered there. It was almost midnight, so most had retired for the evening.

Alone again, she hugged herself, fighting disappointment as she leaned against the balustrade. The sculptures and clipped bushes were shadowy figures between the remaining torchlights.

"Céline?" The whisper was so low, she mistook it at first for the sound of the breeze against her ears. "Say nothing." It was not her imagination. "Just listen."

She stood as still as the statuary, not daring to gaze downward to where she thought the voice came from.

"Meet me at the temple of Apollo in one hour."

She remained there several more minutes, but the voice came no more. Finally, she dared step away, wrapping her shawl more securely around herself to keep from shaking.

She spent the intervening hour in her room, alternately pacing and standing lost in thought, gazing out at the stars. Finally, slipping into a dark gown and shawl, she was ready.

"Be careful," Valentine admonished her. "Do you want me to come with you?"

"Better not." She gave a nervous laugh. "If I do not return within the hour, you know where I am. It is likely Roland, though I could not recognize the voice."

Valentine planted a hand on her hip. "And if it is not?"

Pushing down her fears, Céline shrugged. "I shall soon see."

Before Valentine could protest further, Céline exited the room. No one was about. She went quickly down the back stairs, checking behind her often to make sure she was not being observed or followed.

But the house was silent. She slipped out a side entrance. The night air felt cool against her skin. The gravel path beneath her slippers sounded loud to her ears, so she left it and walked alongside on the grass, using the light-colored gravel to help guide her way. Her slippers were soon wet with the dew.

As her eyes became accustomed to the dark, she was able to make her way more easily. There was a scant half-moon, so the night offered some illumination. She crossed the formal gardens, staying away from the path with its torchlight. The temple in question was situated high on a hill, offering a vista of the entire estate.

She continued glancing behind her but saw nothing. She doubted anyone was still up. There were only a few lights visible behind the curtained windows on the upper floors of the mansion. But most were dark, their inhabitants long since in bed.

Finally, she reached the temple with its domed roof and columns encircling it. Its white stonework shone like a beacon in the night.

Having half run the last portion, she was out of breath by the time she entered its arched doorway. She turned around, her eyes scanning the area, but nothing moved.

She was alone. She shivered, feeling vulnerable and exposed. The temple was surrounded by shrubbery, dark and menacing. She moved farther into the temple, debating whether she should wait outside, perhaps hide herself in the shrubbery. She was about to do so when a shadow detached itself from behind one of the slim columns and approached her.

Her heart pumping furiously, she waited, clutching her shawl tightly around herself.

When the man was close enough to identify, she almost collapsed with relief. "Roland."

"Yes," he said, in as low a whisper as he had used on the terrace. "I thought it best to come myself. We can trust no one."

She nodded.

He took her by the arm and led her back outside to an area of shrubbery. "What can you tell me of things here?"

Quickly, she collected her thoughts and reported everything she'd heard since she'd arrived.

He nodded once or twice. When she ended, he said only, "Good."

He took a step away. "Is that all?" she asked, feeling as if she were being abandoned.

"Yes. I shall convey your findings to France." He suddenly reached up and squeezed her shoulder. "I will return in another few nights. Is there any evening activity planned, where everyone will be distracted?"

She thought quickly. "There is a masquerade three nights hence."

"Perfect. I will meet you"—he pointed toward some shrubbery across the temple—"there by the highest yew. It's better we stay out of sight that night. This same time."

"Very well."

When she turned to look, he was gone.

Rees stood behind a tree and watched as Lady Wexham left the shrubbery and made her way back to the house, almost running.

He continued watching to make sure no one else had followed her. Then he waited until sure her contact had gone. Slowly, he made his own way back to Hartwell House, his heart heavy.

At least de la Roche had not seen her. He felt a vast sense of relief at that. But for how long would she be able to elude him? She was playing a dangerous game. The British were suspicious of her, and now the royalist French as well.

Where would she be safe?

He caught himself.

Safe.

When had his objective gone from uncovering her clandestine activities to protecting her from her enemies?

Céline sat on a blanket on the grass, holding a parasol against the sun. A group of the émigrés was picnicking on the south lawn of Hartwell House.

"My lady, have some more champagne." Monsieur de la Roche lifted the bottle and poured some into her glass. "It will put the bloom back in your cheek."

She glanced at him. There was something about him that repulsed her. Perhaps the way there seemed to be no spare flesh on his bones. "Do I look sickly?"

His pale eyes flickered over her. "A bit peaked, perhaps. Too many late nights, eh?"

She kept her smile in place. What was he implying? "Here? If you think midnight late, you have been away from London far too long."

His lips stretched in what she could only interpret as a semblance of a smile. It didn't reach his eyes.

"What think you of Wellington's chances now that he has reentered Spain?"

"I know little of military matters, monsieur." Why was he so close these days? It seemed she couldn't make a move without finding him at her heels like a lapdog.

"I think you are a very intelligent woman. Your salons are well-known beyond London."

She shrugged. "The secret of a successful salon is to invite people more intelligent than oneself and serve good food and drink."

He chuckled, a dry, barely audible sound, and raised his glass. "I drink to it."

She took a sip from her glass in order to have an excuse to look away from him. The champagne tickling her throat, she let her gaze sweep the company. Tables laden with food had been set up at one end of the lawn and blankets and rugs laid on the grass. Waiters went about serving the guests. She spotted MacKinnon bending to offer her mother something from a platter.

With effort, she turned her attention away from him.

The picnic was set up near the same stream where she'd sat beside MacKinnon but closer to the house. Here the waterway was wider and a pretty oriental-style bridge spanned it. A group of the children—children born and brought up in England by their émigré parents—was standing on the bridge, gazing downward. Others were running around the lawn, their French governesses trying to keep them in order.

Would they grow up as she had, torn in her loyalties between two countries? Or were they thoroughly British? She heard a mixture of English and French floating over to her from their laughing voices. A string quartet playing in the background vied with their childish shouts.

In truth, she found it difficult to sit at ease this afternoon and pretend to have no other thought in her mind but sampling the lobster mousse and lemon ice. Her thoughts were on Hartwell House. She had returned from her early morning ride to find a messenger from London for the Comte.

She had gleaned from a gentleman-in-waiting that the courier came directly from the prime minister's office.

What could be so crucial to bring someone all the way from London to Louis? She must find a way to discover what communiqué the messenger brought.

She tapped a finger against the side of her glass in time to the quartet.

"A strawberry, my dear lady?"

"I beg—" She turned to find a plump strawberry almost at her mouth. She took the fork from de la Roche, not allowing him to feed her and careful not to brush her hand against his. "Thank you."

"The first of the season."

She bit down on its juicy, tender flesh. "Delicious."

As she savored the fruit, her mind went back to her problem. The

Comte rarely left his chambers since he suffered from gout so badly. But she'd heard he was following a rigorous diet in order to be well enough to attend the masquerade.

The *bal masqué* would be ideal. Everyone would be attending, including the servants. It would give her the opportunity to don a disguise as well.

She had planned on dressing as a simple shepherdess, but now she considered something that would hide her identity more thoroughly. It would have to transform her and not hinder her movement. She would have to find a way to enter the Comte's private study and leave quickly.

"Lady Wexham, could you tell us who makes your gowns?"

Céline shook herself out of her absorption. Two young ladies, who were sisters, had approached her blanket. Daughters of émigrés, they were younger than Céline by a decade at least. She felt a twinge of compassion for them. They were of an age to have their first season in London, but their parents probably could not afford to give them one.

"Certainly. Come, have a seat." She patted the place beside her, relieved to have an excuse to end her exchange with de la Roche. "I have a very clever Frenchwoman who makes my gowns. She is the envy of all London but is very selective of whom she takes on."

"Yours are so pretty and so different from what we are forced to wear."

She eyed their white muslin gowns identical except for the color of the sash.

"Your gown is of such a rich hue and such a striking pattern! May I touch it, please, madame?"

"Certainly." She smiled, holding out a length of her skirt, glad to see that de la Roche had moved off. "This is turkey red print. Madame Delantre assures me it is all the crack."

"It is so vivid."

They discussed the merits of embroidered muslin to the newer roller printed cottons. Céline's mind returned to the dilemma of getting hold of the courier's message to the Comte.

Shouts from the stream jolted them from their conversation.

"He's fallen in! Jacomo has fallen in!" A group of children jumped up and down on the bridge, pointing to the water.

Céline stood at once, peering toward the stream. She didn't think it was too deep. Still, if it was a child who didn't know how to swim, it could prove fatal.

She spotted MacKinnon at the edge of the grassy bank. He'd stripped off his jacket and boots and was already splashing into the water. In seconds it was over his waist, so it was deeper than she had supposed.

He swam to the center and reached the boy, whose arms were flailing about as his head bobbed in and out of the water. MacKinnon grasped the boy under his arms and hauled him out. They reached the edge of the stream to cheers from the onlookers who crowded around its grassy bank.

Dripping wet, he carried the boy to his awaiting mother.

The woman hugged the boy to her breast, thanking MacKinnon in a mixture of French and broken English.

"It's all right. I'm sure the lad is fine, just a bit frightened."

The other children had run off the bridge and were clamoring to get near their companion.

The boy finally looked up from his mother's shoulder, tears mixing with the water dripping from his dark hair. Suddenly, he smiled and everyone applauded.

Céline had moved with the crowd and now approached MacKinnon as he turned away from the mother and child. She offered him the blanket she'd been sitting on. "That was very quick thinking of you."

He took it, murmuring his thanks, and rubbed it across his front and head, leaving his hair in disarray.

"Thank you, but any number of people would have done the same," he said, continuing to pat the blanket against his sodden garments. "I just happened to reach the boy first."

She shuddered, looking at the stream. "I didn't think the water was so deep, but the child could have drowned."

"Yes. It only takes minutes. I saw enough men drown at sea."

His story of serving under Nelson must at least be true. His tone was too sober to be otherwise. In the direct sunlight, the small scar on the edge of his chin was more visible. It only added to his allure. Had he received it in a fight at sea?

"It is not a pleasant death, but then none is in war."

Longing to offer him some comfort, she clenched her fist to keep it at her side. "I'm sorry."

He seemed to shake aside whatever memories he was recalling. "It was long ago." He glanced down at his garments with a rueful smile. "I suppose I should go and change."

"Yes, please, before you catch a chill."

He held up the damp blanket. "I'll find you another."

She shook her head with a laugh. "That's quite all right. I can manage."

"Thank you for your thoughtfulness. I'll return to my post as soon as I've changed."

"Please, don't bother. There are more than enough servants here." She smiled at him. "After all, you are the hero of the hour. You deserve some time to recover. You may have the afternoon free."

With a small salute, he turned and left the field. She continued watching him, his stride long and sure. How little she knew about him—and yet how drawn she felt. He didn't resemble Rumford in the least. What sorts of horrors had he seen in battle? How had her old butler become acquainted with him?

She should ask Valentine to search his quarters. Tit for tat. Mulling over this manner of obtaining more information on her butler, she made her way to the mother to ask after the boy.

13

*S*ince overhearing de la Roche's conversation in the storeroom, Rees had been keeping an eye on him. What he saw only deepened his worry over Lady Wexham.

De la Roche approached Lady Wexham at every opportunity. The Frenchman seemed to be at her side at dinner, beside her in the evenings in the drawing room, and when he wasn't talking to her, he was watching her.

Rees didn't like the man's single-mindedness. Lady Wexham, he had to admit—and admire despite himself—never seemed fazed by his attention. She smiled and welcomed him whenever he approached. But whenever he left, her smile would fade and a brooding look replaced the amusement in her eyes.

It was clear from Rees's observation that she did not welcome the Frenchman's attentions. The fact that she didn't let on told Rees more clearly than anything else that she wished no one to know. A normal woman would berate the man behind his back. The more Rees observed Lady Wexham, the stronger his belief that she let few know her real thoughts.

What worried him most was the belief that sooner or later, she was going to make a mistake.

That's when he made up his mind to attend the ball as a guest and not stand against the wall as a footman. He must do it to protect Lady Wexham.

Whatever Valentine had told her mistress about him, Lady Wexham seemed to have a regard for him. He'd seen that most strongly when he'd rescued the lad from the water. Lady Wexham had been right there, not rushing to the child as everyone else but coming to him first with a blanket. He didn't want to allow himself to take it as a sign that it was more than the normal attention a lady would give her servant, but it was becoming harder to keep his hopes and yearnings in check.

He tried to shake aside such thoughts. He must remain objective if he were to finish his assignment. The night he'd followed her had proven she was involved in something clandestine.

She had met a man, that much was certain. Whether it had been an amorous assignation or one involving a French contact, he couldn't be sure, but he'd wager it was the latter. He had discerned no special favor Lady Wexham bestowed on any of the male guests.

Despite inviting her male callers into her bedroom after her niece's ball, Lady Wexham's behavior was exemplary from all Rees had observed. The longer he was in her company, the more convinced he became that she was not bestowing her favors on any man—sinfully or otherwise. The fact would bring him relief if the alternative weren't so distasteful.

Which brought him to his decision. Tonight was the masked ball. He had spent every evening hidden outside after midnight, watching for Lady Wexham, but she had taken no more solitary walks to the temple. If she was meeting this person again, Rees thought it likely to be during the ball.

By donning a disguise and mingling freely with the guests, he would be able to observe without being seen. He'd gleaned enough from the servants to know that many people were invited from as far away as London. One more person in costume among a hundred would attract little notice.

Doubtless, de la Roche would be watching Lady Wexham's every step as well.

Rees was taking a gamble, he knew. Lady Wexham likely expected him to keep an eye on her mother although she had not given him any specific instructions. What would he say if she searched for him during the ball? He decided to make up some excuse that he had been needed down in the kitchens. The palace was so vast it was unlikely she would discover he wasn't there. By the following day, he hoped all would be forgotten. All he knew was he had to protect Lady Wexham this evening.

Carrying out his plan proved tricky. Here, he had no room to himself but shared a small chamber with Tom. He had to find a way to obtain a proper masquerade costume and keep it hidden until the event. He had to find a place to change from his butler's togs into his masquerade sometime during the evening.

Thankfully, Tom had been busy downstairs between the dining room and kitchens since early evening. Rees, too, had been there, but now that the ball was fully under way, he left his post against the ballroom wall and climbed up to one of the many garrets above the mansion.

He retrieved the clothes he'd procured earlier in Aylesbury. He'd found a shop where he was able to rent a pirate's outfit. It had been either that or Turkish garb with a turban. Both offered the advantage of sufficient head covering to hide his hair. He had hidden the clothes and sword in an old trunk in an unused attic. Now, as he donned the black breeches, glossy black boots, and white shirt with wide, brightly colored sash around the waist, he felt a sense of freedom he hadn't experienced in a long time.

He paused, gazing at his reflection in an old, spotted looking glass. He was no longer a serious butler but a daring, dangerous rogue. He took up the fake sword, a curved scimitar, and stuck it into his sash then wrapped a scarf around his head, tying it tightly at the base of his skull. He placed the black domino over his eyes and nose, tying it behind his head. The half mask covered most of his face, reaching down to almost his upper lip.

Would anyone recognize him only by his lips and jaw?

He gave the mask a final adjustment, tugging it downward a fraction, and made sure the knot of his head scarf was tight. Lastly, he picked up the wide-brimmed black felt hat and placed it carefully over everything, tilting it at a rakish angle.

Would Lady Wexham know him? He could not imagine someone less like a butler. His eyes seemed to glitter from the slits, looking almost black in the dim light from his candlestick.

He had not been able to discover what costume she would be wearing. He grimaced, thinking there were disadvantages to being at odds with a woman's lady's maid.

Taking up a pair of black gloves and giving a final adjustment to his hat, he left the attic.

When he reentered the ballroom, it was filled with people in both fancy dress and costume, half masks and full masks, grotesque and elegant. The orchestra was playing in a gallery above the immense room. The various chandeliers blazed their candles the length of the ornate plasterwork ceiling.

Saying a prayer that his masquerade would hold the evening, Rees plunged into the sea of fellow pirates, harlequins, Turks, monks, and ladies in eighteenth-century panniered dresses and powdered wigs, his eyes scanning the crowd in search of his prey.

Céline took a quick look at the crowded dance floor. It was almost half past eleven and the ball was in full swing now. The Comte had come in a short while ago, surrounded by his usual entourage. Céline had to smile at his costume of a Turkish pasha. The balloon pants made his already thick legs enormous and the turban his face rounder.

It was now or never.

She glanced down at her own costume, doubting anyone had recognized her. Her body was encased in a harlequin outfit, the gaudy diamond shapes covering a tunic that came down to mid-thigh, cinched in at the waist with a white belt. Red and blue stockings covered her legs. A black mask covered half her face. Her hair was hidden beneath a large white cap with an upturned brim and red feather.

Thankfully, she was not the only harlequin, though each costume was a different color.

Before she could reconsider her next move, she darted out of the ballroom and hurried down the corridor until she reached the back stairs, looking about her every few seconds. The Comte's apartment was in another part of the mansion. It seemed to take forever to reach that wing. Once or twice she had to press herself into a doorway or alcove when she heard footsteps from around a corner. But it was only an odd servant or two, some on assignations of their own while their masters were at play.

Finally she arrived at the Comte's private suites. She approached the door and pressed her ear against it a moment. Hearing nothing, she dared open it a fraction. A small flame burned low in a lamp. She opened the door wider at the sight of another servant asleep on a striped chair, soft snores emanating from his nostrils. Good. Valentine must have succeeded in putting the sleeping draft in his drink.

Céline stepped inside, closing the door quietly behind her. She crossed to where she knew the Comte's study was located and entered. Another servant sat slumped on the floor, his head lolling to one side.

With trembling fingers, Céline searched the desk, coming upon the packet of papers.

Unfolding them, she saw that they contained correspondence to the Comte signed by Lords Liverpool and Castlereagh themselves, the prime minister and foreign minister. She folded the documents back up, opened the front of her tunic, placed them within her camisole, and rebuttoned her costume, her heartbeat thudding so loudly it drowned out everything else.

With a quick look around, she closed the desk and made her way back out.

Only when she was far enough away, in a back passage, did she allow herself to stop and catch her breath, mopping her brow with a handkerchief.

She would bring this to her rendezvous with Roland in a few hours' time. With a smile she imagined his surprise when he beheld the papers. Finally, she had something of real value to the French.

In the meantime, she would return to the ballroom, mingling with the guests, teasing them with her identity, as if she had no other care in the world but dancing the night away.

She wondered where MacKinnon was. She had searched for him earlier but had seen no sign of him since dinner. He hadn't been near her mother, but perhaps he'd gone to her later. Perhaps he'd taken the evening off, as some servants had. But he didn't strike her as the type of man to be negligent in his duties. At least her mother was not gaming tonight. Perhaps that was why MacKinnon was not at her side.

Pushing aside any disappointment at not seeing him tonight, she reentered the ballroom, pasting a smile on her face.

Rees reined in his growing frustration. It seemed he had circled the massive ballroom dozens of times but still hadn't managed to spot Lady Wexham.

Where was she, or *what* was she?

"A pirate. I've always dreamed of being captured by a pirate."

Rees looked at the woman who had addressed him so boldly. She was dressed as a gypsy in a low-bodiced white shirt and multicolored skirt that only came to her midcalf. A massive head of black curls was kept in place by a bright yellow scarf around her head. She was too short to be Lady Wexham. He executed a bow. "I fear you will be disappointed in me, since I am not in the business of abducting damsels."

She sidled closer to him so she was almost touching his chest. He moved back a pace. "Perhaps you will never have so opportune a moment."

He took a step to the side. "I thank you, fair lady, but I will forgo the temptation." Without waiting for her to reply, he disappeared quickly into the crowd.

This was why he disliked masquerades. It led to unruly, unseemly conduct. People thought that because their faces couldn't be seen, they could get away with licentious behavior.

He continued his search for Lady Wexham, scrutinizing each lady he passed, but with the dominos, it was almost impossible to tell who was who. He focused on women who seemed to be the same height and build as Lady Wexham.

Lord, help me find her. The hour grows late and I sense she's in danger. Please give me discernment.

After another futile turn about the ballroom, weaving in and out of the crowds while ignoring the women who addressed him, Rees stopped by a fluted column, allowing it to half-obscure him. He scanned the dance floor, feeling he'd achieved nothing by milling around. The more he moved, the more the people around him moved, like an endless current, as if searching for amusement among the next group of people.

He was tired of fending off overbold females. His mouth twisted. As if any of these highborn ladies would give him a second look if they saw him tomorrow in his butler's uniform or as a lowly clerk at the F.O.

The wisest thing to do was what he usually did as butler, stand along a wall and simply observe the people passing by him. Yet, he didn't want to chance being accosted again.

He chose a more secluded post behind some potted palms, which acted as a screen while allowing him to view the dance floor from a fairly central spot.

After a quarter of an hour of following each female that crossed his field of vision—shepherdesses, Marie Antoinettes, Turks with baggy pants and scanty tops, huntresses with bows and quivers of arrows slung over their backs—he still had not detected any that caused him to take a second look. He began to think Lady Wexham must be wearing a wig since none of the women he'd seen resembled her in hair coloring once they came close enough.

"What a handsome pirate you make!" A Pierrot in his baggy white clown outfit with wide collar jumped in his path.

Rees stepped back involuntarily, nonplussed at being addressed so boldly by a man. But then he noticed the clown's voice. It belonged to a woman. He narrowed his eyes, to seek more evidence. It would have been impossible to tell, because she was tall enough to be a male of medium height. Her face was painted white and a black domino masked the upper portion. A round, white hat covered her hair, which appeared short, until he saw it was held beneath a stocking cap.

"Thank you," was all he could think to say.

As if sensing his discomfiture, she tossed back her head and laughed, then to his relief moved away.

It hadn't been Lady Wexham, of that he was sure. The timbre of the voice was different; the build slightly more buxom, though it had been hard to tell with the loose clown suit.

As he watched her skip off, it gave him the clue he needed. He began searching for other costumes that could disguise a female figure.

There were several other Commedia dell'Arte characters. Pantaloon in his red hose and short tunic, wrapped about with a wide black cape. Harlequins scampered about in their bright blue, red, and gold costumes; the Doctor, the Captain, Scaramouche—all were male figures. Rees studied each one, but it was difficult to distinguish behind the grotesque half masks, wide ruffled collars, heavy capes, and large, floppy hats.

He studied their contours for any hint of femininity, especially those whose height matched Lady Wexham's.

It took what seemed a long time, but finally his patient observation was rewarded. He fixed on a harlequin clown, following his progress through the crowd. It would be a perfect disguise, the body covered by a multicolored diamond-patterned tunic, the legs by colored hose. A puffy white cap with a floppy brim turned up in the front completely hid the clown's hair. A black half mask hid the upper portion of the face. He strained forward as the clown turned his way. The chin and jaw could be Lady Wexham's. The height and contours were also right.

As the crowd parted momentarily in front of the harlequin, Rees's gaze drifted downward. He couldn't help noticing the shapely legs and frowned. If it was indeed a female, she was wearing an indecently immodest garment. Although her body was fully covered—unlike some of the sheer gowns worn by those pretending to be the huntress Diana—it still revealed too much of her contours.

As he continued to observe her—for the more he did so, the more he was convinced the harlequin was a female—he grudgingly admired her audacity in how far she carried out the masquerade, to the extent of even asking a lady to dance!

It was a French gavotte, danced in a lively tempo. She danced the male part flawlessly, bowing and promenading and turning her female partner around. She was wise to have chosen a lady of slighter build and height, dressed as a shepherdess.

As was the custom, the couple danced two dances in a row before bowing and curtsying to each other and parting.

Rees's gaze followed the harlequin, not wishing to lose her again in the crowd.

A few moments later, the musicians began to play the opening notes of a new piece. Dancers began to shift to form sets on the wide parquet floor.

On impulse, Rees quickened his step, making for the harlequin before she had a chance to ask another partner to dance.

He didn't know quite what he intended.

He bit back an exclamation when a lady wearing a towering powdered wig and feathered half mask stepped in his path. Her panniered dress was so wide on each side that it barricaded him. Ignoring his obvious desire to walk around her, she waved her ostrich feather fan in front of her, blocking his view. "I'll wager I know who you are."

Those words got his attention. "I beg your pardon," he said attempting to disguise his voice.

With a flick, she closed her fan and tapped it against his shoulder. "You are the Marquis de Lalande."

He expelled a breath in relief and was able to smile at her triumphant tone. "You have guessed it, I fear."

She took a step closer, her rouged lips parting in a smile. But he was once more in control and managed to bow and step aside. "If you will excuse me, madame, I must flee. I would have no one guess my identity."

Without waiting for a reply, he walked away from her, scanning the crowd for his harlequin. Good, she was still standing there, surveying the crowd as if seeking someone to partner.

He reached her before the dance began. He could see it would be a cotillion by the squares still forming.

For a moment, he wavered, no longer sure if it was Lady Wexham. The half mask covered most of her face. It was ridged in grotesque false wrinkles over the forehead, the eye slits were so narrow, he could not see her eyes clearly.

"Monsieur?" The voice was low and inquiring, but there was something in the timbre that sounded familiar.

Standing directly in front of her, to prevent her moving elsewhere, he bowed. "May I have the honor of this dance?" He spoke to her in French, hoping his accent wouldn't sound too British.

Her head moved back a fraction as if his request had startled her. But she rallied almost immediately, placing her hands on her hips and smiling. Those were her lips, he perceived with satisfaction. "I think you mistake me for a lady, Monsieur le Pirate." Her colorful arm waved to the side. "There are plenty of fair damsels who would be flattered by your request."

She spoke in French, still disguising her voice.

He knew he was taking a grave risk in revealing his knowledge of French. He didn't understand what devilry possessed him; he didn't take the time to question it. All he knew was that he wanted to dance with her this evening. There would never be another opportunity like this one. "Ah, but it is my desire to dance with Harlequin."

She cocked her head, staring up at him. It was still difficult to discern the color of her irises. "People will think you very strange."

Behind his mask Rees felt a boldness to continue this fantasy. No longer a butler or junior clerk, but a pirate, a lady's protector—or abductor. It was a person he hardly knew but had no wish to stop. "A *bal masqué* brings out the strangest behavior in individuals. A lady in Harlequin's disguise."

Her breath caught. "You would not want to give away my secret, I hope."

He held out a black-gloved hand. "Come, the music is beginning. No one will notice you in this crowd."

Without another word, she placed her white-gloved hand in his, and he closed his own around it.

He led her onto the dance floor to where another couple stood, and they faced one another in the square.

Rees concentrated on the dance steps. He hadn't danced since his last visit home. But Lady Wexham, as he had observed before, was an excellent dancer, moving through the figures and changes effortlessly.

He took her hands in his and performed an allemande turn, her shoulders grazing him as they completed the movement.

As the dance progressed, he could understand how Cinderella must have felt at the ball. For these moments, he was an equal with Lady Wexham. Their movements were courtly and measured, yet with an undercurrent of something more primitive.

His gaze crossed hers. No mask could hide those burnished bronze irises.

"I don't believe I have met you before," she said when they drew together.

"That is true." She had never met him like this.

"You are French?"

He hesitated a fraction. "The son of émigrés."

She nodded. "That explains the accent."

He said nothing.

"In that case, I must know you," she persisted.

He bowed. "Perhaps."

She studied him a moment. "There is something familiar."

He made no reply but guided her in a turn.

When the dance ended, Céline curtsied to the tall pirate with the penetrating gaze and made to move away. It was too dangerous to continue dancing as a woman, no matter how much the pirate's identity intrigued her. There was something about him that tickled the edges of her mind.

But the pirate stopped her with a touch on her elbow. "There is another dance."

She was honor bound to acquiesce. In truth, she didn't mind. It would give her a chance to ferret out his identity. She hadn't recognized his voice, but the longer they spoke, the greater her sense of familiarity grew.

If only she could get a better glimpse of his eyes, but beneath the wide black brim of his hat and behind the black mask with its narrow eye slits, their color was hard to determine.

The cotillion had not given her the chance to study him more closely, but she recognized the next strains of music as a waltz. The French were more liberal in adopting the German dance than their British counterparts.

She smiled. The dance would give her the proximity to discover who her mysterious partner was. How she hoped he danced this new dance as well as he had the cotillion. As an émigré's son, he undoubtedly knew the steps.

As she held out her hands, he halted, cocking an ear to the music. Slowly he turned to observe some of the other couples already on the floor. "It is a waltz."

"Yes, do you not know it?"

"I have not danced it as yet." The words were the first sign of hesitancy the mysterious pirate had displayed.

"It is quite simple," she said, resting her hands on his broad shoulders. Slowly, his hands came to her waist. He was a tall, well-built man, although she knew a domino could hide a hideous face. "Surely you have seen it danced."

"Yes."

Before she could reassure him any more, he took a step in time to the music. Deliberate at first, his movements soon became more smooth.

She began to relax and enjoy the feel of the music. As he led her through the strains of the waltz, she fixed her attention on the part of his face she could see. His chin and jawline were strong, his lips well formed with just the right amount of fullness in the lower one. They reminded her of . . . MacKinnon.

As soon as the thought formed, she sought for the telltale sign.

Her breath caught as she made out the tiny scar on his chin. It was her butler! Her gaze shifted to his mask, which hid everything but his eyes. He was watching her with that same intensity as MacKinnon.

How could it be? His pupils were wide and black, but they didn't completely hide the fact that his irises were gray.

It was too preposterous, so out of place.

It could *not* be a butler. Not this man, so dashing in pirate's clothes. But then wasn't MacKinnon elegant and masculine in his butler's uniform?

But to dance the complicated steps of the cotillion so flawlessly. No butler would have such ballroom dancing skills. Who was he in real life? Could he possibly be a gentleman?

Her gaze drifted downward again, needing to convince herself once more. The tiny scar confirmed that her partner was indeed Mr. Mac-Kinnon. No one else could have exactly the same scar in the same place.

But—MacKinnon didn't speak French. This man spoke it fluently. Her mind flitted to the past when he might have overheard her speaking French, but she took pains never to speak French to Valentine or Gaspard unless she was alone with them. But might he have overheard them speaking to each other? She would have to alert Valentine.

The next second she marveled at how MacKinnon had seen through her disguise that evening. She didn't think anyone had guessed her identity, not even de la Roche.

She narrowed her eyes on MacKinnon, forgetting about her other enemy for the moment. Or, *had* MacKinnon guessed? Was it mere coincidence he had singled her out to dance? No, it couldn't be.

But as the music continued and his steps became more sure, Céline found it hard to care what MacKinnon's motives had been. She was too caught up in the magic of being held in his arms, circling the ballroom.

It was utterly reckless and foolhardy to be dancing with someone whose purpose was to betray her, and enjoy it so much. If not for her own sake, she must remember Valentine and Gaspard, and the others who depended on her.

Yet, she didn't want this moment to end.

Her hands rested on MacKinnon's broad shoulders, and suddenly, for the first time since Stéphane, she felt safe and secure. It was madness. He would no doubt turn her into the Home Office as soon as they returned to London.

A shiver scurried down her spine. What if he knew about the papers she carried tucked away in her bosom? What would he do, staunch, upright Englishman that she was certain hid behind the pirate's mask? Around they danced, continuing to gaze into each others' eyes as if they were the only two persons in the ballroom.

Was it the danger that heightened her enjoyment of the moment, or was it something deeper . . . some inexplicable, unreasonable sense that she could trust her very life to this man?

14

It was long past midnight and Rees had almost begun to believe Lady Wexham merely meant to be having a lark by pretending to be a slim young gentleman dressed as Harlequin. After he bowed over her hand a final time, she continued dancing and wending her way through the crowd like any other partygoer.

Rees continued to watch her from the recess of the potted palms. He regretted having asked her to dance. Why had he yielded to the impulse? Foolish, foolish man. He could not berate himself enough. Had she seen through his disguise?

There had been something unsettling in the smile playing about her full lips during the waltz.

Unsettling! Unsettling had been the feeling of holding her in his arms and having to keep himself from crushing her to him and giving all away. All he'd been able to do was pray for strength and self-control.

Dear Lord, You said You would not give us more than we could bear, but would with the temptation provide a way of escape. Where is my way of escape? I have kept myself from sinning with a woman all these years. He thought of his years at sea as a young man when the ship would be in port and all the other sailors would head to the taverns to drink and carouse with the wenches available. He would stay away, seeking a church mission or library, a quiet place to read and while away the hours in edifying pursuits.

To come now to the ripe old age of one-and-thirty and be bowled over by a lady not only so far above him socially—but a traitor to the country he'd been willing to give his life for!

Yet, as he watched her pretend to be a gentleman, bowing over a young lady's hand then leading her in a dance, all he could think of was the feel of her in his arms. He clenched his hands, willing himself to forget.

His one and only purpose here was to discover what information Lady Wexham was sending back to France. He must never forget their two countries were at war. They were enemies.

Repeating the facts did nothing to strengthen his commitment. It only filled his soul with a bleak desolation as he watched her perform the steps of a minuet.

The hour was growing late, and he wanted only to leave and seek the solace of sleep—dreamless sleep—when Lady Wexham neared one of the arched doorways and gave a quick look about her.

His shoulders stiffened, every sense immediately on alert.

He straightened from the wall to weave once more around the dance floor, his heart pumping from fear of losing his quarry.

He exited the ballroom, peering rapidly every way, no longer seeing the bright blue, red, and gold outfit.

There—disappearing down the wide marble staircase.

Stifling his frustration at the numerous people still milling about the long gallery, he wended his way around them, hoping he wouldn't be too late to see where Lady Wexham was headed.

At the top of the wide stairs, he peered over the balustrade. She reached the ground floor and turned toward the west wing.

He descended the stairs, careful not to arrive at the bottom until she was already well down the corridor.

Where was she going? An assignation? A rendezvous?

Cursing the heavy boots he wore, he had to walk slowly to diminish their sound. Abruptly, she swung around a corner. He reached it, paused, then hearing a door open, he ventured to peer around just in time to see it closing.

Quickly he reached it, about halfway down on the right, and placed his ear to the panels. He thought he heard the click of a door or a latch. Holding his breath, he waited a few more seconds then carefully turned the knob of one of the doors. The room was dimly illuminated from the torchlights outside.

A lacy curtain moved, a breeze blowing it. Abruptly it fell back into place.

He hurried toward it and pushed it aside a fraction. Lady Wexham's dark figure crossed the yard below.

Rees waited only long enough to see in which direction she headed. Away from the terrace and straight ahead toward the formal gardens. She disappeared behind the shrubbery.

The next moment, something moved to his right. He held still. A figure stepped forward from the terrace and followed her.

Wasting no more time, Rees stepped through the casement window, which had been left ajar. He jumped the few feet to the ground and landed on the grass with a soft thud.

He broke into a trot across the lawn, reaching the screen of shrubbery before pausing a few precious seconds to debate.

He couldn't risk being seen. Making a snap decision, he made an abrupt turn left. Gambling that Lady Wexham was heading back to the temple of Apollo, he would circle around and overtake her before the hill leading to it.

He jogged over the soft grass, dodging the trees and weaving around the hedges, arriving winded at the path that led up the slope to the temple. He searched both ways but saw and heard nothing, hoping that neither one had arrived yet.

The next second, he heard a soft footfall along the path. Quickly, he stepped to the side. In the dim moonlight, he saw enough color to know it was indeed a harlequin figure.

Just as Lady Wexham drew near, he stepped into her path, his heartbeat thudding.

She halted with a gasp, almost bumping into him.

He bent toward her, grasping her lightly by the shoulders to steady her. "We meet again, Harlequin," he said in a low tone.

"So we do, Pirate." Her breath came rapidly, as if she, too, had hurried. She made no move to disengage herself from him.

"What game are you about?"

She cocked her head, peering up at him through her mask. "I play no games."

"Then perhaps you are not aware that someone is following you?" he whispered, drawing his face closer to hers.

She drew in a breath, twisting her head around to search the path.

"You needn't bother to look. He will not show himself . . . unless you are expecting him."

She shook her head, turning her attention back to him. "Are you my guardian angel?" she asked, matching his low tone.

He stared down into her face, unable to see her expression, the question taking him aback. "Perhaps," he ventured, realizing his only thought in running to intercept her was to warn her of the one following her.

"Are you sure he is following me? There are many about tonight."

"He followed you from the house."

Again she drew in a breath.

"Or is he perhaps the one you are to meet? An assignation?" He scanned her eyes, his heart pounding as he awaited her reply.

She seemed to swallow a laugh before shaking her head vehemently. "Indeed not!"

A sense of relief filled him at the denial. "Why else would a damsel be out so late at night?" he growled low in his throat.

"I was merely taking the air."

He couldn't help a smile at her absurd reply. The next second, he stiffened, his hands tightening on her arms, as he heard footfalls.

Straining to look beyond her, he spoke softly, "Here comes your shadow." A sudden thought occurred to him. "Perhaps you could fool him by pretending you *are* here on an assignation—"

Before he could finish the thought, she reached her hands upward, entwining her fingers against his nape. "What a perfect ruse," she breathed, drawing his face down to hers. "But we must make it look convincing." His mind was swimming with the scent of her. Whoever was following her would see her in an embrace. Would it fool him? All he needed was to stand still, hold himself in check, and pray for control, Rees told himself, keeping himself rigid under her light touch.

He was unprepared for her whisper. "You may kiss me."

Kiss her? Had he heard aright? He stood paralyzed, the doubts assailing him. Kiss her? How? Where? A peck on the cheek, or bend down just enough to make it look as if he were kissing her on the lips? No one would be able to tell in the dark.

The blood thundering in his ears, he lowered his head until his lips almost touched hers. The scent of roses filled his nostrils. At once she drew closer. Before he could decide how to proceed, her lips met his full on.

Reacting purely by instinct, his lips responded to hers tentatively. He expected her to pull away at any moment in disgust.

Instead her lips parted beneath his.

He lost all reason.

His fingers dug into her shoulders, drawing her closer. Her mouth was more than he had ever dared dream—soft, pliant, warm, sweet. He couldn't help himself. He wrapped his arms around her, until her body was flush against his.

Instead of pulling away in shock, she only clasped him more tightly about the neck, deepening the kiss.

For the next few minutes, all thought was drowned out by the roar of his own blood. Nothing mattered to him but the warmth of her lips eagerly searching his.

He touched her cheek, soft as down, and trailed his fingers over its curve, down her arched neck, feeling the pulse at its base. He rubbed her chin with his thumb as his fingertips caressed her earlobe, as if to memorize every bit of her.

His hands moved downward the length of her back, feeling her contours through the thin silk of her costume. He forgot his purpose for being there, forgot the war, his position at the Foreign Office, all his ambitions and goals . . . all he wanted was Céline. He wanted to shout out her name.

He envisioned laughing with her, talking, sharing everything. But where, how? How could their two lives ever be joined here on earth when their countries were at war? When he was betraying his own by kissing her like this?

Did she even know who was kissing her? Would she kiss a stranger with such abandon, or was she merely toying with him?—these thoughts collided with the overwhelming desire he felt for her, sobering him and bringing him back to some semblance of reality. With an effort of will, he drew apart enough to search her eyes. Her chest was heaving, like his, her eyes watching him. Yet, she didn't remove her hands from around his neck.

"Do you think he is gone?" she mouthed barely above a whisper.

The words jolted him as nothing else could. He'd completely forgotten the reason for their kiss, too caught up in his dreams.

But she had not.

Unlike him, she had not lost her head. She was probably accustomed to playing such games of deceit. The bitter thought spread like acid in his gut.

He eased away from her some more, this time both physically and emotionally, though still unwilling to let her go completely. He glanced behind her, studying the dark path and surrounding bushes. "I think we can trust so. Or, at least, that he is fooled by our . . . performance."

"Will you . . . will you escort me back, please?"

He hid his surprise that she still wanted his company. What of her rendezvous? "Yes." Almost mechanically, he offered her his arm, and she slipped her hand into the crook of his elbow. Without thought, he covered it with his other hand, as if to keep her closer to him, loath to break the contact between them, even now. He guided her over the dark path, no longer mindful of how much sound their footsteps made.

Neither spoke. His thoughts were too full of what he'd just experienced with her to be able to think of the reason she'd been out there in the first place.

When they neared the terrace, before emerging into the torch-lit portion of the path, she stopped and gently extricated her hand from his. He let her go and stepped away from her.

"I think it best if we part here," she said softly.

"Yes—" He stopped himself before adding "my lady."

She reached out and cupped his cheek with the hand she'd just loosened from his grasp, startling him with her warm touch.

"*Merci, mon cher* pirate."

He gazed down at her, a profound disappointment—and longing—filling him. Ruthlessly, he shoved the feelings down. Too much was at stake for sentiment. "At your service." He bowed and forced himself to walk away from her.

Céline waited just long enough for MacKinnon to disappear into the palace before following him inside. Her legs shook so badly she was afraid she would collapse before reaching her rooms.

What had she done? Not only kissed but passionately embraced a man who was out to destroy her. She'd surrendered herself completely the moment his lips had touched hers, with no thought to her own safety.

She had not abandoned herself so to a man, not even to Stéphane, and never to her own husband.

He spoke almost flawless French. He was employed in her household, and it was clear after tonight that he was watching her every move.

Where had he learned French so well? It only made her realize how little she knew of him.

The questions went around and around in her head with no answers. And yet a part of her didn't care—would give anything to be in MacKinnon's arms again. She smothered a wild laugh—she didn't even know his real name! She couldn't think beyond the kiss she had just enjoyed with him . . . who above anything else was strong, watchful . . . and kind. He had warned her of someone following her.

Her mind homed in on that fact, forgotten until now.

It wouldn't have been Roland. He would have been at the temple ahead of her.

Taking up a taper and lighting it from a branch of candles, Céline made her way to her room. She had to think.

Finally reaching it, she closed the door behind her and affixed the taper in a stand without bothering to light any more candles. She didn't want any brighter light to see herself at the moment. Would her wantonness be written all over her features?

Thankful that Valentine was nowhere about, Céline sank down on her bed, removing her hat and taking off the mask. She gazed at it in the dark. Hateful thing that had unloosed a wild, unknown fiend in her.

She had lived for years without giving herself to any man. What was it about this . . . this butler—this spy—this Brit—that had her forgetting all propriety, all caution?

How could she have kissed him like that? Heat filled her face at the memory of her boldness in offering MacKinnon her lips. How could he have responded so passionately? Had she given him any indication before tonight that she would accept such an improper advance from her butler? Shame and consternation filled her. What must he think of her?

And why did it matter? She covered her mouth with her hand, forgetting everything else in the memory of the feel of his lips on hers.

If he indeed was her enemy, why hadn't he betrayed her? Why had he come to warn her tonight?

The thought brought her to a standstill. Why would an Englishman do this?

She didn't know who he was or what his game was. She remembered his question to her. *What game are you about?* She patted her chest and felt the crinkle of paper. It was no game.

She would have to think of another way to give the papers to Roland before they were discovered missing.

After scouting the grounds for some minutes more, Rees returned to the ballroom. He hadn't seen anyone more—other than couples on genuine assignations.

He surveyed the ballroom again, but he didn't see Lady Wexham's harlequin costume. As his gaze returned to the doorway, it narrowed on Monsieur de la Roche. Dressed in a somber black outfit with a white ruff of the Commedia dell'Arte's doctor, he stood there doing the same thing Rees was doing, surveying the company.

A chill traveled up Rees's spine. He'd seen a patch of white like the collar in the dark, and the wide-brimmed hat was the same as that of the dark figure who had followed Lady Wexham.

De la Roche's gaze crossed his then doubled back as if he'd seen something of interest in Rees. Rees quickly looked down then pretended to focus on a lady. He walked toward her and bowed, asking for the dance.

When he was able to glance back at the doorway from his position on the dance floor, de la Roche was gone.

Forced to continue the dance, Rees couldn't leave the ballroom to go in search of him. All he could do was fret about Lady Wexham's safety.

When he was finally free of his dance partner, Rees left the ballroom but saw no more sign of Lady Wexham. He returned to the attics and stripped off the costume and donned his butler clothes.

Off with one role and back to the other. Harrison MacKinnon, butler. *At your service, my lady. As you wish, my lady. I am yours to command . . .*

It was exactly what he'd done this evening. She had led, and he had followed like a pup. He clutched the pirate garments loosely in his hands, reliving those moments in her arms. What had he done? *Like a lamb led to the slaughter* . . . He gave a dry, humorless laugh. Except he was no innocent to claim he'd been forced into something. He'd gone along eagerly, fully participating in the kiss.

His thoughts turned reluctantly to Jessamine, the young lady he considered himself promised to, although nothing had as yet been declared between the two of them.

How little romantic feeling had come into his choice of wife. He'd found her company pleasing, but beyond that, he'd measured her assets: a well-brought-up young lady, demure, modest, well able to take care of a man's household, and who would be satisfied with a man such as he—one who could provide adequately but who was by no means wealthy. She had been raised frugally. He knew her mother and approved of her having taught her daughter all the important aspects of running a house.

Now, Rees frowned down at the garments in his hand, contrasting the man he'd been tonight with the one he'd known all these long years of abstinence and sacrificial toil to achieve . . . what? Bringing his mother and sister back to the level they used to be—deserved to be—before his father's business had gone bankrupt . . . and to be able to support a wife and children someday?

He'd never thought of himself as a romantic person . . . not since he'd been a youth and found himself deep in the throes of calf-love for the daughter of a wealthy, neighboring baron.

Priscilla Edgecomb. They'd lived in Bristol then, his father a successful merchant. Rees had been home on a brief leave from the navy. At eighteen he'd been full of ambition. Although his father's fortune had not yet undergone the reversals brought about by the blockade, the baron had made it known to him in no uncertain terms that a suit was unwelcome from a merchant's son.

Rees had learned the hard lesson back then not to aspire to a lady above his station. A baron and a tradesman came from two different worlds.

His thoughts came full circle. What about his regard for Jessamine? He couldn't even name it love. Was he so coldhearted?

An image of Céline as his wife once again rose to his mind.

No! He mustn't even entertain such thoughts.

15

*C*éline forced her thoughts to what she must do next. Banishing all foolish yearnings, she picked up the taper, which had burned halfway, then turned the key in her lock. This time she lit a branch of candles and placed it on her desk.

Unbuttoning her costume, she extracted the papers she had stolen from the Comte's room and spread them out. She'd have to put it in code before dawn no matter how long it took her.

Then she had best return to London. It was becoming too risky to meet with Roland at Hartwell.

With a sigh, she picked up her pen and drew her inkwell forward. It would be a long night.

A few hours later, she sat back and eased her aching muscles. The sky was becoming pink on the horizon. But she was finished. She glanced down at her papers with satisfaction.

She folded the original documents and stood, debating a moment.

It was too late to try to return them to the Comte's room. It was too risky. By now the servants would have awakened. Too many people surrounded him. By daylight, the documents' disappearance would be discovered. She would have to destroy them and hope that no one linked their disappearance to her departure. With all the people leaving Hartwell after the masquerade, she would be only one among dozens of departing guests. She'd have to invent some pressing need to suddenly return to London. She'd dash a note to the Comte, which Valentine could give his valet later.

She glanced around her room. In a short while Valentine would come by. Kneeling by the hearth, Céline laid the papers on the sooty stone surface then touched a corner with the remains of a candle. The paper began to smoke and curl and finally caught light.

It flared, and in a moment the pages were in flames. With a stick of kindling, she nudged them to ensure that all were consumed.

It had been a long night, but she was still not through. She had come to some decisions in the predawn hours.

She would take only her own traveling coach and leave Valentine behind to finish packing and to organize the other servants to follow at a more leisurely pace later. She knew Valentine would protest, but Céline would insist.

She would take only Jacob and MacKinnon, who could act once again as outrider. Tom would stay behind to accompany Valentine and the other maids when they returned by hired coach.

As for how she would face MacKinnon . . .

Biting her lip, gazing down at the ashes on the hearth, she determined *not* to let on that she had recognized him. She pictured his tiny scar and wished she could touch it now.

No! She must forget this kiss.

Last night had been an aberration, but a new day had returned her to sanity. That person she had allowed to break free for a few minutes was back in its secret place.

Brushing off her hands, Céline went to the washbasin to rinse her hands and shed the clothes of dreams and fantasy. After hiding the new encoded papers behind the covers of a portfolio of other writings and household notes, Céline put on her nightgown and collapsed in her bed, hoping for an hour or two of sleep.

It seemed she had just closed her eyes when she heard Valentine's off-key singing in French. But a glance at the clock told her it was almost eight. She had too much to do and very little time. Throwing off her covers, she braced herself to give Valentine her instructions. As she had expected, Valentine's first words were protest. "I will not be left behind! How are you going to do without me for even a day?" As if to emphasize her words, she gave a jerk to the corset laces.

"Ouch!" Céline placed her hands on her waist to regain her balance. "I can do very well for a day or two. Virginia can help me with any gown I cannot button for myself."

Valentine snorted. "That clumsy girl. I do not want to think how I will find your armoires when I return!"

"Well, I am sorry for it, but you must stay behind. I depend on you to finish packing my things and see to everything else." She sighed, feeling tired and out of sorts. "I shall have to bid *Maman* adieu." Not a task she relished.

Valentine motioned her to her dressing table to begin her hair. "I will see to her after you leave."

She glanced at her maid in the mirror. "Thank you." Behind her gruffness, Valentine would do anything to protect Céline.

Her abigail narrowed her eyes at her. "You look pale. When did you finally retire?"

Céline couldn't help a yawn. "Late is all I will say. But no matter, I will nap in the coach." She looked at herself in the mirror, too aware of the shadows under her eyes. "Perhaps a little rouge." Would MacKinnon indicate by word or look that they had been locked in an embrace just hours before? She couldn't help touching her lips, still feeling the imprint of his.

Would it throw him when she behaved as if last night had never been?

Or was he too hardened a British spy to be scandalized by her behavior? Would it merely confirm for him the loose morals of the French? Her face burned at the thought that he would think she would allow herself to be kissed by any man.

Slowly, she lowered her hand. Better he think her licentious than suspect the feelings his kiss had exposed in her.

"Very well." Valentine began brushing Céline's hair, which only aggravated the pain in her temples from her lack of sleep.

"Please convey my instructions to the other servants," she said abruptly to Valentine, deciding she didn't want to face MacKinnon yet. She ignored the longing in her heart to see him again. No! She would not succumb to such feminine weakness.

By eight o'clock Rees finished helping set the dining table for breakfast. No one was up but the servants, and they all looked the way he felt. Eyes full of grit, head in a vise. He had drunk nothing but hadn't slept a wink when he'd finally been able to return to his room. All he could think of was Lady Wexham's kiss and the danger she was in.

He returned to the vast kitchens to drink a cup of coffee before seeing what other tasks there were to be done. He expected he would have to help clean up the remains of the ball.

He stifled a yawn as he entered the kitchen and headed for a table that usually had coffee and tea urns for whoever happened by. He had just poured himself a cup of the strong coffee when he heard someone behind him.

He turned to see Valentine. Had she just come from Lady Wexham's room? How was she this morning? The thoughts flitted through his mind in rapid succession as he struggled to put in place an impassive demeanor.

Valentine came toward him, her look of dislike evident. With a brief "good morning" he moved aside to allow her access to the urns.

Instead of serving herself, she stood and folded her arms. He lifted an eyebrow, lowering his coffee cup a fraction from his lips.

"You are to accompany madame to London zis morning."

It was good he hadn't yet taken a sip of coffee. "I beg your pardon?"

She sniffed with a toss of her head. "You heard me."

"Lady Wexham is returning to London today?" When had she decided this?

"Yes." As if begrudging every crumb of information she was forced to give him, she turned toward the tea urn and tossed over her shoulder, "You will pack up your zings and go to the stables to assist Jacob with anything he needs. You will ride my lady's mare, as you did coming here."

"Shall I go and see about hiring another coach?"

"*Non*—the rest of us will follow in a day or so."

He drew his brows together, his surprise growing. "You are not returning today?" What would others say? Would it look strange that Lady Wexham was returning all of a sudden to London?

He stopped the rapid progression of his thoughts. He seemed to care more about her welfare than the fact that Lady Wexham must have a pressing reason to return to London—and it was his duty to find out what it was.

"*Non*," she snapped. "My lady returns by herself in her traveling chaise."

"I see." No wonder the maid was so disgruntled. Probably miffed at being left behind.

What was Lady Wexham up to? What did it have to do with last night? He didn't like it. Not when someone had been following her to her rendezvous.

"Well, what are you standing around for? Madame wishes to leave within ze hour."

"Does Jacob know?"

"*Non*. That is for you to do."

"I don't know if he'll be ready in an hour."

She sniffed. "Zat is your affair." She poured her tea, ignoring him.

Seeing he would get no more from Valentine, Rees gulped down his coffee and left for the stables.

He didn't like it.

After some effort on Valentine's part, Céline was finally satisfied with her appearance. A little powder and some rouge hid most of the ravages of so little sleep. At least her dark green traveling outfit set off her complexion well.

With a final adjustment of her bonnet, she picked up her reticule and turned to bid Valentine good-bye.

"Don't look so glum. We shall see each other soon."

"Hah. You have left me with all the work here." She glanced with contempt at the small valise at Céline's feet. "That is all you are taking, and I must make sure nothing is left behind."

"I have more than enough back home."

Valentine picked up the valise. "I shall take this down to the carriage—if that butler managed to tell Jacob to have it ready."

Céline paused at the door. "You told him my plans?"

"Of course." Valentine gave her a sharp look. Before she could question her, Céline walked out of the room. "I shall run to my mother's apartment and then go to the carriage."

"Very well. I shall see you at the front."

Céline knocked on her mother's sitting room door. Her maid opened the door a crack.

"Is my mother awake yet?"

"Yes, my lady, she is just having her chocolate now." She moved aside to let Céline enter.

Céline made her way to the bedroom where her mother sat up in her nightcap and peignoir, a tray on her lap.

Her mother blinked at her over her reading spectacles. "*Ma chérie*, are you going somewhere so early after last evening?"

Céline leaned down and gave her a peck on the cheek. "Good morning, *Maman*. I am returning to London."

"What? How is this? Why didn't you tell me?"

"I only decided last night."

"Why ever for? You only just arrived."

Céline chuckled, pretending a nonchalance she didn't feel. "It has been at least a week and a half. I left many things pending in the city. Don't worry, I shall return again soon." Not sure when that would be, she patted her mother's hand. "Take care of yourself. Valentine remains behind to finish packing my things. She will see to anything else you may need."

Her mother shook her head at her. "I shall never understand you. Always flitting about." She shooed her away from the bed. "Well, be off with you. I want you to arrive before sunset."

Céline straightened. "Very well. I will write you when I arrive." Blowing her a final kiss, she turned to leave, feeling the same vague emptiness she did every time she bid her mother good-bye.

Céline reached the main staircase and was just about to make her way down to the ground floor when someone called her name.

She turned to find Monsieur de la Roche at her elbow. The man had a way of appearing silently where he was least wanted.

She hid her displeasure and smiled. "Good morning, monsieur. How are you this day?"

He inclined his gray pate. "Very well, dear lady. How are you . . . after last night's nocturnal activities?"

She tensed under his steady scrutiny. A vision of embracing MacKinnon came to her, and she struggled to keep her smile steady. "A little worse for the wear, but nothing a good night's rest will not restore."

"Yes." His gaze drifted downward. "I noticed Harlequin wore himself out on the dance floor."

Fear pricked along the back of her neck. Had he recognized her? Before she could react, he asked, "You are going somewhere?"

"Yes."

He waited, his pale eyes never leaving hers. "At a distance?"

She gave a careless laugh. "I fear London beckons me back."

He raised a gray eyebrow. "London." At the inflection, an image rose in her mind of his brain studying the word from all sides, cataloging it, and filing it away for some nefarious purpose.

She shook aside her fanciful imagination. Really, a lack of sleep was rattling her more than merited. With a careless wave, she proceeded down the staircase. "I shall see you in town one of these days, I imagine."

"Doubtless you shall, perhaps sooner than you think."

"I shall count the days!" Without another glance, she walked down the staircase, keeping a dignified pace.

Rees stood beside his pawing mount, waiting for Lady Wexham. It was scarcely past nine o'clock when she appeared.

He braced himself before looking at her, hoping to have himself well in hand before she approached. But his breath caught and a knot formed in his chest at the sight of her. In a dark green pelisse with a matching hat and plumy ostrich feather, she looked as elegant as any fashionable lady of the *ton*—and a far cry from the roguish harlequin she had played the evening before. She smiled and nodded at Tom, stopping to exchange a few words with him.

Rees stood too far to hear what they said. He had deliberately positioned his horse behind the traveling chaise in order to see her before she saw him. Now, he pretended to adjust the mare's girth.

Valentine's nasal tones reached him and then Lady Wexham's quiet reply, though he couldn't distinguish the words.

Rees kept his head lowered, focusing on the leather strap between his fingers, straining to hear the sound of the carriage door opening. Maybe he would not have to speak to her at all this morning.

Instead, it was the scrunch of the gravel drive before him and then her soft voice. "Good morning, Mr. MacKinnon. Is all well with you?"

Slowly, he looked up, feeling at once the impact of those brandy-hued eyes on him. He swallowed back the gnawing ache in his gut.

"Y-yes. Yes," he repeated more firmly.

"Forgive this sudden decision to return to town. I hope you had no trouble readying yourself for departure?"

Clearly she had no notion that he had been the pirate who had accosted her on the path last night.

Not sure whether to feel disappointed or relieved, he searched her face, wondering again why she was returning to London. "None at all, my lady."

"You are all set to ride back then? Not too fatigued after last night's ball? I hope you were not kept up too long." She paused, tilting her chin at an angle. "I didn't see you after dinner."

Was there something behind the words? Or was she waiting for his explanation of why he'd shirked his duties as butler?

"I was kept busy below stairs," he finally managed.

She continued regarding him a moment longer before saying softly, "I see."

The words reminded him sharply of her whispered commands of the previous night. *You may kiss me.*

Finally, she gave a nod and stepped back from him, allowing him to resume breathing. "We shall be on our way then."

Céline settled back against the squabs as the carriage lurched forward.

Well, that was over. Not sure how she would confront MacKinnon, she was relieved he had no idea she knew of his disguise. Or, was she?

Alone in the vehicle, with a few hours to do little else but think, she was hard-pressed to ignore the part of her that wished MacKinnon had acknowledged what had transpired between them last night. She touched her lips, reliving those moments of abandon.

She tried to rein in her feelings, telling herself that once in London, she would have to decide what to do about her butler. She'd have to consult Gaspard and Roland and assess the damage.

And Valentine? Her maid would demand some immediate action against MacKinnon.

Why did Céline yet feel reluctant to expose him? He was her enemy, yet . . . he had protected her last night. She leaned toward the window, even now fearful that de la Roche or whoever had followed her last night would come after her.

But she saw no one but MacKinnon riding atop her mare, a cloud of dust kicking up around its hooves, and she felt strangely secure.

She picked up her book and opened it. She might as well occupy her mind until they reached the first posting house.

They had been riding for a while since stopping at the last tollgate north of the market town of Watford. Rees calculated they would soon enter Middlesex and then it was only a few more miles to London. But first lay Bushey Heath and Stanmore Commons, open areas with few farmhouses.

He rode behind the carriage, trying to avoid the sight of Lady Wexham as much as possible. The market road to London was in terrible shape, deeply rutted from the heavy cart traffic.

How he wished he were elsewhere. Even a post aboard a cutter with the tedious task of blockading the French ports would be preferable at this moment.

He had spent most of the ride figuring out what he would do when they returned to London. What would he tell Bunting?

He would be truthful . . . as far as he could. That there were certain suspicious signs, but no hard evidence against Lady Wexham. If she was spying on the Comte de Provence, that was not grounds for treason. Let the French solve their own problems of succession. As long as Bonaparte was defeated. He doubted anything Lady Wexham did or didn't do would affect the outcome of that.

Napoleon had sealed his own downfall with his invasion of Russia. The loss of troops was irreparable. And Spain was proving a continual bleeding sore.

It would be a matter of months, perhaps a year, but Bonaparte would be defeated.

And what then for himself? Would he receive a promotion? Could he hope for a diplomatic post—a place on Castlereagh's team on the Continent?

The more time he was away from his clerical job at the Foreign

Office, the less he wanted to return to it. Yet, he saw no way out. And without the Foreign Office job, what future did he have?

As he'd told Lady Wexham, he'd run away to sea at fifteen. What he hadn't told her was that it was because he had been unwilling to follow in his father's footsteps and become a merchant.

He'd quickly taken to the life aboard ship, working his way up from powder monkey to midshipman in a few months. He'd seen plenty of action—enough to convince him that there had to be a better way for the nations and principalities of Europe to settle their differences than through the shed blood of their men. That's when the dream had been birthed in him to enter the diplomatic field.

But after a decade of toiling away at the Foreign Office, Rees had come to the conclusion that he was destined to molder away there unless something miraculous occurred.

And that had been when Oglethorpe had offered him the chance of a promotion for spying on Lady Wexham.

Yet now, he found himself questioning his loyalty, he who had never swerved in his allegiance to king and country.

He clenched the reins in his hands. He had to show Oglethorpe something if he hoped for any promotion. *Dear God, what am I to do? Why am I in this situation—torn in my loyalties as never before? Show me what to do . . .*

Would You have me expose Lady Wexham?

Protect her. The words brought him up short, they had been so clear and emphatic. The mare seemed to sense his consternation for she whinnied. Rees patted her neck while attempting to get his own thoughts in order.

Protect her. Had those been the Lord's words or his own impulse? How could he be sure?

He'd never had to wrestle with right and wrong before. He was a British subject. His country had been threatened by France for almost two decades. France was the aggressor, not England. He had fought in His Majesty's navy, been wounded in the service of his country, and now, although his work seemed obscure and unimportant, he knew it was valuable in the overall scheme of things.

Intelligence gathering was vital to the military and government. Any leaks of information were potentially detrimental to the war effort. It could mean a prolongation of hostilities, which would only result in the death of more soldiers.

It was simple. Rees would have to tell Bunting what he knew. He had no other choice.

Rees was so caught up in his internal debate that his horse had begun to lag. He looked ahead with a start at how far ahead the chaise had gotten. He began to urge his horse forward when a group of horsemen brandishing guns sprang out of the trees lining the highway along that stretch of road.

Rees spurred his mount into a gallop, shouting to Jacob to spring the horses. Cursing the lack of groom to load the blunderbuss, Rees prayed Jacob would be able to outdistance the five horsemen.

The highwaymen shouted for the coachman to stop. One of them spotted Rees gaining on the carriage. Rees jerked on the reins, veering away from the road in hopes of distracting some of the riders. Wheeling his horse around, the highwayman lifted a pistol and aimed for Rees. The blast knocked him backward, jerking his hands from the reins. He flew off his horse, landing with a thud on the grassy roadside, the wind knocked from his lungs. Pain radiated from his right shoulder.

In the distance, Jacob shouted, the horses neighed, and the wheels ground against the hard-packed mud. Rees attempted to roll over. To his frustration the chaise had come to a stop. "Go, Jacob—go!" he shouted, but his voice came out a hoarse rasp.

The next second, the door flew open and Lady Wexham sprang down, running to kneel at his side, ignoring the shouts of the highwaymen.

"Why . . . why didn't you ride on?" he gasped.

"Hush." She hiked up her skirt and began tearing off strips of her petticoat. Wadding it up, she pushed them against his shoulder. He stifled an exclamation at the jolt. "I'm sorry," she said immediately, her eyes filled with concern.

Jacob came puffing up behind her, with one of the masked highwaymen brandishing a pistol.

"You, madame, up!" The bandit gestured with his gun.

She didn't spare him a glance, her focus on Rees's wound. "This man needs my attention."

He thrust the pistol against her cheek, and she flinched from him.

Ignoring the burning in his shoulder, Rees grabbed her arm. "Do as he says."

Her gaze shifted from him to the highwayman. Finally, she let the wad go and backed away, addressing the coachman. "Hold it to his shoulder, Jacob."

The older man knelt at Rees's side. "Yes, my lady. You just give them what they want," he said with a glare at the highwayman. "They have the horses."

Through the haze of pain, Rees noted the highwayman training his pistol on him had a French accent. Had they been sent by someone at Hartwell House? His thoughts went to the man who'd followed Lady Wexham the night before. She had been right to leave when she did, except she'd been too late.

As the cloth became soaked in blood, Jacob pressed more of the cloth strips to Rees's shoulder. "This is going to hurt like the dickens, but I've got to bind it up 'fore you bleed to death."

"Yes." He braced himself. Jacob began to undo the buttons on Rees's coat and waistcoat. As he eased them away from his shoulders, Rees clenched his jaw to keep from screaming out. Jacob grunted. "If you don't mind, I'll just cut away your shirt. No sense to trouble you any more than I have to."

Rees only jerked his head.

The coachman took out a pocketknife and slit the muslin apart. "All right then, bite down."

Rees said nothing, fighting the nausea, and praying for Lady Wexham's safety. *Don't let her do anything foolish, Lord.*

Jacob took the remaining strips of petticoat and wrapped them around Rees's shoulder, having to support him with his arms as he brought the strips around his back and under his arm. Rees prayed he wouldn't pass out before he knew what was happening with Lady Wexham.

He looked across Jacob's shoulder and couldn't help an exclamation. One of the men was accosting Lady Wexham, his posture threatening.

"Easy there," Jacob cautioned, "or you'll dislodge these bandages."

Rees searched for the others. One highwayman was holding the horses, while another had Rees's mare. The last was inside the coach.

"There are only five of them," Rees managed. "You could have outrun them."

"Nay, sir, not when Lady Wexham heard the shot and saw you fall. She had me stop."

"Hopefully, all they'll want are any valuables and they'll let us go on our way." Even as he said it, he was afraid this was no ordinary holdup.

"Aye, I imagine you're right."

He cursed himself for not being more alert. He hadn't seen anyone following the carriage, but that didn't mean they hadn't taken a different route. What did she carry of value? And if they found it, what would they do to her? Cold sweat broke out on his forehead at the thought. He would be able to do little to defend her now. He continued to pray.

Jacob sat back with a final tug on the knot he'd fashioned. "There, that should hold you till we can get you to a surgeon. You've got a ball lodged somewhere in your shoulder."

Rees tried to sit up. Jacob put an arm around him and guided him. "Thanks. Do you think you can help me stand?"

Jacob glanced at the highwayman standing a few paces from them, his pistol pointed at them. "Best not. You've lost a lot of blood. Let's wait and see what happens."

Light-headed from the effort to sit, Rees fixed his eyes on the chaise, wondering what the man would find. Finally, the highwayman emerged, speaking in French to another, who must be the leader. "Nothing in here. We must search her."

Rees leaned forward, only to be stopped by Jacob. "What's going on?"

Rees debated and finally said, "I don't like it. It doesn't seem he found"—he hesitated—"anything of value. I hope he doesn't want to search her."

The coachman uttered an oath and turned to study the men.

The two masked Frenchmen stood before Lady Wexham. To her credit, she evinced no fear but stood straight and eyed them in disdain.

"Where is it?"

She lifted her chin. "I don't know what you are speaking of."

"I think you do, madame, and if you are not forthcoming, we will be forced to search your person." The man who spoke took a threatening step toward her.

"If you do, you are a coward." She thrust her reticule toward him. "Here, take whatever notes and jewels I have."

After rummaging through it, he tossed it to the ground. "I think you know what we want."

"I have no idea what you are talking about."

He motioned to his companion. "Take her into the coach."

She fought them, but they overcame her. Rees struggled to stand, but Jacob held him back and he was too weak to overpower him. "We must protect her!"

"We haven't much choice. They have the weapons. We don't need another bullet in us. Let's hope they'll find what they want and let her go."

All Rees could do was continue praying . . . and hope Jacob was right, that all they wanted was whatever she had and didn't intend to harm her in any other way.

He breathed a sigh of relief when they emerged a short while later from the coach, without Lady Wexham. "She has nothing. Let's be off before anyone happens by."

Rees pushed Jacob toward the carriage. "See if Lady Wexham is all right."

Rees attempted to stand, but a wave of dizziness overcame him. In a few seconds, the highwaymen remounted and galloped away, leaving a cloud of dust in their wake. They were heading along the road now, in the direction of Hartwell House.

Jacob stood with a grunt. "Very well." Before he reached the coach door, Lady Wexham descended, straightening her pelisse. The next second she rushed to Rees's side.

She knelt beside him, her gaze on his bandaged shoulder.

"My lady, are you all right?" Jacob asked.

"Yes, yes," she answered impatiently, waving him away. She looked at Rees. "Is it very bad?"

"I'll live. It . . . looks worse . . . than it is . . ." Speaking was becoming an effort as the waves of pain washed over him.

Before he could ask her what they'd done to her, she turned to Jacob. "Please, help me to lift him. We must get him help as soon as possible." She looked about her, biting her lip. "What are we close to?"

Jacob considered. "Bentley Priory is just ahead a ways."

"We have no idea if the marquess is in residence." With a shake of her head, she stood. "No, it's best we head directly to London." She glanced at Rees. "We risk more bleeding with these abominable roads, but once there I can summon my surgeon."

He preferred being in London where he could have a hope of keeping watch over her. "I'll be . . . fine."

The two stooped to begin lifting him. "My lady, I can . . . walk on my . . . own . . . with Jacob's assistance."

"Nonsense. We'll support you on either side." As she spoke, she was already helping him to his feet, her arm strong around his waist.

He almost passed out when he tried to walk.

Jacob supported him on the other side. "Easy there, lad . . . put your weight on me . . . only a few steps . . ."

By the time they reached the carriage door, he remained conscious only by sheer will.

Shaking off Lady Wexham's arm, he made a herculean effort to manage the carriage step on his own. Finally, he was in the coach, collapsing across the seat.

Jacob propped him up in one corner of the coach, lifting his legs across the seat as Lady Wexham put pillows under his head and shoulders.

A second later, she exited the coach. Before he had time to wonder where she'd gone, she was back, her reticule in one hand and a flask in the other. "Those blackguards left everything in such a mess, but I have managed to locate my things. Here, take a sip of this." She leaned toward him, pouring a thimbleful of the flask's contents into its top and bringing it to his lips. Brandy burned down his throat.

"Thank you," he managed, letting his head fall back on the cushion.

She made no reply but spread a blanket over his body.

"I'm sorry—"

She stopped in the act of tucking the blanket around his legs. "For what?"

He waved with his hand. "This."

Her dark eyebrows drew together. "For getting shot defending me? Don't be daft. I'm sorry to have put your life in danger."

Again she turned away before he could say anything and leaned out the door. "We must go."

Jacob closed the door, and the next moment the coach was in motion.

Each sway and bump of the carriage jarred his shoulder. He closed his eyes, praying he wouldn't be sick.

He felt her hand on his forehead. "We'll be home as soon as we can. Jacob will get us there quickly, I know."

He nodded, feeling too ill to open his eyes.

She sat on the seat opposite him.

He remembered the words he'd heard within him. *Protect her.* Is this what the Lord had meant?

What kind of protector had he been? When she'd needed him most, he'd failed her. Who would protect her now?

16

*C*éline sat opposite MacKinnon, wincing with each jolt of the chaise. The makeshift bandage Jacob had fashioned was beginning to bleed again. As the fresh bloodstain expanded on the white cotton, she gripped her hands and prayed.

Dear God, please don't take him. Please—

She bit her lip and looked outside. It had been so long since she'd prayed that she felt unsure. God had no reason to listen to her prayers. The last time she'd really prayed for something had been to be reunited with Stéphane. Instead the Lord had taken him.

Her gaze came back to MacKinnon. His skin was almost as white as the bandaging. How much more blood could he lose? *Please keep him alive. This is all my fault. I shouldn't have brought him along.*

If he died, she would be as guilty as the highwayman who had shot him.

Highwayman! Henchmen sent from Hartwell. How had they discovered the loss of the documents so quickly—and pinned it to her?

She remembered her encounter with de la Roche.

Of course. He could have sent out some of his servants. With good horses and traveling across country, they could have overtaken the coach.

Rees moaned softly.

Unable to stand it any longer, she knelt beside him, touching one of his hands with hers. "We're almost there."

"I . . . beg . . . your pardon. Don't . . . mean to be . . . such . . . trouble."

She drew off her glove and touched his forehead, which felt clammy, the edges of his hair damp. His eyelids flickered open, the gray irises laced with pain. "Nonsense," she said with a briskness she did not feel. "Trouble it'll be if you dare to die on me."

He grimaced. "No chance of that. Not as long as I'm to be your guardian angel—"

Her gaze dropped to the faint scar on his chin, and she remembered how he had warned her the previous night. She looked upward to his lips tightened with pain. Would she ever feel them upon hers again? Her cheeks flushed at how much she desired it.

How could she be thinking such things when his life was held in the balance?

"I didn't . . . do a very good job of protecting you . . . back there."

She laid a finger across his lips. "Shh. Don't try to talk."

Despite the well-sprung coach, it bounced and jostled along the rutted road. But she'd told Jacob not to spare the horses but to return with all haste to London.

She leaned out the window. Would they never arrive? They were going through St. John's Wood. Soon they'd be at Tyburn, the last tollgate before entering London.

MacKinnon moaned more loudly this time. Immediately she was at his side again. "We'll be in London soon," she murmured.

"Did they . . . did they—" He swallowed as if every word caused him effort. "Hurt you?" He reopened his eyes, his gray eyes searching hers.

So caught up in her concern for him, it took her a moment to understand his meaning. She flushed, remembering the men who had groped and pawed at her, searching for the documents. She shook her head. "No. They did nothing—nothing too unpleasant. Please, don't trouble yourself about that."

He groped for her hand, and she gave it to him. His hold was surprisingly strong. "Blackguards! If they did anything—"

She covered his hand with her other. "Shh! They did nothing but have me remove my pelisse and pat my gown a bit. They seemed embarrassed to do more." All the more reason they were not ordinary highwaymen.

His grip loosened and his eyes closed, as if the effort had spent his remaining strength. Digging into her reticule, she extracted her bottle of Hungary water. Moistening her handkerchief with it, she used it to dab his temples.

Jacob had removed his jacket and waistcoat and cut away his shirt. Céline tucked the blanket farther up around him when she noticed him shivering.

"Th . . . thank you."

Once again, the coach slowed. She glanced out the window.

"Where . . . are we?"

"The Tyburn Gate toll." *Thank God.* She squeezed his hand gently.

"You . . . don't have to kneel there . . . soil your gown . . ."

"Hush." She bit her lip at the blood beginning to soak through the blanket. By the time they reached Mayfair, his wound would be dripping on the floor. She flipped up her skirt and began tearing more strips from her petticoat.

"What're . . . you . . . doing?" His voice sounded slurred.

"Don't talk, save your strength." She folded the strips and laid the squares against his shoulder.

His face seemed drained of all blood. How much could a person lose and . . . and . . .

Stéphane had bled to death on the battlefield.

No, she wouldn't think about that! Oh—when would they arrive? Finally the coach began to move again.

She continued kneeling, holding the cloths against the wound though her knees grew numb, and prayed for his life.

Rees murmured something she couldn't distinguish.

". . . fought the good fight . . ." His words were growing weaker.

"You have done no such thing. You haven't even begun to fight!"

"Been fighting . . . all my . . . life."

What did he mean? How she wanted to know who he was and where he'd come from.

How could a stranger, an enemy, have grown so dear to her? *Please Lord, don't take him! You took Papa and Stéphane. I know this man can never be mine, but please don't let him die because of me.*

She covered his hand once more with hers.

He stirred and tried to speak.

She squeezed his hand. "Shh."

"I . . . didn't . . . protect . . . you . . ."

"You protected me very well. You were a fine guardian angel. Now, we're almost home and you shall have the best surgeon in London."

Finally they were turning down her street. The additional wadding was once again soaked through, and MacKinnon had lost consciousness. His pulse felt feeble, but he was still alive. For that she was grateful.

Before the carriage had come to a complete halt, she was at the door, pushing it open. "We need a surgeon immediately," she said as soon as William reached the door. "MacKinnon has been shot."

Her footman's mouth gaped open.

"Fetch Mr. Simmons," she told him, naming the most eminent surgeon of Mayfair. "Hurry!"

"Yes, my lady. I'll go at once."

As he hurried off, Jacob came to her side. "I'll carry him in."

"Bring him to his room," she shouted over her shoulder, already running toward the basement entrance.

Spotting a kitchen maid at the end of the corridor, she called out to her, "Bring basins of hot water and clean towels and bandaging. Hurry!"

Once inside MacKinnon's room, she hurried to his narrow cot and turned down the blankets. Jacob came behind her, huffing with the weight of MacKinnon in his arms. She motioned for him to lay the butler down. "Careful, he's lost so much blood."

"Aye, my lady," Jacob said.

"Don't move him any more than is necessary."

"Best get him a swallow of brandy in case he wakes up again," he said.

By this time, other servants were peering in the doorway of the small bedroom. Céline motioned to Gaspard. "Some cognac."

"*Oui*, madame." He ducked out.

A moment later he returned with a tumbler.

Jacob proceeded to remove MacKinnon's boots. Thankfully, her butler didn't stir. Then Céline panicked, thinking he was dead. "Is . . . is he breathing?"

Jacob leaned down and put his ear to his mouth. "Yes, shallow, but he's still with us. Why don't you wait upstairs for Mr. Simmons, my lady? We'll take good care of MacKinnon here."

Unwilling to leave her butler's side but wanting to be on the lookout for the surgeon, Céline reluctantly agreed.

Once upstairs, she paced the entry hall, glancing out the narrow window every few minutes. When the surgeon finally arrived with his bag, Céline led him immediately down the stairs, explaining as they went.

Mr. Simmons clucked his tongue. "A holdup in broad daylight? There hasn't been a highwayman at Bushey Heath since the one was hanged more than a decade ago. It's this confounded war. Hard times bring out the worst in men."

MacKinnon stirred when they approached his bed. Mrs. Finlay, who had been sitting at his side, rose from her chair.

"How is he?" Céline whispered.

"The same, my lady."

Mr. Simmons cut away the soaked bandaging and examined the wound, probing it with his fingertip. Finally, he straightened and turned to them. "The ball shall have to come out."

Céline gripped her hands, as if feeling the cut of the knife herself. "But he'll be all right?"

"I can't say, my lady. But he seems fit enough. He's fortunate it hit no vital organs."

Fear paralyzed her limbs. Mrs. Finlay patted her arm. "I'm sure Mr. Simmons will do all in his power, my lady. Why don't we leave him to his work?"

The surgeon was opening his bag. He motioned to William. "You can hold him, young man. Get on his other side."

Mr. Simmons looked around at those still in the room. "If you will excuse me, Lady Wexham."

"Perhaps I can assist you."

The surgeon shook his head. "It won't be pretty. I'm sure he won't appreciate a lady in the room."

Céline took a deep breath, feeling a new strength now that Mac-Kinnon was receiving the attention he needed. Not wanting to delay things, she nodded. "Very well. Let me know as soon as it's over."

She decided to wait in Mrs. Finlay's parlor, which was in the basement, closer to MacKinnon.

"Here, my lady, have a nice cup of tea. It should settle your nerves."

"Thank you, Mrs. Finlay."

"We didn't expect you so soon. It's a good thing I was here. I gave some of the girls a holiday since there was so little to do. But if I'd known you were returning today, I'd have—"

Céline struggled to focus on what her housekeeper was saying. "Never mind that. It—it was a sudden decision on my part. I'm sure everything has been well looked after."

"How did Mr. MacKinnon come to be shot?" Mrs. Finlay shuddered. "I heard something of highwaymen."

Taking a sip of the hot tea, Céline braced herself to go over the story again. At least Mrs. Finlay could then convey it to the other servants.

The housekeeper clucked and tsked as Céline relayed the events.

"I always say traveling is dangerous. Better to stay close to home. At least we have the watch here in London."

Finishing her tea, Céline stood, too restless to remain sitting. She glanced out the door toward MacKinnon's room, but all was silent, the door still shut.

Had the surgeon found the ball? She knew Simmons was the best. He'd patched up Rumford when he'd fallen on the ice a year ago; and stitched up Tom when he'd been hit by a dray a few years back.

Her thoughts returned to the attack. She hadn't recognized either the voices or faces of the men behind the stocking masks, but there were so many servants at Hartwell. As she'd told MacKinnon, the one who'd searched her had seemed ashamed so had not done a thorough job. The men had also searched every inch of the traveling coach, dumping out everything in her reticule and valise, but had not found where she'd hidden the coded documents.

Someone at Hartwell had discovered she was spying for the Republicans. And MacKinnon was working for the British. She was no longer safe from either side. She shivered. What was to become of her?

She had never thought it through when she'd agreed to keep her ears open for information. It had almost been a lark, a way to give meaning to a life that had become a dreary round of parties and social obligations.

And now, she might hang for it.

That or go into exile.

The prospect she'd avoided until now stared her full in the face. Did she want to return to France for good?

Her thoughts came back to MacKinnon. Would she ever see him again? Did it matter?

She stopped in the middle of the small parlor, filled with an overwhelming sadness, as if denied an opportunity before it had ever had a chance to be explored.

She'd have to consult with Roland and the others and decide what to do.

The door opened, and she jumped. William poked his head into the room. "Pardon me, my lady, I didn't mean to startle you."

She rushed to the door. "Is it over?"

"Doctor's all finished up. He says you may come in if you'd like."

"Is—is he all right?"

William smiled. "Sleeping like a babe."

She brought a fist up to her mouth to hold back the tears. "Thank God," she whispered.

MacKinnon lay on his back, his bare chest swathed thickly in bandages. He appeared to be resting quietly and no blood was staining the white strips. She turned to the doctor, speaking in a low voice. "How is he?"

"Weak. But I got the ball out, and it appeared a clean entry."

"What must we do for his care?"

The surgeon wiped off his last instrument and put it away. "Just keep the wound clean and change the dressing every day. I've left some basilicum powder to sprinkle on it. You can give him laudanum or willow bark tea if he is too uncomfortable." Mr. Simmons closed up his bag and lifted it off the chair.

"Make sure the patient gets plenty of rest to recover from the loss of so much blood. He'll be awhile mending. He'd best stay put for a fortnight. No resuming his duties till he's regained his strength."

"No, of course not." She moved closer to the bedside. Mrs. Finlay bustled about removing the basin and dirty linens.

MacKinnon still looked unnaturally pale.

"I've given him some laudanum so he should sleep for some time," the surgeon said behind her. "It's better for him. When he wakes, perhaps some broth and a little brandy."

"Yes, we'll look after him well."

"Very good, my lady. I shall be on my way. I'll call tomorrow to inspect the wound and see how he's progressing." He drew in a breath. "The biggest danger is fever, but if your servants heed my instructions, the patient should make a full recovery."

Céline's heart recoiled at the word *fever*. With his weakened condition, could MacKinnon survive an infection?

After the surgeon left, Céline looked once more at MacKinnon. He continued sleeping, William sitting by the bed. Céline wanted to stay but knew it wasn't wise. It was not seemly for the lady of the house to be nursing a servant—not even her butler.

She tarried a moment longer, unwilling to let him out of her sight. As she stared at his sleeping features, she prayed silently. *Dear Lord, thank You for not taking him. I don't understand You and why You take some and leave others, but I thank You for sparing MacKinnon's life.*

Reluctantly, she moved away from the bed. "Let me know if he awakens or if there is any other change," she told her footman.

"Yes, my lady."

She closed the door softly behind her.

As soon as Rees awoke he wished he could fall asleep again. His entire body ached from head to foot, but as his senses sharpened he realized the most acute pain was in his right shoulder.

Memory tumbled into place. He'd fallen from his horse after being shot. The fall explained why his entire body was so sore. He lifted his left hand, gingerly feeling the right side of his chest.

He was trussed up in a thick layer of bandages. More recollection returned. The ghastly carriage ride . . . Lady Wexham . . . her hand upon his . . . the soft touch of her fingertips on his forehead . . . her whispered words of encouragement when he'd truly felt he was at the end.

He took in his surroundings, having no recollection of how he'd arrived back in his bed in London. It must be dawn by the dim light penetrating through the narrow window.

He wore only his small clothes. The light covers were drawn up to his chest. His mouth felt dry. He looked over to see if a pitcher of water had been left by his bed.

Excruciating pain shot through his shoulder at the movement. There was a pitcher of water and a glass on the table. As he debated trying to raise his right arm, there was a soft knock, and his door opened. William peered in. Seeing him awake, the footman entered, a smile splitting his face.

"How are you feeling? Lady Wexham wanted me to check on you first thing to make sure you were all right."

"I'm fine," he croaked. "Just some pain."

William felt his forehead. "A mite warm. The doctor said there could be fever. Would you like some water?"

He gave a bare nod. "Yes, please."

William propped his head up and touched the glass to his lips.

"Thanks. Just what I needed."

"How's the shoulder feel?"

He made a rueful sound. "As expected, I suppose. Did they get the ball out?"

"Yes, sir. I was here, helped the surgeon." He grinned. "The way he dug around in there, you're lucky you were passed out. But he found it, left it for a souvenir, he said." He nodded toward the table. "He says you should be all right as long as you stay put."

William pulled up the chair and sat down, his eyes bright with curiosity. "Jacob told us a band of brigands appeared from nowhere just alongside Stanmore Common after Bushey Heath. What do you remember?"

Rees rubbed a hand over his eyes. "Yes. They came upon us, took us unawares."

"Jacob said you spurred your horse and charged at them."

A sound of scorn issued from Rees's lips. "No . . . I had hoped to draw at least one or two away from the chaise to give Jacob a chance to outrun them. But it was a vain hope." He looked at William. "Did Jacob say anything more about it?"

William leaned forward. "One o' them searched the coach, and even demanded to search Lady Wexham herself! He said they were frogs, couldn't understand a word they said."

"Yes . . ." Rees did not elaborate. He hadn't been able to think about it, but now he wished to be alone to ponder it all. Where had they come from? Hartwell. He thought of Monsieur de la Roche.

Had he hired some thugs to go after Lady Wexham? What had he been looking for? It was definitely a specific item. What had she taken? He didn't remember if they had stolen any of Lady Wexham's valuables. He would have to ask her.

Would she come to see him? He feared and longed for it.

Céline waited as long as she could before going down to Mac-Kinnon's room. If she'd had her way, she would have been down at dawn—would have sat up the whole night with him. Thankfully, her sister-in-law was not in residence, so Céline did not have to dodge Agatha's acid remarks about any concern she showed for her temporary butler.

By nine o'clock she was standing outside MacKinnon's door. It was ajar, and she knocked softly.

"Come in." At the sound of his voice, a wave of relief swept through her, so vast she had to clutch the doorjamb a moment. His voice, though weak, sounded normal.

Her heart beating erratically, she pushed open the door and went in, unsure of what she'd see. He was half-propped up on a few pillows, the covers draped to midriff. The white bandages covered most of his bare chest, but she couldn't help but notice the wide set of his shoulders and his muscular biceps now that she was no longer fearing for his life. She wondered fleetingly what he did in his "real" life.

"Good morning," she said, her gaze drifting up to his, her lips curved upward in a tentative smile.

"Good morning, my lady." He attempted to sit up farther.

She hurried forward, pushing him gently back. "Please, don't disturb yourself. I just wanted to make sure you were comfortable."

Releasing him, warmth enveloping her cheeks, she stepped back and clasped her hands before her. "Has anyone been to see you this morning?"

"Yes . . . I've been well taken care of, thank you, my lady."

She noticed an empty bowl and spoon beside the pitcher and glass on the small table. "Good, I'm glad someone brought you breakfast." She cleared her throat. "How are you feeling?" No one had been to shave him, however. A dark stubble covered his cheeks and jaw, the same dark shade that sprinkled what was visible of his chest.

His mouth crooked upward on one side. "As well as can be expected, I suppose, for someone who had a surgeon 'digging around in there,' as William put it."

She returned the smile. For a few seconds, joy and light filled her after a night of darkness and recriminations. "Are you in very much pain?"

He shrugged and immediately winced. Suddenly they both laughed.

"Oh—that hurts," he said, his laughter breaking off.

She brought a hand to her mouth. "I'm sorry. I didn't mean to cause you more pain."

He shook his head. "It was worth the pain."

As he continued looking at her, she thought of their kiss. Was he thinking the same?

To mask her growing awareness of him lying there half-naked, his hair sleep tousled, she leaned forward, inspecting the bandaging. "I'm glad the wound hasn't reopened. The doctor said he would be by today to see how you fared. Perhaps some willow bark tea will help ease any discomfort."

"I'm sorry to be so much trouble. I'm sure in a few days I can be up again."

She drew back, sorry that his tone was once more that of a butler, his face a mask. She folded her hands in front of her and returned his look steadily. "Most certainly not. You are to be abed at least a fortnight."

His straight dark eyebrows drew together. "I'm sure that's not necessary. It's a mere flesh wound."

"Are you questioning Mr. Simmons's treatment? I'll have you know

leave so soon. She'd have little reason to visit him
the surgeon arrived.

She picked up the black, leather-bound
It was a Bible. "Perhaps you'd like so
the hours."

"Don't trouble yourself. I . . .
"Yes, I see." She rememb
the day before and smoot
"God was merciful to
They looked a
swered softly.
She sigh
have ma
sust

n
des
was
was
Valer

Hi
disput

She eyed his small table crammed with porridge bowl, book, water pitcher, and glass. "I shall have William bring you a larger table to place things at your reach, and perhaps a lap desk when you're up to it. Would you like some fresh water?"

"That's all right. I can pour it myself . . . or someone should be by in a bit . . ."

She shook her head at him. "Are you afraid I don't know how to pour a glass of water for an invalid?" At the startled look in his eyes at the reference to "invalid," she laughed. Picking up the glass, she took it to his washstand and dumped it out in the large bowl. Returning to his bedside, she refilled it from the pitcher. "Is this water fresh?"

"Yes, Virginia brought it this morning."

"Good." As she replaced the now full glass on the table within reach, she sought for something else to detain her. She didn't want to

...gain until perhaps

...book and flipped it open.

...e more books to while away

...have that Bible, as you see."

...red how fervently she'd prayed for him

...ned the cover with her palm, gazing at him.

...you."

...each other a few moments. "Yes, He was," he an-

...ed, feeling a sense of peace at his words. "But you shall

...ny hours to fill before you may get up. If this is all you have to

...in you, I fear you shall try to get up before you are able."

"It is my daily bread."

She considered his quiet, sure tone. The God he believed in and the one she had cried out to the day before sounded like two different entities. "Perhaps a few novels could serve as dessert then," she quipped.

"You sound like your late queen."

She raised her eyebrows then inclined her head in understanding, "Ah, 'let them eat cake.'" Satisfied at the glimmer of amusement in his gray eyes, she pressed her advantage. "Do not fear, Mr. MacKinnon, I shall give you nothing to injure your sensibilities or corrupt your morals. Perhaps some poems by Scott, edifying and entertaining at the same time." She paused. "In return, perhaps you can tell me about this God you feed upon daily."

His eyes scanned hers. "It . . . would be my pleasure."

Afraid of what he might read in her eyes, she looked down at her hands. "I prayed for you yesterday. I feared you wouldn't make it— you'd lost so much blood." She halted, finding it hard to continue. "I hadn't truly asked God for anything since . . . I lost someone dear to me." Slowly, reluctantly, she raised her eyes, meeting his once more. "God did not spare his life."

MacKinnon's regard did not waver. "I did not think He would have spared mine."

She swallowed painfully. "Yet He did."

"Perhaps He heard your prayer."

She shook her head, looking away, afraid he'd see the sheen of tears. "I don't know. There was no reason for Him to do so."

"Perhaps you could read me some of the Scriptures. It's difficult for me to hold a book right now."

"Of course." She rushed forward with the heavy Bible. "Where would you like me to read?"

"Ah . . . perhaps a psalm. I have much to be thankful for." As she sat down and opened the book, he said, "Psalm 103 is a good one of thanksgiving."

She flipped through the pages, remembering her studies at boarding school. Finally she found the indicated psalm and began to read the verses. "Bless the Lord, O my soul: and all that is within me, bless His holy name."

As she read the words, she marveled at their meaning. "Who healeth all thy diseases . . . the Lord is merciful and gracious, slow to anger, and plenteous in mercy . . . like as a father pitieth his children, so the Lord pitieth them that fear Him."

When she finished the psalm, she sat back, feeling a deep satisfaction. It had expressed what she hadn't been able to express in words.

"Thank you."

MacKinnon's words startled her. For a moment she had been alone . . . with her Lord and maker. "You are most welcome. You were correct; the words were very comforting," she ended, feeling her description inadequate.

"I have found everything I need in times of trouble or hardship, as well as in thanksgiving and joy, in that book."

Her gaze rose to his and she wondered if he were speaking to her or merely of himself. Was he alluding to the danger she found herself in? How easy it would be to confess all to him and ask for his help.

But what could he do? He was still in a vulnerable position. It would have to be she who protected him now.

With effort, she closed the Bible and set it back on the table. With a smile and brisker tone, she said, "I shall remember that. Now, my library is overflowing with reading material, so it would be no trouble for me to bring you a few novels and lighter fare."

"I have noticed your library." If he noted her deliberate change in topic, he made no sign. "Do you like to read? Or . . . was it the late earl?" He hesitated at the last question.

"Yes, I like to read very much. I must be one of Hookman's most assiduous patrons since I am always bringing home stacks of books."

He nodded, his gray eyes attentive.

Afraid he was tiring, she searched her mind for something to say before excusing herself, but instead he filled the silence. "Was anything of yours stolen yesterday?"

The horror of yesterday returned. "No, nothing," she said with a shake of her head. "I had no valuables to speak of," she added. "Valentine is bringing my jewelry case. I have sent a messenger this morning to warn them to travel better armed."

He nodded. The fingers of his left hand plucked at his blanket, and he looked away from her. "Was—did the scoundrel make it . . . very unpleasant for you . . . when he . . . er . . . searched . . . your person?"

He had asked her the same thing yesterday. Perhaps he didn't remember. She blushed once again, more at his obvious concern and the discreet way he was asking her than from the indignity of the act itself. "No . . . that is, he . . . behaved in a . . . a gentlemanly manner despite being a . . . brigand."

His eyes met hers as if to assure himself that she spoke the truth. "Good." The word was curt. "They were French."

Once again, he'd managed to throw her off balance. "Who?" she asked carefully, realizing MacKinnon had now had time to think about the holdup and its significance. She would have to tread carefully.

"The 'highwaymen.'" The way he said the word sounded as if he didn't believe they were.

She rubbed her chin, pretending to consider his statement. "Yes, yes, they were, weren't they?"

"Don't you find that odd?"

His scrutiny was relentless. Her pulse quickened, finding the trick of eluding his questions challenging and strangely exhilarating more than frightening. She pursed her lips, tilting her head as if giving his question more thought. "I don't know. There are so many émigrés about, many as poor as their fellow Englishmen. With the war, times are hard."

Finally, he nodded. "Yes, I suppose. So, you think they were merely highwaymen looking for valuables?"

She widened her eyes. "Why, yes, who else could they have been?"

"Someone from Hartwell House?"

She brought a hand to her mouth. "From Hartwell House? Could it be possible? You think someone would be so dastardly as to think he could get away with robbing my coach?" She shuddered. "Oh, it's infamous. The Comte would be so distressed over such a thing."

"Perhaps they didn't mean to rob you. Perhaps you have an enemy there."

She met his relentless gaze, realizing she could not treat him like an imbecile. He knew. Perhaps he even knew who had pursued her.

At her silence, he added, "I would imagine there is much intrigue in a place like Hartwell. It is, after all, a royal court."

"Yes," she whispered. Reminding herself that he could do nothing to protect her, and in fact, would probably do everything in his power to betray her, she finally stood and smoothed down her skirt. "I mustn't tire you. Try and get some more rest. I shall bring you the reading material from my library. Thank you for the Scripture."

"Perhaps you can read me another tomorrow."

She nodded, glad of another excuse to sit with him. "Yes, I should like that very much. Well, I shall leave you. Please, if you need anything, ring for a servant to attend you." She looked around, realizing he had no way of calling a servant. "I shall bring you a bell."

Aware of his gaze still on her, she left the room. If she were not careful, she would betray not only herself and the French cause but her friends. She must think of Gaspard and Valentine.

Rees sat looking after Lady Wexham, his heartbeat only gradually subsiding. Was it his imagination or was she as affected by his presence as he with hers? He shook his head. It couldn't be.

He remembered their earlier conversation. He didn't know what to believe. Did she really not suspect that the highwaymen had been sent from Hartwell? If she was lying, she was well practiced in the art.

He punched a fist at his bedcovers then immediately regretted the movement. Lady Wexham had told him not to get up. How was he to get word to Bunting? How soon before word of his accident reached someone at the Home Office? If he didn't show up soon, they would wonder what he was about. They would have to send someone, and that could prove more dangerous for him than bleeding from his wound.

His head fell back on the pillows, his thoughts in a coil. What was he to do? It was the worst possible time to be laid up. Someone else knew of Lady Wexham's role, and the French monarchists would perhaps be less forgiving than the British. Either way, all he could see in her future was a noose.

He glanced over at the Bible and remembered Lady Wexham's words. His heart contracted remembering how her voice had broken. Her words and emotions had seemed genuine. She had been afraid for him. Could she be that good an actress? Or did she care something about him? Enough to reach out to God?

Ignoring the stab of pain, he reached over and picked up his Bible. Only God could get them both out of this dangerous mess.

As he opened the book, already he looked forward to Lady Wexham's next visit when she would read the Scriptures to him again.

17

$\mathcal{V}$irginia informed Céline when the surgeon arrived—as she'd been instructed to. Céline made her way back downstairs, pausing at a mirror in the entry hall to glance at herself before proceeding down to the basement.

Her color seemed high. She patted her hair. She wore a flimsy lace cap over her dark curls. Did it make her look too matronly? She didn't think so. Her pale green morning gown enhanced her coloring. Adjusting the sheer muslin fichu around her neck, she finally turned away.

When had her appearance become so important in regard to MacKinnon?

She entered his room to the murmur of voices. The doctor was tying the new bandages around MacKinnon's shoulder and chest. Both Virginia and William stood behind the surgeon, watching the proceedings.

The doctor finished and stood back. "That should do for a day, if you don't go making any unnecessary movement." He glanced at the two servants, ignoring MacKinnon's thanks. "The two of you can take turns changing the dressing. Remember, keep it clean, sprinkle the wound liberally with the basilicum powder the way I showed you, and wrap it with fresh linens each day. If you see any change—if it reopens or looks putrid, send word. Think you can manage that?"

"Yes, sir," they murmured, Virginia bobbing a quick curtsy.

Céline moved into the room. "Good afternoon, Mr. Simmons, how is our hero?"

They all turned toward her. "Doing fine," he said, putting away the tin of powder in his bag. "As long as he behaves himself until the wound is good and closed."

Céline's gaze finally went to MacKinnon. She felt shy after her display of emotion earlier in the day. But he nodded to her. "We shall have to ensure that he does," she said, approaching the bed.

"I shall be on my way then, unless any of you have any other questions for me?" When the surgeon was satisfied that his instructions would be heeded, he shut his bag and turned to leave.

"William, please show Mr. Simmons out."

Before Céline could give any instructions to Virginia, the young maid curtsied to MacKinnon. "Is there anything I can get for you, sir? Gaspard made a batch of ham-filled pasties for our tea. I could fetch you some with a cup o' tea, if you'd like."

MacKinnon shook his head though he smiled at the girl. "No, thank you, Virginia. Perhaps in a little while."

She bobbed another curtsy. "I'll check in on you later then."

"You mustn't trouble yourself about me."

"Oh, no trouble at all, sir. I'll see you in a bit." With a quick glance at Céline, Virginia skirted around her and left.

Céline smiled at MacKinnon, though inwardly she experienced an unfamiliar annoyance with the young maid. "You'll have every house and kitchen maid fetching and carrying for you."

"They needn't," he said stiffly. "I'm not helpless."

She laughed. "What, and deny their pleasure?"

His eyes widened in what seemed genuine disbelief.

Her irritation at Virginia's solicitous manner dissolved. "Confess—you know how popular you are among the female servants."

"I know no such thing!"

She chuckled at his outrage. He truly seemed unaware of his allure.

"With all except Valentine, I suppose." Deciding to continue teasing him a little, she drew closer to his bedside. "Whatever did you do to earn such dislike from her?"

His eyebrows drew together. "I assure you, I have done nothing to her." But he was watchful now.

"Don't worry, it is probably nothing personal. She dislikes all British on principle. Your being handsome and aloof undoubtedly gained her immediate rancor. You didn't by chance spurn a flirtatious advance of hers?"

A flush covered his face and ran down his neck and shoulders, but he remained silent.

She let out a triumphant sigh even as she admired him for keeping silent. "I thought so. You must forgive her. She cannot help herself."

Settling herself in the chair, she couldn't resist drawing out more from him. The relief she felt at the doctor's optimistic report was enough to forget for a moment the dangers that still lurked. Resting her chin in her hands, she couldn't help running her gaze over the breadth of his bare shoulders. "Why haven't you married?" She narrowed her eyes, pretending suspicion. "Or are you a womanizer?"

His blazing eyes threw her aback. "I assure you, I am not!"

She smiled, his words mollifying her, and persuading her that perhaps his kiss had revealed his true feelings for her.

As soon as the words were out of his mouth, Rees realized Lady Wexham was teasing him, and once again he felt only the impropriety of their positions, particularly in his state of undress.

She continued to watch him, amusement dancing in her eyes, even as he remained silent. After a moment, she said, "Is she very pretty?"

"Who?" he answered more brusquely than normal, still irritated by her assumption that he would engage in flirting with the female servants.

Her lips curled upward though her eyes lost their humor. "Your sweetheart."

"I have no sweetheart." But he looked away, thinking of Jessamine.

"Now you are acting coy, Mr. MacKinnon."

He fiddled with his blanket. "I assure you, I am doing no such thing." Why was he denying his friendship with Jessamine?

"Well, then you are behaving as one who is not being wholly truthful. Are you secretly engaged?"

His gaze shot up to hers. "No—that is, I have not declared myself to . . . to any woman."

She arched a brow. "I am surprised. How old are you, Mr. MacKinnon?"

"One-and-thirty."

She gazed at him, a speculative look in her eyes. "Most men are married by your age."

"It takes money to set up a household," he said shortly.

"Oh, dear, I am sorry. Does it take so very much?" she asked softly.

A lot she would know about money. Immediately he remembered she and her mother had come from France impoverished émigrés. He grimaced, remembering her marriage at eighteen to a wealthy earl some thirty years her senior.

Glad for a reason to hold onto his anger, he added, "I am also supporting a mother and sister," then immediately became irate with himself for not being able to hold his tongue.

She looked down at her clasped hands. "Of course. I could help you, you know . . ."

His anger was real now. "I need no such assistance. I am quite able to manage for myself."

"Forgive me, I didn't mean to offend you."

He didn't know how to answer. Her sincere tone disarmed him.

"So, you have held off your own happiness for the sake of others."

"It has been no sacrifice."

He said nothing more—for how could he explain about Jessamine, when he himself no longer understood his own feelings? All he could think of at that moment was the kiss he had shared with Lady Wexham.

"I see."

Was she, too, thinking of their kiss? Or didn't she realize he had been the pirate who had ravished her lips?

Her next words dispelled any such thought. "You must bring her one Sunday when you are better. I should like to meet her."

How did she know . . . ? Was she clairvoyant, as well? He scrambled around for a reason. "Uh—that's not possible."

She lifted a graceful brow. "Why is that?"

"She lives . . . too far."

"Oh, dear, I'm sorry. I . . . I could pay her fare—please don't take offense."

"Th-thank you," he managed, making a valiant effort not to lose his temper again. Did she think it was only about money? "I—she could never accept that. It . . . it is not the expense. She . . . she dislikes travel."

"If I had a gentleman such as you, I would travel across Europe."

Gentleman. Is that how she saw him? She sounded as if she meant what she said. And the way she was looking at him, he could almost believe she meant him. Or . . . the thought crept in like an unpleasant odor, permeating everything . . . was she referring to someone dear to her? "Would you?"

"Once." It was said in so low a tone he almost missed it. She was no longer looking at him but down at her clasped hands.

She *had* meant someone else. He swallowed, not sure if he wanted to know more. He thought of her words earlier. Someone she had deeply loved had been taken from her. "Was he young and handsome?" He kept his tone light, part of his mind suspended to receive the answer, the other part working furiously. Who was he? Could it be possible there had been someone besides the late earl?

Had she met and fallen in love with a young Frenchman in Paris during her brief sojourn there?

His gaze hardened as he continued regarding her. Or, had she fallen in love with someone after she'd been married? Had she been unfaithful to the old earl? It happened all the time in her circles—and being French!

Her answer, when it finally came, startled him because he'd been so deep in conjecture. "Yes."

Rees struggled to remember his original question. So, Lady Wexham's lover had been young and handsome. He felt something shrivel up inside of him, some hope or ideal he'd harbored about her. He made an effort to keep his tone detached. "What happened to him?"

"He died." The words confirmed what she'd mentioned in the morning. She had lost someone she'd loved—a man. Their impact on Rees was all the more devastating because of their simplicity. All anger and suspicion fled and only a profound sadness remained, as if he shared her grief.

Had she been only seventeen? Or, had it been a forbidden love while caught in a loveless marriage? He wanted to know who had captured her heart.

"He was a French soldier."

She'd caught him off guard again. Before he could think what to say, she offered more details. "It was during the Peace of Amiens. My mother had wanted to return to France . . . to try and reclaim our family's lands." She laughed dryly. "Needless to say, she didn't get very far. She was sorely disappointed in all she found there."

So, his first supposition had been correct. Impatient now to hear about the young recruit, Rees tried to figure out how to maneuver the conversation back to him, but he needn't have feared.

"When I met him, he was but a cadet in the military academy, but when I left France, he'd received his first commission as a *sous-lieutenant*—I believe that's second lieutenant in your army—and joined a division of the light infantry."

Rees waited, hardly breathing, for more.

"We fell in love." She spread her hands as if in appeal and gave a shaky laugh. "What else does one do at seventeen?"

"Fight." The words came out unbidden.

Her amber eyes regarded him a moment. "Like you and Stéphane."

Stéphane. He hated the name already. The next second, shame filled him for his pettiness.

"You and Stéphane, both fighting at the same time yet on different sides. If you had been in the army, perhaps you would have met on the battlefield . . . one of you killing the other." She shuddered, holding her arms together. "What a mad world we inhabit."

"A fallen one."

She took a deep breath as if leaving the past behind her. "You have a certain bearing of a military man . . . Stéphane had it too." She nodded her head slowly, as if seeing the resemblance.

They fell silent. What was she thinking? About Stéphane? The name was branded on Rees's memory, its syllables seared into his brain.

Or was she thinking of the things he had told her, detecting the fallacies in his story? From stable boy to navy midshipman to footman. Did she see how absurd the facts sounded? Or was she thinking solely of her lost cadet?

To distract her, he asked, "Why haven't you remarried?"

Instead of putting him in his place for his impertinence, she merely pursed her lips as if the thought was a distasteful one. "One marriage was enough."

She stood abruptly. "I have tired you enough for one day and had better leave you to your rest or Mr. Simmons will scold me. Do you need anything before I go?"

Clearly, the topic of marriage distressed her. He shook his head, still dazed by her revelations.

"Please ring your bell if you do," she said with a nod to the bell she had had one of the servants bring him earlier. "I shall bid you good afternoon for the present."

With a haste contrary to her previous lingering, she quickly turned and left the room.

The next afternoon, Céline used the excuse of bringing the books she had promised MacKinnon to go down to him again. Although she'd regretted telling him about Stéphane, something drew her back to his side. It was as if she couldn't keep away from him, like a moth drawn to its destruction.

No one except Valentine and her mother knew about Stéphane. Only Valentine knew about Stéphane's death.

She shook her head to shake aside the memories. It was only when MacKinnon had asked her why she had never remarried that she'd come back to her senses. He knew too much about her now, making her feel more vulnerable than she had since she was eighteen.

She turned instead to analyze his own words. She'd brooded over them for the rest of the day and evening.

A man truly in love didn't kiss another with the passion he had exhibited to her. Nor did lack of money stop a person head-over-heels in love . . . which meant Mr. MacKinnon had never been in love . . . which meant he wasn't in love with the young lady he stammered over. Her conclusion helped alleviate the terrible jealousy his words had caused her.

Despite her teasing tone with him, she did not see him as a man to toy with a lady's affections. He was much too serious and high-minded. He was also pious. No . . . the more she had thought it over, the more she doubted his attachment to the supposed young lady he was promised to. Had he fabricated the story? Or, was there indeed a young lady, but his affections were not so sure as he believed?

She approached his room, relieved to find the door open. The next second she frowned, hearing feminine giggles. She hastened toward the door, to find a pair of the kitchen maids standing beside his bed.

Pausing at the threshold, she frowned at the sight of them, chatting and laughing with MacKinnon.

They were acting like barmaids. Opening the door wider, Céline marched in. "Goodness, you sound as if you are having a party in here."

The maids whirled around, looking guilty.

Her annoyance dissolved at the sight of their faces. MacKinnon looked as worried as a boy caught with a forbidden sweetmeat.

The maids curtsied and moved away from the bed. "Beg pardon, my lady . . . we didn't mean to disturb anyone—" they spoke at the same time.

Céline waved aside their stammering excuses and walked farther into the room. "You needn't beg my pardon. You must beg Mr. Mac-Kinnon's if you were tiring him." She arched a brow at him. "Well, Mr. MacKinnon, must I send these young women about their business, or have I interrupted your fun?"

"No—no—you have interrupted nothing. They have merely been looking in on me—they were only here a few moments."

She almost laughed at his embarrassment. "You needn't worry on my account." She held up the books she carried in her arms. "I brought you the reading material I promised you."

The maids backed out of the room. "If you'll excuse us, my lady . . . ring if you need anything, Mr. MacKinnon . . ."

When they'd left, an awkward silence fell. Céline placed the books on the table, glad to see a larger one had replaced the smaller one. She turned back to MacKinnon, a smile in place, to see him watching her. "Good afternoon. How is your shoulder?"

"Better."

She eyed the bandaging. "Are you taking the laudanum at night or the willow bark?"

"The willow bark. It has helped. I should be able to get up soon."

"Don't speak such nonsense. You'll get up when the good surgeon gives you leave." Her attention returned to the table. The Bible had been supplemented by another volume. She picked it up and read the title. "*Rights of Man?*"

"I asked William to bring it from your library. I am merely attempting to understand your Revolution."

"*My* Revolution?"

"The French one."

"Ah." She didn't know what to think. Was he truly interested? Or merely trying to incriminate her more? "Then you must also read Voltaire and Rousseau. Have you done so?"

"No. I haven't had much opportunity to read in recent years." He added, "I read most during my years aboard ship, but it was not always easy to obtain books."

She nodded. "Well, I have brought you some lighter fare." She read the titles as she set the other books atop the ones on his table. "*Pride and Prejudice*—that just came out a few months ago, I'm sure you shall enjoy it—*The Absentee*, and *The Lady of the Lake* for some poetry. There, perhaps those will amuse you." *So you needn't depend on the housemaids.*

"Thank you, my lady, but it was really not necessary."

"Do you never read novels?"

"I am not in the habit of doing so."

"Well, you have really missed out on some wonderful stories. Here, let me introduce you." On the spur of the moment, she picked up one of the books and seated herself on the chair, opening the book on her lap.

"My lady, I beg of you, it's—"

She looked up from the book. "Yes?"

He worried the blanket between his fingers. "It's not proper."

She raised her eyebrows, pretending ignorance. "Whatever do you mean?"

He waved a hand in a gesture of helplessness. "You—here—in my chamber—"

She was touched by his sense of propriety. It only confirmed her good opinion of him. She widened her eyes and then smiled. "You mean because you are a man and I am a woman?"

"A *lady.*"

She bowed her head. "Thank you, sir. So, you think it not proper for the mistress of the house to look in on the man in her employ who took a bullet to defend her and almost lost his life in the process?"

She flattened the pages of the book, preparing to read. "Fie on those who judge it improper of me to sit by your bedside and read a little to distract you from the pain I have no doubt you are in."

He opened his mouth to speak, but no words came out.

She waved her hand toward the door. "You see the door is fully open. Anyone can enter at any moment. I see no impropriety." Before her butler could object any further, she began to read the opening chapter of *The Absentee*.

About an hour later, when Lady Wexham left his room, Rees didn't know whether to be comforted, amused, or insulted by her ladyship's strange behavior. Clearly, he was so beneath her notice as a man that she saw nothing inappropriate in sitting alone in his bedchamber reading to him.

He had to admit, he had found the reading material interesting. Her voice was clear and melodious, assuming amusing accents when reading the dialogue.

How he wished he could disdain her, keep her at arm's length. She was a traitor! His indignation disappeared as his gaze landed on the books on his table. Paine's *Rights of Man* was indeed giving him insight into the thought behind the revolutionaries.

Lady Wexham had promised to bring him the works of the great French thinkers of the past century. Despite his resistance, he found himself wanting to know her mind better and looked forward to reading what she brought him. If Lady Wexham was indeed a Jacobin, as he began to suspect more and more, he wanted to know her arguments.

Yet, with all the pleasure he had experienced in the past hour, he could not forget his fear and worry for her.

Whoever had attacked the coach and searched her person was not going to give up.

How could he protect her when he was lying in bed like an invalid?

Dear Lord, You sent me here for a purpose. Please help me to get up soon so I may be of use to Lady Wexham. Please keep her and those around her safe. Confound those who mean her harm.

When had Lady Wexham's safety and well-being become his number one objective—above his duty to his country?

18

Céline left MacKinnon's room and headed up the service stairs back to the main floor.

"With the butler again?"

Her sister-in-law stood at the top of the stairs, removing her gloves finger by finger. Agatha had only just arrived the previous afternoon and was already making her presence felt.

Ignoring her remark, Céline paused on the step. "I trust you had a pleasant round of morning calls."

"Yes." She began on the next glove. "Until I came back and heard that you were once again by your butler's bedside. It's indecent."

Céline struggled to keep her anger in check. "Listening to your abigail's tales?"

"If my abigail tells me such things, it is because they are all talking of it below stairs."

Céline moved past her, her mind considering what she must do about the servants. Have a talk with Mrs. Finlay or ignore their gossip? Saying anything would only aggravate matters. Servants would always gossip about their employers, but Céline was shaken with how quickly her visits to MacKinnon had become fodder for them.

Agatha moved out of her way but followed her as Céline made her way to the sitting room. "You are behaving in a manner unbefitting an earl's wife."

Céline said nothing until she had entered the room and shut the door behind them. She looked steadily at her sister-in-law, her tone calm. "Would you care to enlighten me as to what you mean?"

Agatha's gray-blue eyes so like the late earl's pierced her. "A lady of the house does not sit reading to her butler. It's disgraceful."

Céline struggled to keep her voice steady. "*Mr.* MacKinnon saved my life. I am merely doing what any human being would do to look after someone in her charge, and to whom she owes a great debt." She picked up her sewing basket and settled in a chair. "Now, if you will excuse me, I have things to do." Her fingers shook as she took the needle from her embroidery hoop.

"Someday you'll go too far!"

Céline stopped, her needle half in the linen. "I beg your pardon?"

An ugly flush colored Agatha's sallow cheeks. She lifted her chin. "I don't need to explain anything to you."

Feeling a desire to jab the thick needle at her sister-in-law, Céline poked it instead into the linen and took a deep breath. "Nor I to you."

The two stared at one another for a long moment. Finally, Agatha's lips stretched in a semblance of a smile. "As you wish."

The next moment her soft footfalls on the carpet and click of the door told Céline she was gone. The colorful embroidery threads swam before Céline's eyes. Agatha's words, no matter how mean-spirited, had shaken her. These past days she had been living for that scant hour of sitting beside MacKinnon's bedside, as if she were his nurse—or his wife—forgetting all that was around them.

Her embroidery hoop fell on her lap forgotten, as she allowed herself to wonder for a few moments at the feeling of companionableness and comfort she derived from sitting by MacKinnon's bedside, conversing and reading.

If she had met him in a drawing room, would she have given him a second look? Would he have noticed her? Would they have allowed themselves to get to know each other better, as she longed to do now?

Was it only some silly notion that he was beyond her reach that drew her?

She shook her head, bringing her hands to her temples, as if such movements could contain her thoughts.

It was time to wake from that illusion and face reality. Too much was at stake for her to pretend that things could be otherwise.

She sighed, setting aside the embroidery. She must see Roland.

Her sister-in-law would like nothing better than to discredit her and see her lose her place in society. Jealousy at the fortune the earl had left Céline was eating away at her. It mattered little how generous Céline had been to her.

If Agatha only knew how much more serious things were than merely carrying on with a servant. Too restless to sew, Céline rose and went to her desk. She eyed the pile of unanswered correspondence, bills, and invitations.

Since arriving home with the wounded MacKinnon, she had had no time or desire to attend to her mail, much less go out in society. The fewer people who knew she was back in London, the better.

She should be more concerned with her safety—and those of her compatriots—instead of going about like some debutante in the throes of calf-love.

She had known that kind of love once. Then she had been naive and innocent. Now she had no such defense.

She needed to make plans . . . plans if things should unravel quickly. She had not heard from Roland since getting the dispatches to him.

The watch called out the hour, half past two, then his voice receded as he made his way down the block. Rees stared at the dark ceiling, his concern growing with each passing day that he lay abed, not just over Lady Wexham's safety but about his own duty. It was now three days since he'd been shot, but he knew he could delay informing Bunting no longer. His legs felt shaky when he attempted standing. Gritting his teeth and ignoring the pull to his shoulder, he bent to put on a pair of breeches.

He had to stop and gulp some air until the wave of weakness passed before attempting the shirt. Gingerly, he lifted his arms to draw it over his head, praying the wound would not reopen. Imagining Lady Wexham's scolding, he couldn't help smiling. The smile vanished almost instantly as he remembered why he was risking such a thing.

He'd decided late that afternoon that he must go to Bunting's lodgings. It would mean a fair walk, but he saw no other recourse. He doubted he'd find a hackney at this hour.

Rees buttoned his coat as he considered what he would tell his contact. The attack on the coach and his own injury, obviously. But the masquerade and the man who had been shadowing Lady Wexham at Hartwell House? Whatever he divulged would immediately implicate Lady Wexham.

Dear Lord, he prayed as he'd been praying every day, *direct my words*.

He'd overestimated his strength. By the time he arrived at the end of the block, Rees was ready to collapse. Thankfully, there was a hackney stand at the next corner with one lone carriage and a driver slumped over in sleep.

Exhausted, holding his elbow to lessen the pressure on his shoulder, Rees arrived at the door of Bunting's address, a narrow house near the waterfront. It took some minutes and several knocks with the head of his walking stick before Bunting appeared. His nightcap askew, a dark dressing gown clutched over his nightshirt with one hand, Bunting widened his eyes at the sight of Rees. The next moment, he beckoned him in, closing the door quickly behind him.

"Good gracious, man, you look half dead. I've had someone posted outside Lady Wexham's house the last few days and heard you were wounded, but it was too chancy to get someone into the house to see you." As he spoke, he ushered Rees into the dark sitting room and began lighting a candle. "Sit down before you fall down. Are you sure you should be up?"

Rees collapsed into the wing chair, cradling his arm to ease the impact.

Bunting brought him a tumbler and stood over him as he swallowed the brandy, as if to make sure Rees drank it all down. "You look as pale as if they'd fished you out of the Thames after a week."

Feeling somewhat revived, Rees told Bunting, whose keen eyes never left his face, how he'd kept an eye on Lady Wexham as much as he'd been able, hampered by all the people surrounding her at Hartwell. He added that much of his evenings had been spent looking after Madame de Beaumont at her daughter's request.

"The whole place seems to be a mass of intrigue," he ended. "I spotted someone following Lady Wexham a few times, but it could have been for jealousy as much as anything else," he suggested. "She seemed to be a favorite of the Comte's, and of course, they are jockeying for position around him and his nephew, the Duc d'Angoulême."

Bunting nodded. "What else did you notice?"

"They are all waiting for Louis to be able to return to France and be crowned king." Rees paused.

Bunting scratched his unshaven chin, his eyes narrowed in consideration. "What about the gunshot?"

Rees breathed in, praying for the right words—how to be truthful, yet implicate Lady Wexham as little as possible.

"We were attacked by highwaymen around Bushey Heath. There were five of them, too many to outrun. They shot at us when I shouted to the coachman to go on. I was hit in the shoulder." He attempted a shrug then winced at the pain. "It didn't hit anything vital. The coachman was forced to stop. The brigands searched the carriage." His jaw hardened, remembering that they had searched Lady Wexham herself.

"What did they take?"

"Nothing that I know of. Lady Wexham wasn't carrying anything of value." At the man's raised eyebrow, he explained. "She had left a day or so ahead of her servants. The rest of her luggage was coming with her maid."

Bunting continued rubbing his chin. "Why did she travel on ahead?"

"I don't know. Perhaps she had an engagement in London she needed to return for." Would Bunting buy that?

Bunting shook his head slowly. "It doesn't make sense. Ladies don't travel without their maids or an entourage." He eyed Rees. "Tell me more about these highwaymen. What time of day was it?"

"Around three o'clock."

"In the afternoon? That's unusual in our times, to attack in broad daylight. And you say they found nothing of value on Lady Wexham?"

"No." Rees shifted, his shoulder beginning to throb, knowing he'd better confess the next thing before it became obvious he was withholding information. "They were speaking in French."

The man looked down at him a long moment. His features flickered in the candlelight, making him look like a ghoulish specter who could see into his very soul. "From Hartwell?"

"Possibly."

"Did you recognize any?"

"They were masked. There were so many servants—more on account of all the guests at the ball."

Bunting cocked a gray eyebrow. "The ball?"

Rees nodded slowly. "A masked ball, the night before we returned to London."

"How many guests would you say?"

"At least a hundred, possibly more."

"Anything out of the ordinary happen?"

He swallowed, fighting to keep his gaze steady. "Nothing extraordinary that I could see. Crowds milling about in disguise. It was difficult to distinguish who was who. The usual mischief people get up to at such events."

Rees hardly dared breathe as he watched Bunting's reaction. "Yes . . ." he murmured, considering. Then as if coming to a conclusion,

Bunting shook himself and focused on Rees once more. "You look ready to collapse. You'd best get yourself home and into bed."

"Yes." Grateful that the ordeal was over, Rees pushed himself off the chair, feeling light-headed for a few seconds. The sudden movement brought a sensation of moisture against the bandages.

"Here, take another drink if you want to make it back." Bunting splashed another finger of brandy into his glass.

Rees tipped his head back, downing the remainder. It helped clear his head and warmed his insides as he went back out into the cool night.

By the time he returned home, the bandaging was soaked. He kept a handkerchief pressed against it under his coat during the ride back to keep it from seeping into his shirt, but that, too, was beginning to feel wet beneath his fingertips when he alighted from the hackney.

When he entered the house, he shoved the bolt of the service entrance back in place, then staggered to his bedroom. He unbuttoned his coat with his left hand, struggled to take if off, then followed it with his waistcoat. Finally, he braced himself to pull his shirt over his head.

Dawn was beginning to tinge his room. He stared at the large red stain covering the upper right portion of his discarded shirt. What was he going to do about the bloody garments?

Looking around his room, his glance stopped at his basin and pitcher. Since he wouldn't be able to hide the evidence, he'd have to think of some reason he'd gotten up in the night and dressed. Perhaps it would be Tom or Virginia who came in the morning, and he could fob them off with some excuse.

He dropped the shirt and waistcoat into the basin and poured water from his pitcher into it, doing his best with his left hand, which slowed his efforts.

He eyed the bandage, deciding he wouldn't be able to remove it since it was tied too far from his reach to change single-handedly.

Sitting wearily on the bed, he managed to remove his shoes and stockings.

Finally, he was back in bed, with another handkerchief over the bandage.

Dear Lord, let it have stopped bleeding by the time someone comes by in the morning . . .

Which would be all too soon.

Valentine, who had been delayed a few days longer at Hartwell, had done nothing but complain since her arrival. Now, she tugged Céline's hair, her dark eyes meeting Céline's in the glass. "If you had not left in such haste, I would have been able to return sooner."

"But then you would not have been able to tell me what talk my abrupt departure caused." Among most guests, her departure had not aroused any suspicion, since so many had left for London the day after the ball.

Valentine sniffed. "A lot of good that did since de la Roche noticed. Perhaps if we had been with you, they would not have dared hold up your chaise."

Céline was tired of going around and around with Valentine. Her head hurt. Already Gaspard was consulting with Roland about what should be done now.

She was relieved by a soft knock on the door. "Come in."

Virginia peered into the room. "Beg pardon, my lady." Instead of her usual smile, the young maid seemed to hesitate at the threshold. "What is it?"

Virginia took a step into the boudoir. "It's Mr. MacKinnon, my lady."

Céline swiveled around on the stool, unmindful of Valentine's protest. "Is he all right?"

"I went to see him early this morning to bring him his breakfast—either one of the kitchen maids or I brings it to him, ma'am. It was my turn this morning."

"And?" She stood, her hands clenched at her side, unable to hide her impatience.

"His wound, my lady—"

Alarm choked off her breath.

"It's bleeding again. I thought you should know. He said it was nothing, but it didn't look good to me, his bandage is all red and it's soaked into his nightshirt—"

Céline hurried to the door. "Excuse me, Valentine, my hair shall have to wait—"

"But, madame, you cannot go like that—"

Céline was already in the corridor. "Did he say anything more to you?"

Virginia hurried to catch up with her. "No, my lady. Just that it must have opened in the night. I didn't wait but came right up. I thought you should know."

"You did right. Has Mr. Simmons been sent for?"

She shook her head. "No, I came straight up to you. The other servants don't even know. But I'll send a footman right away if you wish."

"Yes, do so." By the time she reached the service stairs, she was running. She pushed open MacKinnon's bedroom door as soon as she knocked, without waiting for permission to enter, and strode straight to his bed.

He was propped up in bed, his breakfast tray on his lap. His eyes widened at her appearance. "My lady—what—?"

She strode to his bedside, her focus on his bandages. "Virginia says your wound has reopened." Her maid had not exaggerated. A large stain, bright red still at its center, spread across the snowy cloth. More blood covered his bedding.

"She shouldn't have disturbed you. It's . . . it's nothing."

She placed a hand to her breast to steady her breathing. "When did this happen?"

"I—I don't know. I mean . . . I got up in the night—"

She frowned at him. "I told you to ring for help if you should need it."

His cheeks flushed and he made an uncertain movement with his hand. "I didn't think . . . didn't want to bother just for my personal . . . needs."

Ignoring his obvious embarrassment, she snapped, "It was clearly too soon to be up."

He began to move the tray off his lap.

She stopped him with a hand on his wrist. "No, you mustn't put any more strain on your shoulder. Mr. Simmons has been sent for."

"There's no need, I assure you."

She paid him no heed but removed the tray from his lap and then leaned over him, looking for the knot of his bandage.

"My lady, what are you doing?"

"Getting this off. I must staunch the bleeding."

He tried to resist her efforts but soon sat still, realizing no doubt she would not be deterred. Her fingers shook, worry clawing at her insides at the thought of how much blood he'd already lost. How could his wound have reopened so fully from just getting out of his bed?

"Goodness, why didn't you ring for someone sooner?" Dark blood edging the bandaging showed that his wound must have been bleeding much earlier in the night. She picked up his bell and ran to the doorway to ring it.

Tom appeared almost immediately, still chewing from his breakfast. "Get me some clean linens. Hurry!"

After a startled look toward MacKinnon, he snapped to attention. "Yes, my lady."

As soon as he left, she peeled the last bandage off carefully. As she had feared, the wound was still bleeding. She fought against the nausea that rose in her.

She went to MacKinnon's dresser and pulled open the top drawer. "Where do you keep your handkerchiefs?"

"Right there, my lady."

A neat stack lay in one corner. She pulled out as many as she could clutch in her hands and brought them to him. Gently, she placed a couple of them against the wound. "Hold these, please, while I hunt for something with which to tie them."

He smiled weakly. "I fear I have no petticoats you can tear into strips."

Her gaze was already searching about the room, but before she could find anything, Mrs. Finlay entered with a stack of linen. "Oh, dear me, Mr. MacKinnon." She tut-tutted, eyeing his wound with concern.

"I assure you, it must look worse than it is," he answered, but to Céline his voice sounded weak.

She was already rummaging through the linens her housekeeper had brought in. Touching MacKinnon's hand, she nudged it aside and removed the handkerchiefs. "Mrs. Finlay, could you please put these to soak before they're ruined?" As she covered the wound with the thicker squares of cloth, her gaze flickered to MacKinnon. "I shall have them replaced for you if they are."

His gray eyes looked into hers briefly before he said only, "There's no need."

She focused on her work, wrapping the long strips of bandaging around his shoulder, helping him to sit forward as she drew the bandage down over his back. When she was satisfied, she tied the last strip in a knot and straightened. "There, that should do until Simmons arrives."

She found him staring at her. "What is it?"

His gray eyes flickered away. "Nothing."

She remembered her loose hair and blushed. She pushed the long locks back over her shoulders. "Goodness, I rushed down so quickly, I forgot. Valentine had not finished with my toilette yet."

He cleared his throat. "You shouldn't have—"

Her lips tightened. "And leave you to bleed to death?"

"I thank you."

Only now that the immediate danger was past did she consider how warm his bare skin had felt under her fingertips.

She swallowed, feeling the room very small and intimate at that moment. To disguise her sense of awareness, she picked up one of the soiled bandages Mrs. Finlay had forgotten and took it to the washstand.

"Oh, dear." His washbasin was full. Frowning, she lifted the sodden shirt . . . and waistcoat. The water was red with blood. Her glance met his across the room. "Where did you go?"

His gaze shifted away. "Nowhere. I . . . I was just restless lying here so many days."

An exclamation of disbelief burst from her throat. "It has been but four days since you were shot. Were you mad?"

He swallowed, still not looking at her. Her eyes narrowed as she tried to decide what to make of his strange behavior.

"I realize I was foolish, but there is no major harm done. I do beg your pardon, as this probably means my convalescence shall be delayed a day or so more and I shan't be able to resume my full duties—"

She waved his words aside, anger rising within her. "Fie on your duties! You shall remain in your bed as long as the doctor orders. If I have to have both Tom and William tie you to the bedposts, I shall not hesitate."

The look of alarm in his eyes turned to amusement. "Seeing this cot has no bedposts, they shall find that order a bit difficult to carry out."

Once again, their gazes held. All she could think of was him as a man and how much he meant to her—whether or not he was in her household to spy on her. Tearing her gaze away, she set the bandage in the water and approached the bed once more. "But it has a sturdy set of iron rails," she ended dryly.

"I shall follow the doctor's orders to the letter," he promised meekly.

She sighed. "You had best finish your breakfast if you are to mend quickly. I can ring for more tea or coffee if yours has grown cold." Her words made her realize she didn't know what he drank for breakfast. "This is fine, thank you," he said softly.

She lifted the tray and replaced it on his lap, realizing how weak he must be with the loss of blood. "There you go." She released the tray.

His chest rose and fell inches from her fingertips.

"Thank you, my lady." His voice sounded strained. She told herself to move away. But before her limbs could obey her, her gaze fell to his mouth, then dropped lower until she detected the tiny white scar on his chin, reassuring her that it was indeed the same man who had displayed such passion the night of the masquerade.

With effort she straightened. "Well . . . I shall leave you to eat your breakfast."

She took a step away from the bed. "Please ring for someone to take the tray away as soon as you've finished so it won't be in your way. Mr. Simmons will be here shortly, I'm sure. Try to rest until he comes."

"Yes, my lady."

It was not until she was back upstairs, sitting before her mirror, Valentine once again in charge of her hair, that Céline was able to think more clearly about her butler's strange foray.

"Rushing off to a butler! If he bleeds to death, it is no more than he deserves—" Valentine's outraged tones washed over her, making little impact as Céline replayed MacKinnon's words in her mind.

Why had he gone out? And if he'd only gone out to stretch his legs and get a breath of fresh air, would it really have caused his wound to reopen?

Where had he gone? To his contact in the Home Office?

She must have Gaspard find out what Roland had decided. Time was growing short.

Rees sat looking at the empty doorway several minutes after Lady Wexham had left his room.

The pain in his shoulder receded as he thought over her visit. She'd rushed down from her bedchamber as if she'd just stepped from her bed. Her hair—that glorious, chestnut mane tumbling over her shoulders, tickling his chest as she'd leaned over him—he tightened his fist, longing to feel her hair between his fingers.

Had she believed his story? It was a flimsy one at best, all he could think of at the moment. She'd startled him so with her sudden appearance.

She'd seemed genuinely distressed over his wound. He shook his head, forgetting his own worry for the moment, at how she'd fretted over him, the way his own mother used to when he was a lad and arrived home battered or bruised.

Did she care about him so much? Would she show the same concern for any of her servants? Would she sit and read to them and share things about her past? Would she look at them the way she had him? His gut hurt from clenching it so hard to keep from grabbing her to discover if she would offer her lips to him willingly a second time. Did anyone have her heart? Or was he only one of her many admirers?

He'd never wanted a woman as he wanted her. It tormented him to think of anyone else enjoying her favor. Why this woman who was completely out of his reach, he asked, looking heavenward. He'd never known until now what it was to feel this passion, torment, need. He was poised over a precipice that had nothing but a rocky fall below.

Last night he'd taken the irrevocable step off the ledge by lying to Bunting. He had chosen to protect Lady Wexham over protecting his nation.

19

*C*éline finally met Roland that night. As she'd foreseen, he was pleased with the document she'd stolen from the Comte.

Roland and Gaspard both agreed she must leave England as soon as possible. Roland promised to make the necessary arrangements to smuggle her past the blockade into Normandy. He and Gaspard had agreed that only Valentine should accompany her. "Three French people traveling together would arouse suspicion."

"But what about Gaspard?" Would the British arrest him if he stayed behind?

"Do not worry," Roland told her. "He will travel a different route, farther down the coast."

Céline paced her private sitting room now, wishing for things that could not be. She had put in motion this move to France by agreeing to spy for her former country, and she had no one to blame but herself now if she no longer knew what she believed.

Valentine was overjoyed at leaving England. Gaspard had shrugged, saying it mattered little where he lived as long as he had freedom in his kitchen.

Céline's steps slowed, and she paused at her window, looking down at the narrow garden below. If this were her life a year ago, she would be making plans already to go into the country for the warmest summer months. Usually she visited several acquaintances, spending a few weeks at each country estate, before paying her obligatory visit to the new earl at his seat in Warwickshire. By August, she would be once again at Hartwell to look in on her mother, before heading to Scotland for the hunting season.

She tapped a finger against her lips. Perhaps . . . perhaps if she made her usual plans, pretending to travel north and westward into the country, when in reality she'd be making her way south to the coast.

It would buy them a little time perhaps—before it was discovered she'd crossed the Channel.

According to Roland's latest information, things would soon be coming to a head in France. Napoleon's days were numbered, although he seemed to be regrouping after his disastrous Russian campaign. But Wellington had made major advances into Spain, and Céline had no doubts from what she knew of him that he would not give up until he crossed the Pyrenees and was at the French border. How long would it drag on?

Roland had told her of the growing dissatisfaction and outright revolt in France against Napoleon. The French were tired of war; too many of the country's young men had died. The thousands upon thousands left to perish from cold in Russia had been the final insult. It was clear Napoleon cared very little how many of his people he sacrificed for his own glory.

Céline straightened her shoulders. It was time to return to her native land. A new government would be forming and she wished to have a say in its formation. It was time to put away foolish dreams of love and romance. She was no longer an ingénue.

She must travel while MacKinnon was still bedridden. He would soon be up and about, and she couldn't be sure how long her ruse would hold.

Her hand clutched the curtain. Yet, she couldn't just leave him. How could she tell him good-bye?

When she went down to his room with her book the next afternoon, she found him as usual sitting up in his bed with a book already on his lap.

With an effort, she smiled the way she usually did, pushing aside thoughts of her impending departure. "Good afternoon, Mr. Mac-Kinnon. How are you feeling today? No more nocturnal excursions?"

He had the grace to flush. "No, my lady, though I feel more than ready to get up from this bed."

Though she knew he was in no shape to leave his room again, she had told Gaspard about MacKinnon, and her chef had kept a watch on his door during the night.

She drew up the straight-back chair to MacKinnon's bedside and sat down, smoothing her gown. "Well, you have only yourself to blame if you are confined to it several days longer than we had hoped." She opened *The Absentee* to the place she had left off the day before. "Let us hope Mrs. Edgeworth will help take your mind off your restlessness."

After she'd read a chapter, she closed the book. He was watching her as she usually found when she read to him. "What were you reading when I came in?"

He glanced down at the book on his lap. "The first volume of Voltaire's *Philosophical Dictionary*."

Gratified with how much he was reading the books she had brought him, she cocked her head. "And how are you finding it?"

"Enlightening."

She returned the smile playing around his lips. "*Touché*. Seriously, Mr. MacKinnon, I would like your opinion."

His hands rested on the coverlet. "He is not the antireligious philosopher he is credited to be. He is merely against the injustices he perceives the established church, particularly that in France, has committed."

"Is the church any different anywhere?"

"Perhaps, perhaps not. It is made up of imperfect vessels. But even Voltaire never renounces a deity. He was merely against organized religion."

"Do you belong to a church?"

His gaze remained steady on hers. "I belong to the body of Christ."

"The difference being?"

He fingered the edges of the book in his lap. "The body of Christ is what He left behind. It is composed of those who choose to accept His deity and to follow Him and His call to 'make disciples of all men.'"

"Do you consider yourself a disciple?"

"Yes."

How she wanted to ask him why he was involved in spying. How could he reconcile the two, a man of God with a spy?

She inspected her buffed fingernails. "So your actions are exemplary and open to inspection?"

Once again, she detected a deepening of color along his jawline. "I consider my actions open to the Lord's inspection. If I do wrong, I trust that He will convict me by His Spirit, and grant me the grace to renounce whatever is not to His glory."

"You put the rest of us to shame, sir."

"It is not a matter of shame. It is a matter of life and death."

She arched her eyebrows. "Are you trying to fill me with fear?"

"Not at all, my lady. I have lived long enough to know that anything that is not in Christ leads to death—whether physical or spiritual makes little matter. My life only has meaning when I am walking with Him."

"So all of man's struggle for freedom"—she motioned to the book in his lap—"is all meaningless and futile if it is not dictated by Christ?"

"That is so." His tone was quiet, robbing her of an immediate rejoinder.

"You seem very certain of yourself and your ideas."

"Perhaps because they have been tested in my life." His gray eyes looked intently into hers.

Her eyes traveled down to his chin and the tiny scar that was not visible from where she sat and then farther down to his muscular chest and arms. He had another scar, a longer one on the lower left side of his torso, like the slash of a sword. What ordeals had he been forced to endure?

She would never know now. She cleared her throat softly. "By the bye, Mr. MacKinnon, I meant to mention to you that I shall be giving a small dinner party tomorrow."

"I should be up—"

She held up a hand, cutting off his words. "You most certainly will not. Not until Mr. Simmons pronounces you fit to do so.

"No," she continued when he fell silent, "this will be a very small affair. Tom and William will be quite able to handle it. I merely mentioned it to you so that you would be aware of my plans and not fret yourself that you will not be supervising things."

She moistened her lips, preparing for the heart of the matter. "It will be composed of a select group, individuals I have known for a long time . . . the Duc d'Angoulême and the Duc de Berry, who I believe are back in London from Hartwell, and Lord Castlereagh and Lord Bathurst and their spouses, of course."

She closed her book and stood. Let him ponder those names. "Well, I hope I haven't tired you overmuch. Don't tax yourself with too much Voltaire."

His smile was brief, but his eyes looked thoughtful. "No, I shan't. Thank you for reading to me. You really should not take time from your schedule."

She ignored his words. "I will look in on you again tomorrow. Have a pleasant afternoon." She would not give up any moment of his company.

Rees rested his head back against his pillows, his thoughts troubled. In the last week, he'd gone from frustrated to impatient to ultimately resigned to his bedridden state.

But the news that Lady Wexham was hosting a dinner party with the guests she had named filled him with deep foreboding. He had to find a way to discover what she intended.

He thumped his fist against the bed. If only he weren't still bed-ridden! He couldn't risk reopening his wound and being laid up even longer.

How could she take such risks? She must know that the holdup of her carriage had to do with her spying and not with a band of highwaymen looking for jewels and money.

Didn't she know the danger she was in? He was barely able to keep back his information from Bunting, risking his own integrity, his duty—his very future—but clearly there was someone else aware of her clandestine activities, someone who would not hesitate to use force to stop her. Monsieur de la Roche's chilling words came back to him. *If she should prove detrimental, she will be stopped.*

He closed his eyes. *Dear Lord, please protect her. She doesn't realize what she's doing. Have mercy on her. Show me what I can do. What would You have me do? I have a duty to my country . . . yet, I—*

He paused, opening his eyes and staring across the room yet seeing nothing but Lady Wexham's face, her smiling brown eyes. *I cannot bear the thought of any harm befalling her.*

He dropped his head into his hands, seeing no way out. He knew he must trust God in this. God, who saw much beyond what he himself could see. Finally, he was able to whisper, "I trust You, Lord, with her life. Please guide her, keep her in the palm of Your hand."

Céline sat at her escritoire the evening of her dinner party. The guests wouldn't arrive for another half hour, but she was already dressed and coiffed by Valentine. Now, there remained only the most important detail.

She picked up her pen and dipped it into the inkwell.

When she had finished, she sprinkled it with pounce then shook off the excess.

Valentine entered at that moment. "Is everything ready?"

She nodded to her maid. "Yes, you may take it and give it to Gas-pard."

Valentine took the paper from her without a word and glanced at it. Seeing it was dry, she folded it once and placed it in the pocket of her apron, a grim smile on her face.

Céline frowned, not liking the glimmer of triumph in her maid's eyes. Of course, Valentine didn't know what the message contained. She thought only that Céline was throwing out a false lure to MacKinnon.

Céline stood and smoothed down her satin skirt. "How do I look?"

Valentine eyed her critically then gave a sharp nod. "Very well."

"I shall go to the drawing room then." She took a deep breath, feeling more nervous than she normally did before a dinner party. Perhaps because so much more was riding on this one. In a few hours she would know if her butler had taken the bait. Gone would be the fantasy of the past week.

As she walked down the hall to the drawing room, she tried to ignore the yearning in her breast for something that could not be. What if she had met MacKinnon under different circumstances? What if he was on her side, shared her sentiments about her country? She gave a bitter laugh. In short, what if he were not British, much less a veteran of its navy?

Once he heard the carriages arrive on the street, Rees snuffed out his lamp and stood by the narrow window, watching the dinner guests disembark.

As the hour advanced, and he calculated everyone was seated around the dining table, he got up several times from his bed and went into the hallway, walking to the stairwell when nobody else was about. But he didn't dare advance any farther, since the footmen and maids were still going up and down from the kitchen.

His shoulder hardly pained him. How he wished he could have convinced Lady Wexham to allow him to resume his duties of butler this evening. But she would have none of it.

Even with all she had to do before a dinner party, she had still looked in on him for a few minutes, admonishing him with a laugh to stay abed and not worry—as if she knew how hard it would be for him to comply.

She had looked resplendent in a gold-colored gown that brought out the golden highlights in her hair and eyes.

"And if Tom or William should spill some soup on a count or minister, well . . . I shall simply smile and distract the guest from the discomfort of a wet waistcoat or pantaloons."

Looking into her golden eyes, he was quite certain she would succeed. What man could withstand the power of her smile?

How he wanted to dislike her—to condemn her for what she was doing! But he could not. Every day found him more and more entangled by her web of charm.

Hours later, he stood at his window again, this time watching each guest depart. The last to leave was the Duc de Berry. As the echoes of his carriage wheels faded, Rees turned away from the window and went to his door. He opened it a crack and left it ajar.

He made his way back to his bed, prepared to wait, for he knew not what, but most likely for the sound of someone leaving the house. He had not dressed but sat in his nightshirt and dressing gown. It was futile to attempt to follow anyone if indeed anyone were to leave this night, but he did want to find out if anyone were to go skulking about.

He fought drowsiness since he'd slept little the previous night, frustrated with his immobility.

To pass the time, he went over this week he'd spent bedridden. Despite the pain and discomfort of a bullet wound and the frustration of being out of service, he would not trade this time for anything.

He thought over every moment with Lady Wexham, every expression on her face, every nuance of every word spoken. It had been a magical interlude—one he knew could not last. Soon he must carry on his work for his country—and she? What had she been planning since her encounter with the masked men from Hartwell?

Each afternoon he had looked forward to that hour when she descended from above stairs to his room in the basement and sat reading and conversing with him. For that time, he could pretend they were two equals who enjoyed each others' company to the exclusion of anyone or anything else.

He tried not to think of the future.

What would happen to . . . Céline? He had not dared think of her as anything but Lady Wexham, but tonight, tense as he was about the danger she was in, he dared enunciate the syllables to himself. "Céline," he whispered in the dark. A beautiful, feminine name for a beautiful, passionate woman. He imagined what it would be like to whisper it to her in the dark, against her neck, her hair tumbling around them both, as he breathed in the essence of her.

Something sounded in the hallway. Rees stiffened, his fantasies evaporating, every sense alert.

It came again, this time the sound of a door closing. He'd almost missed it, so intent was he on thoughts of Lady Wexham. It was back to Lady Wexham—and his reason for being in her household.

Footsteps echoed down the corridor from the back of the house—it must be Gaspard's room—and passed in front of his door. They continued on to the service entrance, pausing only once.

As soon as they'd passed by, Rees hurried to the door. He pushed it open a few inches more and looked, but the person was already out of sight around the corner.

He heard the bolt being drawn back, so he went to the window.

A dark, cloaked figure walked up the steps, pausing and looking about him. Then he reached the street, looked up and down before heading quickly down the pavement—the same way Valentine had the night Rees had followed her.

But he was certain it was not a female tonight. The figure was too large to be either Lady Wexham or Valentine. Rees rubbed his finger across his chin, thinking. The most likely person was Gaspard. The only way to know for certain was to go to his room.

Making up his mind, he spun around and headed back to the corridor.

When he arrived at the chef's door, Rees grasped the knob and put his ear to the panels. Silence met him. He turned the knob and paused again before pushing the door open an inch. Holding his breath and straining his ears, he still heard nothing. He dared push the door open fully. Silence greeted him.

He walked slowly forward, his eyes already accustomed to the dark. If the room were indeed unoccupied, he would go back and retrieve a candle.

He arrived at the bed, remembering the room's layout from his previous search. He felt around it; it was empty as he expected but still warm from recent occupation.

Rees returned quickly to his own room, lit a taper, and walked back to the chef's room. He closed the door behind him and used the taper to light a lamp then blew out the taper. He doubted Gaspard would be back anytime soon, so he wasn't afraid of the light.

He didn't know what he expected to find in the room. If there was anything, Gaspard would surely have taken it with him tonight.

He began a methodical search, beginning with the area by the bed. There were no more scraps of paper under it. He shook out the clothes piled on a chair by the bed and tried to lay them back down as he had found them, continued on through the stacks of French newspapers then to the cookbooks atop the chest of drawers. Once again, a few folded recipes fell out. He refolded them to place them back, then paused, his fingers on one that looked more recent. The paper looked new.

33.41.21.72.83.55.65.61.21.17.89.25.41.512.74.512.74 . . .

Rees's hands began to shake. There were two rows of numbers. The series looked just like the encoded messages their undercover operatives stole from French couriers on the Continent. Many contained messages from Napoleon himself to his marshals in the field.

Rees had seen enough of these ciphers in his work as junior clerk in the Foreign Office. It was his job to break them.

He placed the folded paper in his breast pocket.

Here, at last, was irrefutable proof of Lady Wexham's treasonous activities. With this, she and Gaspard could hang.

Giving the room one last glance to ensure that he was leaving it the way he had found it, he blew out the lamp after relighting his taper and made his way out of the room.

When he returned to his own room and lit a lamp, he got back into bed and unfolded the ciphered message. As he did so, a thought occurred to him. Gaspard's room had not been locked.

He pondered this a moment but came to no conclusions, not knowing if the locked door the previous time had been out of the ordinary or not. Perhaps in his rush to leave for his rendezvous, Gaspard had neglected to lock it.

He turned his attention to the more important matter of deciphering the message. Praying for wisdom, he studied the numbers.

The various combinations of numbers stood for letters. All he needed was to find a pattern.

Reaching over to the table Lady Wexham had been so kind as to provide him, he took a pencil and piece of paper and began to write, playing around with the ciphers to see if there were any rhyme or reason to them.

20

Céline looked up at Gaspard, who stood beside her desk in her private sitting room, bracing herself for what she knew was to come. "You are certain?"

Gaspard snorted in his Gallic way. "*Mais oui!* The paper is gone. I noticed a few other things moved as well, though he left little trace. But I made sure to arrange things in such a way so I would know if anyone had been in my room."

She sighed. "It could have been no one else in the household, could it?"

His lips flattened, his dark eyes looking at her as if in pity. "You are letting your heart deceive you."

Her cheeks colored. Was she becoming that transparent?

He touched her cheek with his calloused thumb. "Never fear. You have done nothing so *terrible*, but it's perhaps time to put an end to it, *non?*"

She lifted her gaze to meet his once again. Like Valentine, he had been with her since she was seventeen, and many times acted as the father she lost so young. "What do you mean?"

He gestured with his chin to the upholstered chair against the wall.

"Of course, please take a seat."

When he sat facing her, his hands folded atop his white apron, he explained. "Roland has fixed it for two days' hence."

She swallowed, knowing he referred to their departure. She had been expecting the news any day, yet the prospect filled her with sorrow. "Tell me."

"You must prepare everything as you said."

Roland had approved her plan of leaving for their annual country visits. She nodded. "Very well."

"I will travel with you as far as Deptford then head west."

His rough hand cupped her cheek lightly. "Do not worry, *ma petite*, I will see you in France."

Her eyes teared up. Would they all survive? "Please, do so."

He took a step back. "Have no fear. *Bien*, I shall leave you and begin my preparations to leave for the country."

"Very well."

"Remember, two days."

Céline stared at him, realizing her heart was not ready to leave.

Rees clenched and unclenched his hands, feeling at a crossroads. Even though he hadn't yet broken the code, his mind battled with what he was going to do with the slip of paper he'd found. At the moment, it lay under his mattress like a live coal, burning a hole through the ticking.

With it, he would condemn Lady Wexham as a traitor.

But what choice did he have?

At that moment, there was a knock on his door. He knew it was Lady Wexham, since it was the time she usually spent reading to him. He'd thought all morning about the visit, fearing and longing to see her all in one. "Come in."

She entered, looking as fresh and delightful as ever in a sprigged muslin gown of tiny blue flowers and matching ribbons at the waist and cuffs. Her hair was dressed simply, coiled about the back of her head in a loose knot, with soft tendrils escaping from it.

She paused a moment on the threshold, holding the book in her arm, a tentative smile on her lips. "Good afternoon. I'm not disturbing you, am I?"

He made a motion at his semi-prone state. "Very little, I'm sorry to say."

She approached his bed. "You must be patient a little longer." Her focus shifted to his shoulder. At least he was dressed today. "Has one of the footmen been in to change the dressing?"

"Yes, this morning."

"Good. Mr. Simmons will be by tomorrow, I believe?"

"Yes." He sensed a barrier between them today and wondered if it was all on his side. Had something come from Gaspard's late-night visit to wherever he'd gone? Had she received some bad news?

She took her accustomed seat and opened her book. "Well, let me begin. I need to finish soon."

"Yes, I'm hoping the surgeon will give me permission to get up and at least begin a few light duties about the house."

She blinked as if surprised at his words. "Oh yes, indeed. Of course there is no hurry about the tasks, but I do understand how bored you must be." She paused, her fingers pressing the pages open. "But I was actually thinking of another reason."

She was looking at him so strangely, a disquiet began to grow in him. "Yes, my lady?"

"I shall be leaving London."

Her words reverberated in the stillness. If time could be said to stand still, he imagined it must feel like this. "Leaving?" he could only echo.

She nodded slowly, her gaze fixed upon him. How he wished to be able to translate the meaning of her glance, but he had no way of knowing what she thought, could only imagine it was anything like his own thoughts.

"You . . . only just returned," he murmured.

"Yes, that is so. But summer approaches." She sighed. "I always leave the city before it becomes too hot." As she spoke, her words grew firmer as if she were recollecting what she was saying. "There are several friends who have invited me to visit. Then I shall spend the latter part of the summer with the new Earl of Wexham and his family. The country seat is at Warwickshire. Do you know it?"

"No." It sounded as if he were not to accompany her. Of course not. He was useless as a butler for the time being. It sounded, moreover, as if she were to be gone for the rest of the summer. His spirits plummeted. "Will you wish me to go there?" he couldn't keep himself from asking.

She moistened her lips, not quite meeting his gaze. "No, that is . . . not necessary. They have an excellent butler there."

So, it was over, this little interlude that was but a ripple in Lady Wexham's sea. He drew his focus away from her and stared at the wall across the foot of his bed. "You will close up the house here?"

"I shall leave the staff here, but they are free to have a holiday if they so wish. Lady Agatha usually spends the summer at the young earl's estate. Mrs. Finlay will most likely shut the house up when all have left for their own homes. She has a sister in Derbyshire she enjoys spending the months of July and August with. I will, of course, take Valentine and Gaspard with me."

"I see."

She hurried on. "Mr. Rumford should be well enough to resume his duties by the time I return. I shan't be back in London till well into the autumn. The hunting season begins in the north, you know."

He nodded, knowing nothing about it at all.

She opened the book, smoothing down the pages.

He spared her the uncomfortable chore of saying some trite nicety of how well he had filled in for the older man. "In truth, my—uncle is probably well enough now. I can write him if you wish—or I can stay on here a little while longer if Mrs. Finlay should require any help in closing up the house. It is wholly up to you." He was satisfied that the words were spoken calmly, as if the prospect of leaving or staying meant nothing to him. He was, after all, only a man masquerading as a butler who had known his assignment would be but a temporary one.

"Oh." She seemed at a loss for a second but quickly recovered. "That is most kind of you. You may write your uncle that he is to take his time there. I don't expect him to return until the autumn. Actually, he may await my instructions until then.

"As for you . . ." She showed the first signs of hesitation, biting her lip, her caramel eyes gazing at him, almost in supplication, but that must be purely fancy on his part. She was probably just wondering how to tactfully put an end to his employment.

"I can leave now if you wish." He forced the words out through stiff lips.

"Is that what you wish, Mr. MacKinnon?" The words were barely audible.

With them, she effectively turned the tables on him and tore down his defenses. There was no mockery in her gaze, only questioning.

When he said nothing, she moistened her lips again. "I don't . . . wish to keep you from your family. Or . . . from the young lady who holds your heart."

Jessamine. How distant his sister's friend seemed now. What had this lady done to him that he was ready to wreck his carefully constructed plans for the future for the sake of—what? Some rash dream that had no basis in reality, that could never be? "There . . . is . . . no young lady who holds my heart," he said in halting syllables.

"Th-there isn't?"

Did she sound relieved or disappointed?

She gave a slight laugh. "I could have sworn the other day it sounded as if you had a young lady waiting in the wings until you had saved up enough to marry her."

He swallowed, feeling as if something were obstructing his throat. "I—you misunderstood me." He rubbed a hand across his eyes, searching for an explanation that would sound satisfactory, when he knew there was no such thing.

"I . . . I meant that there is—*was*—a young lady with whom I . . . I *had* contemplated—I mean, if ever I thought of marrying anyone, she would have . . . been my choice, but . . . but . . ."

His words dribbled away as he removed the hand from his eyes and stared at her bleakly. What was he trying to say? Hopefully, she would not understand. He continued more firmly. "But, at the moment, I am not contemplating matrimony. My life is too uncertain."

She gazed solemnly at him, no teasing light at his stumbling words. "I . . . understand perfectly."

They stared at each other for another moment. Perhaps the only words that could be communicated to each other were to be silent ones.

She shook herself with a slight laugh. "Goodness, I must begin reading if we hope to finish the story before my departure. And, to answer your question, you are to stay here as long as you please until Mr. Simmons pronounces you fit enough to travel. And you are not to worry about resuming any duties."

She looked down at the book, her long dark lashes obscuring her eyes. "I wish to express all my gratitude for your service—"

"Please—my lady!" He held out an arm as if to fend off her words. "Please," he continued more gently when she fell silent in midsentence, "don't say it. I did what I had to do, no more."

She nodded slowly. Finally, with a long sigh, she took up the book and began reading.

Once night fell, Rees took out the coded message and pored over the ciphers again. He'd analyzed which numbers repeated themselves the most often. All he needed to do was find which vowels they corresponded to. What complicated it was not knowing what language it was in. He assumed French, but it could also be in English. Each had its own set of most-often-used letters. Another complication he had found when decoding messages was that the creator would use more than one combination of ciphers for the same vowel in order to make it harder to break.

Feeling restless and frustrated after a few hours, he got up.

He felt his shoulder wound was no longer in danger of reopening, especially if he were only walking around the house. After dressing in only his trousers and shirt, he opened his door a crack. The house was still, the servants retired to their rooms, and Lady Wexham and her sister-in-law out. He had seen them depart earlier in the carriage.

Lady Wexham had resumed her evening activities, so she was rarely at home until at least midnight.

He decided to continue searching her room. Perhaps it would yield a clue to unlocking the code.

Once he was inside her private sitting room, however, it proved more difficult than the first time to riffle through her personal belongings. This time, he knew the person . . . had held her in his arms . . .

No! He ruthlessly cut off the direction of his thoughts. He mustn't let any sentimental considerations sidetrack him now. Too much was at stake.

He focused on her escritoire, having to pick the lock. He dug through every cubbyhole, every drawer, but all he found were dressmakers' bills, quills, a few steel nib pens, a penknife, and piles of correspondence, all things he'd searched through once before.

He didn't know what he hoped to find; it was doubtful he'd find a key to the code, but perhaps there would be information about her impending departure. Was she leaving London to escape de la Roche?

He paused, his hands on the back of her desk chair, when he'd gone through everything. What stumped him was the absence of any correspondence about her departure. He would think she would have the invitations to the house parties she had mentioned. Perhaps she didn't need invitations—perhaps she went to the same houses every summer.

He closed and relocked the escritoire.

He proceeded to Lady Agatha's room. He wasn't sure why he bothered now. Didn't he have enough damning proof against Lady Wexham? What did her sister-in-law's business concern him? From all he'd observed of the two, they were like two strangers inhabiting the same house, each going her own way with rare exceptions, as this evening.

But perhaps her desk would yield some information about their travel plans for the summer.

Virginia had told him earlier that Lady Agatha's personal maid was laid up with a light cold so he knew he'd have her rooms to himself for a few hours.

He was surprised when he first entered her bedroom. It seemed at odds with her austere, disapproving personality. He stepped into a fanfare of lace and gilded furniture, striped wallpaper, plush carpets, paintings and statuettes of shepherdesses and mythological figures.

He made a cursory search of the room, because it didn't hold many pieces of furniture where things could be tucked away. Instead, he made his way to her sitting room next door. As with Lady Wexham's room, he began at her desk, the most likely place for information about their travel plans.

Her desk wasn't locked, and it contained similar things to Lady Wexham's, the main difference being more of everything. Stacks and stacks of old letters, tied in bundles with ribbons. She didn't seem to have thrown away anything. He riffled through one bundle with his thumb but decided against taking the time to untie it. Most of the tied stacks looked quite old by the color of the paper.

He came to a narrow locked drawer at the back, beneath the cubbyholes. He tried the other drawers, but they weren't locked. So he returned to that one and stuck in his skeleton key.

Sliding it open, he found only a notebook. He drew it out and flipped it open. A journal.

He read the first entry. It was dated a year ago. He saw by subsequent entries that she rarely missed a day. So, somewhere, he surmised, she probably had a whole set of journals detailing the minutiae of her life from getting fitted for a gown to visiting Lady So-and-So on such-and-such a day.

He flipped through the pages, stopping here and there to peruse an entry. The name Céline caught his eye.

Céline thinks she can get away with her presumptuous behavior. For too long she has been lording it over me. Ever since Geoffrey died, she behaves as if she were still a countess, when all she is is a penniless émigré. If not for my brother, she'd be working her fingers to the bone in a milliner's shop.

Instead, she parades around every event of the Season as if she is the first lady of fashion.

Well, she has had her day. I have finally hit upon the way to bring her low. It shan't be long now!

Rees frowned, wondering what her ominous words meant. He had sensed her antipathy toward Lady Wexham but had never imagined the extent of her resentment. He read further.

After this evening, everything will change. I managed to drop a hint in the viscount's ear. Ha! All I needed to mention was the word "spying" and I had his attention quick enough. They all think I'm nothing but an embittered old spinster. I showed him I know more of what's going on. The way they all fawn over her, it sickens me!

Castlereagh gave me his attention soon enough. Took me by the arm into a private room to inquire further.

All I did was drop enough hints that Céline is well placed to spy on both the English and French. Lord Castlereagh patted my hand, promising to investigate further. To leave it all in his capable hands.

Rees held the notebook in his hands, staring at the ladylike penmanship. So, it was her own sister-in-law who had betrayed Lady Wexham. He wondered if she had had any evidence of spying or had merely acted out of spite. He would hazard the latter had been the case.

He checked the date of the entry. March 2.

Only a couple of weeks later, Lord Oglethorpe had given Rees his assignment to go into Lady Wexham's household masquerading as a butler.

He scanned the remaining entries for mention of Céline's name, but there were few references involving Agatha's role in bringing her sister-in-law to the attention of the British foreign secretary. One or two expressed impatience that the British authorities had not yet exposed Lady Wexham as a traitor.

The more recent ones showed that Lady Agatha had questioned Lord Castlereagh and had been promised that things "were proceeding along the proper channels and not to trouble herself." She expressed resentment over being brushed aside. That entry was dated a fortnight ago . . . before his wound.

He closed the notebook and set it back in the drawer and relocked it. Little did Agatha know that it was he himself who would ultimately be the one responsible for exposing her sister-in-law—nor yet how reluctantly he would do it . . . *if* he would do it.

He closed the desk and stepped away from it, not liking the conclusions he was coming to.

How could he contemplate not carrying out his duty to his country?

Clearly Céline was in trouble.

The next day Céline looked around her room. Everything looked neat and tidy. There were no signs that she might never return to it. Sally and Virginia had already made up the bed and tidied the room. She touched the counterpane.

This room held few memories for her, unlike the earl's house she had vacated upon widowhood. She thought about all the times she had hoped to be carrying the earl's child, only to be disappointed time and again.

Her glance rose to the rest of the room, thinking of the three years within its walls. Much living that was only "existing" had occurred. Céline hadn't realized it herself until Roland had shown up and recruited her services . . . but more recently—and much more intensely—since Mr. MacKinnon had come into her life.

The fact that he was both enemy and lifesaver only added to the sensation. Would he betray her to the British? He hadn't . . . yet. But he was not her only enemy. She had not seen de la Roche, but even now, she felt his eyes upon her every time she left the house.

Gaspard was right. She had no time to lose—whether it was Mac-Kinnon or the Comte's agents who betrayed her, her life in England was no longer safe.

She picked up her reticule and gave herself one final inspection in the pier glass, not wishing to appear anything but her best when she left this house . . . this city of adoption.

She would not see MacKinnon again. She willed herself not to walk down the stairs to the basement. She had bid him adieu yesterday afternoon when she had finished reading him the novel.

They had parted as mere lady and servant. Gratitude, all politeness, a hint of indifference in his tone, which would have cut her to the quick if not for the memory of his searing kiss.

What secrets must you hide deep in your soul, my dear butler?

But it was not to be her lot to discover them.

There was a war to be fought, and a country to save.

With a final glance behind her, she lifted her arm in farewell and left her room.

She was leaving this morning.

Rees had only discovered it when he'd appeared at breakfast for the first time since his return from Hartwell. It had been an effort to continue forking up his food, his features schooled to reveal nothing but passing interest.

She had wasted no time since informing him yesterday of her departure. Besotted fool that he'd been, so distraught by her news, he'd not even thought to ask her the date of departure.

As soon as he'd finished breakfast, he returned to his room, fighting the hope that he would see Lady Wexham one last time before she left for her supposed sojourn in the country. More likely to France! All he'd been able to discover at breakfast was that she was headed for Somerset. He could have donned his butler uniform and stood in the entryway upstairs, but he did not want to bid her farewell in the company of others, as servant to lady.

But as the morning wore on, he heard no footsteps outside his door. He stood like a sentinel by his window, watching the post chaise draw up to the front of the house. Tom had told him she would not be taking her own carriage but leaving it for her sister-in-law, who would stay in London for a few more weeks before retiring herself to the country.

Tom and William loaded the corded trunks and other valises onto the boot of the yellow coach.

Still tiring easily, he finally turned back to his bed and continued working on the encoded scrap. He had little fear that anyone would knock on his door. The servants were too busy with Lady Wexham's departure.

He had dressed earlier with no aid, only leaving off his jacket. Thankfully, his wound, though still tender, was closing nicely. In the back of his mind had been the thought that he wanted to appear presentable if Lady Wexham should stop by his room before her departure.

But no one came.

He stared at the series of numbers. He had a few sheets of notepaper filled with possible letters replacing them, using the knowledge he had gained of patterns in previous ciphered codes he had studied.

He didn't know how much time had elapsed, perhaps an hour, when he heard voices in the street. He jumped off the bed and went back to the narrow window.

Lady Wexham stood outside, Valentine beside her.

He rubbed the back of his neck, observing Tom help Lady Wexham into the carriage then turn to assist Valentine. Gaspard already stood mounted on Lady Wexham's mare. She would not need Rees to protect her this time, he thought bitterly, remembering how useless he had been. Pray to God that the chef would prove more adequate.

Lady Wexham disappeared into the carriage without a backward glance.

She was departing his life as simply as she had entered it, with no fanfare, no warning of the effect upon him.

He should be glad.

Instead, his worry only deepened. If she planned to flee to France, she might very well be heading to even greater danger. She didn't realize what the decades of war had done. Chaos was coming, if Bonaparte fell.

Wellington had advanced as far as Vitoria, Spain. It was only a matter of weeks—perhaps days—before he reached the French frontier. In the meantime, the Prussians and Austrians were closing in on Bonaparte's armies in Germany.

Would she look back one last time? He shook his head bitterly. The last thing he wanted was for her to see him like this—staring out the basement window like an unwanted dog being left behind when the master went on a journey.

But he couldn't tear himself away until the postilions climbed aboard the horses, one on the lead horse and one on one of the wheelers behind. The fact that she had hired two teams of horses meant speed was of the essence. Where was she going? France, Scotland, America? He had to know.

With a blow of the horn, the groom behind gave the signal and the horses were off.

Once the vehicle was out of sight and the sound of the wheels and hooves had faded from the street, Rees left his watch post and headed back to his cot.

He sat against his pillows, unseeing for long moments.

What now, Lord? Go back to the Home Office, end my assignment officially, and report to Oglethorpe at the Foreign Office? Tell them the countess has left the country?

Instead he felt a sudden urging to take up the note in his hand once more and continue working on it. He rubbed the edge between his thumb and forefinger. So far he had made little headway. Perhaps he'd lost his knack for discerning patterns.

But if the Lord was quickening him about it, perhaps he should ask for wisdom. *Dear Lord, if this is important, help me see what it means.*

With a renewed will, he studied the numbers.

And he knew what one of the words was.

About an hour later, he had cracked the code and read the message in French:

When you read this, I shall be gone. It was an unforgettable experience making your acquaintance, Mr. MacKinnon.

He stared at the letters. She'd known. All along she'd known.

She'd never by sign or word let on. Yet she'd let him continue his game. Why?

His thoughts jerked to a stop at the night of their kiss. Had she known then that he was the pirate?

She must have.

The realization filled him with fierce elation, hope—and fear. Fear of what it could all mean.

He read the message again. She had known the danger she was in.

France. The word formed instantly in his mind. He would bet his life she was headed across the Channel.

If there was any chance Lady Wexham had fled to France, Rees mustn't dawdle here conjecturing. He would go after her, he decided in that moment—if nothing else, to ensure that no one stopped her flight, his mind picturing de la Roche and Lady Agatha, even Castlereagh himself.

He stood, the paper crumpled in his fist, and went once more to the window. She had an hour's lead on him, and before he could leave, she'd have another hour. But a good horse was always faster than a coach-and-four.

He must think . . . plan. The closest port was Dover, but it was also one of the most heavily fortified against a French invasion and patrolled for smugglers.

If she were heading to one of the tiny harbors along the southern coast, it could be like looking for a needle in a haystack. But with a hired chaise and postilions, she would likely stop at all the posting houses on the Kent Road.

He gathered a few things for a journey and stuffed them in a satchel, his mind already on what he would say to the other servants. He'd ask Jacob for a horse—the fastest one available. And he'd arm himself. With his butler keys, he would select one of the late earl's fine pistols and get enough shot for the journey.

It would be the last liberty he'd take as Lady Wexham's butler.

21

$\mathcal{R}$ees crossed London Bridge into Southwark and took the road southeastward toward Dover. As he paid his fourpence at the first tollgate, he glanced behind him, realizing he was leaving London without letting anyone know. He had given Jacob the rather flimsy excuse that Lady Wexham had left something behind and he would endeavor to catch up with the carriage. No one knew he was heading southward.

Jacob had offered to go himself or send a footman, but Rees was adamant and silenced Jacob's protests over his gunshot wound with a sharp word, using his authority as butler for the final time.

He left the last houses behind him and rode through open fields with only an occasional inn or posting house along the way.

The journey gave him plenty of time to think. Going over all Lady Wexham had said and kept hidden since his gunshot wound, he marveled anew at her audacity. Knowing she housed a British spy under her very roof, yet she had not confronted him or dismissed him but befriended him! He shook his head. She'd even taken him to Hartwell—into the lion's den.

She must have suspected him since Valentine had found him outside Gaspard's room. He thought about the night he'd followed Valentine to the tavern. Had it all been a ruse? Likely.

Lady Wexham had proven one step ahead of him all the way.

Even her final move showed her cool head in the face of ever-growing peril. What a perfect way to disguise her escape to France. Make preparations for her usual sojourn to the countryside, where she did not reside in any one place but traveled all over for several weeks, even months.

News traveled slowly. Her servants here would have no reason to communicate with her or expect any news from her until the end of the summer. All they cared about would be making their own getaways to their various families.

Only Lady Agatha would remain for a short while in London, and likely would not suspect a thing until Lady Wexham did not appear at the earl's country seat sometime well into August.

Lady Wexham had covered her tracks well.

He frowned, wondering at the timing. Had Lady Wexham been warned of some impending action? Or was it merely that since the holdup on the road, she knew her time was limited? He had not spoken with Bunting since the night he'd dragged himself to his lodgings.

He sobered, knowing tonight he should have gone to report instead of running after her half-cocked.

At the third tollgate, he left Surrey and entered Kent, soon afterward reaching the town of Deptford. There he stopped at a posting house to refresh both his horse and himself, banking on the fact that if Lady Wexham were heading anywhere on the southeast coast of England, she would likely stop at the same posting house.

He hadn't been in the saddle since the gunshot, and after five miles, he was already sore. He rubbed his shoulder, his wound throbbing, and prayed it hadn't reopened.

He followed a stable lad who led his horse to a watering trough, then handed him an extra coin and asked if a post chaise had stopped there in the last few hours.

After receiving an affirmative for one carrying a single lady and her lady's maid, Rees remounted with renewed energy and will. She couldn't be too far ahead of him.

He spurred his horse on, hoping to overtake the chaise at Shooter's Hill. Many a carriage had a difficult time on the steep rise. But first were the miles of Blackheath. He pressed on past the farms and fields until the road began to climb. It was a well-traveled highway, so he passed several wagons, farm carts, and an occasional rider on their way to London. All of these would surely slow her chaise down.

As the incline grew sharper, he made out the dusty cloud of a carriage a mile or so ahead of him. He frowned, seeing no outriders. What had happened to Gaspard? The road entered a wood, so the carriage disappeared from his view.

He slowed his mount's pace, keeping well behind. By the time he arrived at the top, he had a good view of London and the Thames in the distance behind him. He peered forward but saw no signs of the coach ahead of him. It must have entered the next wooded stretch.

Hoping it was Lady Wexham's coach, Rees began his descent, wondering if they would stop somewhere for the night or change horses and ride all night to Dover.

Céline sat viewing the miles pass by the carriage window. In a day or two, depending on tide and weather, if all went well, she would be in France.

She had not been on her native soil since she was seventeen. What would it be like at eight-and-twenty, as a widowed countess? No longer the girl who had fallen in love with a handsome French lieutenant.

But perhaps just as foolish.

When and how she'd allowed herself to fall in love with a man whose identity she didn't even know . . . it was beyond belief.

"Regrets, madame?"

She turned to Valentine and attempted a smile. "Perhaps, but—no." She shook her head. "My life was useless, going from party to ball, before Roland contacted me."

"What will you do in France?"

"I don't know. I haven't had a chance to think about it."

Valentine knotted her thread and picked up her sewing in the swaying coach. "Roland will find you something to do."

Céline smiled. "And where will I flee when my life is once again in danger?"

Valentine shrugged. "You will not be in danger in France."

"You think not? And if the royalists come to power?"

"Bah! That fat old man? He can't even rule those parasites at Hartwell."

Wishing she had her maid's certainty, Céline fell silent. She didn't want to think of her future across the English Channel, not when she felt as if she had missed the present somewhere along the way . . . not while she felt so adrift.

With a mental shake, she smiled at Valentine. "And you, do you have any regrets leaving England?"

The Frenchwoman didn't hesitate. "That foggy island full of ignorant *bêtes*? *Certainement pas!*"

When they stopped at one of the posting houses, the postilion came up to her. "Are you up to riding through to Dover?"

She felt weary to the bone, and the prospect of jostling along on the rutted road for several more hours held little appeal, but Gaspard had urged her to push on.

"Yes, we must continue our journey."

Hours later, exhausted and dusty, Rees entered the village of Sittingbourne. As he followed the boy who came out to take his horse, he exchanged some pleasantries as he had at each stop, then handed him an extra coin with the question about a post chaise carrying a fine lady.

"A half hour or so ago," he replied promptly. "Changed horses and stopped for dinner then went on."

It wouldn't be long now. He had time for a quick meal in the taproom. He needed to keep up his strength.

He changed horses in Canterbury. Between tolls, tips, and arranging for the stabling of his horse, his expenses began to mount. Thankfully, he had recently been paid his wages. Lady Wexham had also added an extra amount, ignoring his protests, as compensation, she told him with a droll look in her golden eyes, for getting shot.

By the time Rees arrived at the last tollgate before Dover, he was hunched over his saddle in exhaustion. It was nearing midnight, but the sky had only just become fully dark a short while ago. He eyed the inn beside the tollgate with longing, wishing for nothing better than a bed to fall upon.

Instead, he dismounted and rang the bell to alert the toll guard.

As soon as the gate was opened, he pushed on, pausing only at the top of the hill overlooking the port. A few streetlights twinkled in the distance below him. He had ridden this road many years before on one of his leaves during his time in the navy.

He knew Lady Wexham had not broken her journey along the way. So, she was somewhere down there in one of Dover's six inns. Because it was wartime, the city didn't receive as many travelers as it had been accustomed to in peacetime. With the blockade, almost all traffic from the Continent had ceased.

He decided to head for the center of town and find an inn near the harbor. With a weary sigh, he nudged his horse forward, having to pick his way along the dark, rutted road.

He ended up at the Golden Lion. After seeing his horse stabled, he resisted the urge to lie on the inviting bed in the room he was shown. He made his way back down the stairs. The taproom still held a few drowsy patrons—some sailors, a couple of soldiers in uniform, and a local citizen or two.

The port was a garrison town as well as the headquarters for the preventives, the branch of customs officers in charge of patrolling the coastline. The worry that had been hovering under the surface throughout his journey, which had driven him onward despite weakness and fatigue, grew as he realized the risk Lady Wexham was taking if indeed she was leaving from Dover. And if Gaspard had left her, she and Valentine had no male escort.

She was in a town with a military barracks in the medieval castle on the cliffs to the north and another newly constructed barracks on the cliffs to the south. The harbor was filled with customhouse cutters and man-of-war ships.

She might as well have entered a pit of vipers. What was she thinking? She could have gone to a smaller village farther down the coast and had a better chance of getting across the Channel.

Rees left the inn and walked down the narrow, crooked streets toward the waterfront. A mist had risen and the few street lamps cast a glow but did little to illuminate beyond their small sphere.

It was a dark night. He had to find where Lady Wexham was staying. Would she lodge or leave tonight? It all depended on the tide, unless she was not sailing across. He knew some smugglers rowed the twenty miles in the "guinea boats," carrying the gold needed by Napoleon to finance his war—gold in exchange for the tons of goods smuggled across from the Continent, from hogsheads of brandy to bolts of lace and silk.

Rees heard the lapping of water against the beach before he arrived at the enclosed harbor. Very little was visible on the water, only a scarce light here and there marking the cabin of a vessel farther out in the bay.

He turned back and made his way to the most prominent hotel on the waterfront, the Ship Inn.

A clerk was dozing at the front desk. Rees slapped his hands on the desktop, causing the clerk to jump.

"Yes!" The man blinked groggily.

"Good evening. I have an urgent message for Lady Wexham. Is she a guest here?"

The man rubbed his eyes and yawned. "Lady Wexham? No one here by that name."

"A lady traveling with her abigail, a Frenchwoman.

The man shook his head. "No, no Frenchies here tonight."

Rees took a step back. "I must have been mistaken in my information. This is where she usually stays when in Dover. Pardon my disturbing your slumber. Good evening, sir."

Leaving the man staring at him openmouthed with another yawn, Rees backed out of the inn. Well, she wasn't at the most likely hotel for a lady of quality. Where could she be? Would it be better to wait until morning to make his inquiries? But she could be gone by then.

And if she wasn't? What did he hope to do if he found her? His brain too muddled with weariness to know what to do, he stood a moment in the silent street, debating.

Dear Lord, show me where she is. I've come this far . . . and I'm not really sure what I'm supposed to do. All I know is I want to see her again. I need to know she is all right.

After praying some moments more, he felt a calm in his spirit. Slowly, he turned around and headed for his own inn. If Lady Wexham departed in the night, he must trust to God to take care of her.

If she were still here in the morning, he must trust that the Lord would show him where she was.

Rees fell asleep as soon as his head hit the pillow and didn't arise until midmorning. He panicked when he saw how high the sun was in the sky, but he remembered his prayer of the night before. After a hearty breakfast, he emerged and began his hunt.

The day was a fine one, a light breeze blowing off the Channel— good for sailing across to France. He frowned at the sight of navy frigates, customs cutters, and a few English merchant ships filling the harbor.

He walked the length of the wharf, down the ropewalk to North Pier and all the way around the harbor to the other end to South Pier, two jetties protecting the harbor. Where would Lady Wexham find passage across the Channel? Two French persons would arouse immediate suspicion.

His next step was to inquire at every inn. Most likely she had gone to a smaller fishing village farther down the coast.

Smugglers would do anything for the right price.

He went methodically to each hostelry, choosing the most frequented and closest to the harbor first. After a brief refreshment at the inn, he braced himself to continue his search. If Lady Wexham was in Dover, he didn't think it would take too long to locate the party of two travelers, one of them with a noticeable French accent.

It was at the third inn that he stopped short on the threshold at the sound of a masculine French accent ahead of him.

"Yes, I am to meet a lady here. She is French by birth but sports an English title. Has she booked her room yet?"

"No, sir. No French lady here."

Rees drew back, recognizing Monsieur de la Roche from Hartwell House.

Rees exited the inn and crossed the street, wrapping his cloak more securely around himself. He found the alcove of another doorway where he could watch the Frenchman.

So, de la Roche was on Lady Wexham's trail as well. Rees waited until he came back out. He walked away and entered the next inn, one Rees had been to. Would the Frenchman discover that someone else had been inquiring after Lady Wexham?

Rees had to find her first.

He finally located her at the last inn, the smallest, meanest one on the western end of town. There was no one by Lady Wexham's name, but there was a guest, a lady by the name of Mrs. Avery, accompanied by a French maid.

He also inquired about the tide and was told it would be going out around two that night.

He spent most of the evening in the taproom, listening to the conversation around him. At one point, someone asked him what his business in Dover was. He replied that he was there to meet someone from one of the packet boats from Holland. They seemed to accept that.

Once it neared midnight, Rees armed himself and headed to the small inn. He posted himself in a nearby alcove where he could remain hidden and watch the entrance.

He hadn't been there more than half an hour when the two cloaked women exited. Even though their figures were hidden from him, he was sure the two were Lady Wexham and Valentine. They carried only a small valise each. Had their trunks been part of the ruse?

They kept to the shadows, heading west.

As Rees waited a moment to give them a lead, another shadow disengaged itself from a narrow alley and followed after them.

De la Roche. So, he, too, had located Lady Wexham.

Without thinking, Rees drew out his pistol and crept up behind the Frenchman.

Giving him no chance to react, Rees swung the butt with all his force against his head. De la Roche fell.

Rees dragged his body back down the dark alley.

Having nothing to bind him, Rees brought de la Roche to the end of the alley and left him in a garden shed, securing the door behind him.

Then he ran back out into the main street.

Afraid of being detected, he forced his steps to slow, guessing the two women were headed to Shakespeare Beach, a shingle beach just outside the town limits, the only possible location for a small craft to land. The road split, the higher road leading up to the cliffs just beneath the military garrison. Despite the cool sea air, he broke out in a sweat thinking of the risk they were taking—meeting a smuggler's boat right under the eyes of the sentinels above.

Leaving the last street lamps behind, Rees decided on the higher path. He'd spent much of the afternoon exploring the various roads leading out of town both east and west.

Refreshed from a good night's sleep, he was alert, every nerve on edge. His muscles still ached from his hard ride yesterday, but thankfully his wound was dry.

He arrived at the cliff overlooking the beach on the southwestern outskirts of the harbor and positioned himself flat on his belly just below the garrison.

The night was pitch black. He could not even make out his hand in front of him, could only hear the endless crashing and sucking sound of the surf on the pebbly beach below.

This cliff was low in comparison to the other, white-chalk cliffs distinguishing Dover. He had not seen the two figures again since leaving the inn. He could only guess they were down below on the beach.

Céline would need to be far from the coast by dawn. If they were spotted by a customhouse cutter . . . he didn't want to think of that.

Suddenly, he saw a small, blue flash. It lasted only an instant, then blackness enveloped everything once again. He could have imagined it, but he didn't think so. He knew what it was. The flash of a flintlock pistol without a barrel, an oft-used signal to alert smugglers on land that a boat was offshore ready to unload its cargo. Rees had spent enough time in the navy in the Channel patrolling for ships to know all the ways of smugglers.

He glanced over his shoulder. Would the sentries along the high ridge have spotted the flash? And if they did, what could he do?

He could only pray.

Training his eyes on the darkness below, he endeavored to make out a return signal from the beach. But he saw nothing. Likely they had a covered lantern, being so close to the garrison, whose light would only be visible an equally short time seaward.

Was that the sound of a boat scraping against the shingle beach? The tide was going out. He thought he made out the sound of footsteps upon the small pebbles, but it was lost in the sound of the incessant waves.

Then a thud like that of an oar against wood.

He kept glancing upward toward the Western Heights to the garrison for any sentries, who could quickly come down to his level by way of a special set of spiral stairs built inside a shaft leading to the road he was on. From there it would be a quick path down to the beach. If he had not stopped de la Roche, how easy it would have been for him to alert the soldiers.

His lips moved silently, continuing to pray.

But he heard no shouts, just the sloughing of the surf in and out upon the shore. He strained, thinking he heard the footsteps of a sentry on the ramparts above him, but only the sound of the waves came to him, one after the other in unbroken succession.

Many moments later, the emptiness in his heart told him Céline was gone. He gazed across the blackness, knowing on the other side of a narrow strait lay France. In about five hours, she would be there if their small boat was not detected by an English vessel.

From what he'd heard around the taproom earlier in the evening, the guinea boat rowers were swifter than the sails of the revenue men.

After a long while, Rees got to his knees, feeling stiff and cold. Slowly, he rose to his feet.

He didn't return to his inn. Instead, he walked back to the harbor and stood gazing across the water. As the sun made its way over the horizon, it promised to be another beautiful day. The breaking light cast a white, sparkling swathe over the silvery water. A milky mist lay over the farthest horizons, obscuring the coast of France.

Gradually, the sky lightened, becoming a pale blue, almost white. Rees breathed in deeply of the muted scent of brine upon the air. A gull screeched and wheeled overhead, coming in low then diving into the water.

Once he'd looked toward the sea with longing—for adventure and the sight of distant lands.

Now, he wished only for a home and the quiet of a shared hearth . . . the companionship of a bosom mate.

But that dream was forever out of his reach.

Would he ever see Céline again?

"Godspeed," he whispered to the breeze, then turned on his heel and left the harbor.

In the following days, Rees went about his business as if on a mission, schooling his thoughts and actions with military precision. It was not unlike the self-control he'd had to impose upon himself when he'd first run off to sea and realized, too late, how unromantic life aboard ship was going to be.

The first thing he did upon returning to Lady Wexham's townhouse was to apologize to Mrs. Finlay for having taken off so abruptly—explaining that Lady Wexham had forgotten something and he had gone off to take it to her.

At Mrs. Finlay's worry, he gave her vague assurances that he had managed to overtake the coach above Biggleswade and given her the item.

That night, after packing his things and leaving his room bare and tidy, he reported to Bunting and told him that Lady Wexham had left for France. Before Bunting could ask him why he hadn't let them know sooner, he explained that he had only discovered it at the last minute, laid up as he'd been, and had not had time even to send a message.

He said nothing of having followed Lady Wexham until she embarked for France, only that he had lost the trail in Dover.

He remained mute about the coded message, saying only that Lady Wexham had received a message that a family member in France was gravely ill.

Bunting pondered this. "You think it was only that?"

Rees waited a moment. Finally, he shrugged. "I don't know. I found no evidence that she was passing along state secrets. I think if there was any intrigue it was between her and Louis's court at Hartwell."

"That would be nothing surprising. There will be all kinds of factions jockeying for power once Napoleon falls."

At least he'd done his best to ensure that if and when the British allied armies invaded France, Lady Wexham would be seen as only another "faction," and not as a former traitor to the British crown.

"Another dead end then." Bunting sat back with a sigh. "Well, you had better report back to the Foreign Office. You'll do more good there."

Relief filled him that Bunting seemed satisfied with his report even as shame filled his heart. "Yes, sir."

The next morning, he went back to his old office, and after sitting through several minutes of Oglethorpe's monologue on the events transpiring on the world stage and his own exalted role and prospects, a silence fell.

Rees cleared his throat. "I was wondering if I might have a few days' leave, sir." At Oglethorpe's raised eyebrows, he added, "I have a personal matter that I must attend to."

"You know, Phillips, we are living in exciting times. If you want to move up, you cannot be going off whenever the fancy takes you."

Rees shifted in his chair, trying to hold his impatience in check. "I understand that, sir."

"Castlereagh is looking carefully at who will accompany him when he is finally able to enter France."

Rees's attention was caught. "Does he anticipate that soon?" Had there been some new information since he'd been on assignment in Lady Wexham's home?

Oglethorpe shrugged. "With Austria having declared war on France, for the first time Napoleon is facing all four allied powers at once. He cannot last. Moreover, the duke has not lost a battle since reentering Spain this spring. It is only a matter of time before Napoleon is defeated."

"But the Armistice—"

Oglethorpe laughed. "A tenuous thing at best. There will be a battle before the summer is over, is what I've heard."

What would become of Lady Wexham in a defeated France? Once again, he hoped his lie to Bunting would help to ensure her future security. "I understand, sir. However, with this . . . assignment, I have left many things pending. I only ask you leave to visit my family for a few days."

Oglethorpe drummed his fingers on his desk. "Very well. But be back Monday morning, bright and early."

After leaving his office, Rees journeyed to his mother's house. His next most difficult task, after deceiving Bunting, lay ahead.

He greeted his mother and sister, endeavoring to answer their questions as best he could, and enduring his sister's reproaches about his long absence. When she mentioned seeing him in London, he said only, "You must be mistaken. I was nowhere near London at the time." When she continued to insist, he stuck to his story.

Megan sighed impatiently. "Jessamine says she has received no letter from you in weeks."

"Yes, that is so. Where is she, by the way?"

"Home, I expect."

"Perhaps I shall call on her now."

His sister brightened. "An excellent idea. I shan't accompany you," she added with a sly smile.

His heart heavy, he walked to his neighbor's house.

When he was shown into their sitting room, Jessamine's mother smiled in greeting him. "Hello, Rees! We didn't know you were home. I haven't seen you in an age. Your mother tells me you are so busy what with the war. We thought when you left the navy, we would see you more often." She shook her head. "Dear me, but it seems you are even busier."

He returned her smile with difficulty. "Yes, it does seem so. That is why I begged leave from them for a couple of days so that I could . . . er . . . visit my family."

He turned to Jessamine as he spoke the last words, knowing she was the reason he was here.

His heart felt heavy at the words he knew he must speak. Her shy smile told him how glad she was to see him. It only increased his sorrow. Better if he'd never raised her hopes at all. "Hello, Jessamine. It is good to see you." She was a comely girl with dark brown hair, more ebony than Lady Wexham's, and green eyes—

He shook aside the comparison and forced himself to smile. "You're looking very well." He held her hands briefly then took a seat, feeling like the lowest scoundrel.

After exchanging some pleasantries with the two of them and asking about other family members, he asked permission of her mother to take Jessamine for a turn about the garden. Such a suggestion to be alone with Jessamine would only give them both the wrong impression, but he had to tell her and could see no other way to do so privately.

They walked in silence. It was midsummer, the smell of roses in the air. They reminded Rees of Lady Wexham. He shut out the memories with the ruthlessness of a soldier marching into battle.

"We've known each other quite a few years," he began.

"Yes," she replied with a smile in her voice, although he kept his focus on the ground.

"You were but a girl when my mother moved back to this area after she was widowed." Before she could say anything, he continued, "You've grown into a lovely young lady in the last year or so."

They both stopped as if by mutual accord, and he met her gaze then. It was open and honest. He read her regard—and hope—and felt like the worst blackguard for what he was about to destroy. "I know that . . . someday . . ." He cleared his throat, finding it hard to continue. He was not only destroying her happiness but also his own chance for love and companionship. But he pressed on. "Soon, I imagine, a young gentleman is going to come along and . . . and desire you for his wife."

The hope in her wide green eyes turned to puzzlement and then surprise and finally disappointment as his meaning dawned. Her chin lifted up a notch. He admired her for her bravery.

"I . . ." He wasn't sure what more to say. He looked down. "I thought . . . for a while that I might be that man." He drew in a breath, to give him the courage to look her in the eye as he destroyed her dreams. "But I am not that man."

She opened her mouth, but he hurried on to prevent her from exposing her own sentiments. He didn't want to embarrass or humiliate her in any way. He'd rather bear the burden himself. "I am not worthy of you. I know that I shall never find a woman superior to you, but . . . but I—that is, at this time in my life—my career . . ."

Before he could think how to go on, she reached out a hand and placed it on his arm, stopping his words as he searched for some good reason. "You needn't explain any further."

Her eyes were bright with unshed tears. They tore at him, making him feel worse.

"I'm sorry if . . . if I ever gave you any . . . any reason to hope . . ."

She shook her head, a tremulous smile on her lips. "No, no, don't trouble yourself. You were all that was correct and proper of a . . . an older brother and friend." Her voice began to break. He reached out, but she withdrew her hand and backed away from him.

"Ex-excuse me, please—" Turning from him, she ran away to the house.

He stood there, knowing he could do nothing to ease her pain.

Dear Lord, forgive me for hurting someone so dear. She doesn't deserve it. Was I wrong?

But deep in his spirit he knew it would have been more wrong to pretend to her something he didn't feel.

After knowing what love was, he could never violate the sanctity of marriage with something less.

He would return to London in the morning, back to the Foreign Office to resume his duties. Oglethorpe had said nothing of the promised promotion, and Rees would certainly not bring it up. After compromising his patriotic duty for the sake of a woman, he was grateful to have any job at all, even if it meant continuing in his role of junior clerk with no hope of advancing beyond the tedium of translating communiqués from the field.

One chapter of his life was over. Despite its brevity, it was one that would mark him forever. It was time to pick up the pieces of his former life.

22

AUGUST 1, 1814

Rees stood on the edges of the Green Park just south of Piccadilly. The night brought a relief from the August heat. He stopped and gazed at the lightened sky as the first fireworks erupted overhead.

All of London seemed to have crammed into the park and the surrounding streets to celebrate the victory.

Napoleon had abdicated in April and the allied armies had been occupying France since then.

In London, celebrations had been going on since June when the allied sovereigns had arrived. King William of Prussia, Czar Alexander of Russia, Marshall Blücher, and a host of other lesser dignitaries had been fêted by the Prince Regent. The crowds had lined the Kent Road to catch glimpses of the royalty from their coach windows.

Perhaps the most admired and courted had been the Duke of Wellington when he'd returned from Paris, the conquering war hero.

Hyde Park was turned into a fairground with booths, stalls, pavilions, balloon rides, and all kinds of entertainment for the crowds. Returning soldiers filled the streets.

Tonight marked the beginning of yet another month of celebrations. The Prince Regent had declared the centenary of the House of Hanover, the royal house that had been on the throne in Britain since George the

First. Today also marked the anniversary of the Battle of the Nile when Admiral Nelson had defeated Bonaparte's navy off the coast of Egypt.

Rees had been present at that battle, his first engagement as a young sailor, a lad of sixteen.

He watched the explosions go off now. Smoke covered the large Castle of Discord that had been erected in the park as colorful fireworks burst out over it.

The feat of pyrotechnics left him unmoved.

All summer long he'd been an observer of the pomp and circumstance. Although he'd fought in the war over a decade ago, and he was heartily glad it was finally over, he was not a participant of the peace celebrations. He felt like a traitor.

It had taken all his strength to go to work each morning and come back to his rooms at night.

As he stood watching, rockets shot up into the night sky, others broke into all kinds of colorful shapes—trees, ships, pinwheels, girandoles, rockets bursting out of rockets—all to fall in a fine rain of fire back to earth.

Dear Lord, what am I doing here? Our two countries are no longer at war. I must go there. I must find her. Even if there's no hope, I must see her.

He had tried to forget Lady Wexham. Instead, he still dreamed of her, even found himself speaking a thought aloud to her at times.

He rubbed his shoulder, which still pained him now and again, remembering her care of him. Had she forgotten him as easily as she would any servant who had briefly been in her household? Would she see his face and pass it by on the street?

He must discover.

How could he go to France? The thought thrilled and terrified him now that he had given it free rein.

He would go to Oglethorpe—he'd go to Lord Castlereagh himself—and request a position on the Duke of Wellington's staff in Paris.

With new hope in his breast and a lightened step, he turned away from the awestruck crowd and left the park.

23

PARIS, AUGUST 21, 1814

Céline closed the door behind her. With a weary sigh she faced the street. The day was waning, and pedestrians hurried by on their way home, many carrying their baguettes under their arms for the evening meal.

Coaches and carts rattled past on the uneven cobblestones.

Paris was very different from living in London, and after a year, Céline still had trouble accustoming herself at times. So many of Paris's streets were dim and narrow, making her feel more as if she lived in medieval times than at the start of a new century.

London had been vibrant and modern, expanding continually outward from its borders, while beyond the center of Paris, the city dwindled quickly into fields and small farms.

But that was neither here nor there. This was her city now, and she'd best be about her business before nightfall. She tightened her hold on the roll of papers she carried and made her way down the street.

"Lady Wexham!"

She stopped so quickly, a pedestrian bumped her from behind. After a hurried *pardonnez-moi*, she glanced beyond the people nearest her, searching for the male voice that had hailed her.

She hadn't been addressed by that name since leaving England. She could have sworn it sounded just like . . . like . . . she hardly dared utter his name.

Her eyes scanned the street as a jumble of thoughts of those last months in London went through her mind.

Her gaze was arrested by a gentleman standing across the street, as still as she, his eyes fixed on her as the people pushed past him.

She stared. MacKinnon? Could it truly be? The man resembled him in stature and broadness of shoulder, yet in nothing else. This gentleman looked just that—a gentleman beneath his high-crowned beaver. She tore her gaze from his and took in his appearance. Well-cut tailcoat and white cravat, fawn-colored pantaloons tucked into tall Hessians.

Feeling the pull of his eyes still on her, she met his gaze once more. Only MacKinnon looked at her with that intensity.

She waited, her heartbeat thudding like a kettledrum, as he crossed the street with barely a glance in either direction, like a man with a single-minded purpose. A moment later he stood before her, his gray eyes searching hers.

A kaleidoscope of emotions collided in her—disbelief, shock, longing, joy, wonder. MacKinnon here—why? How? Could it be?

She had never thought to see him again and had spent months attempting in vain to banish him from her thoughts only to be reminded by the merest sound or sight—a man's broad shoulders, a shade of gray, a certain stride or tone of voice.

And now, here he stood mere inches from her, looking so dashing, it quite robbed her of the ability to speak. She wanted to laugh at the thought of how passionately they had kissed and yet had never gotten beyond the formalities in their address.

"Is . . . is it truly you, Mr. MacKin—" She smiled slightly. "But that is not your name, is it? What am I to call you?"

His gray eyes flickered in acknowledgment. "No . . . it is not." His low voice grew firmer. "My name is Phillips, Rees Phillips."

She took the information in, trying to accustom herself to the unfamiliar name. Rees. She allowed the single syllable to linger in her mind, finding she liked it.

The color rose in her cheeks as he continued looking at her. He certainly must see a woman quite different from the one he had known in London.

"What are you doing here—?"

At the same instant, he said, "I tried to fi—"

They both stopped. She gestured for him to finish speaking.

"I arrived Monday last and have been searching for you since then." A smile glimmered in his eyes. "You have proven most elusive."

Natural caution returned. Why had he been looking for her? Was he sent by the British? Were they still after her? "One cannot be too careful," she parried.

A slight frown creased the space between his heavy dark eyebrows. "You are not still in danger, are you?"

She shrugged. "The Ultras in power now would silence all voices of opposition if they could."

His frown deepened. "It is not what Britain wants. That is why they have appointed Wellington as ambassador."

When she said nothing, he cleared his throat. "You left London so suddenly."

"I tried to tell you."

"With your coded message?"

She met his smiling eyes. "It was all I dared give you." She laughed, suddenly feeling happier than she had since arriving in Paris. "After all, you were spying on me. I had every confidence in your ability to decipher it."

He merely tipped his chin in acknowledgment.

She sobered, recalling those days. "I hadn't only my own safety to consider, but Gaspard's and Valentine's—and others."

"And I had my loyalties as well."

"Yes."

He shook his head ruefully. "I fear I made a very poor spy. All the time I was supposed to be spying on you, I was trying to protect you as well."

"From the highwaymen."

He nodded.

"I always wondered. And yet, I could never fully trust you. You were, after all, working for the other side."

"The British were not your only enemies, it seems."

She thought of de la Roche.

"When you left London, I did not think ever to see you again," he said softly.

The words sounded like those of a man . . . in love. Could he have any feelings left for her—a traitor to his country?

Her heart began to hammer as she told herself not to read too much into his tone. She moistened her lips. "Did you wish to?"

"Very much."

"Y-you said you were looking for me?"

He nodded. "I could only guess you were headed to France when you quitted London." He paused. "I deciphered your message shortly after your carriage departed. I followed you."

Her eyes widened. "To Dover?"

"I surmised you were heading for the coast."

She nodded slowly. He was an intelligent man, just as she'd always suspected. She knit her eyebrows, still marveling that he had followed her. "Did you find me?"

"At an inn." He paused. "And then a beach outside of town."

She drew in her breath. "You followed us that night—and didn't stop us?" she breathed, realization dawning.

A shadow crossed his features. "You were in grave danger. De la Roche was on your heels. France was the only place that was safe for you."

"De la Roche! I should have expected him. That is why I was told to leave England so quickly." She shook her head sadly. "Between the British and the French royalists, it was a wonder I am alive to tell the tale." She frowned. "How did you know about de la Roche?" Her mind went back to Hartwell House. "Wait—is that why—at Hartwell—" She stopped before blurting out about the kiss.

But he had followed her thoughts and nodded. "He began suspecting you at Hartwell. I overheard him talking with another gentleman. That's when I . . . I determined to keep an eye on you both and decided the night of the masquerade to go in costume."

They stared at each other, and she knew in that moment he, too, was remembering the kiss. "It took me most of the evening to discover who you were. You were very clever in your choice of costume."

She felt her cheeks grow warm at his gaze. "And you were the dashing corsair," she murmured.

When he said nothing of the kiss, she took it as indicative of his gentlemanly tact. "So, you were after me too, were you not?"

He didn't flinch. "I was placed in your household by the British government to . . ." He paused, as if seeking the right word.

"Spy on me?"

"To ascertain if you were passing on information to the French."

"I see." How she longed to throw herself in his arms. The next second she reined in her emotions. She still knew next to nothing about him. Was he married now? Why had he been searching for her? Her mind returned to that evening in Dover. "You saw de la Roche in Dover?"

"You left in the nick of time. I fear both the British and the French royalists were becoming very suspicious of your behavior. The shooting proved the danger you were in."

She shuddered, remembering. "I never meant to put your life in danger."

"It was not your responsibility. I was working for the British."

"Did Rumford take part in your masquerade? I must admit I could hardly believe it of him."

He nodded. "The Home Office convinced him it was his duty to find where your loyalties lay. Don't think too harshly of him. He was very torn, and refused to believe you would betray England."

She flushed, looking away. "Dear Mr. Rumford. I am sorry to have put him in that difficult position. Perhaps someday he will be able to forgive me." She sighed. "If I should ever be allowed to return to England."

"Would you want to?"

"I could hardly do so now, could I?"

"I expected to find you easily here in Paris. Your family is a prominent one, is it not? Yet, no one seems to know of you."

She smiled without humor. "I am not traveling in the first circles anymore since there is a new court at the Tuileries."

It was her first reference to her political allegiance and the present state of things in Paris. "Is everything all right? You are not in trouble, are you?"

She laughed then and shook her head. "Oh no. If I am not a leading lady of society, it is by choice."

His gaze traveled downward, and she wondered what conclusions he was drawing from her appearance, very plain compared to her gowns in London. "It seems I am keeping you from something."

She remembered the article. It must be delivered to the newspaper office by five o'clock. "I must go." Would she see him again? Did she want to? Was there any hope? It seemed she lived with so little hope these days. Did she want to resurrect the feelings he had stirred in her? Would it be fair to him? With an effort, she took a step away from him. "I . . . must go," she repeated.

As she began to walk away, he seemed to come alive. "Wait! I can take you. Where do you need to go?"

She blinked at him. "You are not on foot?"

He indicated a carriage parked across the street. "I was, when I thought I recognized you."

It appeared a fine-looking equipage. Everything seemed so topsy-turvy, it added to her confusion. She should be the one offering him transport. She lifted a brow, finding it hard to reconcile herself to the gentleman whom she had only known as a manservant. "A butler traveling by private carriage. How odd. But then you were never a butler, were you?"

His mouth tilted upward on one side. "No, my lady."

She smiled faintly. "And I am no longer Lady Wexham."

He lifted a dark eyebrow a fraction. "No?"

She held out her hand. "Just plain Céline de Beaumont."

He took her hand in a firm grip. "I am pleased to make your acquaintance." Then before she could remove her hand from his, he bowed over it. Her breath caught in her throat, thinking for a moment that he would kiss it in the French manner. But he straightened, letting her hand go, and she had to stifle the sense of disappointment.

He shrugged. "In any case, it is not my own carriage. It belongs to the British embassy. The Duke of Wellington has given me use of it."

She raised an eyebrow. "It seems your fortunes have risen if you are on such close terms with the duke."

"They have."

What was it she read in his eyes? Before she could analyze it, she reminded herself that he might be dangerous, if he was working so closely with the British embassy. "I must go—" Again, she forced herself to take a step away.

"Don't run away from me—please!"

She could not resist the plea in his voice. She turned around. "Who are you working for now, Mr. . . . Phillips?" She had to remind herself of his new name.

"I am still working for the British Foreign Office."

"Ah. I thought perhaps it was the Home Office when you were under my roof."

"I was on loan from the F.O. to the Home Office for the duration of my time at your residence." He cleared his throat lightly as if in embarrassment. "As for why I was searching for you—that was for . . . for personal reasons alone." A flush crept up his cheeks as he said the last, and her insides began to melt at that familiar sight. When had she grown to be able to read the telltale signs in his features from the merest flicker in his gray eyes to that heightened color along his jaw?

"Please, Lady Wex—Mademoiselle . . . Madame—" he fumbled in confusion.

"Mademoiselle de Beaumont," she supplied for him, placing a slight stress on her title of single woman.

"Mlle. de Beaumont," he repeated. "Please." He gestured to the awaiting carriage. "Won't you allow me to take you where you need to go? I promise you, I mean you no ill. I am no longer a spy. But I do not feel comfortable talking to you on the street."

She looked from the coach to him, weighing the risks. They were on her soil now. She might be in opposition to the government, but she was doing nothing illegal—yet.

The city had been crawling with British for a year now. If they had wanted her, they could have found her, she supposed. But what would they charge her with now after the peace?

More importantly, she asked herself as she gazed at Rees, did she want him to know anything about her present life, and she his?

"The war is over, you know." His soft voice penetrated her thoughts, as if guessing their direction. "No one is after you."

She gave him a bittersweet smile. "The royalists would silence me if they could." At his puzzled look, she shrugged her shoulders. "Very well, Mr. Phillips, I shall accept your offer."

They crossed the street, his hand lightly on her elbow. "Where can I drop you?"

She thought quickly. Better a public place. "Place St.-Germain-des-Prés, by the abbey."

Once he'd instructed the coachman, he reached into his inside coat pocket and pulled out a calling card case and extracted a card. Without a word, he extended it to her.

She took it from him. *Rees Phillips, British Delegation.* "You are with the Embassy?"

"Yes. I've been appointed to Wellington while he is ambassador here."

"From butler to diplomat. What did you do to merit that?"

A shadow crossed his features. "It's a long story, one which I should like to share with you if I may. But a rattling coach is no place for us to catch up with one another." His gaze fixed on her. "Would you do me the honor of dining with me this evening?"

"Before I reply, I think I should tell you I write for the opposition press." She lifted the roll she carried. "Your government might not approve of me."

His own eyes widened. "You write?"

"Under a pen name, C. de Valois. People assume it's a gentleman, but those who have the power to shut us down know very well who I am," she added bitterly.

He nodded thoughtfully. "That is why I had such trouble finding you." Instead of pursuing the topic, he repeated his invitation. "Will you honor me with your company at dinner this evening?"

She found herself yielding to the plea in his eyes. "Very well, Mr. Phillips. Where shall I meet you?"

"At the Palais Royale. I have been told there are several restaurants there. But please, let me fetch you in the carriage. It is not safe for a lady at night."

She acquiesced, though with a warning that it was somewhat different from her London residence.

They arrived at her destination, and the groom opened the carriage door for her. She gave Rees her hand. *"Au revoir, monsieur."*

He held her hand a moment, his eyes never leaving hers. "Until this evening."

Rees chose the Café de Chartres, a restaurant made famous during the Revolution. A fellow Englishman from the embassy had shown it to him a few days ago. From what he had seen in the week he'd been in Paris, the British were spending most of their time on the town, discovering the delights of the Continent.

At least it appeared a warm, cozy place for him to spend a few hours with Lady Wexham. The small restaurant was located along the stone galleries of the famous—or infamous—Palais Royale.

The quarter teemed with civilians, both highborn and low, and soldiers—British, Prussians, and Cossacks in their colorful uniforms. But Rees had little interest in the hordes milling about in the street outside. He only had eyes for the woman sitting across from him at the small table.

After losing hope that he would ever be able to find her, it was as if the Lord had led him to be on that street corner at that precise time of day. He'd hardly believed it to be Lady Wexham at first, her appearance was so altered.

Instead of a lady dressed in the height of fashion, she had appeared almost drab in a gray gown and simple straw bonnet adorned with only a ribbon. At first glance, she looked like someone's governess or a lady's companion. But once he'd stood in front of her, in close proximity, he'd been captivated as quickly as in Mayfair. She could dress in sackcloth and she would still take his breath away.

This evening, she looked more the lady, although her gown was simple by her London standards. It was a pale green and she wore a gossamer shawl draped loosely over her shoulders. Her glossy hair was looped in a thick coil with no ringlets loose around her face. The style highlighted her fine cheekbones and dramatic dark eyebrows.

She sat gazing at the other patrons in the crowded restaurant. French people tended to eat out much more than their British counterparts. Restaurants and cafés abounded in the city, Rees had quickly found.

A waiter approached their table. After conversing with him a few moments, they made their selections, Rees content to follow his companion's recommendations.

When the waiter departed, Lady Wexham turned to him. "It is plain fare, but I think you will like it. Their fish and game are very fresh. And their wines are good."

He wondered whether she came here often and with whom.

"Your French is very good," she said.

"Thank you."

"You hid that fact well all the time you were in my household."

He didn't know whether she was angry or teasing him. She had kept her feelings concealed up to now. "It wasn't always easy, believe me, especially when we were at Hartwell House." He eased back in his chair, curious himself. "How long before you knew I was not a real butler?"

"Not long." She shrugged. "Valentine alerted me that you were not all you appeared."

"Of course."

She paused, taking a sip of her wine. "You made an enemy of her."

"Yes, I realized that. How is she?"

"She is well—as well as can be expected in a city that has known nothing but shortages for too many years." She shrugged. "She will survive. That is what she does best."

"Does she still . . . work for you?"

"Not precisely. She still lives with me and insists on looking after me. But I have told her she must find herself a new occupation. I think she will open a shop."

He digested this information, wondering if it was a matter of Lady Wexham's not being able to afford a lady's maid. "And Gaspard?"

Her smile grew wider. "He has opened a restaurant of his own. I should take you there."

He returned her smile, feeling for the first time that something of the walls that separated the two had fallen a fraction. "Yes. You should have told me and we could have gone there tonight."

Then his smile disappeared. The fact that she kept neither chef nor lady's maid pointed to reduced circumstances.

Her expression also sobered. "First I needed to find out for myself whether you were . . . sent by the British."

"I see." He rubbed a hand across his jaw, wishing he could prove to her that they were no longer on opposing sides. "I was not. They are no longer after you."

She looked at him a long moment as if weighing whether to believe him. "Perhaps not, yet they run this city for all intents and purposes. While Louis sits on his throne and does whatever the British tell him."

"You cannot blame England if it wants to see some stability in France before it leaves."

"I suppose not." She gazed at a point over his shoulder. "I sometimes wonder if the regime they have installed here will not be worse than anything previous." Her golden eyes were somber. "The royalists are out for blood—the blood of anyone they judge to have been either a Bonapartist or a Jacobin."

"That is precisely one of the things Wellington is here to prevent."

She sat back and folded her hands upon the tablecloth. "So, tell me what you have been about since I left London."

"I think perhaps I should first tell you how I came to be in your household." If he hoped for her trust, and any future with her, he had to be truthful about his past dealings with her.

"Very well." Her tone gave nothing away.

He recounted how he had been offered the opportunity to spy on her in exchange for a chance at advancement in the foreign office. "I soon discovered that hard work and merit play very little part in how promotions are given out."

She toyed with her spoon. "So, you had to agree to something that was not palatable to you?"

Feeling himself diminish in her estimation with this part of his narration, he forced himself to answer truthfully. "Yes. I know now it was not honest, but I also wanted to protect my country. Too many men have died."

"I understand," she said softly, and in that moment, hope stirred in his chest. He clenched his hand to keep from reaching across the table and taking her hand in his.

"I did not want to believe that a lady as beautiful . . . and intelligent and amiable as you could be involved in spying on the British." He cleared his throat, having trouble keeping his thoughts clear as he watched the expressions flit across her eyes—surprise, amusement, sympathy. "Not when you had lived the major part of your life in England and called it home," he added.

She looked at her hands as if acknowledging what she'd done. "Yes, it was my home, and I would not have done anything to—to harm it." She bit her lip. "But a Frenchman convinced me that Napoleon's armies would not survive long, and I had . . . a duty to help with the future." Her troubled eyes met his once more. "The Comte de Provence was the worst possible choice for France, but he was the only one the British would consider. They are so afraid of revolution on their own shores that they are content to suppress all democracy across the Channel."

She looked away again. He had the sense she had more to stay, so he remained silent.

His patience was rewarded. "But that is not the only reason," she said in so low a tone he had to lean forward to catch her words. She swallowed, as if unable to continue.

"It happened when you were seventeen and returned here, didn't it?"

Her eyes widened. Then collecting herself, she took a deep breath, as if delving into the past took all her effort. "Yes. I told you I fell in love with a young soldier. It was not my choice—or his—for me to leave him, or France. My mother discovered the attachment and forced me back to England." Her voice grew flat. "You see, her ambition was that I must marry a wealthy gentleman. She had lost everything during the Revolution and her only hope lay in me, her daughter."

Her lips twisted. "So, I know what it is to be obliged to do something that goes against one's inclinations."

She had been forced into marriage. The realization shifted all he knew of her. Mere events listed by dates in a file had done no justice to the tale of a young woman whose mother had pinned her whole future on her daughter's marriage, an eighteen-year-old who bore the responsibility of providing not only for her mother's future but for that of her French servants as well.

As she filled in the details of the things he'd read in her dossier, his heart went out to the young woman who had had to give up her first—her true—love for the sake of an ambitious mother. "I was a prize on the Marriage Mart that year." She emitted a humorless sound. "*Maman* even managed to procure a coveted invitation for me to Almack's through Princess Esterhazy. I'm sure she has some tenuous claim to relationship if we trace our lineage back far enough."

"That is when you met the Earl of Wexham."

She nodded.

The waiter interrupted them, laying out a tantalizing array of hot dishes.

"Roast quail," Céline explained with a graceful motion of her hand. "A roebuck pâté with a gooseberry compote, trout with a truffle ragout, an artichoke pie, side dishes as you see."

He inhaled. "Smells delicious." Rees hesitated then asked, "Would you permit me to say grace?"

She inclined her head in assent.

"Dear Lord, thank You for leading me to Lady—Mlle. de Beaumont. Please bless our evening together, as well as this food we are to partake of. In Your precious name we pray, Lord Jesus."

He looked up before taking up his cutlery to gauge her reaction.

She was unfolding her thick napkin. "I think if you are having such trouble remembering my name, you should call me by my given name."

He swallowed, feeling another wall between them come down. "Céline," he ventured.

She smiled.

"If you will call me by mine."

He waited, breathless, for her to utter the word.

"Rees."

He released his breath, realizing he'd waited a long time to hear his real name on her lips.

"I like your name."

"It's Welsh. My grandmother on my father's side was Welsh. It was a family name from one of her relations. But I use the English spelling." He fell silent, realizing he was talking too much.

But she didn't seem to mind from the way she was listening.

She took up her fork. "So, you are thankful for having found me. You said you were searching for me?"

She had listened to his prayer. "Yes, I was. But please, I'm more interested in your story before I get back to mine."

"Very well." She gestured toward his plate. "Please, don't let your food get cold."

They ate for a few moments before she resumed. "I had many admirers that first season. But as one quickly discovers, very few make a serious pursuit once the parents inquire into a young lady's dowry and expectations. I was but a poor émigré.

"That did not weigh with the earl. He was wealthy enough to choose whichever bride struck his fancy. He had already been married once, in his youth." She paused, looking down at her place. "He had only one overriding concern."

He remembered her dossier and could hazard a guess. "He needed an heir."

24

*C*éline stared across the candlelit table at Rees. "Yes." Was her barrenness so evident, even to him? She thought she'd grown used to this failure, but seeing the knowledge in his eyes reminded her afresh.

He coughed behind his napkin. "Forgive me, but when I . . . I chose to accept the task of going into your household, they gave me a file to read."

"You know all about me then?" Somehow hearing it from his lips made it harder to bear.

He shook his head, his smile rueful. "Hardly that. I know facts, facts that anyone can discover with a little digging. I know you married the earl at the age of eighteen after your first season, and I know he died childless."

She moistened her lips, somewhat appeased. "You can imagine then how important it was for him to marry a healthy young woman of impeccable pedigree who would produce a healthy male child."

"As far as anyone in my station can imagine such a thing, yes."

She smiled faintly at the irony in his tone. "You have never given an heir any thought, Mr.—Rees?"

He set his fork and knife down on the edge of his stoneware plate before answering. "Not in terms of an 'heir.' Like any man, I would like to have children someday with my wife."

Of course, he would. Another reason she must never think of a future with him. She shook away the instant of self-pity and forced another smile. "Would you? Yet you've delayed your marriage."

"I was never betrothed," he reminded her.

She remembered his words to her that afternoon in his bedroom. "I thought only financial considerations were keeping you from proposing."

He fingered his napkin, his words hesitant. "I had desired to be married and have a . . . a family. But I had never met the woman with whom I wished to share my life."

When she raised her brows in disbelief, he hastened, "It is true, there was a young lady. She was a close friend of my younger sister," he continued, "and I had watched her grow up. I respected and admired her greatly, and as my situation in life improved where I could finally think about marriage, she seemed an ideal candidate."

"But?" she ventured softly when he paused.

"I wasn't in love with her."

He held her gaze, and she found herself spellbound by what she saw in his smoke-gray eyes. "No?" she whispered.

"When you left . . . I didn't think I'd ever see you again. I had no hopes of ever being able to come over here after the war—not after having compromised my spying assignment so thoroughly."

His words reminded her of the reality of his role in her life. "Compromised? I wouldn't say so. I would say you have done very well for yourself." She eyed his evening clothes, which sat very well on him.

A flush spread on his cheeks but his gaze didn't waver. "On the contrary, I never betrayed you to my superiors."

"No?"

"I never told them I had proof of your spying activity, that you had undoubtedly fled to France knowing both the French and the Home Office were after you. I merely gave my superior the bare minimum of information and let them come to their own conclusions." He gave a bark of laughter. "I went so far as to say you had gone to France when you'd received a message from a sick relative." He shook his head. "If they'd ever wanted another spy, they certainly would not have needed one as gullible as I."

Her heart pounded in her chest. "Why did you do that for me?" she whispered.

"I think you know the answer to that."

They continued gazing at each other. Before she could gather her wits, his mouth crooked upward. "I never thought I would be given the chance to come to France and find you. Yet it didn't stop me from asking to be sent here. No one was more surprised than I when my superior gave his approval." He shrugged. "Perhaps my knowledge of French—and the fact that I was well qualified for clerical duties—convinced them I'd be useful on Wellington's staff." He paused. "My only goal was to look for you." His gaze traveled from her face to her hand. "Though I expected to find you spoken for."

"It is bare, you see."

He cleared his throat. "After you left, I went to . . . visit this young lady . . . and I spoke very candidly with her. Even though there had been no declarations between us, I admired and respected her as a dear friend, and I . . . I didn't want her to hold out any hope that I might . . . someday offer her marriage." He swallowed, his stilted words reflecting his difficulty with the topic.

Céline tried to picture this young lady—far younger than her now twenty-nine years, she was bound. She felt a sudden, irrational jealousy for this unnamed woman. "What was her name?"

He looked surprised at the question, and Céline wished she had not asked it. Finally, he replied, "Jessamine."

"What a beautiful name." She hated it. "It's lovely."

She was being childish. In an effort to get hold of her emotions, she said, "That was kind . . . and brave of you, Rees. A woman does not like to be kept waiting, and it was unfair to keep her hopes alive if she indeed was expecting a declaration."

"My sister had always encouraged the suit and perhaps had spoken to her about it. I'm afraid I may have hurt her, but it was unintentional though not excusable—"

He was a noble man. She couldn't help admiring his behavior. "You cannot marry someone you do not love."

"No." The way he was looking at her told her he was no longer referring to himself. "You know that from experience, do you not?"

She looked down. "Yes." A moment later, she let out a shuddering breath. "If it had not been for Valentine's shoulder to cry on after I received word of Stéphane's death, I don't know what would have become of me."

This time he reached for her hand on the table and covered it with his own. She remained still, although she felt the touch of his warm hand throughout her body.

"I went about in a state of numbness for a long time. I didn't care what happened around me. When my mother insisted I accept the earl's suit, I thought it would at least help my mother out—and end the drama of another season for me. I had vowed never to go through that again."

He waited as if for more. But she didn't want to talk of her marriage. After a moment he bent to his plate again.

They ate in silence. When the waiter came to remove their dishes, Rees thanked him and sent his compliments to the chef.

Céline shook her head with a smile. "I cannot accustom myself to your command of French."

"I learned most of it in one of your prisons."

She gasped softly. "You were a prisoner of the French?"

He sat back in his chair. "I told you the truth when I said I had been in the navy. What I left out was that I was captured off your coast. Our ship sank. I survived and was taken prisoner by your people. I suspect my French is not of the finest variety."

Now she began to see more. "It sounds quite polished to me."

"I had a French governess as a child, but it was during that year in prison that I grew proficient. It was only because of the brief peace that I was released and able to come home."

She gestured toward his chest. "When you were shot in the shoulder, I noticed a scar."

He glanced downward. "Yes. It was a nasty sword wound."

Leaning her chin in her hand, she smiled faintly. "I always wanted to ask you how you obtained the scar on your chin. Was it also during your time in the navy?"

He fingered the area on his chin. "Yes. Another fight on deck, this from a knife blade. I didn't think it noticeable."

"Not unless a person is very close to you."

Her breath caught at the look in his eyes. Was he, too, thinking about their kiss?

Rees left Céline, his mind and heart full. He spent the next hour walking the streets of Paris, knowing he would not be able to sleep for a long time. Thankfully, Céline had agreed to see him again on the morrow. This time, she had asked him to meet her at the Jardin du Luxembourg on the Left Bank. She promised to take him to Gaspard's restaurant afterward.

For the first time, he felt hopeful that maybe he had a chance with her. He could scarcely imagine that she might care for him, but he felt that at least he could begin to court her as a proper suitor. He was relieved in a way that she appeared in reduced circumstances. He wanted to provide for her, take care of her, even if it would not be in the manner she had been accustomed to.

The next day, he arrived at the appointed hour and breathed a sigh of relief when he saw her already there, beside the central basin in front of the palace. She walked toward him when she saw him. His heart lightened immediately, and he realized he had been afraid she wouldn't show up today.

"Would you care to take a stroll?" she asked after their greeting.

"If it's not too warm for you."

"Not at all. I have my parasol."

He offered her his arm, and the two walked over the wide path. "Paris is very beautiful. Much more so than I imagined."

"Despite what you English think of him, Napoleon did make some improvements to the city. Although it was Marie de' Medici who had the palace built, it was Napoleon who improved and enlarged both the palace and park. This was his home for a few years before he declared himself emperor, you know." They stood in front of the palace a few moments.

"And now he is sitting on a small island, still calling himself emperor."

"Yes."

"'Their inward thought is, that their houses shall continue forever, and their dwelling places to all generations,'" he quoted.

"That sounds like Scripture."

"It is, a psalm of David."

"I've been reading the Bible."

He flashed her a look. "Have you indeed?"

She looked away from him. "Since that day I prayed for you—" Her words came out softly, as if she were uncomfortable uttering them. "I have sought to know God . . . more deeply . . . to know the God that you held so dearly."

"And have you?"

She nodded.

Rees felt more moved than he could express in words. All he could do was press the hand resting in the crook of his arm.

She tilted her head up to him. "Perhaps you are an answer to prayer now."

"Why do you say that?"

She turned away from him, making a vague gesture with her free hand. "The way you found me—" She laughed shortly. "Don't pay me any mind. It's foolish."

He scrambled around, seeking to prolong this line of conversation. "No, I don't think so."

"Why do you say that?"

He swallowed. "Perhaps because I was praying to find you."

Her amber eyes looked searchingly into his. The tip of her tongue moistened her upper lip.

Then she turned away from him again, saying in a brisk tone. "Come, let us walk down this alley here. I shall show you another of Marie de' Medici's lasting works."

His hopes plummeted. He was deluding himself that he could ever win her.

He followed her lead, content for now to be in her company, vowing he would be patient and win her.

Céline looked beautiful, and he felt proud to be seen with her. Today, she was dressed in a deep yellow gown that brought out the warm tone of her skin and the reddish tints in her dark hair. She looked more like the fashionable lady he had grown accustomed to in London. Had she dressed for him?

He shook aside the vain thought.

They walked under the shade of the elm trees planted along the avenue. The vast park was filled with couples and families strolling its many formal gardens and tree-lined alleys.

They spoke some more of what had happened since she'd left England and finally turned to the topic of her present work in France.

She waved an arm in outrage. "The British were determined to put Louis on the throne. Well, you have succeeded."

"I know he is not the perfect solution."

"Hah! Not even approaching perfect."

"There was no one else who could bring a modicum of stability to France at this time," he began, knowing it was a weak argument.

"He will do more than bring stability. Don't you see what the royalists are doing? They will turn France back to its prerevolutionary state. Already, the press is having a hard time publishing anything that goes contrary to the royalists' view. Anyone who served under Bonaparte is being punished."

Rees could only gaze in admiration at the passion she displayed in her tone, her eyes, her very gestures when speaking of the political situation in France. "Wellington won't allow the far right to take away the freedoms of the people," he countered.

Her lips thinned. "You English can be so idealistic at times." Instead of arguing further, she sighed. "I hope you are right, but I have seen so much corruption and desire for retribution since I've returned that I wonder what will become of France."

It was the first time he had detected any discouragement in her. "With people like you fighting for democracy, France has a chance."

She stared at him, her lips slightly parted, and it was all he could do not to lean toward her. "I feel like a very small drop in the desert."

They arrived at a grotto made of rustic stone at one end of the park. Two jets created a refreshing splash of water in its basin. A marble statue was tucked into the arch. "Very pretty."

"Yes, it is. It, too, has been refurbished by Napoleon's architect." Céline trailed her fingers in the pool. "Have you seen the Arc de Triomphe? It is Chalgrin's work as well."

"Yes. I am lodging at the British embassy, not far from there. It is quite impressive, though not completed."

She gave a sardonic laugh. "Perhaps good King Louis will do so."

"I'm sorry the area is so overrun with British soldiers at the moment. Wellington will doubtless bring them to order."

She shuddered. "They are nothing compared with the Cossacks and Prussians. They are out for revenge for the French having destroyed their cities."

He frowned at her. "It's not safe for a lady to go out alone. I hope you have someone to accompany you."

She dismissed his concerns with a toss of her head. "I have become accustomed to taking care of myself."

Her answer didn't satisfy him, but there was little he could do at the moment. How he wished he could protect her.

They continued to walk. The park was so vast he couldn't see the city on the opposite end of it.

She questioned him about his background. "I have not had the benefit of reading your file, you see."

He acknowledged her barb with a smile. Then his tone became serious. "My father was once a prosperous merchant, but the blockade ruined him, since the majority of his trade was with the Continent. As a staunch Christian, he did not believe in indulging in the smuggling trade."

"I see where you come by your principles then."

"He was a fine example as a father—and as a man."

The shouts of children came to them from afar.

"I remember very little of my father."

"I am sure he was a man to be proud of as well."

"Thank you. My mother has always spoken highly of him. Perhaps that is why she needed so much to be wealthy again. She felt she must regain what was taken away from him during the Revolution."

He smiled, recollecting her mother's gambling. "How is your mother?"

"She is here in France at the moment. Perhaps you shall see her at the British embassy. She spends her days badgering any public official she can obtain an audience with. She is trying to regain her lands, you see." She shook her head. "I don't know how she will succeed."

"Perhaps I can help in some way."

She tilted her head at him. "Why should you do that?"

"Because she is your mother." He smiled ruefully. "I haven't much influence. I've only arrived here myself. But if I can mention something to the duke, perhaps he will look into her case."

"You are sweet."

Her tone was tender, but instead of encouraging him, it filled him with despair. Is that how she saw him? As a kindly man who meant well, but was, after all, still little more than a poor clerk with pretensions of a gentleman?

To mask his thoughts, he asked, "Is your mother staying with you?"

"Oh no. My house is not grand enough. She is staying with old friends in one of the imposing *hôtels* in the Place Vendôme. You are bound to run across her at one of the functions you will doubtless attend. Young British gentlemen are in high demand at all the balls and soirees at the moment."

He grimaced. "I'm hardly that."

"Of course you are." She narrowed her eyes at him. "You mean because you are a merchant's son?" She laughed outright. "Goodness, you are worse than the ultra royalists. Didn't you read any of those works I gave you?"

His lips curved upward, unable to disguise the pleasure her words—her scold—gave him. "Yes, I did."

Before he could say anything more, she pressed his arm. "But please continue with your own story."

He skimmed over the details of his youth and return from a French prison. "My father had to sell his business. And then he fell ill. At the time, I was serving in the navy. I had been a restless youth, seeking adventure and longing to see the world. When war broke out, I ran away and signed on to the navy. I think it broke my father's heart not to see me educated. But when I was promoted to midshipman, he boasted of me to all his friends and associates."

"I'm sure you were a brave sailor."

He fell silent at the unexpected praise, not sure how to receive it. "I returned to find my father gone. He had died while I was sitting across the Channel in prison. My mother and sister needed me then, so I returned home.

"My mother had moved back to her native village on the southern coast in order to live more modestly. I was able to secure a position as a private secretary to a local landowner, on the recommendation of a naval officer I had served under. He and this baronet were good friends.

"That position led finally to a post in the Foreign Office." He shrugged again. "Until that day I was offered the job of spying on you. Since I had been toiling away for nigh on a decade with little advancement, I knew I must accept it. As I told you, I have supported my mother and sister for some years."

"You have sacrificed a great deal."

He shook his head, uncomfortable with the praise. "Not more than many."

They walked in the dappled shade of the trees until they arrived back at the palace. She paused at the vast basin of water where children were sailing boats. "Shall we walk to Gaspard's restaurant?" she asked.

"If you are not too tired?"

"Oh no, I am used to walking."

He wondered if she no longer kept a carriage. "Very well." Before they could move, they were interrupted by a soft masculine voice behind them. "Good afternoon, Mlle. de Beaumont."

She turned with no smile of welcome. Even though it had been more than a year since he'd heard the voice, Rees recognized it at once. Monsieur de la Roche approached them, his thin ebony cane tapping against the path. His gaze rested on Rees. "You look familiar, monsieur, though I cannot place you." He spoke to him in English, which made Céline realize he had overheard them speaking.

"I worked in Mlle. de Beaumont's house last year when she stayed at Hartwell House. Doubtless you saw me there."

She admired his aplomb in admitting to his position on her staff.

A tiny line formed between de la Roche's gray eyebrows. "Ah, a private secretary, perhaps?" He turned to her for confirmation.

Before Rees could admit to having been a butler, she replied, "He was sent by the Home Office to spy on me. He pretended to be a butler."

She wanted to laugh at his expression. It was not easy to throw de la Roche, and she had succeeded. Clearly, he hadn't been privy to what the English were doing.

De la Roche studied Rees as if for some clue to his former profession. Rees merely inclined his head. "I fear it is as Mlle. de Beaumont says. We were working for the same side, but not in tandem."

The older man's thin lips pressed together until they almost disappeared. "Perhaps it would have helped all our efforts toward a speedier peace if your government had thought fit to inform me of your role."

"Perhaps." When Rees volunteered no more, de la Roche addressed her. "You continue your activities?"

She feigned nonchalance. "As a matter of fact, I just turned in my latest article yesterday."

He said nothing, merely regarded her in that expressionless way he had. Finally, he took a step back and bowed to them both. "Well, I see you are occupied. I shall not interrupt your tête-à-tête further."

When he left, she shuddered. "Insufferable man. He means to shut down the paper if he has his way."

Rees frowned. "The one you write for?"

"Yes." She sighed. "Thus far he hasn't succeeded, but he works closely with the police commissioner. They are always coming up with ways to fine us. I won't be surprised if the paper soon folds and we all end up in prison. In a few months, there will be no free press in France."

"Have a care."

She read true concern in his gray eyes, and she longed to—

What? Accept the warmth and friendship she read in his eyes—and more?

How easy it would be to follow her longing.

But she could not do that to him. He had said it to her plainly. He wished for a wife and family.

Only the first could she give him.

25

*R*ees insisted on dropping Céline off at her house. He was still puzzled about why she chose to dwell in a modest, almost shabby, building, when her mother was living in the highest circles. Had the British confiscated her wealth? He had not been privy to that information.

No matter. He didn't care if she hadn't a sou to her name. In fact, he'd prefer it, if it would help his suit.

For the first time since beginning this venture, he felt optimistic. The Lord had led him to Céline only days after his arrival. And now he faced at least a few months of living in Paris. He would court Céline as a proper suitor.

He knit his brow, remembering their encounter with de la Roche. He didn't like it. The man meant trouble, he was sure of it. He was probably still smarting over Céline's escape to France.

The sooner Rees married Céline, the sooner he'd be able to protect her properly.

But first he must speak to the Duke of Wellington.

It would be a tricky situation to ask to marry a Frenchwoman who had been suspected of espionage against the British just a year ago. Would he again risk his career, his reputation? Who would have thought a merchant's son could aspire to a countess? The idea still left him shaking his head. It was only because of the upheaval war and the Revolution had brought about. Or was it true love?

He smiled at the sentimental thought, then sobered. He could not offer Céline what the gentlemen of her station could, but his prospects now at least were hopeful. Being part of Wellington's delegation at a critical time in France could mean the dream of a career in diplomacy becoming a reality. He knew his knowledge of French had been a primary reason he had been selected. He also knew from speaking with Wellington's private secretary and observing how the duke dealt with those underneath him, that he was an exacting, demanding man, but that he rewarded those who were faithful in carrying out their duties.

Rees felt he would get along well with him.

After seeing Céline to her door and asking to call upon her on the morrow, Rees went back to the Right Bank to the temporary quarters of the new British embassy.

They were lodged in a fine mansion not far from the Tuileries Palace, where the former Comte de Provence had taken up residence as King Louis XVIII.

When he had the opportunity that afternoon, Rees consulted with Wellington's secretary to secure a moment with the duke before the end of the day.

When he stood before the famous commander, Rees began with, "Your grace, I am intending to propose to a lady here in Paris."

Wellington lifted a dark brow. "Indeed? And who is the lucky woman?"

Rees swallowed. "Céline de Beaumont. Lady Wexham."

He pondered the name a moment. "Ah, Lady Wexham. The lady you were sent to spy on last year in London."

Wellington had been well briefed. "That is correct, your grace."

Wellington listened to him as he explained how he had met her again since arriving in Paris. The duke asked a few questions about his time in her household when he was spying on her, but kept his thoughts to himself, so Rees had no idea if he approved or disapproved of Rees's desire to marry her.

"I may be presumptuous—or premature, since I don't know if the lady will accept me. But I also feel a sense of urgency since seeing Monsieur de la Roche. It's apparent to me that he means her ill."

Wellington mulled this over. "He's an influential man in the new government." He eyed Rees across his desk. "Why do you think Lady Wexham left England so precipitously?"

Rees had anticipated the question. "I believe she knew France was losing and she wanted to be here to join the voice of opposition to the royalists."

"It's not an enviable position to be in at present. Even if she becomes your wife, it will not be pleasant in Paris with the Ultras gaining more and more influence over the king."

"No, your grace."

The duke sat silent several minutes. He appeared to have forgotten Rees's presence, since he sat looking down at the correspondence on his desk.

Abruptly, he looked up and focused on Rees again. "You know Castlereagh is arriving Friday."

Rees shook his head. "No, I thought he was going directly from Belgium to Vienna."

"The Duc de Berry convinced him to stop in Paris en route. I advised him to accept. Not many know of his visit, and we'd prefer to keep it that way. With the Fête de St. Louis beginning Thursday, Paris will be thronged." Wellington shuffled some papers and set them aside. "Lord Castlereagh expects to arrive the following day and then leave on Sunday."

Rees nodded, wondering what all this had to do with him.

"I can assign you as an envoy to Castlereagh. He can use your linguistic skills. It will offer you multiple opportunities to advance."

To be part of the British delegation to the Congress of Vienna. Rees could scarcely imagine it. The Congress would be a stage for all the leaders of Europe to redraw its map in order to prevent another war.

It was the opportunity of a lifetime for someone seeking a career in diplomacy. And it would mean Céline would be safe, away from Paris.

The next moment his spirits sank. But if he had to leave in a matter of days, how could he hope to convince Céline to come with him?

Wellington stood and came around the desk. Rees immediately followed suit, knowing the interview was over.

"You needn't answer me now." A twinkle shone in his eye. "After all, you don't know the lady's answer."

The duke accompanied him to the door of his office. "I shan't wish you happy yet, but rather I offer you my best wishes for your success in persuading Céline." He gave Rees a keen look. "At least as her husband you will be able to keep the lady under round-the-clock surveillance."

Rees started. Did he suspect she had spied on Britain? For an instant, the duke's serious mien displayed a glimmer of a smile. "I'd prefer to have her working for us than against. Perhaps she can help keep tabs on that wily fox Talleyrand."

The next second, Wellington once more was all business. "It's not in our interest that France become too reactionary. Lasting peace will only be achieved by a balance of powers in Europe, and within France, where all voices can be heard."

The two shook hands and Rees left, his thoughts in a daze—foremost among them, how would he persuade Céline to marry him and come away with him? Would she be willing to leave everything and take her chances with him?

He spent that night praying, thinking, pacing. By morning, he was resolved. Impatient for his meeting with Céline now that he had decided to ask her to marry him and come to Vienna, he had a hard time concentrating on his work all morning.

By midafternoon, he was standing at her iron gate. He opened it and walked through the small courtyard in front of the narrow, sandstone building sandwiched between others like it. The pavement was cracked. Everything looked worn and in need of sprucing up. But most of Paris was like that, he'd noticed, with the exception of the monuments and the great *hôtels*, those mansions of the rich. The years of war had taken their toll. The absence of young men was the most evident sign. He'd noticed on his ride from Calais the desolate farms run by women and old men.

And in Paris, the returning soldiers, many ill, maimed, and for the most part unemployed, resented the swaggering occupying armies in their finery.

Rees rang the bell, his heart beginning to thud, his palms to sweat. His heart sank when the door opened and he faced Valentine.

She looked unchanged, her dark hair pinned back mercilessly. "You!"

The single accusation almost brought a smile to his lips, but he bit it back in time. "Yes," he answered meekly. "Is your mistress at home?"

"*Non, mademoiselle n'est pas là.*"

"Do you know when she is expected to return?" he replied in her language.

She eyed him up and down. "So, you do speak French. Hmph!" She folded her arms across her chest. "*Non*, I do not know when she will return."

"May I wait for her?"

As she was considering his request, he added, "It's very important."

With a long measuring look the length of him, she finally swung away. "Come."

He followed her to a front parlor. Despite the outwardly decaying appearance of the building, this room was surprisingly light and cozy. A few good pieces of furniture were arranged around a thick Turkish carpet. A fine fireplace was situated along one wall, and a pair of windows, their shutters opened to let in the light, were filled with flowering geraniums in exterior window boxes. A shelf of books stood against another wall, and he remembered Céline's love of reading.

Fingering the brim of his top hat, he took the sofa Valentine indicated to him. "Tea?"

He started at her offer. Perhaps she feared Céline's reaction, if her mistress were to discover she had not offered a caller some refreshment. "No, thank you."

He sat to wait.

Céline arrived within the hour. He tensed, hearing the front door opening, followed by two sets of footsteps as Valentine came into the corridor. Then soft voices in French.

A minute later, Céline appeared in the doorway of the parlor, her cheeks rosy. "Hello. I didn't expect you so early. Were you waiting long?"

He stood as soon as she entered and helped her remove her pelisse. "Not at all." He cleared his throat. *Dear Lord, may she accept me.* "I am early. I . . . that is . . . something has come up, which I wished to . . . to discuss with you."

Her eyes showed immediate concern. "What has happened?"

He shook his head. "Nothing. That is, nothing bad. Please, I don't mean to cause you alarm when you've only just stepped in the door."

She smiled, relief evident. "I would have returned earlier if I'd known you would be here. Has Valentine offered you anything?"

"Yes, she did. I didn't need anything. But you must be parched if you have been walking—"

"No, I'm fine. Please, have a seat," she said, motioning back to the sofa. "Are you sure you don't care for some tea?"

He tried to smile in reassurance but couldn't quite pull it off. The stakes were too high, and the moment of truth had arrived.

She peered into his face. "What is it?" she asked softly.

He didn't bother to sit down but took a deep breath. "I've been asked to accompany Castlereagh to Vienna."

She blinked as if not having expected that. "I thought you were part of the British Legation to Paris."

"I was . . . am. But, I've just been told that Castlereagh is coming through Paris on his way to Vienna. Wellington has asked me if I wish to be assigned to Castlereagh for the congress."

Céline's hands were clasped in front of her. She took a step back and looked away from him. "I see. Goodness, what a surprise. But it's a good thing, is it not? I should think it an honor to be involved in the work of the congress." She smiled, holding out a hand. "I . . . offer you my congratulations. When will you be leaving?"

He took her hand, grasping it firmly, as if needing her support. "In three days—Sunday. Castlereagh is expected tomorrow."

Her eyes widened. "Oh."

As he felt her hand pulling away, he tightened his hold, bringing his other hand up to cover it. "I wished to . . . that is . . . will you marry me?" The words came out in a rush.

Her eyes rounded. She tugged at her hand, and he let it go. She stepped away from him, turning her back to him. "I . . . I don't know what to say."

Had he miscalculated? Misread her? "I know it is all very sudden. It's not the way I had planned—"

"You hardly know me, Rees."

"I know you are a kind, brave, compassionate woman, who regarded her lowly butler as a human being worthy of her time and attention."

Still she didn't turn around. "I . . . I did as any . . . any mistress would do for one of her servants."

"I don't think so." Although his voice remained firm, his hope was slipping. Of course she wouldn't consider marrying him.

"I would not have you destroy your new career just as it is beginning. I believe you have an impressive future ahead of you. You do not need to be saddled with a traitress."

He gave a laugh of disbelief. "No one has accused you of anything."

"But you and I know the truth. What would your British government say if they knew your loyalties were divided?"

He had wrestled with the problem and come to his own peace. If he had to choose, he knew he would give up the diplomatic service.

"Our countries are no longer at war. The future demands we work together. France will be the poorer if individuals like you stop working on her behalf for the freedom of her people. And . . ." He forced himself to continue, despite his fear. "And, together, we can work to help uphold the peace of Europe."

If his words affected her, she did not let on. She raised a fine eyebrow. "And how would we ever be able to trust one another? Would we be loyal to one another first, or to our respective countries?"

"To God, I would hope."

Céline stared at Rees, silenced by his words. His proposal caught her by surprise. She had suspected his feelings, certainly, but she'd hoped for more time.

Time to plan . . . time to harden her heart. Now, he caught her when she was vulnerable. It would be too easy to give in to his moving words, the tender look in his eyes, to her very own deepest needs and desires.

No! She wouldn't saddle him with a barren woman. She wouldn't make him come to hate her as the earl had. As the minutes ticked by, she knew she could not marry Rees and destroy his future. She must be strong.

To escape his keen gaze, she stood before the window, looking out to the street as she formulated what to say.

He took a step toward her. "Marry me and come with me to Vienna. You are in danger here in Paris. I saw how de la Roche spoke to you yesterday. He means to harm you."

She gave a short laugh. "I don't think he's forgiven me for besting him in England."

"Then it will only be a matter of time before he discovers how I bested him."

She turned to stare at him. "How you bested him?"

"If he woke up in a garden shed the night you left Dover, with the door jammed on him, and a knot on his head the size of a bowline, he has me to thank."

She gasped. "What did you do to him?"

"I stopped him the night you crossed the English Channel."

She shook her head at the image of de la Roche bested by Rees. "So, I have much more for which to be grateful to . . . my butler than I realized."

"I don't want your gratitude."

How she longed to reach up and touch his face.

"There is something else you should know. I debated whether to tell you or not, but I think there should be only truth between us."

Her heartbeat began to quicken. What other awful revelations were still to come? When would her sordid history of spying be finished?

"It was your sister-in-law who betrayed you to the British. That was why I was sent to spy on you."

"Agatha?" she breathed.

"Yes."

She brought a hand to her face, her thoughts trying to make sense of it. "I knew she disliked me, but I never thought she'd go to such lengths."

"I found her journal shortly before you left London. Perhaps you didn't realize how intensely she disliked you."

She stared at him, feeling the blood drain from her face.

"I didn't mean to upset you more."

She shook her head. "No, that's quite all right. I appreciate knowing the truth. It's just that—" Words and looks of her sister-in-law's came back to her. She should have suspected. Céline gave a short laugh. "I should have known, yet I scarcely thought her competent enough."

"It doesn't take much competence to whisper a suspicion in someone's ear, especially when they are a guest in your house."

Céline had to sit down. "I haven't been in contact with my sister-in-law since I left England. Where is she now?"

"Continuing to live in your London townhouse."

"She must have blackened my reputation among the *ton*."

"Actually, she has said little about you. As far as I know, she has allowed the story to circulate that you went to France to aid a sick relative. Perhaps now that she has achieved her aims, she feels it would reflect poorly on herself, as well as on the late earl, to lord it about that you were a French spy."

Céline smiled. "You are doubtless right. Poor Agatha."

He seemed surprised. "You are not angry with her?"

"Would you be? Isn't her bitterness punishment enough?"

"Yes." When she said nothing more, he said, "You are a noble woman."

She knotted her hands together when the silence drew out. He came toward her. "Let me protect you. I know de la Roche won't rest until he enacts his view of justice. Come to Vienna."

When she said nothing, her heart torn, he knelt at her side. "I know I have little to offer you; I'm only starting out in the diplomatic service, but I have spoken to Wellington." He smiled ruefully. "Forgive me for my presumption in bringing up your name, but I wanted to have him know my intentions toward you . . . in case the British held anything against you."

Ah, perhaps, there she would have him. His job security. "And?"

"Wellington would welcome you with open arms. It was he who suggested bringing you to Vienna with me." He smiled. "He said he would prefer you work on our side than against us." He sobered. "Even if the British did accuse you of something, we could emigrate to America."

He would give up his dreams for her?

"I hadn't meant to ask you in this way, but things changed all of a sudden. I had wanted to spend this time in Paris to court you properly. I realize I am not a gentleman to aspire to so noble a lady—"

"What nonsense!"

His gray eyes stared into hers. "Have I been a pretentious fool to suppose you felt something for me? Tell me now—and I shan't bother you anymore—I promise."

She couldn't let him think that. "You have not been at all pretentious! You shouldn't be wasting yourself on someone like me! Much less sacrifice your career. All you need is a brilliant marriage to a wealthy debutante, and you will quickly rise to the top of the diplomatic corps—"

"Like the one forced upon you?"

His words left her speechless. How could she fight his onslaught? For every argument, he had a solution. Suddenly, she teared up. No, she mustn't let him see she was weakening. She blinked back her tears and stood. "Oh, please don't make this harder for me!" She took a turn about the room and came to a standstill before him, swiping angrily at her eyes. "You haven't thought this through. You are so high-minded, and I'm frivolous . . . and I will hurt your career—"

He smiled down at her indulgently. "Do you think I spent ten years of my life in the Foreign Office to let that monstrous edifice come between me and the woman I love?"

She swallowed, stunned by his words. "L-love?"

He put his hands on her shoulders and gave her a little shake. "Yes, my dear, sweet republican. Love. Do you truly think any of the other is worth losing you—and any chance for happiness?"

Her lips trembled.

"What is it—why won't you have me?" he asked gently.

It was her undoing.

"You said you wanted a family—" she blurted out at last. Her voice broke. "Don't you see, I am barren!"

The ugly word stood between them.

Instead of bowing his head in acquiescence, he strengthened his hold on her. "Is that all it is?"

She stared at him. "Is that all! Isn't that enough?" Her voice firmed. "No, Rees, I will not destroy your life. Go home to England and marry your English girl."

When Rees at last left—unwillingly—Céline sank down on the sofa with her head in her hands. She had done the right thing, she kept repeating to herself.

Why then did her heart feel so empty?

"You fool!"

She lifted her head at Valentine's contemptuous tone. She should have known her maid would have heard the whole thing. "I hope you weren't standing there when Rees—Mr. Phillips left."

"Is that what he calls himself now?"

"That is his real name." She leaned back against the sofa, too tired to get up. "I thought you didn't like him."

"I don't."

"Then why did you call me a fool?"

Valentine folded her arms across her chest and eyed Céline as if she were a recalcitrant child. "What does is matter whether I like him or not? It's clear he is besotted with you. He'll do anything for you." She jutted her chin at her. "Does he know of your wealth or does he think you live in poverty now?"

"I don't think so."

"He's not even a fortune hunter! If I know that one, he'll rise to the top."

Céline bit her lip to keep from crying. Even Valentine could see Rees's sterling qualities. "B-but . . ." She tried again, her lips trembling over the words. "But I c-can't give him children."

"Bah! What of that. If he doesn't care?"

"But he will someday." She brought her fist up to her mouth, determined not to give in to tears, for she knew if once she began to cry, she wouldn't be able to stop.

The next day she received a note from Rees.

My Dearest Céline,

Yesterday I didn't mean to make light of your fears of being childless—or, rather, of not being able to give me children. Children are a blessing of the Lord, and while it is true that I would have loved to have children, given the choice, I would much rather have you. There is no question in my mind about that.

I have loved you almost from the moment I met you. Even though we were on opposing sides during the war, I came to admire your courage and abilities in carrying out a very dangerous mission for your country. I also admired you as the mistress of a large household. You cared for every single person working in it. Even yesterday, when you knew of your sister-in-law's perfidy, you showed no signs of rancor toward her.

You are a jewel among women. Any man would be privileged to gain your heart. I know I am not worthy of your love. I would be satisfied with your mere affection and regard, if you would but give me the chance to care for you.

Please come to Vienna with me. You will be under the protection of the British government, as well as my own. I pledge you my life. I know that together the two of us can work to build a lasting peace in Europe. The time when we sat and read and discussed things together during my recuperation in your house showed me that we are not so very different in our outlooks and beliefs. We both want what is good for humanity as a whole. We believe in democracy and the rights of man.

If it is childlessness you fear, did it never occur to you that perhaps it was not you who was at fault, but your late husband?

And if it turns out that it is you who are barren, the Scriptures say that the Lord makes the barren woman to be a joyful mother of children.

In closing, the only words I can offer you are to trust in the Lord. You said that you had made your peace with God.

Well, perhaps now it is time to trust in His goodness toward you. Trust that He will bless our union whether we beget children or not.

I love you, Céline. Please marry me and come with me. I leave on Sunday morning.

Your servant, Rees

He had written the address of the British embassy at the bottom.

Céline was unable to sleep that night. She lay for hours, staring at the darkness. She had reread Rees's letter more than a dozen times.

Dear God, how can I marry him? What if I am condemning him to never seeing a son grow up, a daughter smile at him in love and admiration?

The tears finally came, drenching her pillowcase.

The next day dragged on. Valentine gave her no sympathy. When she visited Gaspard, Valentine had already been to him. He gave her a look of understanding.

"Think hard before you turn this man down. You have been unhappy with one man and alone for too many years. Perhaps *le bon Dieu* has put this man in your path."

She could find no words to refute him.

He sighed. "France is no place for you now, *chérie*. It will only make you unhappy."

She fought with everything within her to keep from going to the British embassy.

Sunday finally arrived. Céline heard a rooster crow in someone's yard and arose while it was yet dark. She was sitting in their small kitchen when Valentine came downstairs.

Thankfully, her maid said nothing but went about stirring up the fire and putting a kettle on to boil.

Céline drank a cup of black and bitter coffee, her mind imagining the preparations at the British embassy. How many would be going? How early would they leave?

Help me to be strong, Lord. Help me to let him go.

When she went upstairs, she pulled out his letter again, from the Bible by her bed.

She reread the words. *Trust in His goodness.*

Had she ever trusted in the Lord's goodness?

She had learned to accept God's will. She had learned to accept Him.

But had she learned to accept His goodness?

Dear Lord, what does that mean? Her eyes slid to the next line in the letter.

Trust that He will bless our union . . . I love you, Céline. Please marry me and come with me. I leave on Sunday morning.

Suddenly, those words "on Sunday morning" hit her full force. He was leaving. Perhaps he was already on his way.

Oh, dear God, no! She might never see him again.

No! She must see him. One last time.

It was Stéphane all over again. Except this time she had a choice. The Lord had given her a choice.

Her heart racing and her hands shaking as if with the palsy, she grabbed her clothes, not bothering to call for Valentine, praying the Lord would delay Rees in time for her to arrive at the British embassy.

26

*R*ees was ready and waiting outside the embassy as servants loaded the last things. Castlereagh was already down, and Rees knew it would only be a matter of minutes until they were off.

Castlereagh had accepted Wellington's recommendation to have Rees join the British Legation to the Congress of Vienna. The foreign minister remembered him from a brief encounter at the Foreign Office shortly after Céline had departed England.

That was when Rees was racked with guilt, questioning his own patriotism and loyalty. He'd tendered his resignation, but Castlereagh had refused to accept it, offering him a leave of absence for a few weeks instead.

Now, the foreign minister welcomed him, telling him he needed someone fluent in French, as well as another pair of eyes and ears in all the hobnobbing. For he had made it clear to the younger men accompanying him that they would be just as useful at all the social events he anticipated as sitting in meetings or translating documents.

There were two other men his age, one Castlereagh's private secretary. They had three coaches in all, the last one for the servants and the bulk of the baggage.

Castlereagh would ride in the first carriage with his wife. Rees could only be grateful to the minister's wife. Any delay in departure was due to her last-minute preparations and leave-taking.

But as the minutes wore on, Rees's hopes that Céline would have a change of heart dwindled. *Lord, Thy will be done*, he kept repeating to himself.

Céline had not contacted him since the day he'd proposed to her. He had no idea if she had even read his letter. He grimaced. Perhaps Valentine had destroyed it before her mistress even had a chance to see it.

The heavy doors to the *hôtel* opened, and the two men came out.

Lord Castlereagh turned to his secretary. "Everything ready?"

"Yes, sir."

Castlereagh handed the bag he carried to the younger man. "Well, as soon as Lady Castlereagh appears, we shall be off," he said with a chuckle. Then he turned back to Wellington.

At that moment, Rees heard footsteps coming into the large court-yard from the street. His heart leaped at the sight of Céline, who stopped short at the opened gates, her gaze on the carriages.

With a brief "Excuse me," Rees hurried over to her, afraid to hope.

They both began to speak at once. "You came—"

"You haven't left—"

They stopped and smiled self-consciously at each other. At the sound of the stomping of a horse's hooves, Rees glanced back. Castle-reagh was looking his way. "Come and greet Castlereagh and the duke."

Putting a hand to her bonnet, she hesitated. "I am scarcely dressed for the occasion. I—I hurried over, afraid you had already left."

He pressed her hand. "You look beautiful as always."

She allowed him to lead her to the group of gentlemen. Both Wellington and Castlereagh greeted her fondly. After a few moments of small talk, Céline glanced at Rees.

He cleared his throat. "If you would excuse us—"

"Certainly, certainly," they assured him at once.

He pulled her aside and took her hands in his. "Dare I hope this means you've changed your mind?"

She squeezed his hands in hers. "I . . . I don't know."

Hiding his disappointment, he returned the pressure of her hands. "Please come to Vienna. I can ask Castlereagh if his wife wouldn't mind having you along. She may appreciate the companionship."

She shook her head. "Oh no, I can't come today. I haven't made any preparations."

Today. He fixed on that one word. "Does that mean you will come?"

Her brandy-hued eyes met his, her hands resting trustingly in his. "Are you very sure?"

"Yes."

When she still hesitated, he thought of a possible reason. "I can give you money for whatever arrangements you need to make."

She shook her head. "I have money." She smiled. "I am not destitute, you know."

He returned her smile. "I am glad to hear it." Then he sobered. "We can be married once you arrive there."

He read the wavering in her eyes. How he longed to pull her to him. "Please come. I'll find you—us—a house. If you change your mind when you get there, I'll arrange for you to travel back." He was going on, grasping at anything to have her promise.

He waited, hardly daring to hope, his gaze fixed on hers.

Finally, she took a deep breath. "Very well."

He smiled, his spirit soaring at the two words. Then he frowned. "I don't like the idea of your traveling alone. It's not safe."

"I shall find someone to accompany me. I'm sure there are hordes going to Vienna for the congress."

He nodded in relief. "Yes. That's perfect."

She seemed to have something more on her mind. "What is it?" he asked softly.

"You said in your letter"—she paused, moistening her lips and looking away from him—"that perhaps the fault was not with me but with . . . with . . ."

He knew at once what she was referring to. He touched a finger to her chin, turning her back to face him. "First of all, the good earl never begat an heir through his first wife, did he?"

She shook her head.

"Then it stands to reason the problem lay with him and not you."

Her brow began to clear. "Do you really think so?" she whispered.

"Yes," he said emphatically. Before she could speak, he held up a finger. "But, if it is indeed you who are barren, we can adopt a child. There are certainly enough children left each day at our foundling hospitals to establish a whole dynasty." He smiled tenderly at her. "You may have as many children as you wish—or your diminished fortune allows—since I am still only a salaried man. You are getting the paltry end of the bargain."

Her lips twitched, and her hands came up to rest on his chest. "Oh, I don't know about that. Your prospects are quite decent, with Castlereagh and Wellington both befriending you."

"Perhaps with you at my side in Vienna, I will quickly rise to prominence." He leaned in close to her, the last words whispered against her lips. Would he be able finally to taste them once again?

"La, is that what I am to expect of romantic language from you?" she whispered back.

He cupped her cheek in his hand. "I am not a Frenchman of fine words. I can only tell you I have never loved anyone as I love you."

She closed the gap between their lips, breathing against them. "Do you remember the first time?"

"Do I indeed . . ." he only managed before being lost to the kiss.

It had been so long, and yet the moment his lips touched hers, it felt as if it had only been yesterday that they'd stood in the garden at Hartwell House and embraced.

How he longed to deepen the kiss now, but he knew they weren't alone.

Slowly, reluctantly, he drew his lips from hers, though he kept his hand on her face. "Don't delay. I shall count the days until your arrival."

She nodded, her eyes warm and loving, her lips rosy and still half parted.

He heard a discreet cough behind him and turned, taking Céline by the arm. It was Castlereagh's secretary. "We are ready to depart, sir."

"Yes. I'll be right there." He turned to Céline.

"Go." She loosened his hold and stepped away from him. "You mustn't keep them waiting."

He swallowed. Would he see her again? He took her hand and bent over it. Then, reluctantly, he let it go and moved away.

He ascended the second carriage. The door slammed shut, and the horses' hooves began to clatter against the cobblestones. Rees pushed down the window and leaned out of it, his gaze fixed on Céline until the carriage left the courtyard and headed down the street.

Epilogue

$\mathcal{S}$carcely a fortnight after Rees left Paris, Céline arrived in Vienna.

He had sent her a few messages by courier, telling her of his arrival, giving her the details of where he was lodging, and finally sending her the address of the apartment he had found for her. It was located in the center of town, near all the activities of the congress.

She arrived late at night and sent him word the next morning.

Rees came as soon as he received her note.

An Austrian maid he had hired showed him to a sitting room. Too nervous to sit, he stood at a window overlooking the street below.

A few moments later the door opened. All he could do was stare. She had really come. She stood in the doorway as if she were unsure of her welcome.

"You're here," was all she said as she wiped her hands against the sides of her gown.

He walked toward her with a gentle smile, afraid she would turn and run at any moment. "I should be saying that to you. I hope I am not too early. You must be exhausted after your journey."

Céline looked at Rees as he came toward her, feeling suddenly very shy. Did he still want her?

Encouraged by his smile and outstretched hands, she met him half-way. "No, I'm fine, nothing to signify."

His hands clasped hers as he smiled at her.

"Are you happy to see me?" she whispered, her courage returning at the warm look in his eyes.

"How can you even ask that?"

Then she was in his arms, her bones in danger of cracking, and he was twirling her around. "I was so afraid you'd change your mind," he said against her neck.

He halted and gazed down at her.

"And I was afraid after so many days away from me you'd come to your senses and hope I wouldn't follow after you."

"I certainly have not changed my mind, if that is what you are implying," he said sternly. "In fact, I have taken the liberty of finding a pastor who can marry us this very day . . . if that is not too soon for you." He searched her eyes for confirmation.

She smiled slowly. "Today? And then . . . you would move here with me?"

He nodded cautiously. "If you have no objections."

"None at all," she whispered, her cheeks tinting.

He cleared his throat. "Castlereagh said he and his wife would stand as witnesses at the wedding."

"Oh, my. You have certainly come up in the world."

He chuckled. "If they come, it is only because of you, my dear."

She rested her hands against his chest. "That must mean they have forgiven me my activities of last year."

"You know what they say—all's fair in love and war. Besides, I think he wants to use your influence and talents for the British at this congress before Talleyrand gets to you."

Her eyes sparkled. "He already has!"

The two laughed as he bent his head and touched his nose to hers before taking her lips once more with his.

*I*f this is what a London season is, I'd say it's a silly waste of time." Jessamine Barry folded her arms in front of her, frowning at the hordes of people milling past her in the Grecian-style drawing room.

"It is rather difficult to speak to anyone in this situation," admitted her closest friend, Megan Phillips.

If it weren't for Megan, she'd know no one in this sea of glistening, gleaming faces. Her handkerchief was already limp from patting it against her forehead and neck. "All this trouble to dress one's finest just to be ignored. I don't know how long I shall be able to stand it."

Megan turned worried eyes toward her. "Oh no, don't say that. You know it's such an opportunity we've been given by your godmother. I'm sure things will soon improve." Megan craned her neck above the crowd. "Where did she go? I haven't seen her since we arrived."

"In the card room, I would say," Jessamine said sourly. The picture Lady Bess had painted Jessamine's father of a London season was far from the reality. Jessamine shook her head. If her father could see her now, he'd whisk her back home in a thrice, lamenting the cost of her gowns and all the other falderals deemed necessary for a young lady's coming out in London. She flicked her fan open, eyeing the ivory brisé sticks with distaste, and stirred some of the warm air against her face.

"Look at that gentleman there." She snapped the fan closed and pointed it toward a young man whose florid jaws bulged over his neck cloth. "He looks close to asphyxiating any moment from his own cravat. How can men be so ridiculous?"

Megan swallowed a giggle behind her own fan. "Careful, he'll hear you."

"How anyone can hear anyone in this babble is beyond me, yet they all go on as if anyone cares what they say." She studied the ladies and gentlemen making a slow progression past her. As far as she could make out, a rout was merely a place to see and be seen. No one seemed to be listening to anyone, yet their mouths kept moving, their smiles pasted on their faces like painted dolls.

She shuddered at the amount of rouge she'd observed on women's faces, both young and old. What went on in London! And the gentlemen were worse, dressed like popinjays with more jewelry than the women.

"Perhaps if we smile at some of the young ladies our age, we'll be able to meet them."

"My lips hurt from all the smiling I've had to do since arriving in London," Jessamine muttered. "I refuse to do so any longer, since it hasn't done us a bit of good." To illustrate her point, she scowled at a lady sporting a purple turban with three curled ostrich plumes of the same shade, which thrust themselves against her male companion's upswept curls, so full of pomade they reflected the light from the chandeliers hanging above them.

"I know you're not in the best frame of mind, but things will get better, I'm sure. Things just . . . just take time."

Jess's lips tightened in displeasure at Megan's reminder. How she wished at times that Megan weren't her best friend. It would have made things easier. To be constantly reminded—but no, she would not think about *him*! *He* was as good as dead to her.

She felt like one of those families that had exorcised a wayward son from their midst, the father banning the mere mention of the loved one's name in his hearing.

It would be humorous if it still didn't hurt so much—and weren't nigh on impossible to avoid hearing her beloved's name since he was Megan's brother. Thank goodness he was no longer in England.

It should have been the happiest time of her life, yet she was miserable. A year ago she would scarce have imagined herself among the fashionable world in a London drawing room, enjoying a season.

Her mouth turned downward, and the tears that were never far threatened to cloud the vision of the glittering array of ladies and gentlemen parading before her.

A year ago, she'd have envisioned herself betrothed by now, perhaps even married, to the finest, handsomest—no! The streak of rebellion and bitterness, a streak new and foreign to her which had invaded her nature almost a year ago and poisoned everything around her, reasserted itself.

The man in question—Rees Phillips—was not the finest, handsomest, noblest gentleman. He was the lowest, most despicable, shabbiest cad she'd ever known! He had no right to be happy when he had made her so miserable!

"Your frown could crack marble."

Jessamine jumped at the lazy drawl. Turning, she glared to see if the gentleman standing beside her had indeed been rude enough to address her.

Glaring in this case entailed craning her neck upward if she didn't want to waste the effort on a bleached white shirt front and pristine cravat.

"Are you addressing me, sir?"

Amused brown eyes stared down into hers. They might have been attractive if the pale forehead hadn't been topped by a mop of red hair. The gentleman's lips quirked upward. "You recognized the description?"

Jessamine drew herself up to her full height. How dare he mock her suffering!

"Excuse me, sir, we have not been introduced." With that setdown, she turned away, her chin in the air, and took Megan by the arm.

Before she could move, he stepped before her and bowed. "I beg your pardon." Then he turned and wandered off.

She fumed, watching him move with ease across the crowded drawing room.

Ruth Axtell has loved the Regency period of England ever since discovering Jane Austen and Georgette Heyer in high school. She knew she wanted to be a writer even earlier. The two loves were joined with the publication of her first book, *Winter Is Past*, a Regency, in 2003.

Since then she has published several Regencies, as well as Victorian England and late nineteenth-century coastal Maine settings.

With *Moonlight Masquerade*, her fourteenth novel, Ruth returns to Regency England.

Besides writing, Ruth always yearned to live in other countries. From three childhood summers spent in Venezuela, a junior year in Paris, an au pair stint in the Canary Islands, and a few years in the Netherlands, Ruth has now happily settled on the downeast coast of Maine with her college-and high school–age children and two cats.

Learn More About

Ruth Axtell

RuthAxtell.com
RuthAxtell.com/Blog